A RISKY PROSPECT

RIVER REAPERS MC, BOOK 2

ELIZABETH BARONE

ALSO BY ELIZABETH BARONE

STANDALONE NOVELS

Any Other Love

Crazy Comes in Threes

Just One More Minute

The Nanny with the Skull Tattoos

Sade on the Wall

The Stairs Between Us

RIVER REAPERS SERIES

A Disturbing Prospect

A Risky Prospect

SOUTH OF FOREVER SERIES

Twisted Broken Strings

Diving Into Him

Savannah's Song

What Happens on Tour

Visit **elizabethbaronebooks.com** to purchase!

MAIETTA INK

A Risky Prospect

River Reapers MC, Book 2

Copyright © 2019 by Elizabeth Campbell, writing as Elizabeth Barone

All Rights Reserved

1st Edition

Cover photography by Nestor Rizhniak / Shutterstock

Cover designed by Natasha Snow

ISBN 978-0-9912838-8-0

 Created with Vellum

A RISKY PROSPECT

Brash social worker Olivia has been through her own personal hell and come out the other side, tattered but determined to make things better in her corrupt town—no matter the cost. Her roommate's current situation is the perfect place to start.

When ex-con Cliff's wild ol' lady Olivia comes to him and the River Reapers for help, he's on board. His vigilante motorcycle club can get the job done, and it'll help convince Olivia to take the next step in their relationship.

But when Olivia's traumatic past walks through the club's doors, there's no stopping her from doing whatever it takes to settle her own score. Even if it means crossing a line that Cliff might not be able to pull her back from.

For me.

FOREWORD

A Risky Prospect was the hardest book I've ever written. I took two "men" who hurt me, mashed them into one character, and used Olivia, Cliff, and the River Reapers to help me process those traumas.

Some of the themes in this book might make some people uncomfortable, and may even be triggering for people with personal trauma. I've made a list of potential trigger warnings that I'm including here.

For the sake of realism, I've depicted biker culture from my own experience and understanding. Although that culture and its attitudes toward women is changing, it has a long way to go. My goal for this book and its subsequent series is to help change that mentality.

TRIGGER WARNINGS

I 1,000% stand behind *A Risky Prospect*. I wrote this book for me. I took two "men" who hurt me, merged them into one character, and then got my revenge. However, I realize that this book isn't for everyone. It might not make sense to a lot of people. But to me —and maybe for some of you who have survived hell, too—this book is everything.

However, I'd never want my words to set someone else's healing back, so I've put together a list of triggers so that you don't walk in blindly. I can't count how many fluffy romances I picked up only to find themes I wasn't mentally prepared for. When you have PTSD or something else you struggle with, being equipped is an essential tool in your recovery.

Here are the potential triggers.

Drug and Alcohol Use: Some characters use drugs and drink alcohol.

Childhood Sexual Assault: Several characters have a history of being molested as children.

Guns and Violence: My vigilante bikers use guns to fight the bad guys, as well as other violent means of taking out the trash.

PTSD from Rape: A character experiences flashbacks, anxiety, and other symptoms of PTSD due to being raped by an ex-boyfriend.

Sexual Revenge: A character goes *Full Dark, No Stars* and a little *The Girl with the Dragon Tattoos* and gets their revenge.

If you feel that you won't be safe reading *A Risky Prospect*, please don't risk your health. As a rape survivor and someone with PTSD, I wish many books came with a list of trigger warnings. No book is worth your well-being.

Please also note that I don't necessarily condone or endorse the themes contained in this book. I do, however, wish it was legal to kill rapists.

If you've read *A Risky Prospect* and feel that I may have missed something, please email me at
elizabethbaronebooks@gmail.com.

1

OLIVIA

The fabric of my dress tears as Cliff yanks the top down to free my breasts. The ripping sound cuts through the air, loud enough that I swear everyone in the vicinity probably heard it. The vicinity being the River Reapers' club house.

I always wanted sex so good, clothing had to be ripped. It's a shame that my graduation dress is collateral damage.

Cliff thrusts into me, oblivious to the heat spreading through my cheeks. He wraps one hand around my breast, his other hand caressing my ribs, crossing my stomach, traveling down, down, down, until the pad of his thumb rests on my favorite nerve. As he gives it one quick stroke—like he's plucking a note on a guitar, checking to make sure it's tuned properly—my back arches and I forget that the whole club can hear us, that we just ripped my graduation dress. I fade into him, as in sync with another person as I'll ever be.

There's something about him that absorbs me without erasing me. We orbit each other, a symbiotic relationship. Especially when his hands are on me and he's inside of me.

My hips match his pace, his hand rubbing over my nipple, giving my breast just the right amount of squeeze, drawing me closer and closer to the edge. Without me ever saying so, Cliff instinctively knows the key to me coming with him is his giant hands on my chest. He's attentive like that.

I'm close, so close I feel like I'm dying. Every woman knows this agony: when you're right on the edge but not quite there yet. I'm burning alive from the inside out with his match igniting me.

"Close?" he asks, voice rough. It's always deep and smoky, a rasp that sends shivers through me and makes me wet.

I nod, forgoing words to focus all of my concentration into the final rub he gives me before moving both hands to my breasts. I moan. As long as he keeps doing that, I'll be more than close. This one's gonna be one of those firework shows, the kind that leaves me slightly dizzy, staring at the ceiling.

Except the sharp rap of knuckles on Cliff's door yanks me right out of my happy place and reminds me of *why* I can't focus in the first place.

"Olivia!" my roommate, Esther, calls. "We're gonna be late. Vamonos!"

It's the day I've been working toward for the past four years. In just a couple hours, I'll officially be a social worker. Esther, too.

"Oh, shit," Cliff says. He pulls out, but just as his crown brushes my clit, he shudders and lets go. The hot pulse takes me with him, a mini spark instead of the fireworks I'd hoped for, but I'll take it.

I lay back with a smile.

"Shit," he growls. "I'm sorry."

"You're sorry?" I laugh. "I'm pretty sure this is my fault."

"I'm the one who grabbed your ass," he says as he pads away from the bed and ducks into the bathroom.

I sit up on my elbows. "I'm the one who wasn't wearing any panties."

Esther pounds harder. "Let's go," she calls, drawing out the two words. To think, a few months ago, my bookish roommate was the one dragging her ass, making me play time games so neither of us were ever late. *Now* she's in a rush.

I glance down at my ruined dress and sigh. It's not too big a deal, considering no one's going to see it under my gown anyway. But still. I kinda liked it.

"I'll get you a new one," Cliff says, handing me a washcloth.

"I should punish you by just wearing my gown and nothing else." I clean up as quickly as possible, then start hunting through his dresser for something else to wear. I don't stay overnight with him in the club house often, but this winter I learned to keep extra clothing stashed in as many places as possible.

A girl never knows when she's going to get dirty.

Or bloody.

I slip out of the remains of my dress and tug on the romper.

Cliff groans.

"What?"

Instead of telling me, he closes the space between us and touches my hard nipples through the fabric. "You're killing me," he whispers, and I'm immediately wet again.

"I'm leaving!" Esther threatens.

"I liked her better when she was quiet," I tell Cliff, grabbing my clutch bag. "Donny is a bad influence."

He chuckles. "And vice versa. Donny was as cold as ice. I saw him *smile* the other day, and Esther wasn't even in the room."

"Please kill me if I ever change for a guy."

His eyes drop from mine as he picks up his keys. He shrugs into his cut without a word. I wish I could have a moment to run my fingers over the stitching where the arms would be on a normal leather jacket, feel the silky patches and rocker that make him a member of the River Reapers. That make him a Sludge Specter. I pull the door open and come face to face with Esther.

"Ready?" I ask her.

She gives me a look—a death glare that is all Esther and zero percent Donny—and flounces away in her cornflower blue sundress and white canvas sneakers, the color and the dress complimenting and accentuating her long, dark legs.

I roll my eyes at my pale legs, mottled with scars and bruises. There's also the scar at my hairline.

Cliff catches my hand, drawing me in for a kiss. His warm lips touch mine for a full second, then he pulls back. "See you there," he says.

Nodding, I leave Cliff's room and the other club rooms, heading toward the stairs that'll take me down into The Wet Mermaid, the MC's strip club and my place of employment. For now, anyway. After graduation, it'll be a whirlwind of state job interviews and shopping for business casual.

I make my way through the club, my brothers in leather nodding at me and raising their glasses. Girls spin on the poles, and Vaughn mixes drinks behind the bar. Good thing it's not anyone else. I don't know where Mark—my boss and the MC's treasurer—finds some of these girls. They can't tell top shelf vodka from bottom.

As I exit the club, the heat hits me like a wall, humidity wrapping around me and wrecking what was left of my hair. Gotta love New England weather—it always jumps straight from winter into summer.

I spot Esther's car, but she's not in it. Glancing around, I scan the parking lot. Two minutes ago she couldn't hold her horses, and now she's nowhere to be found. Typical fucking Esther. Scowling, I grab a cigarette from my clutch and light up. At this rate, Cliff and Donny will be at the campus before we are.

A sob cuts through the thick air, and I whip around. I know that voice. I've heard my roommate cry at *Finding Dory*. I follow the sound, my fingers closed around the handle of the knife in my clutch. I don't go anywhere without it.

Rounding the corner of the building, I nearly crash into Esther, who's sagged against the wall, her ass on the ground, knees drawn to her chest. Her shoulders shake and her limp hand loosely holds her phone. Her face is dry, but her chest rises and falls in rapid breaths. She gasps for air, and I drop to my knees in front of her, taking her hands.

"Esther? What's wrong?"

2

CLIFF

"Everything good?" I lean into Mark's office, gripping the doorway.

He nods from his desk. "Don't you worry your pretty, grizzled—" He glances up and the words cut off. "Face," he finishes, blinking at me.

I run a hand over where my beard used to be. Now there's just a chin strap—a short beard accenting my jawline. I even let Abraham trim my hair—a *little* bit. Just enough to keep it healthy.

He whistles. "Tell me she didn't make you do that."

"Yeah right."

Olivia likes my beard, as long as I don't let my mustache get too out of control. She says it pokes her in the nose when we kiss. I've let it all grow out so long, I don't know any different.

Today is a special occasion, though.

More than just Olivia's graduation.

"Well, you look good, son," Mark says, eyeing my black jeans, black T-shirt, and the cut I hardly ever take off. That piece of leather marks me as a River Reaper until the day I die. "Just don't change anything else, or I won't recognize you."

"You worry about tonight, and I'll worry about my personal

grooming." I fish out a cigarette and light up, then hold out the pack to him.

He waves it away. "We're all set. The band playing, Oh Vile Eye, will be here to set up around four. Bar's stocked. Caterer starts setting up at three. I think that's everything. I've never thrown a graduation party before."

"How about the cake?" I suck in a long hit of nicotine.

"Beer Can was all over that. Let's just hope it says 'Congratulations, Olivia,' and everything's spelled right. He was a little lit when he put in the order."

"It's gotta have Esther's name on it, too, brother," I say, glancing into the club behind me. "Donny'll slit all our balls off if we forget her."

"I'll check on it." He lifts the phone out of its cradle, then puts it back down. "You good for this afternoon?"

I bow my head, moving it back and forth to work the kinks out of my neck. "No, but there's no helping it. I've done all I can."

"Including making yourself look like a twelve-year-old boy." He laughs, getting even louder as I thumb the strip running down from my lower lip to my chin.

A hand clasps my shoulder. "We're out of here," Donny says.

"A'ight." I point my cigarette at Mark. "Check that icing." Turning, I fall into step with Donny.

"That soul patch is making you bossy," Mark calls after me.

I shake my head and make my way through the club, Donny at my elbow. "You got plans after?" I ask him. We break through the doors and into the heat. It's going to be a bitch riding in this weather.

"Nah," he says, striding toward our bikes. He straddles his and straps his helmet on. "Essie's having lunch with her grandparents, and I ain't ready for that shit yet."

"I hear you." I hold my helmet in my hands, bike between my legs. I'm not ready to meet the parents, either. Meeting Olivia's means facing my aunt and uncle for the first time in twenty years.

I'll have Lucy there as a buffer, but that won't make things much easier. While I was away, they adopted Olivia, and that complicates our already tense relationship now.

"Why are the girls still here?" Donny nods toward Esther's car.

I follow his gaze. It's empty. No sign of Olivia or Esther. "No idea."

Dismounting, I pull my phone from my pocket. I glare at it before typing in my password with a thumb. Ever since the last update, the thing's been acting like a Y2K crash test dummy. Texts show up out of order. Calls don't go through—either in or out. For a smartphone, it's pretty fucking useless.

I punch in Olivia's number and hit the call button.

"Walking fuckin' phone book, right here." Donny grins.

"Faster than scrolling through," I tell him. Olivia's phone rings and rings, but she doesn't pick up. "Jesus Christ."

Donny and I exchange glances.

"Should we go to the campus? Or just say 'fuck it' and have a beer?"

"Esther was in a hurry," I say.

"I know," he agrees, "which is why I kinda don't wanna know." He gives me a pointed look.

"Amen to that, brother."

With those two, it could be anything. Especially Olivia. I reach for my beard, then remember it's gone. I grab another cigarette instead.

I hold the flame to the end, inhaling. As the flame goes out, movement from the other side of the building catches my eye.

"Over there."

I approach at an angle, giving me a wide enough view to spot Olivia kneeling in front of Esther.

"Shit!" Donny takes off toward them.

I follow, scanning the parking lot and watching Donny's back. It's empty except for River Reapers' bikes—typical for ten in the morning at The Wet Mermaid. My shoulders drop a half notch, my hackles still up. Call it prison sense, but something doesn't feel right.

Maybe it's the weight of the air, or the crows cawing from a nearby telephone line. Maybe it's the knot in my stomach that tightens every time I think of seeing my aunt and uncle.

Maybe it's flat out paranoia.

I approach slowly, flanking Olivia as Donny kneels next to her. She slides over, giving them some space.

"What happened?" I ask, dropping my voice.

She reaches for the cigarette I've forgotten about. Putting it between her lips, she takes a long drag.

"Plans have changed," she says.

3

OLIVIA

Cliff watches me for a long moment. I hold his gaze, realizing that he tied his hair back from his face. The sight of that ponytail sends a rocket of heat to my center—completely inappropriate timing, I know.

What I love most about myself is that I can feel like utter, terrible, absolute shit death, and still be thinking about the next time I'm gonna have sex. I'm a gremlin like that. I'm the same with food. I can always eat. I've got a healthy appetite and I love that about me.

What I don't love is the way Cliff is looking at me: all soft brown eyes, so dark they're almost black, brows furrowed just enough to put a slight crease in the middle.

Despite the fact that shit just hit the fan for Esther—his brother's old lady—he's looking at *me* with a tenderness that pools in those eyes, so transparent I can see straight through it.

I frown, too.

That's not supposed to happen.

"I'm taking her inside," Donny says.

I use Esther as an excuse to break away from Cliff, although I still feel his eyes on me. Taking one of her arms, I hoist her to her feet, Donny supporting her other side.

Once we get her sitting in Donny's room upstairs, I run back down to get her a shot of vodka. The bottle comes with me, just in case. Mark can yell at me later. Handing her the shot, I sit next to her, tucking my legs underneath me.

She holds the shot between two fingers, staring through it. Both men stare at me. I occupy myself by rubbing her back.

Donny kneels in front of her, each big hand clasping one of her knees. "What happened, baby?" he asks, voice calm on the surface but steely underneath. There's a reason he's the club Enforcer.

She downs the shot, shuddering as the sharp vodka slides down her throat. I hold the bottle out to her, but she shakes her head. "Maybe in a minute." She sucks in a deep breath. "That call I got," she says, looking at me, "was my grandma."

I nod, trying to be patient. This isn't some drama queen. It's Esther.

"The kids," she breathes, closing her eyes and holding out the shot glass.

I bite my lip as I pour her another one. For the past four years, her grandparents have been fostering her younger siblings. There's some sort of unspoken agreement that when she graduates, she's supposed to become their guardian. I don't know much more than that.

She throws the vodka back, closing her fingers around the empty glass. Her hand curls so tightly around it, I'm a little concerned it's going to bust. "They're going to give them back," she whispers. "My grandma didn't want to wait 'til after the ceremony to tell me."

Donny gives her a stricken look. "I'm sorry, Essie."

"That's good, right?" I ask, glancing from her to Donny.

She laughs, a bitter sound from those sweet lips. "It was all I could do to get DCF to take them out of there." Her hand tightens.

Gently, I pry her fingers from the glass and take it away. "Doesn't that mean that your parents got their shit together?"

"Damn, Olivia. You of all people should know people never change."

I think of Bree, of all the men she paraded in and out of our apartments. Suppressing a shudder, I shove down the memories. Esther knows more about my past than I know about hers. That's because, all throughout college, she plied me with Netflix and wine, and I gave up little pieces here and there. All this time, she's sat next to me on that couch, being my friend, when I've done shit for her.

"The system is bullshit," she continues.

"Yeah," I agree. Before Cliff's aunt and uncle adopted me, I bounced from family to family. No happy memories. I don't want to press Esther, but we're both social workers now. If anyone can figure this out, it's us. "Look, I know I've been a shitty friend, but let me help. What exactly did DCF tell your grandma?"

"You've been a wonderful friend." She pats my knee. "Especially if you give me that bottle."

I hand it over.

"Essie, there's still some time, if you want to walk," Donny says.

Between chugs of vodka, she gives Donny a dirty look.

He holds up his hands in surrender. "A'ight." Standing, he nods to Cliff. "Let's step out, have a smoke."

"It's okay," Esther says. "He can stay." She closes her eyes again and sighs. "It's not that I don't want to tell you guys. I just don't want to talk about it." She swallows.

"If you're gonna fight for these kids, you better get used to it," I say.

Cliff nudges me with his elbow. "Jesus, Olivia."

"What? It's true."

"She's right." She draws her knees to her chest, her dress pooling around her waist. She keeps the bottle in her lap. "When DCF finally took the girls out of there, they hadn't eaten outside of school in weeks. Cierra tried to make ramen for herself and Abril. She didn't know what to do for the baby. She ended up burning herself. Ximena's diaper hadn't been changed in a few days." She shakes her head.

"Where was your mom?" I ask.

She snorts. "Bitch was right there the whole time. Just didn't feel like it."

"And your dad?"

Her face pales by several shades. "My *father*," she says, her voice cracking. Her eyes dart toward Donny, then close. He places a hand on top of her head, his mouth a tight line.

"College was my ticket out," she says, a pleading edge to her voice.

My hands go numb, dread pitting in my stomach. I don't want to hear this. "Your ticket out of what?" I ask anyway.

Against my better judgement.

Because I know this story. The details might be different, but the structure is all the same. College was my ticket out, too. Still, I have to hear her say it. I can't jump to conclusions. Not everyone's story is like mine.

"I can't say it." She takes another drink from the bottle.

I want to ask her to pass it over, but I don't. "You have to," I hear myself say. "You keep it a secret, you give him power. Shine your light on the truth—on what he did to you."

I'm a hypocrite.

"My sisters, and me. All the time. He'd leave for a little while, and things would be okay. My mom would slack off, but I'd pick up the pieces. She always let him come back, though. She's just as much of a monster as he is." Her lips tremble.

I think of Bree's boyfriends again. Statistically speaking, they should've been the biggest threat to me. They never touched me.

Most of them barely even acknowledged my existence. They were too busy getting high with my mom.

I lick my dry lips. "Your father sexually abused you and your sisters?" With each word I speak, my blood boils a little higher.

Esther nods. "Not the bab—Ximena. I mean, she's five now. She isn't his—his words, not mine. That's why he let her be." Her voice rises with each word, the tears flowing faster.

My stomach curdles. I want to dart into the bathroom, slam the door shut behind me.

"Jesus Christ," Cliff says, reminding me that Esther and I aren't alone.

I have to get my shit together. If not for Esther, then for Cliff. It's bad enough that he looks at me so tenderly.

I don't need him to look at me the way he's looking at Esther. Like he feels sorry for her. He can never look at me that way.

4

CLIFF

I squeeze my hands into fists so tightly, my knuckles hurt. I see my father looking at Lucy a little too long, can hear her cries late at night. He's dead, he's gone, and Lucy is *safe*, but these little girls aren't.

Donny's fingers move like dancers through Esther's hair, stroking and comforting. It's weird, reconciling this tender man with the one who just a few months ago helped me disassemble a body. Then again, it's weird compartmentalizing myself, my own hands that have taken lives and given love. He glances at me, brown eyes so dark they're nearly black.

"DCF says they've done everything they're supposed to," Esther says with a sob. "My mom went to all of her parenting classes and therapy sessions. And my . . . *He* can't pass the psychosexual evaluation, but he has a job and their apartment is a two bedroom." Esther lowers her legs, crossing them and then letting her hands rest in her lap.

"What's a psychosexual evaluation?" I ask, but I think I already know. My hands itch for something to do. A cigarette to smoke. A rapist to choke. Anything.

"It's a test for sex offenders," Olivia explains bitterly. "Tells the clinician how much of a risk they are, if they'll sexually assault someone again. It's also supposed to tell the clinician what kind of *treatment* they need." Olivia practically spits the word. "Treatment." Shaking her head, she paces the small room. "If he can't pass the psychosexual eval, isn't that a fail?"

"That's what I thought," Esther says with a shrug. "But their social worker is working toward reunification."

"Reunification?" I repeat.

"Means they're slowly going to give the kids back to Esther's parents," Olivia explains, still pacing.

"I was supposed to take care of them," Esther whispers. Tears slide down her cheeks.

I rub at the strip of hair on my chin, every muscle and nerve in my body on fire. Olivia is the kind of woman who doesn't have many friends. She keeps to herself, staying loyal to the few friends and family she does have. Esther has been an angel in my Olivia's life. When my girl has nightmares about Eli and I'm not there to soothe her back to sleep, Esther climbs into bed with her and holds her close. No questions asked.

To think that someone hurt this quiet woman who so sweetly holds Donny's heart and tames Olivia's sends a fresh surge of fire through my veins.

"We'll take care of them," I say, giving Donny a weighted look. He nods.

"'We' the club, or 'we' the three?" Olivia asks. She's finally stopped pacing but her arms are wrapped so tightly around herself, there'll probably be bruises later.

Esther holds up a hand. "*We* need to handle things my way. At least, we have to try."

"What do you want to do?" Donny asks, sitting behind her and wrapping his arms around her.

Glancing at the digital display on the alarm on the nightstand, she takes a deep breath. "Well, I've officially graduated. I guess my first step is to meet with the social worker." Her lip curls. "She was supposed to get TPR moving ages ago. I need to find out what's up with that."

"TPR?" I prod.

"Termination of parental rights."

"We can put pressure on her," I offer. "Just get me an address."

Her lips part, probably to tell me to let her handle it, but Olivia speaks over all of us.

"We've got this, Cliff. We're both in the system now, remember? We're the good guys." She sits next to Esther and squeezes her hand. "We're gonna figure this out."

I don't trust the system. Everyone in this town looked the other way when my father was hurting Lucy. They've obviously been doing the same for Esther's parents. Before I can say so, my phone rings.

I pull it out of my back pocket, wincing when I see who it is. "Yeah," I answer, swallowing.

"Where the hell are you two?" Lucy demands, enough heat in her voice to let me know that she's been stuck with her parents at the ceremony, and she's pissed.

"Lucy," I mouth to Olivia.

Our time's run out.

5

OLIVIA

"I'll see you tonight," I promise Esther. "Call me if . . ."

I don't finish. Esther doesn't need me. What she *needs* is the relief that comes with her family's safety. She doesn't need me to hold her hand. She needs me to get her some answers. I won't be able to do anything for her until Monday, when I start my new job with the Waterbury Department of Children and Families.

"Thank you," she says, squeezing my hand. "And I do need you, chica. You keep me calm and focused just by being here. So thank you."

I leave my hand in hers, too stunned to say anything. Being wanted sends a spark of warmth through me. I squeeze her hand back, then release it. "Let's go," I say to Cliff, hurrying past him and out of the club house.

On to the next emergency—my biographic title.

"Hey," Cliff calls after me.

Shoulders tightening, I dangle between pretending not to hear him and riding off, or actually dealing with him right now. Except I'm not dressed for riding, so it's either go back into the club house and grab my gear, or warm the seat behind him.

Smoothing away my emotions, I turn around. "How pissed is Lucy?" I ask, hoping that's all he wants to talk about.

He grimaces. "Pretty pissed. Want a ride?"

I try not to mirror the look on his face. I don't want to hurt his feelings. I just need a little distance right now. Plus, I'll use any excuse to take out the Street Glide.

"I get it," he says when I don't answer right away. "Why ride with me when you can ride your own?" His grin lights up his face. There's nothing but affection there.

I nod, even though that's not it. I really need to clear my head.

"Go get changed," he says. "I'll wait for you."

I take a step back toward the club house. "That's okay. One of us should get to Lucy before she explodes."

"I'm not really looking forward to facing Livid Lucy *and* your parents on my own," he admits.

No matter how muddled my head is, I can't subject him to that kind of torture. "You're right. It's safer if we stick together." I laugh, and his face softens as he reaches for me.

"I want to talk to you about something." He places a hand on each side of my waist and pulls me into him, and I nearly dissolve in his arms.

I swallow. "We should go."

"It'll take two minutes. I'll ask, you'll say yes, and then we'll handle your parents and Lucy."

The heat radiating from his body, from his eyes—it will burn me alive. My heart races faster and faster, and I'm not sure if it's from exhilaration or fear. Because as much as I'm dreading what I think he's going to say, it feels nice to be wanted.

Even if I can't give him what he wants.

"Where are you planning on going when Esther moves out?"

Here we go.

I shrug as if I haven't put any thought into it. "Not sure I'm going anywhere. I mean, my salary with DCF should cover rent." Barely. "I'll probably keep my bartending job to fill in the gaps."

"What if you didn't have to?" The corners of his lips lift, brown eyes pools that I could dive into. Drown in. He's the water and I'm the stone.

"I like bartending. Besides, it's a way out of Prospect pranks." I roll my eyes, but my smile is fond. Along with club dues, Prospects—potential members of the MC—get the grunt work. That's how it is. But I swear the guys are giving me the extra special treatment, because there's no way that regular Prospects have to do things like buy hemorrhoid cream and magnum condoms. Then there was the time they sent me to pick something up, and there was nothing at the address they gave me—not even a building.

It's like having a gang of older brothers. Their brand of torture is harmless, but it's a huge pain in my ass. Not to mention a waste of gas. If I'm too busy with work and bartending for them, they can't send me wandering all over the state. At least, that's what I'm banking on.

"Just wait 'til you find out what they've got planned next," Cliff says, kissing the tip of my nose. His hands slide up and down my waist. A hot breeze moves my skirt around my thighs. All I want to do is drag him upstairs with me. I have to get undressed anyway.

He kisses the side of my neck, just under my ear, and I'm melting into him again. My neck arches back, exposing my throat. Leaning down, he licks the slope from my chin to the hollow of my collar bone. His lips rest in the space, notching in as if they were made to fit my body.

"Let me take over Esther's half of your rent." His lips move against my skin as he speaks, and my knees go weak.

Traitors.

"Cliff," I moan. "We have to go." Putting a hand on each side of his chest, I push him away, even though I don't really want to. I want to take him upstairs with me, let this fantasy envelope me for another little while.

It doesn't work that way. Things with Cliff need to stay easy if I'm going to remain intact. No tangling up our lives until he's so deep inside me, I'll never get him out. A man almost ruined me once before. I'll never let it happen again.

"I'll be down in five," I tell him, tone firm. Without looking back at him, I head into The Wet Mermaid.

THE STREET GLIDE hums between my thighs, a constant vibrating purr that reverberates through my bones. This thing is power. It's the crash of ocean against land, the crush of a flower in a hand, the punishing whip of a sandstorm across the desert.

It already feels like an extension of me.

I push it faster, leaning forward into the wind. My hair lashes out behind me in a stream. If it were possible to do so without getting sand in my mouth, I'd be smiling. I'm the happiest I've been in a long time—and the most free.

Cliff draws even with me, throwing an annoyed glance my way. I lift one shoulder. He motions for me to slow down and pull over, his hands and fingers in black leather gloves.

I roll my eyes. We're just getting to the good part. I'm not exactly sure where we are, as far as town lines go, but I do remember that the road curves ahead, snaking wildly this way and that. It's a fun stretch to drive in a car. I'm dying to find out how it is on the Harley.

Cliff makes a more fervid motion. His message is clear, but I pretend not to understand. Lifting a hand in a wave, I take off. For a second, I swear I hear a sigh behind me, but that's impossible. My engine is too loud.

The first curve begins. I don't slow, but I do lean into the turn just like Cliff taught me. The Harley leans so far, if I glance to my right, the road is only inches from my face. My heart thrusts blood through my veins, and despite the wind, I do smile. Pitted gray gravel blurs past me. A black spot could be an ant or a droplet of grease. I pretend it's the former, that I'm some Greek goddess looking down on my Earth.

Taking it all in.

As the turn ends, I right the bike. Being vertical again makes blood rush from my head and I feel slightly faint. Dizzy. My hands go numb, my legs heavy. I let my body go limp on the bike, tipping my head back. The air rushes up my neck, a cold caress. I'm a little tempted to let go of the handlebars, but I know Cliff is right behind me and I'm sure my little stunt already gave him a heart attack.

I'll hear all about it later.

For now I just ride, uniting my body with the machine between my legs, leaning into curves, pushing myself closer to the road every time. It's an edge that I'm riding—too far and I'll get myself a nice tattoo of road rash up and down that half of my body. Maybe even wreck myself entirely. It's the line I'm strad-dling that gives me a high. Every time I sit upright again, every time adrenaline flushes my system, I feel invincible.

I decide I'm going to name the bike Até, after the Greek goddess of mischief. She's another part of me, like we were made for each other. It feels like I have to put barely any effort into this. Then again, both Ravage and Donny have said several times that I ride like my father.

Mercy—the first man who taught me how to ride.

Not for the first time, I wonder how different things would've been for me if he'd stayed out of prison. If Bree had stayed put. I would have a family much different from the one that adopted me. Even though I wouldn't trade Lucy for anything, being adopted has its complications.

Mainly, Cliff.

As I cross the Middlebury line, heading south on Route 63, he appears at my side. We're doing a slower 40 mph, so I actually hear him when he shouts over to me.

"Are you trying to scratch up that Harley?" His silky black hair flies out behind him, and the urge to run my fingers through it makes my hands twitch. I'm always wet after our rides, and today is no different.

Yet this damned ceremony is the only thing Lucy and Cliff have been able to talk about for weeks.

I'm glad we missed it. My adoptive parents have no idea about my second life, but they will soon enough. They've done a lot for me over the years, and have always treated me as their own, but I haven't told them about Cliff yet. It's bound to cause an argument.

This is *my* life, not theirs. It's not even Lucy's or Cliff's. Even though I'm not entirely sure what I'm going to do with this life yet, I want the freedom to figure it out. Patting the Street Glide, I slow down as I veer off Route 63 and onto Park Road, toward the restaurant.

At the restaurant, we back our bikes into spaces side by side. I kick down the stand but don't move. I'm not looking forward to telling my parents that I'm banging the nephew who ruined their lives—according to them.

Never mind what Cliff's father was doing to their daughter.

I've never known two people more in denial.

Cliff pulls me into his arms—thick, muscular limbs that wrap around me. He presses full lips to mine, the metal of his septum piercing cool against my skin. Another change he's made lately. Yet here I am, still the same.

"It's going to be okay, Olivia."

The way he says my name sends warm tingles down my spine. Again I'm overcome by the urge to hop back on our bikes, go to my place, and ride *him*. But then I'd have to deal with his questions.

I'm not sure who I'd rather face right now—him or my parents.

"Thanks," I whisper.

I lead him to Elena's, an expensive Italian restaurant that my parents are obsessed with. They didn't ask where I'd rather have *my* graduation brunch, same way they didn't ask where Lucy wanted hers. Nora and Collin always assume that they know best, end of story.

I step inside, Cliff at my back, both of us still wearing our cuts, jeans, and riding boots despite the humidity. Better to sweat than to get third degree burns from the bikes.

The cold air is a welcome caress. I glance around for my parents and Lucy and, spotting them at a table in the back, ignore the hostess.

"Come on," I say in a low voice. I weave past the tables, trusting that Cliff is following me and not heading for the hills.

It's funny, the things that send us running.

For me, it's the prospect of moving in with him. The unspoken feelings he carries in his eyes.

For him, it's my parents. The history they share, long before Nora and Collin welcomed me into their home.

Mom smiles when she sees me, her face freezing and falling when she spots Cliff on my heels. Dad follows her gaze, his mouth hardening into a thin line.

"Hey, guys," Lucy says, rising from her seat and giving us hugs. It's good to know she's on my side, no matter how pissed off she is at us for making her wait.

"We only reserved a table for four," Mom sniffs.

I'm in for a long day.

6

CLIFF

It's been over twenty years since I last saw Lucy's parents—my aunt and uncle. From the little that Lucy's said about them since I got out, they don't like me. Or, rather, they don't talk about me or what happened. In just a little while, we're going to have to at least endure small talk with each other.

I'm more worried about Olivia.

Lately she's been pushing me further and further away. She completely avoided answering my question back at The Wet Mermaid, and on the road, she blew past me. I know she's been having nightmares about Eli, even if she won't talk about them. I'm sure she's nervous about starting her new job, too, especially with this Esther thing going on.

Ever since we started her riding lessons, she's been pushing the limits. It's been obvious from her first lesson that she's a natural—another reason for my aunt and uncle to hate me. Not only did I burst their bubble of denial, but I've also managed to corrupt their younger daughter.

Adopted daughter, I correct myself.

Olivia and that Harley are like two reunited souls. I'm not the biggest fan of the way she speeds and takes turns like she's begging for road rash. Olivia's reckless riding is going to give me more grays.

But it's what happened before we started lessons that crawls under my skin.

Before the River Reapers made her a Prospect.

Why the club made her a Prospect, actually.

Now Olivia and I have even more in common than when we started out, and if her parents or even Lucy ever learned the truth, prison would be the least of my fears.

She won't even look at me as we stand in front of her parents. I can't tell whether it's because she is ashamed of me or blames me for what happened. Or if it's just that she simply doesn't want to be with me anymore.

"We can squeeze in one more," Lucy says, thawing some of the frost in the room. She signals the waiter. "Can we get another chair and place setting?"

"Of course." He hesitates, hanging around a moment too long.

Lucy frowns. "Thank you." She turns from him, her voice ice.

I glance at Olivia. She settles into the seat next to Lucy, her eyebrows lifted but her lips immobile.

My aunt and uncle smile woodenly at the waiter until he disappears.

"Do we have a problem with the guy serving our food?" I ask.

All four of them glare at me.

I extend a hand. To who, I'm not sure. "It's, uh, good to see you, Aunt Nora, Uncle Collin."

Their faces are equally expressionless and they avert their eyes from me as if they agreed upon it before leaving their house.

Immediately memories from the last night I saw them flash before my eyes. Lucy's never-ending scream. The growing pool of blood on the floor. My aunt and uncle bursting into the room, ordering me away from her.

The sickening crack of my father's skull.

My stomach roils, my appetite gone.

Lucy, as always, saves my ass. "Are you nervous about Monday, Olivia?"

"Nah," she says with a wave, her eyes on the drinks menu.

"You know Olivia. She's always thinking about what's next," I say.

"As if *you* know her," Aunt Nora says. She still won't look at me, but her voice drips with disdain. As if she knows me. She never did, not really. Neither of them ever tried. They were too busy partying to bother with their daughter or nephew.

"Mom." Lucy huffs. "This is Olivia's special day."

"I just don't understand why *he's* here," my aunt continues.

Lucy puts her hands on her hips, looking every bit the schoolteacher she is. "Like it or not, Cliff is a part of our lives, and our family."

"And what? We just ignore that he ripped our lives apart?" My aunt's voice goes up an octave with each word.

My uncle, of course, remains silent throughout the exchange. Nothing has changed.

"Let's just try to have a nice time," Lucy says, eyeing her own menu.

I stand awkwardly over the table, feeling every bit out of place as I should. This isn't my scene. Nor is it my family. And, apparently, it's not my girl, either.

Lucy gives me a small smile across the table. She is the closest thing I have to a sister, and my best friend. I would kill for her.

And I have.

If nothing else, I'll always have her.

The waiter returns with a menu and cutlery, a bus boy dragging a chair behind him. "I'll give you guys a few more minutes," he says, and they both hurry out of the dining room.

"We're going to the bar for drinks," Nora announces, standing. She wraps an arm around Collin's, practically dragging him up with her. Neither of them offer to get anyone else something.

They hightail it from the table like we've all got contagious rashes.

Lucy's green eyes are dark with memories and anxiety. "They don't blame you for . . . what happened to me," she whispers. "At least, I don't think so."

"It's okay. We don't have to talk about it." I settle into my seat, my knee bumping Olivia's. She draws away from me, her gaze intent on her menu. I scoot my chair back a little to give her space, accidentally bumping the chair into a man at the table behind us.

People don't make room for people like me. The world is built so that, no matter how hard I try, I can never make myself invisible.

The man and his family stare at me without trying to hide their disgust. With my long hair, what's left of my beard, and septum piercing, I look like a criminal. Since I'm wearing my cut, I fit the part of the murderous biker rampaging through their imaginations.

Lucy sighs beside me.

"What?" I ask her.

"Did you really have to wear those?" She gives Olivia and me a pointed look.

I cock my head at her. "Is there a closet full of suits in your condo that I don't know about?"

She rolls her eyes. "You could have tried."

I gesture to my clothing. Under the leather vest, I'm wearing dark jeans and a solid black T-shirt that doesn't have holes in it. This is as dressed up as it gets for me. "What's wrong with my outfit?"

"Would you wear jeans to your own wedding?"

I snort. "Luce. Do I look like the marrying type?"

Lucy laughs. "Yes."

Next to me, Olivia stiffens.

I can't help but think of the conversation Lucy and I had, back when Olivia and I were just starting . . . whatever it is we're doing. Lucy warned me to be careful, accusing me of being the marrying type and warning me that Olivia is not.

Her parents sit down beside her and our conversation grinds to a halt. I half listen to my aunt and uncle as they catch up with their daughters. They make no effort to learn about my life, and I don't bother to ask them anything. They've already made up their minds about me. Right now I'm just an ugly fixture in the restaurant that they're tolerating.

I could just leave. I should. If I do, I'd just be proving them right. So I sit at their table while they ignore me, Olivia only acknowledging me long enough to ask me to pass the salt.

I definitely spooked her by asking her to move in with me. All I can do is hope that, once we're away from our family and in the club house, we can go back to just being us. Everything else is just details.

Or so I'd like to believe.

ON OUR WAY back to The Wet Mermaid, I let her take the lead. Something inside my chest swells, expanding until I can barely breathe. Pride and other emotions thicken in my throat. Despite everything, here she is, a real life hero ready to step out and save the world.

I just hope she hasn't become tainted by me, the villain.

Away from my aunt and uncle, I feel less on edge. Everything is simpler. I don't have to watch what I say or how I eat my food. By the time we reach the club house, I'm myself again. I let Olivia go inside first.

The guys whoop and whistle, holding up drinks to toast her and Esther.

"Congratulations, sweetheart," Mark says, giving her a hug and kiss on the cheek.

"Let me hug my goddaughter," Ravage interrupts. He engulfs Olivia in a bear hug. "I'm proud of you, baby."

"Thanks, Pres." She moves away from me through the crowd, toward the bar.

"You good?" Ravage asks me.

"He's had a rough day," Lucy says from beside me.

"Hey." I wrap her in a hug, careful not to crush the flowers she brought for Olivia. "I didn't know if you were coming."

"I wouldn't miss the real party." She kisses my cheek. "That was fun, huh?"

"I need a drink." I nod toward the bar, where Olivia is yelling at the poor young woman making drinks in her place.

The crowd parts for me and Lucy, and I lead her toward two empty bar stools.

"Are you two okay?" she shouts over the music. "I caught a vibe."

I scoff at her over my shoulder. "Like the vibe between you and the waiter?"

"Waiter?" She tries to smile, but it doesn't reach her eyes.

"Is he the would-be fiancé, Luce?"

Her eyes tighten, lips flattening.

"I'll take that as a yes. I guess we've both got trouble in paradise." Reaching the bar, I place my hands flat on the lacquered wood, leaving the seats open for Olivia and Lucy. But my girl takes her drink and saunters away as if she didn't see us.

"Guess so." Lucy hops onto the stool. She rests her elbows on the bar and puts her chin in her hands.

"What do you want to drink?" I ask.

"I'll just take a soda."

"A soda? After the 'family' reunion we just had?" I signal the bartender.

"I have to drive, Cliff," she says, giving me her stern teacher look.

"You're not staying long." I tilt my head. "What's going on with you and the waiter?"

Before she can answer, the bartender reaches our end.

"Hey," she says, all burgundy hair and big green anime eyes. "I'm Trish. What can I get you?" Her eyes rake over my muscular arms, pause at the septum piercing, then skim up to meet my eyes. She winks.

From across the room, I can feel Olivia watching us. I turn in my seat and, sure enough, she's leaning against the wall, sipping her drink as she gives Trish the death glare.

Turning back, I chuckle. I guess there's nothing to worry about after all.

"Let me get a couple Snakebites," I tell Trish. I nudge Lucy. "You're having one. It's gonna be a good night."

With a shake of her head, she hops down from her stool. "I'm gonna give these to Olivia," she says, holding up the flowers. "Then I'm heading out. You two have fun."

I watch her as she moves through the club. She says something to Olivia, who replies with a smirk. I wish I could read their lips. Lucy nods toward me and Olivia says something else. Pressing the bouquet into Olivia's free hand, Lucy gives her a kiss on the cheek. Then she's gone.

Olivia downs her drink, setting it down on a nearby table. Eyes locked on me, she heads over.

When Trish brings me my shots, I down them both. Then I meet my girl halfway.

7

OLIVIA

"**A**re we good?" Cliff whispers in my ear. He backs off a little, holding me at arm's length in front of him, those big hands on my waist.

I nod, red painted lips curling into a smile.

"I'm not trying to push you into anything." His brown eyes search mine, a wall of hesitation between us.

"I like it right here where we are," I say, scooting in closer. I stand on my tiptoes and wrap my arms around his neck.

I like being with Cliff. I really do. Right now, everything is simple with him. Easy. There are no expectations. We're just together. The way he's been looking at me lately—those puppy dog eyes that go soft every time he sees me—is far from simple.

I don't know what to do about it. Guys like Cliff want the whole package. He's the type who needs the wedding and three kids. Eventually that's going to shake this whole thing up—probably sooner rather than later.

It won't be fun anymore.

I did the whole promises thing once, and it almost destroyed me. Kind words were replaced by vile ones. It got so bad, I thought *I* did something wrong. Turns out there's a word for that:

gaslighting. I know Cliff isn't like that. He'd never hurt me. I knew it from the moment we met.

Still, we want completely different things. We just haven't said so out loud yet.

"Want another drink?" he asks me.

Bishop Briggs's "Tempt My Trouble" comes on over the speakers, the opening beat already getting my shoulders moving. I don't know who put together the playlist for the party, but it's been a good mix of the MC's favorite music, mine, and Esther's.

Except for her love of boy bands, like 5 Seconds of Summer and ESX.

"I want to dance before another shitty Backstreet Boys song comes on." Or before Cliff asks me to move in with him again.

"Oh, come on, you know you love those '90s jams." He laces his fingers through mine and pulls me to the makeshift dance floor.

"I know *you* do, Mr. Fiona Apple."

Closing my eyes, I let the music take over my body. Dancing is a lot like fucking. You have to give yourself over to it completely. Any lack of confidence, and that body freezes up. If you let yourself go, your body practically does the work for you.

"Fiona Apple was fucking hot in my day," Cliff says over the music.

I crack an eye open. "Oh yeah?" I turn, putting my back to him. As if completely in sync, his arms wrap around me, hands flush against my stomach.

"There's nothing sexier than a pissed off woman." He tugs me closer, and I let him pull me in.

Bishop sings about pretending even though they're neither just friends nor are they in love, and I try not to think about how accurate that is. How things between us are fire when we're between the sheets, but now we're avoiding this next step.

"You keep mooning over Fiona Apple, and you're gonna see

pissed off." I actually love her, but I'll never give him the satisfaction of knowing. Unless he sees who I follow on Spotify.

More reasons not to let him move in.

"Don't worry, baby," he says, wrapping his arms around me and holding me close, our bodies moving to the music together. "You're the only angsty girl for me."

I wriggle against him until we're facing each other again. "I'm *not* angsty." Nor am I the only one for him.

The song ends, the speakers going silent. I put my hands on Cliff's chest, getting ready to put some space between us and get myself another drink. The crowd cheers, lights dimming. Several figures stride onto the main stage, the drummer taking his place behind a kit, the bassist and guitarist strapping on their instruments.

I didn't know we got a band for tonight.

The lead singer steps up to the microphone at the edge of the stage, a guitar strapped across his chest. With the lights down, I can't make out any features. But when he speaks, my skin crawls.

"Hey, what's up," he croons, the sound of his voice churning my stomach. "We're Oh Vile Eye, and this is 'He Said, She Said.'"

The drummer counts them in and they launch into the song, a melody I've never heard before but the lyrics are too familiar. Bile creeps up my throat. Turning from the stage, I run.

I shove past bodies, faces I can't make out, my heart taking shots at my ribs. Pushing through the doors, I burst into the warm evening, the air suffocating. Each breath scrapes my throat. I stumble to the Street Glide, resting a hand on the seat. My knees have turned to jelly. Grabbing my cigarettes, I stagger to the side of the building and sink to the pavement.

I light up with a shaking hand, head spinning. I thought my ex moved out of state. He's supposed to be doing his music shit on the other side of the country. Far from me. If he's really back, I'll never feel safe.

8

CLIFF

One second Olivia's right next to me, the next she's gone. She didn't even say anything. At least, I didn't hear her—it *is* pretty loud in here. Still, I've got a feeling she's given me the slip. I sigh as the band goes right into their next song, and make my way over to the bar.

I sink into a seat, inclining my chin at Stixx, a member I don't talk to too often. It isn't the ink that covers him from the neck down in black, red, and gold that unnerves me. It isn't even the pompadour he rocks, his light blond hair parted, the undercut fade almost down to his skin. It's his pale ice eyes—always a little too wide—that freak me out.

He nods back, hands wrapped around a rocks glass of whiskey—minus the ice.

"You drinking that warm, brother?"

"Yeah." He tosses back the remainder of it, then holds up the empty glass for Trish to refill.

I turn back to the stage while she tends to Stixx. The band actually isn't bad. They're a weird blend of punk, dance, and grunge, but it works for them. It's too bad Olivia is missing this, because I think she'd like them. I scan the club for Esther, but with the club lights strolling through the floor, it's impossible to make out faces. I sigh.

I've been ditched.

"So what's your name?" Trish asks Stixx.

I swivel back around in my seat. "Don't ask," I warn her.

She turns those anime eyes on me long enough to roll them, then bats them at Stixx.

"Stixx," he tells her.

"Sticks?" She blinks.

"That's two Xs." He wiggles his glass at her. "One for each house I've burnt down."

"Okay," she says slowly, taking his glass. She turns back to me. "What can I get you, sweetie?" she asks me, eyes begging me to order something, anything. Stixx has that effect on people.

"Whiskey on the rocks, please." I eye Stixx's warm whiskey and choke back a grimace.

"What's up, boys?" Vaughn claps us each on the shoulder. "Where's the lady of the hour?"

Trish slides our very different whiskeys to Stixx and me, then hands Vaughn an IPA.

"IPAs taste like pine and piss," Stixx says.

"Better than room temp Maker's." Vaughn shakes his head at me. "Seriously, where's Olivia? Ravage wanted to see her."

"I don't know." I suck down my whiskey, a headache cracking across my forehead as I finish it: brain freeze.

"Well, when you see her, send her his way." He lifts the IPA in a salute to Stixx and me, then heads back onto the floor.

The booze works its way through me, but it isn't enough. "Another, please," I rasp to Trish. I thought Olivia and I were okay, but apparently we aren't. I should've known better than to ask her to move in with me. Lucy did warn me, after all. I guess I just thought I was different—that we're different. Olivia spends a lot of nights upstairs with me, anyway. Moving into her place wouldn't change things much.

Or so I thought.

Trish hands me another whiskey with a smile, tucking the tip I give her into her bra. I don't bother telling her that it's not happening. I knock this one back, too, then head outside for a cigarette. Maybe the hot air will clear my head. Or maybe I'll just take a ride.

Maybe it's for the best. In just a couple days, Olivia will be working for the state. I'm not even sure why she's wearing that Prospect cut, because the two don't go together.

There's a lot about Olivia that messes with my head.

The second I step out, I spot her right away, like I'm magnetically drawn to her. Sighing, I light up and walk over to the line of motorcycles.

She leans against the building, the bottom of one boot planted on the brick. Relief floods through me at the sight of her.

She didn't leave.

Still, she didn't say anything. Usually we go out for a smoke together. I'm probably reading too much into it all, but after this morning's botched talk, I'm a little sensitive.

I decide to play it cool. Hanging back by my bike, I follow cars with my eyes as they pass, smoking in silence. Minutes pass, punctuated by each roll of tires and the music thudding from inside. I refuse to be the one to break whatever this is between us. If we're going to work, I have to let her come to me.

"I really do love Fiona Apple," she says.

"Huh?"

"I guess I'm just absurdly jealous of your high school crush." She drops her cigarette and crushes it out. *Even though I won't move in with you*, is what goes unsaid.

I shrug. "It's cool. It's not like Fiona and I are ever getting together."

"A boy can dream."

"I'm a few decades past that, darlin'." I blow smoke through my nose, relishing the sting. Anything to distract me from the bruise of rejection.

She sighs, a soft, sweet sound. Even though her eyes are bright, there's a chink in the armor. I can see it in the way her glance falls down, eyes skating back up to meet mine for a second before she drops them again.

"What is it?" I ask before I can stop myself. So much for playing it cool.

"Just a weird day." The smile she gives me is just as cracked as the wall she keeps throwing up.

It's the beginning of the end.

I *knew* I shouldn't have asked. Some part of me hoped that since she's keeping extra clothing in my room and a toothbrush in the bathroom, it'd be a natural next step.

"Well," I say through a stream of smoke, "Ravage is looking for you."

She scowls. "Did he say why?"

"I didn't talk to him. Vaughn let me know." I extinguish my cigarette under the heel of my boot.

"This was supposed to be my day," she says under her breath. Straightening, she pushes off from the wall.

Normally I'd offer to go with her, at least take the ride for whatever errand he's sending her on. Right now, I just want another drink.

"See you after," I say, lighting up another cigarette.

Her lips part, tongue running along her lower lip. Those eyes that can send me to my knees dance back and forth, hesitation on her tongue. Then she presses her lips together, turns, and marches inside without another word.

I wish I'd never brought it up. I wish I'd skipped brunch.

It's too late to go back.

9

OLIVIA

Cliff is mad at me for not letting him move in.

I realize it as I re-enter The Wet Mermaid, the shitty band's music engulfing me. Well, okay—it's actually pretty good. Greg always was. Between his giant ego, bad boy persona, and actual talent, I always knew he'd go places.

I just didn't think he'd come back to haunt me.

He stands on stage, both hands wrapped around the mic, shirt off—probably somewhere in the crowd. I look away, afraid that if I stare too long, he'll feel me and find me. Head down, I move past people dancing. One of the club's dancers catches me with her elbow.

"Sorry, sweetheart," she calls after me.

I keep moving, rubbing my ribs, wishing I could just as easily soothe away the bruises Greg left behind.

The music stops and the crowd cheers. The doors to the Chapel are just a few yards away. I hone in on them until they're all I see. I just have to get inside. Nothing bad can happen if Ravage is with me.

"Thank you," Greg tells the crowd. "I actually grew up here. It's been a while." He chuckles, and the sound sends shattered icicles scraping down my spine. "I did a stint in the military, saw the world. My one true love is music."

Applause and whistles drown out his next words. The path to the doors opens up and I sprint toward them.

"Well," he amends, "music and this one girl. I hear she's the guest of honor tonight."

My hands go numb. I force myself to keep moving. I just have to get to Ravage. Take whatever bullshit errand he's got for me and get the fuck out of here.

Just as I reach the door, the lights come on.

"Olivia, where are you?" Greg croons. "I came back for you, baby."

Swearing, I push the doors open and burst into the cool calm of the Chapel. I slam them shut behind me, drawing in a deep breath. If I was alone, I'd lean against them, take a moment to collect myself.

Ravage sits at the head of the table, his PRESIDENT patch worn and dirty on his cut. "There she is." He grins. "Have a seat."

"Why?" I blurt. Prospects don't get to sit at the table.

"We need to talk," he says, smile fading. His piercing blue eyes appraise me.

I drop into a chair, knees too weak to keep standing anyway. "What'd I do?"

"Easy, kiddo." He runs a hand over his buzzcut, each strand a deep shade of black. I wonder if his hair is dyed or he just super-naturally hasn't gone gray yet. "You didn't do anything wrong. I'm proud of you."

"Thank you," I say, but my eyebrows remain pinched together. If I've learned nothing else after hanging around the River Reapers these past four years, it's this: never question the President. Especially if I want to be patched in—which, I do.

Still, my stomach wraps itself into a tight knot. It's probably just a culmination of the day I've had: boyfriend who wants to up the ante, parents who can barely stand being around me anymore, my sister who took off after barely saying hi . . . Then there's Greg.

I push it all away, focusing on my President. I'm the fucking master of shoving things down.

Ravage slides a thick envelope across the table, flap side up. It's the kind that graduation cards come in. I wasn't expecting anything, especially considering he and the club threw Esther and me this party.

"Thank you," I say again.

"It's not from me."

I flip it over, and gasp when I see the name and return address: Mercy, Lewisburg. "He's been at Lewisburg this whole time?"

"Who do you think watched Cliff's back all these years?" he counters.

I blink. "Why would Cliff need protection?"

Ravage scoffs. "He killed our President, Olivia. Not everybody was happy about that."

My frown deepens. "Wait. Are you telling me that the club made Mercy go to Lewisburg?"

"We took a vote," is all he says.

I stare down at the card. "I bounced back and forth from foster care to Bree. Every time she fucked up, I got sent to another home." I run my teeth across my bottom lip. "I could've stayed with my dad," I say quietly. I lift my eyes to Ravage's.

He waits.

"So what do you want me to do?"

"Go see the old man."

"That's all, huh? You just want me to drop everything and take a trip to Pennsylvania to see my father, who basically abandoned me." I stand. "No thanks."

"He never abandoned you," Ravage growls.

If I'd gone to live with my father instead of landing in foster care, so much of my life could've gone differently. The few memories I have of him are good ones. Not like the memories I have of Bree, of too many drugs and all of the boyfriends who were too mean. He taught me how to ride, sitting on his lap and holding the handlebars while he steered us around the industrial park. The framed photo in my bedroom of him holding me as a baby is a constant reminder that, even though he hasn't been in my life for years, he still loved me.

But he couldn't have loved me that much.

"He left me for the club!" I slash a hand through the air.

"He did it to protect Cliff." He crosses his arms, lifting his chin at me.

"Enough of the bullshit. Why does the club need me to see him?" I cross my arms, too, and stare down at him.

"He needs a ride home," Ravage says.

10

CLIFF

I glance down at all the cigarette butts at my feet. I've been out here long enough. All I want to do is go up to my room, but this party won't be over for hours. Then there's Olivia, somewhere inside. I don't know if there's anything I could do to erase the past ten hours, but I'd love to go back to this morning, right before Esther knocked on my bedroom door.

I've got to make this right, or I'll lose her.

I pull open the door and duck back inside. Mercifully, the band is packing up and Esther's boy band playlist is back on. Their music wasn't bad, but the lead singer was a little much. I'll take pop prince angst over predator on stage any day.

The doors to Chapel are closed, neither Olivia or Ravage anywhere in sight. I was outside for a while. Whatever Ravage wants from her, it's important.

I join Donny at the bar.

"Another Maker's on the rocks, sweetheart?" Trish asks.

"Thank you." When she turns to make the drinks, I lean toward Donny. "Any idea what Ravage wants with Olivia?"

He gives his head a single, curt shake.

Esther slips between the two of us, planting a kiss on Donny's cheek. Her arms wind around his neck and she nuzzles into him. "Hey guys," she sings.

"Hey, darlin'." I'm glad she's feeling better, even if it's only temporary. That's another reason why I need to make things right with Olivia. Esther needs all of our help. If Donny's going to have any success bringing this to the table, he needs my support.

"That front boy was mackin' on your girl," Esther slurs.

"We gonna have to bury him, too?" Donny jokes.

I stare at the doors to Chapel as if I could wrap up Olivia and Ravage's conversation by force of will alone.

Esther giggles, thankfully not catching the "too." "That might be a yes."

"Yeah?" Donny swivels around and pulls Esther into him, his knees at each of her hips.

"You're changing the subject," she says, but presses into him.

"Damn right." Cupping her face, he touches his forehead to hers, their skin a brown to browner ombré. "How much longer we gotta stay at this party?"

Esther whispers something, but it's in Spanish and I can't hear much of it over her playlist, anyway. The band finishes packing, the lead singer stopping to talk to Mark on their way out. The River Reapers' Treasurer hands him an envelope thick with cash. Smirking, the guy walks out, tucking it into his pocket.

A while back, the MC voted on having a regular band. If this is the band that's going to be our regular, I might have to find a new job. Just the guy's face makes me want to break it in. That cocky shit-eating grin. I haven't even talked to the guy, but the aura of smugness he carries around him is cloying even from here.

Spend twenty years in prison, and you learn to read people really well.

"Another one?" Trish asks me.

I glance down. My drink is empty. I don't even remember her giving it to me.

The Chapel doors open. Olivia comes out alone, her lips crooked, lashes low.

I set my drink on the bar, already out of my seat. I'm pulled over to her as if tethered to her. "What'd he want?" I ask, glancing back at the door.

She stalks to the door leading outside, her strides long. My legs are longer than hers, but I have to jog to keep up. She shoves open the door and bursts into the twilight.

"Olivia?" I ask, catching up to her.

Her hand lashes out, the envelope in it smacking me in the chest. Dropping it to the ground, she goes to her bike for her cigarettes.

Stooping, I pick up the envelope and flip it over. It's addressed to her, care of Ravage, whose real name is apparently Todd Harris. I chuckle. Todd. Not that I'd ever say anything like that to his face.

The return address is from Mercer Reynolds at Lewisburg Penitentiary—Olivia's father.

"Why didn't you tell me your dad is in Lewisburg?" I wouldn't have been in such a hurry to leave. Lucy, either. Not that I would've been in a rush to meet him.

She glares at me through a cloud of smoke.

"You didn't know," I say.

"He's been there this whole time." Tears slip down her cheeks.

Tucking the card into my cut, I close the space between us. "Hey." I thumb away her tears. "You didn't know. We'll just go see him."

She laughs, pulling away. "You've already met him."

I shake my head. "No one from the club ever approached me when I was inside. I was a naive kid. I didn't even know my father was President. I've seen him, but I don't know him."

"Well, he knows *you*," she tosses at me.

"He was my father's VP. I don't really remember him." I

suppose I could have met him at some point. Birthday parties, cookouts . . . Who knows.

"Damn it, Cliff." Her free hand clenches into a fist. She lunges forward and hits my chest with the softer side of it. "He's inside because of you."

"No, baby," I say. I wrap my fingers around her wrist in a loose hug and draw it away from my chest. "I don't even know him."

"The club took a vote," she hisses, words dripping with venom.

"Why?" I shake my head. It doesn't make sense.

"Because someone had to watch your back."

I run a hand through my hair. "What are you talking about, Olivia? No one was watching my back except me." I hold my hands out to her, knuckles up. Even in the waning light, the scars dotting them are stark against my skin.

"Not according to Ravage," she says, stabbing her cigarette into the air between us. "Because of you—because of the club—my dad was taken away from me. And now I can't even start my job. How am I going to help Esther from out in fucking Amish country?" The tears drip from her cheeks onto the pavement, leaving dark splotches.

"Slow down," I soothe, taking a step toward her.

"No!" She sidesteps me, then whirls around. "You don't get to make this better."

"Okay." I hold my hands up. Dropping them, I take a few steps back until I'm leaning against the wall. "All right." I reach for my beard, but my fingers close around empty air. Again. "Why can't you start your job?" I ask, voice haggard.

"You haven't heard? Mercy is getting out on Monday, and I have to go get him. I have to call my supervisor. I don't even know what I'm going to tell her. She's going to fire me before I even start. I'm going to miss my first day!"

Damn. The last thing I want to do is question my President, but that was a bad call. "Ravage should've known better, but he's just trying to help. He probably just thought you'd want to be the first one to see your dad."

"I guess." Her shoulders drop a little. "Still doesn't help me keep my job."

"I'll talk to him," I promise. "Donny and I need to bring Esther's problem to the table, anyway. I'll make him see that he needs you here, in that DCF office."

"How the hell are you going to convince the club that Esther's problem is a club problem?"

Pushing off from the wall, I hold my arms open to her. She shakes her head at me, but steps into them. "That's for me to worry about."

11

CLIFF

U nless there's anything pressing, the River Reapers usually have Church on Sundays—someone's sense of humor, I guess. We typically discuss business, such as The Wet Mermaid's fiscal budget, upcoming charity events, things like that. I've got less than twenty-four hours to figure out how I'm going to convince my brothers to help Esther.

I bend down and kiss Olivia full on the mouth, my lips moving against hers automatically. I suck in her lower lip and she sighs, a dreamy, evanescent sound. Sometimes I wish I could record certain things about her, that way I never have to forget. Like the exact pitch of her moans, the soft exhalations that come out in wave after wave when she's coming.

Then there are the things I could never forget, like the mischievous look in her eyes that first night as she tried car doors. It seems like ages ago and yesterday all at once. It's only been three months, but they've been the best three months of my life.

She presses against me, arms encircling my neck. Because she's so much smaller than me, she always has to stand on her tiptoes. Or I have to support her. I like the latter better.

Gripping her thighs, I lift her from the ground. She squeals, another Olivia sound that I can't commit to memory but appreciate every time I hear it. It's a short, surprised laugh that lilts at the end, an exclamation but not a protest.

"Wanna go upstairs?" I whisper against her lips.

I know my Olivia, my ol' lady. Sex is her language, her go-to no matter the occasion. Finding out her father's been in prison all this time indirectly because of me has to be stressing her out.

I can't change what happened. I'd never undo what I did to save Lucy. Eight years old or eighty, my cousin is my whole world. She's my best friend, might as well be my sister.

I just wish I hadn't hurt Olivia in the process.

The least I can do now is help her keep her job. Give her a safe place to work out her stress. Stop pressuring her to make this more than what it is. If it's meant to be—if Olivia and I are supposed to be together—it will be.

She wraps her legs tight around me. "Yes."

I carry her back into the strip club, by brothers who smirk knowingly, past Donny and Esther—who are probably on their way upstairs, too, judging by how seldom their lips part over at the bar.

Muscles straining, I take Olivia up the stairs, careful to watch her head as we pass under the low ceiling of the stairwell. I open the door to my room, kicking it closed behind me as I back her toward the bed.

"Uh-ah," she chides, unwrapping her legs and falling onto the bed. She hooks her thumbs in the loops of my jeans. Sitting up on her knees, she tugs me down with her, nudging me onto my back. With a wicked grin, she straddles me.

I'm already straining against my jeans, but then she rolls her hips. Even through all the denim between us, I can feel the heat of her. It burns just under the surface of her skin, shimmering in her eyes. I suck in a ragged breath.

She's going to burn me alive, whether I'm careful or not.

I'm not even sure I care anymore.

She leans forward, her knees cradling my ribs, thighs flush against my sides. Her back curls, breasts settling against my chest. She captures my lips with hers, and I'm content to let her do as she pleases. This is as safe for me as it is for her. Only with Olivia do I feel truly alive and free, as much myself as ever.

She takes my bottom lip between her teeth, pulling it into her mouth, running her tongue back and forth across my flesh. I place one hand on each of her hips, pressing her tighter against me. While her lips work mine, she lifts up enough to slide a hand between us, fingers ghosting across my stomach. She finds the hem of my T-shirt and slips her fingers underneath it, down to the waistband of my jeans.

I shiver as her fingernails trace the border between skin and denim, back and forth, teasing me because she's only inches from wrapping that hand around me. She must love torturing me, because she does this all the time.

Not that I mind the anticipation.

With the slight space between us, I have room to do my own exploring. I slide my hands up underneath her tank top, past the barrier of underwire and lace, palming her breasts. Her spine arches and she grinds harder into me. I grin against her lips.

Two can play at this game.

She uses the opening to penetrate my lips with her tongue, sliding into my mouth and gliding her tongue against mine. The contact feels so good, I get a little high, forgetting to control the rest of my body for a moment. She wakes me up by unbuttoning my jeans, her deft little thumb freeing the button from the slit of fabric in one quick motion.

Little thief.

I ease my grip on her breasts, rolling my palms over the nipples until they pebble and poke up. I don't need to see them to know what they look like: berry red and round, ripe for my mouth. She keeps me pinned down, her hand moving lower and lower until the pad of a finger brushes my crown, flitting over the tiny opening and dragging a wet line down my length.

As much as I want to flip her over and tear off her clothes, my job is to let her do what she wants, to give her whatever she needs. Her fingers close around me, pumping slowly up and down. When she reaches the base, she releases me only for a second, cupping my balls and drawing her nails across them until they're tight, aching.

I'm gonna have to move this along a little before I explode in her hand.

Releasing her breasts, I slide my hands down the silky flesh of her stomach, pausing only long enough to trace her bellybutton. Her thighs clench against my ribs, and I grin against her mouth.

I know which buttons of hers to press just as well as she knows mine.

I pop open her jeans and, holding her hip with one hand, slide the other hand past the lace and cotton, palming her throbbing heat. A whimper escapes her lips, floating in the breath that passes between us. I splay my fingers, keeping my index and middle finger together, and slide against her slick wetness until I reach the other little berry that gets her going. I press the pads of my fingers against it only for a second before sliding my fingers back down, running up and down her length.

She wriggles away from me then, releasing me from her grip as she rolls onto her side. With her lower lip between her teeth, she tugs off her jeans. I pull off her cut, tank top, and bra, tossing them onto the floor. She kneels in front of me in only her panties, vulnerable anticipation in her eyes.

Straddling me again, she pulls me free from my jeans. Each side of the zipper is a dangerous border grazing my sensitive skin. Pushing her panties aside, she rubs my head against her, following the same route my fingers took only moments ago.

Sometimes she plays this game, too, letting me in only enough to make me crave more, then pulling me out again.

I hold her hips in place, shivering as she rubs me against her bundle of nerves. The slickness of her almost makes me come undone. One thrust and I can be inside, but I have to be patient.

Let her work it out.

Releasing me, she grinds up and down my length, making me slicker, slippery. I twitch against her as blood rushes through me, my balls hot and tight. I'm impossibly hard, almost uncomfortably so. When she reaches my crown again, I arch up against her, an invitation, a plea.

Rolling her hips, she lets me in, taking me all the way inside her. I keep hoping that, if she lets me in like this, eventually she'll let me into her heart too.

I close my hands around her breasts, rolling my palms against the tender flesh, the tight nipples. She shifts, leaning her body toward mine, deepening the angle. I let her find her rhythm, her hips grinding against mine as she makes little circles, then slides almost completely off me. She sits back down, taking me all the way again. I let go of one of her breasts and catch her hand in mine, pulling our linked hands up over my head. Grinning, she pins me there, riding me while I pass my thumb over her nipple, cup her, then reach across her chest to stroke her other nipple.

I match her thrust for thrust, watching each subtle change of her face. I catch the moment she lets go, the way her shoulders fall, her eyelids fluttering closed. Her lips part and she tips her chin back, shouting my name to the ceiling, to the heavens.

She shivers and bucks against me, and I let go too, falling into the sky with her. The room inverts, hazy gray clouding my vision. Olivia collapses on top of me, her cheek resting against my chest. I twitch inside of her, still filling her.

When I finally stop, I run my fingers through her hair, caress her back. "Feel better?"

She nods, her words muffled as her lips move against my cut. "Thank you."

"You know," I say, reaching for the mortarboard on the nightstand. I place it on top of her head. "It's not a proper graduation until you move your tassel to the other side."

She sits up, adjusting the cap. "It doesn't really matter," she says, but the corners of her mouth curl up anyway.

I take the tassel, stroking the silky fibers for a moment. Then I move it from the right to the left.

"Congratulations, Olivia," I whisper.

"Now it's off to the real world," she says with a sigh, hopping up from me. "Do you really think you can convince the club to take on Esther's parents?"

I grab cigarettes from the nightstand, light one for each of us, and pass her one. "We're a team," I tell her. "You and I can do anything, together."

"We'll see," she says, turning from me. She pads into the bathroom and closes the door. A moment later, I hear the shower start.

She's given me the slip again.

12

OLIVIA

There are times I feel like someone is pulling the strings, just trying to push me to my breaking point. Today is one of those days.

This morning feels like it was ages and ages ago, yet it's not even midnight. It's like someone is just dragging it out, building up the tension until I can't take it anymore.

I sit on Cliff's bed at the club house, alone, my wet hair dripping down my back. I thought about just going home, but it'd look really weird if I ditched my own party. Besides, the guys put a lot of work into the whole thing. It's not their fault that my opportunist ex dragged himself back into the state, or that, even dead, Bastard is still pulling the strings behind the scenes.

I don't even blame Ravage, not really.

Cliff is right—I think Ravage really did mean well when he told me I have to pick up Mercy. It's not even his fault that I didn't know where my father's been all this time. All I had to do was ask, but I never did, not in the weeks since Ravage told me who he was. I never even asked my parents or any of the social workers about him.

Maybe I didn't want to know.

Sighing, I glance at the closed door. I have no idea when Cliff will be back, so I've got to make this quick.

Opening the browser on my phone, I type in Greg's full name, then add "Naugatuck, CT" to make sure I've got the right Greg Byrne. My guess is that he's living in his mom's old house. Before he went into the Navy, he stayed with his dad in an apartment part of the time, and the other half at his mom's. It's a shot in the dark—he could be anywhere, really. He might not even be staying in town.

But if he's really back, I need to know where he is.

Especially if he's going to be playing at my club.

The search engine results load, starting with a Facebook listing of all Greg Byrnes. He might not even have a Facebook, but he does have an ego. I can't imagine him forgoing everything that comes with social media: DMs with tit pics, adoring fans fawning all over his latest selfies, hundreds of likes and comments. All that shit.

Hands shaking, I click on the link.

The page loads agonizingly slowly. I never have good service up in the club house. Downstairs, at the bar, I have full bars. It's one of those Naugatuck oddities.

I stand and pad toward the only window in the room. I pop open the screen and hold my phone out in the humid air, hoping I don't drop the damn thing.

The listings appear on my screen all in one shot.

Pulling my hand back inside, I go back to the bed. Even though Cliff isn't here, it makes me feel safe to sit on his rumpled sheets next to a discarded tee, his scent the only thing I can smell.

I take a deep breath and light a cigarette.

The first result is a direct hit. The profile pic thumbnail is teeny, but I'd recognize that red hair and those dead gray eyes anywhere. It's the same man who was on stage downstairs just a couple hours ago. He's gained a little weight and a goatee since I last saw him, but it's him. He's still chiseled from head to toe with the body of a Navy SEAL god. Once upon a time, I adored those abs. Now I want to kick them in, break some ribs.

I've never hated anyone so much.

I click on his profile, but other than his profile pic and basic information, I can't see shit. Stupid Facebook makes you log in to see any of the good stuff. Snarling, I punch in my email address and password.

I get the spinning wheel up top in the teeny status bar.

The River Reapers need to get themselves some goddamn Wi-Fi.

I stalk back to the window, cigarette clamped between my teeth. Greg's profile loads, every detail mine to peruse. I'm going to have to block him eventually so that he doesn't find me, but for tonight, it's all at my disposal.

You don't need to be a private investigator or cop to find someone. You just need to know what you're doing.

I start to scroll through his posts when something in the information sidebar catches my eye, stopping me cold.

He's married.

He has a wife.

Nausea cramps my stomach, and I drop the cigarette into the ashtray. Running for the bathroom, I barely make it to the toilet before every drink I had earlier comes hurtling up my throat, burning even worse the second time around. I vomit until I'm empty, until my voice is hoarse and tears stream down my cheeks.

He's *married.*

When I let him get away, I didn't just save my own ass. I gave him the opportunity to do what he did to me . . . to someone else.

Bile crawls up my throat, and I bend over the toilet again.

13

CLIFF

I find Ravage sitting at a table downstairs, his wife Shannon in his lap. Shit. I'd hoped to catch him before the party really got going. I don't even see Donny, so he and Esther must be upstairs.

Interrupting Ravage right now would be a bad idea. He's not in business mode anymore. Shannon is snuggled in his arms, so they're not far from going upstairs. If I cock block him, he'll cold cock me.

Or Shannon might.

Hesitating by the bar, I signal for Trish.

"The usual?" She bats her eyes at me.

"Thank you, darlin'." I smile back at her, the crooked one that my mom always said was going to kill the ladies. An unexpected twinge ripples through my chest. It shouldn't be possible to miss someone this much after so long, but I do. Especially because she'd be able to give me some advice about Olivia.

But she's not here. Apart from Lucy, I have no family left. Only my brothers.

Trish shovels ice into a glass and pours the whiskey over it. With a wink, she adds a cherry with a stem, then she sets the glass down in front of me. Stretching out, she leans on the counter, her chest framed by the stained and worn wood. But all I can see is Olivia.

I take a sip, the whiskey cold and refreshing. It's liquid courage, bolstering me enough to interrupt my President. I take my drink over to their table, smiling at Shannon.

Leaning in close, I speak so that only he can hear me. "Can I borrow you for a minute, Pres?"

He turns toward me, surprised. "Yeah, son. Everything okay?"

"Just need to run something past you."

"Sure." Ravage kisses Shannon deeply, then they part. He waves me over to an empty table in the corner of the club. Sitting, he folds his hands on the polished wood. "What's on your mind?"

Even though I want a cigarette, I fold my hands in front of me, too. "The club needs Olivia in the DCF office," I say, looking him in the eyes. It's fire meeting ice.

"Why's that?" His face gives me nothing. I can't tell if he's pissed at me for challenging his decision or if he's bored now that there isn't a warm body in his lap.

"Esther has a family problem that the club needs to handle."

"Donny's ol' lady?" Ravage's eyebrows lower.

"They're pretty cozy," I say. "I think Donny's serious about her."

"If he's so serious, why isn't he sitting there instead of you?"

I lift my eyes toward the ceiling, smirking. "He's a little occupied. Olivia can dig into the state, find out what's going on with Esther's siblings. She's our Prospect, so that makes this official club business."

Even though my tone is even, my heart is racing. I have to step carefully here, pick my words so I don't come off as challenging my President.

"Olivia's heading to Pennsylvania." Ravage spreads his hands. "Mercy's getting out."

"If she loses this job, we have no one in DCF's offices." I pin him with a pointed look. "You and I both know how they like to sniff around, see if they can break up our families. We need her to keep this job."

"Are you asking me, *son*," he says, the force in his voice reverberating in my chest, "or are you telling me?"

"I'm saying I think it'd benefit the club to have someone on our side. It'd also make Donny happy. You know, happy wife, happy life, and all that shit."

Ravage's head bobs as he thinks it over. He points a thick finger at me. "You'll make a good President someday."

I hold up my hands, palms out. "That's not what I'm after, here." Not yet, anyway. Someday, I'm reclaiming that seat. I'm not ready for that responsibility just now, though.

"Olivia can stay," Ravage says. "You'll pick up Mercy."

"Are you sure that's a good idea?" I pluck my pack of cigarettes from the pocket inside my cut and light one.

My President *laughs*. He throws his head back and slaps his thigh. "I only wish I could be a fly on the walls of that road trip." He stands and walks away, still laughing.

I suck in a deep drag and grimace.

I'm going to meet Olivia's father.

When we were inside, he had no reason to hate me. Besides, the MC needed him to keep me alive. Now, he has every reason to choke the life out of me.

After all, I'm the guy he went in for—the guy he gave up raising his daughter for. The daughter that I happen to be sleeping with.

I'm in deep shit.

Courtesy of Google, I find a wedding registry for Greg and Mrs. Byrne—Cami. Turns out they just got married this Valentine's Day—the day I met Cliff. Her registry is full of household appliances, big things like a dishwasher, a stackable washer and dryer. It confirms at least one thing: they live in a house. I'm just not sure whether it's his mother's or a new place.

My guess is, unless his mom died, they got their own mortgage. I tap my lips with a finger, thinking. My stomach rocks, the nausea never ebbing, only building. Secrets will only burn you from the inside out. I thought I could just move on with my life.

I don't know what to do with this.

If this was an inspirational Oprah segment, I'd let go, transforming into a life-loving warrior queen. I'd start a non-profit, help other women like Shannon, Ravage's wife. They say forgiveness isn't absolving the other person from what they did—it's letting go. I've never been the letting go type, though. All I feel is a violent need to make him suffer for what he did to me.

He broke me. Rendered me unable to trust anyone. Gave me

such a heaping dose of paranoia, I killed a man. A man who was probably going to hurt me, anyway, but still.

How do I get revenge for that kind of damage? Putting a quick, quiet bullet in his forehead just doesn't equate the weight I carry.

I click back to Greg's Facebook page, knowing my time is almost up. Instead of looking at his feed, I go straight to his photos. I don't have the luxury of reading statuses.

I scroll through, most of them boring family photos of him, his parents, his siblings. There are selfies—rockstar sex god pics cross-posted from his Snapchat or Instagram. Then there's a single wedding photo, of him and Cami posed together. He presses her against a wall, her eyes closed, her lips curled into a laugh. Her strawberry hair falls in waves around the white lace of her dress. He looks down at her like she's his whole world. They look happy.

She looks happy.

There's no fear in her eyes or body language. A rush of conflicting emotions thuds into me, through me. Guilt, because I never told anyone what happened. I left him free to do it again, to someone else. Anger, because apparently he's capable of loving someone enough not to hurt them. She married him, so things must be perfect between them.

Of course, that's a hell of an assumption. I just don't know what else to think.

The door opens and I close the page in one quick swipe. Cliff ducks underneath the frame, a sloppy grin on his face.

He's drunk.

"How did it go?" I ask tentatively. At least he's still in one piece.

With a grunt, he throws himself onto the bed facedown, nearly squishing me in the process. I scooch out of the way just in time.

"Just remember me when I'm gone," he slurs.

I lift an eyebrow at him. "When you're gone? Did Ravage take your patch?" I didn't think it was that serious, but I've never seen Cliff like, well, *this*. I glance at his cut. Everything is intact. He's still a member.

He buries his face in the sheets. "You're good for Monday," he mumbles into them.

"I still have a job?" He nods. I breathe a sigh of relief. I can still help Esther. I can still afford my apartment. "Why the dramatics, then?"

He lifts his head. The ball of his septum ring is off center. A thick strand of hair falls over his face. "Guess who's picking up your dad?"

I blink. Then I burst into laughter. "You're afraid of my dad?" I squeeze out each word between giggles. This man—who towers over almost everyone, who went to prison for offing his own father, who has scars on his knuckles from doling out so many beatdowns—is scared to meet my father.

There's a strange floaty feeling in my chest, the nausea gone.

"It's not funny," he roars, but there's a grin on his face as he reaches for me, pulling me down to lie next to him. His fingers wriggle into my ribs and I go limp, every nerve lighting up as I laugh so hard, I nearly pee myself.

"You're," I squeak, trying to crawl away. "Scared." I gasp between laughs, his fingers dancing across my belly. "Of." Grabbing a pillow, I chuck it at his head. "My dad!" I suck in a deep breath, rolling onto my back. "Have I found your Achilles?"

Cliff turns onto his side, facing me, his face suddenly serious. "*You* are my weakness," he says, and it's not the booze talking.

I swallow. "You barely know me."

"I know enough." He draws me into him, cradling me against his body. "I know you don't let many people in, but you're fiercely loyal to and protective of those you do let in." His warm lips press against my temple, and I melt into him.

No matter how afraid I am to let Cliff in, I'll always feel safe with him.

"I know you're independent and stubborn," he continues, "and handle a bike like it's your bitch. It's almost a little scary, watching you ride." He kisses me again. "And I know you have a big heart. You want to save all the kids in the system, find them good homes. I do know you, Olivia."

I bury my face in his shirt so he doesn't see the tears.

15

CLIFF

I wake with one arm stretched across the bed, reaching for Olivia even in my sleep. She's gone, the bed as cold and lonely as if she'd never been there at all. What I do have is a raging headache.

I blame Trish, who made me some kind of monster drink after I finished up with Ravage. She might've been trying to get in my drunk pants. At least I had the sense to go upstairs.

I couldn't have been that trashed, because I remember everything, including the things I said to Olivia. They were all true, but even drunk my judgment sucks. At least this time she didn't freeze me out.

Maybe I'm making progress.

This thought boosts me while I shower. I even whistle a few bars of Queen. I throw on a Clutch tee, my cut, and the same jeans from the night before. I'm running out of clothing. Normally I'd take a load of laundry with me to Lucy's, but instead of hanging out at her place like we usually do every Sunday, she wanted to grab lunch.

Of course, her idea of lunch is around eleven, which is breakfast time for me. Bouncing for the strip club these past few months has undone twenty years of waking at the ass crack of dawn for prison work duty. I hope Cara's is still serving breakfast. Or at the least, coffee.

I run down the stairs, booted feet drumming a rhythm on the steps. When I reach the landing and round the corner, I slow.

Trish and one of the dancers sit at the bar. Her name is Pru. She's a cool chick—one of the few not trying to get into my pants.

"Do you think they call him Red Dog because of his cock?" she asks.

Or so I thought.

Trish giggles. "I don't know."

I walk by, smirking, their eyes following me as I pass. By the time I reach the front door, they burst into giggles.

"I'd ride that Red Dog no matter what color it is," Trish says, flicking a glance my way. She bites down on the straw of her iced coffee.

I pull open the door. As I duck outside, I hear Pru say "Oh my god, Trish."

Shaking my head, I amble over to the Screamin' Eagle, lighting a cigarette. I've seen some guys smoke and ride, but I'm not that coordinated. Maybe it'll come with experience, like eating a Big Mac while driving. Or it'll just be one more thing I never quite master.

I suck the cigarette down, then drop the butt, dragging the heel of my boot over it to extinguish it. Straddling the Screamin' Eagle, I put both feet flat on the ground, then use my left toes to nudge the kickstand out. I turn the key in the ignition and kick the shifter into neutral. Then, holding the bars of the bike, I pull in the clutch with my left hand and flip the switch on with my right. The motorcycle hums beneath me, idling.

Back when I first started riding, all of these steps were so overwhelming. Now, it's second nature. This bike has become as much a part of me as any of my limbs.

It's my wings.

I kick the shifter into first gear, give it a little throttle with my right hand, and then I'm off to meet Lucy.

Since moving out this past winter, I've made it a point to keep our Sunday dates. I missed twenty years of her life. I don't intend on missing any more. Sometimes Olivia joins us, but not always. Especially during the last weeks of her last semester. Between studying for her finals and finishing up her internship, I was lucky I saw her at all. She never said why, but I got the feeling she fell behind for a little while.

Before me. Before Eli. I'm not sure why.

I wish I hadn't passed out on her. I don't know if she had her usual nightmares or if her sleep was as black and peaceful as mine. Guess that makes me a bad boyfriend—or "ol' man"—if that's even what I am to her.

I pull into the parking lot of Cara's, the diner Lucy wanted to meet at. I take the Screamin' Eagle past a couple cars, then back it into a spot almost right in front of the restaurant.

"Mommy," a little boy calls, his tiny finger pointed at me. "Vroom!"

"It's cool, huh?" she coos to him, but she's looking at me, too.

I give her a wink and wave at her son, then head inside.

The diner is pretty standard: natural lighting from the huge front windows; lamps hanging over every table; a yellow, orange, and blue color scheme. When I was inside, I read somewhere that the color orange makes people hungry. Apparently it's the best color for a kitchen or restaurant.

I spot Lucy sitting in a booth in the back. Striding down the aisle, I try to decide what to tell her. I should probably let Olivia fill her in on Mercy, but I don't want to say nothing, either. Besides, if she's going to give me the right advice, she needs to know the gist of things. I need to figure out how to survive Mercy and, if I can manage that, how to win the heartbreaker's heart. I don't want there to be any secrets between Lucy and me.

Well, with a few exceptions.

She doesn't know about Eli, and Olivia and I agreed that neither of us are ever going to tell her. That's a complication—and a lecture—neither of us need. How my little cousin became both of our big sister, I'll never know.

Giving me a tiny wave, Lucy frowns down at the glass of ginger ale and plate of toast in front of her.

"Hangover?" I ask, sliding in across from her. I should probably have the same.

She shakes her head, her red hair falling into her pale face. Dark circles bring out her green eyes. "No," she sort of whispers and moans.

"Dude, no offense, but you look pretty rough for someone who isn't hungover." I grab a menu and flip through. They serve breakfast 'til noon. Good.

"Gee, thanks." She takes a sip of her ginger ale and grimaces.

"Still hate the stuff, huh?" Some things never change.

Her lip curls. "More than anything, but it's all I can keep down at this point."

Both of my eyebrows lift. "At this point?"

She sighs, a drawn out, forlorn sound. "Twenty-one weeks." Those green eyes pin me.

"You've been sick for twenty-one weeks? Jesus Christ, Luce. You seen a doctor yet?"

Rolling her eyes, she shoves the plate of toast away. "I'm not sick, Cliff. I'm . . ." She shakes her head, eyes dropping to the table. Taking a deep breath, she stares at the stained formica. "I'm pregnant," she whispers.

I sit back, resting my hands on the table. My mind spins. I can't believe neither Olivia or I picked up on this. Our heads must be really far up our asses. "Twenty-one weeks," I repeat. "So you were already pregnant when you came to get me."

She nods.

My eyebrows knit together. "But you drank with us."

Lucy scoffs. "I had one glass of wine with Olivia. And the only other time, I made you *think* I drank with you. You two dogged those freakin' shots. You barely even noticed." She holds up a finger. "And I really don't need to know why."

"No," I agree. "You don't." Reaching across the table, I take her hand, wrapping her smaller fingers inside my big fingers. "Is this the guy who you didn't marry?"

She nods, over and over, her shoulders rising and falling as she takes a deep breath.

"Is this why you didn't marry him?"

"I don't believe in marriage," she says. "I mean, look at my parents. Look at *yours*." She laughs ruefully.

"Say no more." I squeeze her hand. Mine never married, but that's beside the point right now. "What are you gonna do?"

Running her free hand through her hair, she blinks back tears. "I don't know, Cliff. I'm past the pill. I'd have to have a surgical abortion," she says, lowering her voice. "I'm almost to the point where no one will do it. But I can't have a baby."

"You're twenty-one weeks," I remind her, cutting past the small talk I could drag out. I don't have it in me. Besides, Lucy and I never dance around anything. "That's five months. Set me straight if I'm wrong, but I know you. You would've already done it, if you really thought you don't want a baby," I say gently.

She glares at me but her lips curl upward into a half smile. "You got me. I love kids. I really do. But have you seen how fucked up my family is?"

I slide her a wry look. "That'd be my family, too, kid."

"So you know exactly what I mean." She pulls her hand away and rubs her temples. "I really don't know what to do, here. I need to make a decision soon, though."

"Well," I say, nodding to the waitress walking toward our

booth, "I'm glad you told me. Whatever you wanna do, I've got your back, Luce."

"I know," she says on a sigh. "I still haven't told Livvie. *Please* don't say anything."

The waitress, a woman in her late forties or early fifties, stops at our table, notepad in hand. "Would you like some coffee to get started?" she asks me.

"Sure." I glance at Lucy. "Wanna try to eat something?"

She pushes her toast farther away. "I'll live vicariously through you."

"Let me know if you change your mind," the waitress says. "I'll get your coffee, hon." With a pat of my shoulder, she leaves us alone in the booth.

"I told her I was gonna drop a bomb on my cousin," Lucy says, a little smile poking through her misery.

"Just for the record, it's not really a bomb. If you decide to keep it, I'll be a kick-ass uncle."

"You will." Her smile this time is radiant. "Speaking of babies and marriage, how's things in O Land?"

I lean back in my seat, spreading my arms out across the top of the booth. "I might've asked her to move in with me."

"Oh, Cliff." Sitting up in her seat, she glances around the diner. "Should I have our waitress make it an Irish coffee?"

"I might be drinking tomorrow night. Her father is getting released in the morning and I get to pick him up."

Lucy's mouth hangs open. "Bombs away at this table. Livvie didn't say anything about this."

"Guess we've all got our secrets." I shrug. "I'll let her fill you in, but I'm not looking forward to another round of Meet the Parents."

"And so close on the heels of Round One." Reaching for her plate, she grabs a slice of toast. "I'm suddenly feeling a lot better about my situation."

"I'm glad," I say dryly. "Speaking of parents, how do you think your parents are gonna take the news?"

"About their impending grandchild or Olivia reuniting with biker daddy?"

"Yes," I say.

The waitress reappears with my coffee and a cold ginger ale for Lucy. "Do you need a few more minutes?"

"Please," Lucy says. When the waitress is out of earshot, she turns back to me. "I really don't know. My parents have always been a little distant, what with all the coke and family secrets, but they've been extra weird lately."

"Think it has anything to do with me?" Leaving my coffee black, I take a sip. It warms me all the way through, hitting the spot despite the heat outside. Something about coffee has always comforted me.

"Probably," Lucy confesses. "I'm really sorry. I hoped they'd come around by now, but . . ." She shrugs.

"Maybe they'll warm up when they find out about their grandbaby."

"Maybe," she says, a fresh smile lighting up her face.

"You didn't argue that at all." I put my coffee down and take both of her hands. "Am I gonna be an uncle?"

"For better or worse," she says. "At least I know it'll have people who really love it. Minus Olivia." She snorts. "That girl won't go near babies with a twenty-foot pole. Or boyfriends with apartments," she says, giving me a pointed look. "I warned you, Cliff."

"I know." I sigh. She's right. She did warn me. "Any chance I can turn that around?"

She gives me a sad smile in answer.

16

This is the last day before I start my new job—my last chance to lounge around in a tank top, no bra, and butt-cheek shorts while bingeing *Game of Thrones* or *The Great British Baking Show*.

I'm sort of doing that.

I lie on my stomach on my bed, laptop open in front of me, the tab I was watching Netflix in paused and forgotten. The earbuds are still plugged in, to both the laptop and my ears. Dio sleeps curled up next to me, his paws covering his sweet little face, orange striped belly rising and falling slowly with each content breath. Despite a slight kink in his tail, he's as good as new. It's almost like Eli never happened.

But evil men tend to leave other marks, ones that can't be seen.

I scroll through Greg's profile again, this time careful to read every status, examining every photo. Most of his statuses are really just announcements for his band, Oh Vile Eye. "We have T-shirts." "We're playing Toad's Place tonight." Things like that. Apart from the single wedding photo, there are no pics of his wife. It's almost like Cami doesn't exist.

I keep scrolling, looking for some clue. Anything I can use. She doesn't have a Facebook account. I'm not even sure messaging her there would be a good idea, anyway. I have to get in touch with her, somehow, some way.

I scroll past a photo of a flower bed in front of a teal house, rolling my eyes. "Spent all day getting our yard together," the caption reads. There are about fifty comments and eighty-something likes, loves, and wows, all of them kissing his ass.

I grit my teeth.

How can everyone love him so much when he's hurt me so deeply?

His sister comments on every damn thing he posts, always with a love reaction. The one and only time I met her, she was thrilled to reunite us. At the time I thought nothing of it. Now I know she's just another sycophant—a dangerous thing for a rapist to possess.

Tipping my head back, I close my eyes and wiggle into a sort of cobra pose: forearms flat-ish on the bed, spine curled, legs stretched out behind me. I'm getting nowhere stalking his social media. I'm also inviting trouble, because the more I look at his profile, the more the Facebook algorithms are going to try to connect us. I'll pop up in his recommended friends, opening myself up to even more than a stage shoutout from him.

I have to block him soon.

Before I can do that, I need to figure out how to do a welfare check on Cami. Because if he's hurting her, it's my fault. The least I can do is make sure she's okay.

I also need to know where he is. Just for my own peace of mind. Naugatuck isn't that big a place, so I'm sure we'll run into each other eventually. Still, I need to know.

Opening my eyes, I scroll back up through the last year of posts. Same shirtless selfies, Oh Vile Eye EP blasts, and family get-togethers. I pass the photo of the flower beds again and hit the brakes.

It's his house.

Clicking on the photo, I make it a little bigger on the screen. This time I look past his ridiculous flowers and mulch—as if he could change who he is just by making his yard prettier. I examine the house itself.

It's not his mother's.

The stamp on the Facebook post tells me he uploaded it from Naugatuck. He's definitely living in town and, considering most landlords don't allow their tenants to landscape to this extent, he probably owns it. Finally, something I can use.

I click open another tab and Google "Naugatuck property records." Like I said, it's really easy to find someone online, if you know what you're looking for. All those finder services are a total scam. All it takes is some time and patience.

When the website loads, I search by his name. The top listing is for a property owned by a Greg Byrne, Sr.—probably his father. If I can't find anything in Greg's name, I'll check under Cami Byrne. I don't have to look long, because the second listing is owned by a plain ol' Greg Byrne.

My heart inches its way into my throat as I click on the link. An address loads, along with an outline of the parcel. I stare at the street and number. The street name sounds so familiar.

I open yet another tab and Google the address. The map loads agonizingly slowly—which probably means that my neighbors have kicked me off their Wi-Fi, or maybe their kid is playing Fortnite while watching TV.

I really need to catch up on my internet bill.

Just as the map blinks into place, Esther pushes my bedroom door open, not even bothering to knock. I peer at her over the screen of my laptop, itching to glance down but trying to be nonchalant.

I'm just watching Ned get his head lobbed off again, no big deal.

"You busy?" she asks, as if I'm dressed in a suit and heels instead of rocking PJs and messy Medusa snake curls.

"Yeah." I leave the headphones in, hoping she'll get the hint.

"I'm gonna pick up the kids, take them out for ice cream. Wanna come with?" The corners of her mouth twitch in a tentative smile.

"Sure. Just let me get dressed." I give her a pointed look.

Looking sheepish, she ducks back out, closing the door behind her. "Just don't take too long," she calls through the door.

Dating the MC's Enforcer has made this girl more punctual. Better late than never, I guess.

I lower my eyes back to the directions. Fingers flying over the keyboard, I type in my own address, just to see how far away he is. I've lived in Naugatuck my whole life but there are still streets I have yet to explore.

The screen reloads, the driving distance in neat letters underneath both our addresses.

He lives two driving minutes away.

Pinching my eyebrows together with my thumb and forefinger, I try to rub away the headache forming behind my eyes. For at least the past three months, he's lived two minutes away. He's within walking distance, for fuck's sake.

I switch to satellite mode and manipulate the trackpad on my laptop until I'm virtually standing in front of his house. Then I click back to the tab where his house and flower beds pic is still open.

It's definitely the same house.

Taking a deep breath, I save the address into the notes on my phone. I close everything and erase my browser history, then shut down the laptop.

Then, I get dressed. Nothing goes together like ice cream and stakeouts.

"I 'll drive," I tell Esther, grabbing her car keys from the counter.

"Okay, alpha book boyfriend." She holds her hand out to me for the keys.

"So you can spend time with your little sisters." I smile, letting my eyes go soft.

"In that case," she says, grabbing her hobo bag, "thank you." She tugs down her denim shorts. They're short and scored full of holes. The more time she spends with Donny, the more her wardrobe changes—in a totally hot way. When he came along, he unlocked something inside her, letting her free to come out and play. Her tee is a mural of roses, Belle, and Chip the teacup, but its cropped length makes it nerd sexy.

"The new look is working for you." I slide my feet into wedges, relieved to not have to wear boots for once in the heat of New England spring.

I will never get used to riding around in full gear while the sun beats down on me.

I consider grabbing my cut, but I'd look out of place with that Prospect rocker in the middle of a park full of kids. Besides, I want to show off the orange and yellow floral scoop neck tee I picked up the other day. It's probably more appropriate for fall, but fuck it. It's cute, and it makes my eyes look more orange. I threw on white denim shorts to make it more summer-y, but whatever.

I left all the fashion police in high school.

I plunk one more kiss on Dio's forehead, then Esther and I leave our Sunday nest. Unlocking the car, I pause for a moment before sliding into the driver's seat, fiddling with my bag while she gets in on her side. When I'm positive she isn't looking, I glance at the address in my phone one more time.

"Ice cream, ice cream," Esther chants.

"Man, you are getting so bossy." I get in and start the car, cranking up the AC. Another downside to riding a motorcycle: there's only the humid breeze on a hot day, and the bike itself burns like an inferno. Until I started riding, I had no idea that it's got to reach a certain temperature before it's even rideable.

Of course, that's only during colder months.

So far this spring, I just sweat on the damn thing.

Backing out of the driveway, I ease the car into the street. Instead of taking School Street, I continue down our street, Anderson.

"Abril is in this stage where she thinks she's wearing makeup to school. The worst part is, my abuela lets her," Esther says, clicking her tongue. "If you ask me, I don't even think Cierra's old enough for that shit, and *she's* fourteen. But what do I know? Abuela says her house, her rules. She wonders why my mom turned out so fucked up."

That's the most Esther has told me about her family in the four years I've known her.

"Does your grandma talk to your mom?" I ask, keeping the conversation going. I turn onto Spring Street.

She scoffs. "Hell no. What's that saying? 'Fool me twice, shame on me.' Something like that. The first time DCF took us, Abuela let her see us outside visitation hours. Then my mom took off and disappeared for like a year. That's how we got Ximena. Abuela is *done*." She cuts her hand through the air. "Why are you going this way? My grandparents' house is *that* way." She points in the opposite direction.

"Oh." I chuckle. "Figured I'd get the AC going."

She holds her hands in front of both vents on her side. "It's going."

I don't need to glance over to know she's giving me a look. "It's a motorcycle thing," I say. "Gotta take it around the block, let it warm up." I push the car faster, flying over Spring Street, which might as well be ten miles long right now.

"Okay, but clearly you're driving a car."

"I figured you needed to vent." I grip the steering wheel tighter.

"Sure." She puts her feet up on the dashboard. "It's fine. We've got time for your weird."

I glance over at her, but she's already got her phone out, a game of Solitaire on the screen. "You're the only one I know who plays that shit."

"Blame Abuelo," she says with a shrug. "Damn, this is a shit deal."

I speed down Spring Street, glancing up and down the opposite lane for Cliff or any of the guys. I don't need any of them tagging along so they can say hi. Thankfully it's just cars and trucks. No bikers.

Up ahead I can see his street. I check on Esther. She holds her phone close to her face, eyebrows furrowed in concentration. Good.

My heart rate rises the closer I get. He might see me. I've got to be careful. No slow creep—just a quick drive by.

Wish I could give him a different kind of drive-by.

"No good," Esther says with a sigh. "New deal."

"It's a good thing you met Donny." I turn onto his street—

Mallane Lane. It's a strange name for a street. The word "mal" means bad in Latin, and "lane" is already in there. Mallane is probably some old white fuck's last name, but still.

Bad Lane.

It's fitting.

His house isn't hard to find. It's a nearly teal Victorian, a square turret thrusting into the sky. If only I had one of those wrecking balls.

Just like in his Facebook photos, flower beds hug the front and corner of the house. Two cars sit in the driveway, but no one moves outside.

"What are we doing here?" Esther asks, setting her phone down in her lap. She turns to me, eyes narrowed.

"It's for rent," I blurt.

She rolls her eyes. "Why didn't you say so? Is the landlord around?"

I continue along Bad Lane, passing the house.

"Wait." She cranes her neck, trying to see, but it's already faded into the distance. "Damn, girl. That place looked big enough for you, me, *and* my sisters."

"You don't want me to play mommy," I say, circling back toward Esther's abuela's.

"I like living with you," she says with a shrug. "Besides, I'm a little worried I'll never hear from you once I move out."

I actually did it. I drove by his house, and he didn't see me. Bold electricity rushes through me, tinged with nausea. If this wasn't Esther's car, I'd light up. I clench the steering wheel to keep my hands from shaking. Unfortunately it does nothing for my voice. "Why not?"

"Please. You and I wouldn't have been friends if it hadn't been for my Craigslist ad."

"We *are*, though," I remind her.

She snorts. "Sort of. You don't tell me anything about yourself."

"I could say the same for you." I drive the route to her grand-parents', familiar from the few times I needed her car and dropped her off so she could visit. I've never met her family.

"Touché, I guess." She taps her phone against her thigh to the rhythm of the pop song on the radio. Even driving, I don't get to pick the tunes—Esther's car, Esther's rules.

"We'll still see each other. You've got Donny, and I've got . . . Cliff." I swallow, wondering how long I'll have either of them.

The second I pull up to the house, Esther's sisters tumble out, her grandma trailing them.

"Behave," she chides, lifting a hand to wave at us.

The girls pile into the backseat, their chatter sucking up all the oxygen. I blink, a little taken aback by all of the energy. I've only ever been someone's little sister. I have no idea what it's like to be the oldest of a whole brood, to be responsible for so many little people.

Esther's grandma shuffles to the passenger's side, a hand pressed to her back. Bending, she waves for Esther to roll her window down.

"Hola, Abuela," Esther says. Over her shoulder, she tells the girls to buckle up. "Olivia, this is my grandma, Salome."

"Hi." I wiggle my fingers in greeting. I never had a grandma to care when Bree didn't. I only had Mercy, and he loved his club more than he loved me.

Salome points a finger at me. "Drive carefully. Have them back before dark." Leaning in through the open window, she kisses Esther's cheek, her hand lingering on Esther's face for a moment before she pulls away. "Te amo."

"Bye, Abuela!" the girls—Esther included—call.

I gaze at the unassuming brick ranch, envisioning the over-stuffed couches and chipped knickknacks in the living room, a plate of warm cookies on the coffee table. It's a safe place, a home for these girls when no one else wanted them.

My eyes burn. Blinking, I look away and put the car into drive.

"Jimmy, your seatbelt." Esther unbuckles her own and practically dives into the backseat to help the little one—Ximena—with hers.

We take them to Linden Park. It's not the nicest I've ever been to, but it's close by. I have to work tonight, so time is precious.

Ximena and Abril break for the swings the second I park the car. An ice cream truck idles at the edge of the playground. Cierra hovers by Esther, glancing at the ice cream truck.

"You want some?" Esther asks, running her fingers through her sister's long, silky hair. Unlike the other two girls', Cierra's hair is pin straight—like Esther's. The other two have frizzy curls like mine.

I sit on a bench and light a cigarette. From here I have the perfect view of both Abril pushing Ximena on a swing and Esther French-braiding Cierra's hair. I have dozens of memories of Lucy doing the same things for me, none of Bree doing them.

"Motherless girls," I mutter.

"Mira, it's not that bad." Esther walks Cierra over to my bench, her fingers splayed, strands of hair caught between them. "We've got each other."

I watch her fingers dance back and forth, weaving Cierra's hair into a perfect French braid.

I can't rewind my childhood. I don't even know where Bree is. I *can* make sure that these girls stay together, though.

Securing the braid with a hair band, Esther drops the tail onto Cierra's shoulder. "Go swing," she says.

Cierra traipses to her little sisters, shoulders drawn.

"In some ways they're so normal," Esther says, sitting next to me. "Then sometimes they're so sullen. I don't know how to fix it. I don't even know how to fix *me*."

"Some people say therapy is helpful." I shrug, flicking ash into the breeze. It swirls around my bare leg, then drifts to the ground.

"What's going on with you and Cliff?"

My hand freezes midair, smoke curling upward from the cigarette. "What do you mean?"

She clicks her tongue. "Please." Tilting her head, she pins me with a knowing look. "You've got to talk to someone, Liv. You're helping me—let me help you. I'm excellent at relationship advice. Are you thinking of moving in with Cliff?"

I hold back a snort. Barely. Somehow, Esther's been unscathed by the darkness that's encroached her entire life. She's still an optimist, still sunny enough to assume my problems are boy-related. "He asked," I hedge, wondering if I should tell her what's really on Bad Lane.

That's such a shitty thing to bond over. The woman who was raped by her father and the woman who was raped by her ex-boyfriend. We'd be the sickest of besties. Except her unending optimism might push me off a cliff.

"And?" she presses, grinning.

"I said no." I drop the cigarette and die it out in the park mulch.

"¿Por qué?" she exclaims. "I hear the two of you in your bedroom. And the club house." She grins wickedly. "You could have that every single night. And day, if you wanted." She wiggles her eyebrows.

I sigh. "Cliff is . . ." My voice trails off. I don't know how to describe him. He's sweet, with just enough edge and bite to keep me on my toes. He does shit for me, no questions asked. I think of how quickly he rushed to help me with Eli. How he called Donny and Beer Can, and they just took care of it. He held me for hours, never pushing. He didn't even tell me that what I did was stupid.

Even now, when I have nightmares, he just holds me. Cliff popped into my life and then he stayed, even when he could've—and should've—left. All he wants in return is to share a space with me, and I can't even give him that.

I try to put all of that into words for Esther. "He's been giving me a look."

She lifts an eyebrow. "A look?"

"Like a puppy-eyed 'I love you and wanna have your babies' look."

"Qué lindo," she croons. "You two would make some cute babies."

I glare at her. "This is a baby-free zone." I cross my arms over my stomach in an X.

"As soon as I get guardianship of the kids, Donny and I are getting a place together. We figured it'd be better if he doesn't live with me yet. DCF leans more toward female-only homes when it comes to girls who have been sexually assaulted by a man."

"See, that four years of school is already paying off."

"God, I hope so." She nods toward the girls. "Look at them. I can't imagine my life without them. Can you imagine your life without Cliff?" She nudges me gently.

"I can't go there."

"Why not?"

I don't have an answer for her.

18

CLIFF

Pressing the doorbell for Olivia's place, I step back. Only the porch light is on. No light shines from inside. I can't imagine she and Esther are already in bed. I raise my fist and knock, a soft three-tap, just in case.

From the other side, I hear a soft meow: Dio.

"Hey buddy." He meows again. I picture him rubbing his cheek against the door. "I guess no one else is home. I'll see you later."

Turning, I chuckle. Olivia's got me talking to her cat now.

She's got me doing all kinds of things—like picking up her father. I wanted to see her before I left, even if only to wish her luck for her first day at DCF. Maybe see if there's anything I should know before meeting Mercy, or if there's anything she wants me to scope out before she meets him.

She isn't home, though, so there's not much I can do, other than go back to the club house and try to get some sleep.

I walk slowly back to the Screamin' Eagle. The last thing I want to do right now is go to bed, mostly because I don't want to get up at the ass crack of dawn to drive all the way to Lewisburg. Traveling by train would take longer, and neither Ravage nor

Mark were willing to pony up for a plane ticket. Worst of all, I have to take a cage. It'll be more comfortable than riding all the way down, but the more I ride, the less I want to be in a car.

I swing onto the bike and grab my helmet. Securing it in place, my fingers pause. Olivia might be working tonight. That would explain why she isn't home. There's also a chance she's at Lucy's, but I'd rather not ride all over town trying to track her down. If she's already at the club, I might be able to talk her into staying the night. That way she can crash in my room after work, and I can see her before I go. Maybe even see her naked.

Two birds, one stone.

With that happy thought, I fire up the Screamin' Eagle, wincing a little as I imagine poor Dio hiding from the noise. Ever since Eli, he's been so skittish. If Olivia hadn't already killed him, I'd kill the motherfucker myself. Who the hell tries to kill a tiny, defenseless kitten?

I wish she'd told me what was going on before it got that bad.

That's Olivia for you. She can take care of herself, which is one of the things I love most about her.

I nearly stomp on the back brake.

I love her.

It's a whole-body realization. The road tips upward, the bike falls down into the sky. I float for a moment, fingers and toes tingling. Then I slam back into my seat, the bike firmly on 63. Somehow I still have my balance.

I have to tell her. I've never been good at keeping my feelings to myself. My father's headstone is proof of that. It's either tell her, or walk away, and I already know I can't do that.

I can't tell her, either.

She shut me out when I suggested we move in together. I can only imagine what she'll do if I tell her I love her.

I love her.

The more I repeat it, the more woozy my stomach is, like I've had a few drinks and I'm warmed all the way through. At the same time, it makes me *need* a drink.

There's a good chance I don't *really* love her.

I have no idea what it feels like to be in love. I know what it's like to love someone—Lucy. I know what it means to be loved— Lucy again. But the odds that I wholly, truly love the first woman I laid eyes on after getting out—not to mention fucked in the back of a station wagon—are slim to none.

I've been lonely for so long, I'm just imprinting on her.

That's got to be it. Because there's no way someone like me can really love her, not now. I love Lucy because it's all I've ever known. Those feelings were there long before I went away. What I think I feel for Olivia can't be real.

Not after twenty years of crushing in noses with my fists. I don't deserve it.

She doesn't deserve me.

Yet, when I see her Street Glide in the parking lot of The Wet Mermaid, my whole body lights up from the inside out.

Whatever this is, it's here to stay.

Until someone knocks some goddamn sense into me.

Maybe meeting Mercy won't be so bad after all.

I slide in next to her bike, then just sit for a moment, the engine idling. Whatever I think I feel, I need to keep my mouth shut until I can figure it out. I've just got to figure out how to keep it off my face—that must be what freaked out Olivia. We're practically living together. Talking about moving in shouldn't have landed me a snow cone.

My head throbs. I don't know what the fuck I'm doing. I never dated. I thought moving in together was the logical next step, but maybe that's not how things are done anymore. Like I'd really know, anyway. My parents were a tragedy. They both wound up dead. I doubt things could go any differently for me.

I squeeze my eyes shut. My head is a mess. I can't go in there like this. She'll take one look at me and she'll know. I need to see her before I go, though. I need to know that everything I've done for her is worth it. That there's a chance she might feel the same way. Otherwise, I chopped up Eli and went up against my President all for nothing.

With numb fingers, I reach for the cigarettes in the pocket of my cut. I grasp the corners of the box, then drop it.

"Damn it," I mutter. I shut off the bike and climb off, then retrieve the pack. I barely feel the heat of the flame as I light a cigarette.

The door to The Wet Mermaid opens and Olivia skips out. I drop my cigarette.

"Fuck me," I whisper. "Just kill me now." I squat as casually as I can and pluck the damn thing from the dirt.

Trish follows Olivia close behind. Olivia lets go of the door, and Trish nearly walks into it.

"I told you to stop messing with the bottles on the shelf!" Olivia shouts. She sticks a cigarette in her mouth and, cupping the flame with one hand, lights it.

"I just don't understand why they're not in alphabetical order," Trish counters. "How else do you remember what goes where?"

"By memory?" Olivia sighs. "Top shelf *stays* on the top shelf, Trish. For the thousandth time." Her eyes skip from Trish to where I stand by our bikes. "Hey."

"Hi Cliff," Trish says, pouncing on the change of subject. "You working tonight?"

"The key word there would be *working*," Olivia says.

"I *do* work." Trish's hands clench into fists.

Olivia takes a step closer. "Then stop messing with my fucking bottles."

"Hi," I say, closing the distance between the three of us. I lean down and kiss the tip of Olivia's nose. "You ready for tomorrow?"

Trish might not be the most organized bartender, but she knows better than to pick a fight with a Prospect when a patched member is watching. Shaking her head, she slips back inside.

"Define 'ready,'" Olivia says. She takes a long drag of her cigarette. "My navy blue, button down shirt and khaki pants are ironed, if that's what you mean. I can't believe I'm going business casual."

"Moving on up in the world," I say softly.

"Do you think they'll give me a case right off the bat? Or will I have time to dig into the girls' case?"

Before I can answer, the door opens and Trish's head pokes out. "Olivia, bar's full. I need you." She pops back in, avoiding the dirty look my girl throws her.

"I'm going to kill her," Olivia says.

"I hope you mean that figuratively." I flick the remainder of my cigarette into the parking lot.

"You *do* know how to hide a body now . . ." She disposes of her cigarette in the tall ashtray beside the door.

"Anything for you, darlin'." I pull open the door, holding it for her. "Meet me upstairs after your shift? We can talk more."

"Sure," she says, standing on her tiptoes to give me a quick kiss. Her eyes don't meet mine, though. She falls to the flats of her feet and gives me a half smile. Then she disappears into the crowd inside.

I stand there for a moment, letting Kiiara's "Gold" wash over me. I already know I'll be missing Olivia tonight.

19

OLIVIA

I sit up in the darkness of my bedroom, gasping for air. No, not darkness—it's pitch black. I widen my eyes, glance toward the window, but there's no light. I'm not even sure there's a window. My lungs tighten as if someone's fist squeezes around them, releases for a second, then squeezes again.

"Calm down," I tell myself. "The street probably lost power."

I grope for my phone. I fell asleep reading my favorite novel, *Lex Talionis* by S.A. Huchton, so it's got to be here somewhere. My fingers brush sheets, sheets, more sheets. If I dropped the thing on the floor, I'll never find it. I keep patting the bed, pleading with my mattress to give it up.

My hand lands on a furry, wet mess, still warm.

I scream, mouth wide open, tears running down my face. The light turns on, bathing me in harsh bright white. I glance down at my sheets, my hand, but there's nothing there.

"Hello, Olivia," Eli says, and I scream again.

I sit up so hard and fast, the room sways around me. At least I can see. My T-shirt sticks to me, cold and clammy against my skin. I take a big gulp of air, the squeezing sensation still in my chest but fading. This time, when I reach for my phone, I find it right beside me.

Four a.m.

I have to be up in two hours if I want to eat, shower, and tame my hair. Drawing my knees into my chest, I wrap my arms around my legs, resting my face on my knees. I breathe in slowly, let it out just as slow.

"You're okay," I tell myself over and over.

I should have stayed at Cliff's.

I figured I'd get a better night of sleep in my own bed. Guess the joke's on me. I'd probably be sleeping like a baby in his arms right now, if I'd stayed.

If I hadn't stood him up.

My phone buzzes in my hand with an alert. Glancing down at the screen, I almost scream again.

There's a Silver Alert for a twenty-five-year-old Elijah Moretti from Naugatuck, Connecticut. I guess someone is missing him, after all.

Each breath exits my lungs in a ragged whoosh. I try to keep it slow and steady, but the vice is back.

Someone is looking for Eli.

He has *family*, people who have no idea what happened to him. As much of a monster as he was, I know exactly how his family feels. Every time Bree left me, I worried it'd be the last time I saw her, that someone would find her dead somewhere.

I really should've gone to Cliff's.

I can still go now. I can hop on that Street Glide and slip into bed beside him. Even in sleep, he'll wrap his arms around me and make me feel safe, if only for a moment.

Someone is looking for Eli.

If they find him, I could go to prison. If they don't find him, they'll always wonder what happened to him.

Shivering, I reach for the quilt I keep folded at the foot of the bed. I cocoon myself in it and sit up against the wall that my bed hugs, staring into the dim darkness of the room, tinged with orange from the streetlights.

"Olivia?" Esther calls with a knock. "You okay?"

"Come in," I reply.

The door opens and Esther tiptoes inside, glancing between her feet for Dio. He darts out from a hidden corner of the room, running between her feet and nearly tripping her.

"You should've named him Diablo," she mutters, climbing into bed with me.

Dio ricochets and hops up, too, prancing across the sheets and plopping down in my lap. His purr reverberates through my body. Absently, I rub the top of his head with the side of my thumb.

"Another nightmare?" Esther asks, snuggling up.

I want to tell her everything. How Eli stalked me, that he was the one who hurt our cat. How I asked Donny for a gun, just in case, because even then I didn't feel safe. The night that Eli came after me, and I killed him.

Instead I just nod, then rest my head on her shoulder.

"It'll be okay, cariña." Esther strokes my hair, oh so gently. The last thing I think before I drift off is how good she'll be for those girls.

THE CHORUS OF "BITCH" blares through my bedroom, jolting me awake. I rub my sore eyes, the nausea from lack of sleep already setting in. Showing up exhausted on my first day is *not* how to make a good impression.

"Morning," Esther says, slipping into my room with two mugs of coffee. She passes one to me and I smile gratefully.

"I don't deserve you."

"Don't forget that." She perches on the edge of my bed. "Are you ready for today?"

"Ugh." I take a long sip of coffee, wishing I could just attach an IV and be done with it. I set the mug on my nightstand and grab my phone. The Silver Alert is still out. I sigh. Silver Alerts are supposed to be for the elderly, but for some reason the state of Connecticut randomly uses them for younger people all the time.

A lot of people who go missing are never reported. Maybe it's because no one cares enough, or maybe it's simply that the explanation isn't one they can give to the authorities.

If this were any other morning, I'd open Facebook and see what I can find out about Eli's family. If I don't get moving, I'm going to be late, so I put my phone aside and scoot out of bed.

"You know," Esther says while I grab my outfit, "you don't have to fix this thing with my sisters. You've got a lot on your plate already, and I don't want to pile more on you."

I turn, holding up a hand. "This is exactly why I became a social worker, Essie: to help people like you and me. Let me help."

She beams. "You called me Essie."

I smile back. "I've gotta get in the shower."

"And I'm going back to bed." Squeezing past me, she pads across the living room to her own bedroom. "Have a great day, dear."

"Have fun being unemployed and sleeping in, dear!"

"I *have* a job!" she fires back before shutting her door.

As much as I'd love to tease her more, I really do have to get ready. I trudge into the bathroom, hoping that the rest of the day will be easier than last night.

20

CLIFF

The sun bleeds over the horizon just as I cross into New York. I grab my sunglasses from the dashboard and don them against the light. I've been on the road for almost an hour; the drive there should take just under four. I thought I'd hate being trapped in a cage for so long, but I don't mind it. I drive with a wrist draped over the wheel, just me and the road.

Until I hit morning rush hour traffic.

Against my better judgement, I took I-84 W. Even with all the road work and traffic, it's still the fastest route. It's also the most frustrating. So far, though, I'm enjoying the peace of the road.

It was a long night.

I tossed and turned, so first thing, I grabbed a big ass coffee with three espresso shots. I wish Olivia didn't have this effect on me, that I could sleep like a baby without worrying that I'm driving all the way to Pennsylvania for nothing. Yeah, it's for my club, but I offered to do it for her—and she still stood me up.

I don't know what it means, if we're still on or what. She's been hot and cold from the beginning. I knew who she was when I got into this. She's not the kind of girlfriend who needs reassurance and insurance. She's more like a cat.

Hell, I'm not even sure she's my girlfriend.

Maybe it's the lack of sleep, but I'm not sure of anything anymore.

My phone buzzes, the vibration inching it away from me across the dashboard. Keeping one hand on the wheel and an eye on the road, I stretch out my arm, closing my fingers around it.

I know the laws about texting and driving in the tri-state area. I also know the statistics. But there's a good chance it's Olivia, or Lucy, or the club. I right myself in the driver's seat and drop the phone into my lap. The last thing I need is to get pulled over for texting. It'd also violate my probation, and that'd land me right back in the pen.

Except this time there'd be no Mercy looking out for me.

It's weird, knowing that for twenty years there might've been guys inside with me who wanted me dead. I have a lot of questions for Mercy. I know the club was split over whether or not to kill my father for what he was doing to Lucy. There were a lot of people who loved Bastard, devil or not. Growing up, I remember my father always surrounded by friends. I need to know that there isn't anyone else inside or out who wants a bullet in my head.

My phone buzzes again—the two-minute reminder, I think. Unless someone's rapid texting me. I scan the highway for cops. All I see are other cars. It's times like these I think Lucy's right, I should learn how to use Siri. There's just something so unnerving about talking to a computer.

I unlock the phone with one hand and open up my texts. There's just one.

Olivia: Be safe.

No way I can type with one hand, so I toss the phone onto the passenger seat. Maybe I'll call her when I get to Lewisburg.

Maybe I won't.

Seems like playing it cool is working in my favor.

Even then, I want to tell her to have a good first day. I want that kind of relationship.

Lucy's words echo in my head: *Be careful with Olivia. She's not the marrying type, but you are.* She's right. The longer I've been out of prison, the more I see that. By all right and reason, Olivia and I are no match for each other. But I can't let go.

For better or worse, I love her.

I just need to decide whether I can live with that.

LEWISBURG IS JUST AS FORLORN as I remember it. From this side of the barbed wire and in the sunshine of May, it should be less depressing. Behind the gothic arches and carvings is a hell I'm still trying to forget.

A hell I'm about to walk right back into—this time as a visitor.

Dread makes my limbs heavy. I sit in the Jeep Wrangler that Mark let me borrow and smoke cigarette after cigarette. I don't even have to walk those halls, past the D block cages that I once called home, but I can't make myself go in. Part of me holds this silly fear that they'll take one look at me and realize they made a mistake.

I have to do this. For the club. For Olivia. For myself.

Just the thought of the narrow solitary cell I spent most of my time in sends a chill down my spine. In the pen, you're either predator or prey. My size and crime made me a wolf, but there were many men inside with me who weren't strong enough to defend themselves.

See, it's not just rapists and murderers that go to fed. There are a lot of nerdy guys who used the internet to steal money, a few accountants who got caught up in RICO cases but couldn't prove their innocence. There are a few men who need medication in order to function, who did something bad but have no memory of it, and after a few years inside, they don't know up from down anymore. Guys who wouldn't hurt a fly—really.

Then there are the animals who enjoy the hunt. They don't care who those men were outside. All they care about is establishing dominance, showing the rest of the pack that they're not to be fucked with.

So they pick on the dweebs.

I couldn't stand for that.

I spent a lot of time in seg for it.

The doors to the cells in SMU—the Special Management Unit—are so narrow, I had to walk sideways to get in and out. The ceilings are so low, even inmates of average height have to crouch to take a piss. Each cell was built for one person, but often they'd cram two or even three of us into one.

I can still hear the screams of men who saw things that weren't really there. I can still smell the blood, taste the fear. After twenty-four hours in seg, even guys without schizophrenia start to lose their minds.

Dropping my fourth cigarette out the Jeep window, I shake away the memories. I've got to go in. I don't have to go far. The visitor side is by far nicer than the rest of the place. I just need to meet Mercy, then I can get the fuck out of here.

And drive four hours back to Connecticut, trapped in a cage with Olivia's father.

I open the car door and step onto the pavement, asphalt I haven't set foot on ever since climbing into that taxi last winter. In some ways it feels like ages have passed. In other ways, it'll never be long enough.

From the outside, Lewisburg looks like a nice place—a cathedral or a museum, even. It kind of reminds me of the old train station turned newspaper in Waterbury. If you ignore the thirty-foot wall and barbed wire fence. Instead of a clock tower, there's a watch tower. I pass under brick with angels carved into it, move through an arched doorway. Armed COs patrol the compound grounds on foot, while still more sit inside eight gun towers.

I pass through a metal detector and get patted down by still more COs. Seems they've added a few to the roster since I left, because I don't recognize these guys. They're younger, eager. Probably young enough that they still think they can make a difference.

Inside, I step up to the desk, protected by bulletproof glass. On Mondays, there's no visitation. At least I don't have to wait in line.

"Back so soon?" CO McKennan asks. His dark bald head gleams under the florescent light.

"I'm here to pick up Mercer Reynolds." I try not to look as uneasy as I feel. My fingers twitch for something to do, my feet itching to move.

He picks up a clipboard and scans the list of names. There aren't many. Picking up the receiver of a phone, he punches a few buttons. "Yeah," he says. "Inmate Reynolds's ride is here." He hangs up. For a moment, he eyes me up and down. "You look good, Demmel. Still getting into fights?"

"I'm a bouncer now."

He laughs. "That's a good fit. Have a seat. Reynolds will be out shortly."

I sit on the hard wooden bench, a fixture that's probably been here since the prison opened in the 1930s. Most of Lewisburg is original, except the cameras they added. When I was inside, inmates couldn't scratch their asses without someone seeing. Those cameras made things really hard for the entrepreneurs among us.

A lock clicks and the heavy metal door opens. I glance up from the red tile. A man with hair as black as Olivia's—what hasn't gone gray yet, anyway—fills the doorway. Brown eyes hard as steel appraise me. I know those eyes.

Olivia is the spitting image of her father, only a hell of a lot prettier. Her bones are finer, too. They have the same eyes, the same lips, and the same cheekbones.

Standing, I hold out my hand. "Cliff," I say.

"Red Dog," Mercy rasps. He clasps my hand. "I know you." He releases my hand and shakes a finger at me. "You don't recognize me?"

"Sorry."

"It's been a long time." He shifts a brown paper bag to his other arm. "Your old man was my best friend." Saluting CO McKennan, Mercy turns and strolls toward the exit. "Get me the fuck out of here, Red Dog."

I lead him out to the Jeep, letting him hang back, enjoy the fresh air and sunshine. I remember that feeling all too well, the knowledge that there are no longer walls and guns keeping you inside.

Unlocking the Jeep, I reach into the backseat for the things Ravage gave me. "Your cut," I say, tossing it to Mercy.

He catches it with one hand. Putting down the paper bag, he shrugs into the cut. It hangs a little loose on him. "Guess I've got some burgers to eat," he says with a grin. "You got my house keys, too?"

I grab them from the backseat and pass them over.

"All right," he says with a nod. "Let's roll." He picks up the bag and strolls to the passenger side.

I climb in too and start the engine, mind reeling. I don't know where to start. My father was his best friend. Even more questions funnel through my head.

It's just as well. We've got four hours to kill. That's plenty of time to get some answers.

Unfortunately, it's also plenty of time for him to grill *me*.

21

OLIVIA

My new supervisor, Diane, wastes no time getting me settled in.

"We're overloaded," she says the second I sit down in her office. "I wish I could take some time and teach you the ropes, but I don't have time to hold your hand. I'm putting you with Glace. She's been with us for seven years. You'll pick up everything you need to know just by watching her."

Someone knocks at Diane's door.

"Come in," she calls.

I turn in my seat to see the newcomer. A curvy woman with long curly hair and copper skin leans in through the doorway. Behind purple frames, her brown eyes are warm yet observant. In just a few seconds, I sense her taking in everything about me, from my clothes to my own curls to the scuffs on my riding boots.

"Glace," Diane says, pronouncing it like a shortened version of "glacial," "this is Olivia, your new trainee."

"Hello." Glace waves. "I hope those boots are comfortable. We've got a home visit in twenty." Without another word, she turns and bustles from the office.

My mouth falls open. "I thought I had paperwork to fill out."

Diane waves a hand at me. "Stop in later, we'll get those tax forms handled. Go."

Pushing back my chair, I hurry to catch up with Glace. She works her way around cubicles toward the entrance, pausing only long enough to say hello to a few of the other social workers. From behind, I study her gray jeans and long sweater.

I might've overdressed.

Glace bursts through the double doors, holding one open for me. I slip through and follow her to a blue Hyundai Elantra.

"State vehicle?" I ask, glancing at the plates. They look normal to me.

She gives me a funny look. "Yeah right. Hop in."

"Where are we going?" I ask as I jog to the passenger's side.

"A home visit," she says, as if I didn't hear her the first time.

"Yeah, but where?" Opening the door, I slide into the seat. Her car smells like vanilla. A Yankee Candle air freshener hangs from the rearview mirror.

"Mapleridge Drive." Glace gets in and starts the car, air conditioning blasting out of the vents. "Disabled kid, depressed mom. I'm trying to help them out, but the mom makes it really hard."

Mapleridge is in one of the few remaining nice neighborhoods in Waterbury—not the kind of place that usually comes to mind when I think of DCF taking kids.

"How so?" I ask as she pulls out of the parking lot.

"The kid is a wheelchair user. Nice. Quiet. He won't go to school, though. He's been truant for so long, pretty soon we'll have to place him with someone. The mom's husband up and left, and she pretty much gave up."

"Damn," I say. Even middle class people have their problems. "So what can we do?"

"I'm holding out as long as I can, but eventually I'm going to have to start the paperwork for placement. I tried setting her up with therapy. She won't go. I tried having someone come for in-home services. When they knock, she won't answer." Glace sighs, a long, weary sound that rattles my bones. "Not only is he missing school, but he's also missed a year's worth of doctor's appointments. They're behind on bills. Facing eviction. She even let her food stamps go."

"There's really nothing else we can do?" I stare through the windshield, watching the city pass as we head to the East End neighborhood in Waterbury.

"Can't help someone who won't help themselves," Glace says with a shrug. Flicking on her turn signal, she glances at me while she waits for traffic to pass. "This job can eat you alive. I suggest you don't get too attached."

With those words, she turns the car up Meriden Road.

We lapse into silence. I knew being a social worker wouldn't be easy, but I'm already frustrated. When DCF took me from Bree, I didn't like it, but I got it. Bree left me for days at a time, often without food in the house. All for her flavor of the week. This mom that Glace describes sounds like someone who's just fallen on hard times—someone the state should be helping, rather than punishing.

Glace pulls into the driveway of a green single-family home. It's all on one floor—perfect for a child with a disability. My fists curl at the thought of a landlord tossing a single mom and her disabled child out onto the street.

Opening her door, Glace steps out of the car. "Grab those files on the backseat for me," she says, walking to the front door.

I lean over the center console and find a black laptop bag stuffed to the brim with folders. I buckle it closed—barely. Wrapping my fingers around the strap, I yank it toward me. It practically sinks into the backseat.

"What does she have in here, rocks?" I mutter. I yank the bag free, hoisting it onto my lap. Apparently part of my duties as a trainee is lugging around heavy files.

It's not much different from being a Prospect.

I didn't expect to be given a case on my first day or anything like that, but I went to school for four years and got licensed so I could help people, not so I could be someone's bitch for a day. Squaring my shoulders, I carry the bag inside the house.

The first thing I notice is how normal everything looks inside. The living room is tidy, and the scent of apple cinnamon wafts through the air from candles on the coffee table. It's nothing like Bree's house, that's for sure.

The mother sits on the couch, her hands folded in her lap. Her son sits in his wheelchair, an Xbox controller in his hand. On the TV, a game sits paused, the sound on low. Once again, I'm struck by how completely normal it all is. This isn't a case of child abuse. It can't be. I stand in the living room and fix my gaze on the framed photos on the entertainment center rather than staring. Most of them are of the kid, from infancy to now, his teen years.

"Renee," Glace says, "this is Olivia. She's just started her training with the department, so she's going to observe. Is that okay?"

Renee shrugs. "As long as she isn't here to take my son."

Glace opens her mouth, but I interject.

"I'm not here to take your son, Renee." I take a seat on the other end of the couch and drop the bag on the floor. "We don't make the rules, do we, Glace?"

Glace blinks at me, stunned. "No," she says. "We don't." She pinches her eyebrows together and narrows her eyes at me.

Rifling through the bag, I pull out the Thomas file. I tap the manila with a fingernail. "On our way over here, Glace briefed me on your situation. Renee . . ." I let my voice trail off, hold my eyes to hers. Let her see me. "I was a foster kid. The state does the best it can, but it was still hell for me. At his age and with his condition, your son—" I flip the folder open and scan the names inside. "Rhett will probably be placed in a group home." I slap the folder shut. "Do you want that for your son?"

Rhett lets out a low, guttural moan.

Eyes wide, Renee places a hand on his shoulder. "No one is taking my baby."

"That's my point," I snap. "Do you think you're the only case we've got?" I pick up the bag and drop it onto the couch for emphasis. It sinks into the cushion, the whole couch shaking as it lands. "Glace has been extraordinarily patient with you, but it's just about out of her hands. The state is stretched thin as it is. They're not going to keep working with you. Do you understand me?"

Tears spill from Renee's eyes. She shakes her head. "Please," she sobs.

"You've got to meet us halfway," I tell her.

"No," she cries. "I didn't do anything wrong!"

"You didn't," I soothe. "I know your scumbag of a husband took off and left you with a child who needs around the clock care because of his Lou Gherig's disease. I know you can't work because no job is going to fit your needs. I know you're heartbroken and you feel like you've got no one on your side. But I'm telling you, right here, right now, that Glace and I are all you've got. So are you gonna let the therapist come in here and talk to you? So we can check this box off on our list, and close your case?"

Renee's eyes meet mine, hope blooming in them. "Okay," she breathes.

"And are you gonna send your kid to school?"

"I can't," she says through tears. Her face reddens in splotches.

"Why the hell not?" I demand.

"Olivia," Glace warns.

"They're awful to him," Renee cries. "He's not even learning anything there. I know—" A hiccup cuts off her words. "I know there's not much they can do for his condition. It's degenerative. I know that. But all they do is let him play on an iPad and give him candy. That's not school." She buries her face in her hands, shoulders heaving.

I glance at Glace. Her eyebrows reach her hairline. "I had no idea," she admits.

"Glace, are there better programs we can look into for Rhett?" I ask.

"Absolutely." She pulls her phone out of her purse and holds it up. "I'm going to call Diane, pick her brain. Just give me one moment." Pressing the phone to her ear, she steps outside.

I slide closer to Renee and rub her back. "I'm sorry. I know you're hurting. I can't promise you that it'll stop, but I can promise you that if you do what Glace has been asking you, things will get better."

Lifting her face from her hands, Renee reaches out and squeezes my hand with a soggy hand. "Thank you," she whispers.

I squeeze her hand back. I probably just got fired myself on my first day, but at least I know I made a difference.

22

CLIFF

"So," I drawl, lighting a cigarette. I hold out the pack to Mercy. "You mean, I can have another cigarette that ain't stale?" He plucks one out and sticks it between his lips. "Red Dog, you're spoiling me."

I roll the Jeep toward the only toll booth on the way back to Connecticut. Naturally, it's the one closest to home. Now that it's afternoon and all the rush hour traffic has cleared, we're making just as good time as I made coming down.

It's taken me the whole trip to work up the balls to ask Mercy about Bastard. About Olivia. We've mostly been listening to the radio and trading war stories—that is, stories about Lewisburg.

"Did you know it only takes twenty minutes to boil water using one of the pipes in the SMU cells?" Mercy exhales smoke while he talks.

"Never had a craving for ramen while I was in seg," I say, pulling up to the toll booth window. "Hand me those singles in the center console?"

"Sure." When the attendant announces the fee, Mercy counts out the ones and passes them to me.

I hand the money to the attendant. She waves me through, and I press down on the gas. Tolls are one of the worst things about living in the tri-state area. Can't go anywhere without paying out the nose in gas and tolls.

I drive in silence for a few minutes, continuing along 84 and crossing the Connecticut state line. "I've gotta know something, Mercy," I say finally.

"You're gonna get off at Straits Turnpike," he says.

"Straits Turnpike? Don't you want to go to The Wet Mermaid?"

"Nah." He flicks the remainder of his cigarette out his window. "I wanna go home. See my dog."

"You've got a dog?"

He laughs. "Yeah, a Red Dog." Reaching across, he clasps my shoulder. "It's good to have someone to talk to who gets where I'm coming from."

"To think, we'd have nothing to talk about, had you not gone inside for me." I shrug his hand off. "Why, Mercy? Why would you do that?"

"I told you. Bastard was my best friend. I was his VP, for Christ's sake. Who do you think initiated the vote to take him to the river? The goddamn club, though . . ." He reaches for my pack and holds it up in question.

"Go for it."

"The vote had to be unanimous, and some brothers thought we made up the story about Bastard so I could be Pres. They'd rather believe that than believe their precious Bastard was molesting a little girl." He spits out his window. "I could've killed them all, the cowards." He flips the Zippo open and lights the flint, then snaps it shut without lighting his cigarette. It dangles between his lips, wiggling and jutting from his mouth as he speaks. "You took the burden off Ravage, Mark, Beer Can, Donny, and myself. No more internal fighting, thanks to you. But there were a lot of brothers who weren't happy about a boy killing his own father, either."

I mentally flip through all the faces from my time at Lewisburg. "Guy with the long, nasty white hair? Scar running down his cheek?"

He grips my shoulder again. "That greasy old fuck wants you dead, Red Dog. Lucky for you, he's going to rot in there. Serial rapist, across four state lines, I believe. He had a thing for mothers and young daughters." He spits again. "He and Bastard were cut from the same cloth."

Grimacing, I reach for the cigarettes and light my own. There isn't enough nicotine in the world for this conversation. I need a drink. "Why would you want to watch my back? Why would you leave—" I almost say "Olivia" but catch myself last minute. "—the club for a kid who isn't yours?"

"I love my club," he growls, patting his cut. His palm slaps the leather, the sound reverberating through the Jeep. "I was fucking VP, Red Dog. I put my blood, sweat, and tears into that club—literally. But I knew that if you were gonna live long enough to take your father's place—take your birthright—someone had to keep you alive. You're not cut from his cloth, Cliff. I knew that even back then. I hope you know it, too."

I concentrate on the road. I know I'm not my father. I'm some other kind of monster. Bad things run in my blood.

He lights the Zippo again, holding the flame to his cigarette. "You're gonna be Pres someday, kid."

I say nothing. I need to clear my head.

"Straits Turnpike," he reminds me, pointing to the upcoming exit.

He directs me to a white Cape Cod style home. I pull into the driveway, brows pulled together.

"This is really you?"

"My pride and joy." Opening the passenger side door, he extends a hand to me. "Thanks for the ride."

"Will I see you later at the club house? I've got a shift tonight. I think your daughter does, too." I can't wait to hear about Olivia's first day at DCF. I've got no idea how we're going to work this whole thing now, especially with Mercy around, but that doesn't change how proud I am of her.

"Nah." Mercy climbs out of the car, his brown paper bag tucked under an arm. "I'm gonna hit the road. Thank Beer Can for watering my plants for me, will ya?"

It takes a second for my mind to catch up. I imagine Beer Can coming to this house every week for the last twenty years, keeping the house in shape for when Mercy returns. My chest tightens. Despite my initial misgivings about the MC, I've walked into a real family.

Then the other thing he said hits me.

"Hit the road?" I repeat.

Mercy unlocks the door to the one-car garage. Placing the brown bag on the ground, he hoists the garage door open. There's no car inside, only a white, chrome, and black Softail. "It's a beauty, isn't it?"

I get out and approach the garage. "To think they gave me a Screamin' Eagle when this baby was sitting out of commission."

"Hey, be grateful," he says, flipping on a light so I can see better.

Before the club folded me into its arms, I never would've considered myself a motorcycle guy. Looking at the Softail, I think I might be turning into one.

This thing is sleek. Classic, even. To my uneducated eye, the Softail is the definition of a motorcycle. My eyes roam over the exposed gears, the low handlebars, the sort of caps that helmet the wheels. I don't know what to call them.

"Oh, I'm grateful," I say, walking around the Softail in a circle. "I'm grateful I've got a job so I can save up for one of my own."

Mercy straddles the bike and flips up the kickstand. He turns the starter and gives it some throttle. The Softail roars to life.

Unhooking the house keys from his bike key, he throws them to me.

I catch them with one hand.

"*You* water my plants," he says, pointing a finger at me. Then he puts both hands on the handlebars, a smile creeping across his weathered face.

"Where are you going?" I ask. "Don't you want to see Olivia?"

"I'm going to find Bree," he shouts over the engine. With a final nod, he rolls out of the driveway. Then he takes off down the street, disappearing out of my sight.

I stand there, rubbing a hand over where my beard used to be. How the fuck am I going to explain this to Olivia?

23

From the hall I watch Glace throw her hands up over and over, her lips barely pausing for breath. Diane leans on the edge of her desk, her arms crossed, head bobbing with everything Glace says.

I'm *so* fired.

I turn away, but my view of the cubicle maze isn't much better. Everyone in the office either openly stares at me or they keep glancing over, trying to be inconspicuous but failing. This is probably the most entertainment they get. Maybe they even throw bets down on how long each newbie will last. I remember reading somewhere that there's a high turnover rate of DCF social workers.

Not everyone is cut out for this, and apparently neither am I.

The door opens. I straighten. If I'm going to get fired, I can at least do it gracefully.

Glace slips out, holding it open for me. As I pass, she smiles, her lips tight. Not a good sign. I step into Diane's office, not sure whether I should take a seat or remain standing.

Glace shuts the door behind me.

I lift my chin, clasp my hands in front of me. It's better to make the first move, give myself the advantage. "I was out of line today," I tell Diane. "I was only supposed to observe, and I over-stepped."

I don't say that I'm sorry, because I'm not.

"You're damn right," Diane says from her perch. "Glace said you weren't even in there for five minutes before you started yelling at the mother."

I cross my arms. "I told her like it is."

"Glace said you made her *cry*." Diane gives me a stern look.

I refuse to wither. I won't apologize. She can fire me if she wants, but I know I did the right thing. Because of what I said to Renee, she and Rhett will stay together.

"Renee called Glace to set up a therapy appointment for this afternoon," Diane says.

"Good."

"It's *very* good. Glace has been trying to crack that woman for months. Because of you, we'll be able to close the case soon." She gestures to the chair in front of her.

I put one foot in front of the other on my way to it. It's got to be a good sign that she hasn't kicked me out of her office yet.

"Your approach is . . . not something we use here," she says. "We're supposed to follow protocol, nothing more. I should be firing your flaca blanca ass right now, but you've got heart, and we need that now more than ever. We're about to be inundated with cases, and I'm going to need people who'll fight for these kids. While not going off script, of course. Do you think you can handle that?"

I nod, because I don't want to make any promises. I'm not exactly sure I can keep them. Not if we have more parents like Renee, who just need a gentle kick in the ass and a little bit of empathy in a system run by checklists. "I just want to help," I say instead.

"Good." Diane pushes off from the desk and returns to her

side of it. She passes me a folder. "Let's get those tax forms handled."

Taking the folder, I glance up at the standard issue clock on the wall. Cliff and Mercy should be back by now, maybe knocking back shots at The Wet Mermaid. I'm supposed to work tonight, but I'm sure the guys are throwing a party, so maybe they'll let me off the hook.

As I write my last name on the form, I try to imagine what it'll be like to have a beer with my dad after so long. When the Demmels adopted me, I could've taken their name but I didn't. I didn't know who he was or where he was, but I liked to hope that one day, my dad would be back for me.

I could never count on Bree, but I know I can count on Mercy.

I CLOCK out for the day and stop at home. I need to wash the stuffy, mildew tinged scent of working for the state off of me. I can't believe I'm working for the same people who were once my enemies. I hope Mercy understands the same thing I've come to realize: I can do more from behind enemy lines than I ever could from without.

"Hi, Esther," I shout to her closed door. I nudge the front door shut with my foot and scoop Dio from the floor. He's almost perfect, minus the little crook in his tail. If it weren't because of Eli, I'd think it's cute.

Esther moans from her bedroom in response. I smirk. Must be Donny in there. In my hurry, I must've missed his bike outside.

"I'm taking a shower. You all set with the bathroom for a few?" I settle Dio into one arm and march into my bedroom.

"Oh God, yes," Esther yells in response.

Jealousy wraps around my spine, tightening its grip. Esther and Donny have it so easy. They just . . . are. Neither of them have any misgivings about moving in together. Hell, Donny's even willing to play house and help raise the girls. Cliff, I know, would do the same for me.

The only thing standing in our way is me.

I've already broken so many rules with Cliff. I can't give in any further. Right now I've got to focus on my career, on repairing things with Mercy. Maybe get fully patched if I'm lucky and don't kill anyone else.

"What do you wear for a father/daughter reunion?" I ask Dio. I stare at the clothes in my closet. A dress feels so childish. Besides, I've got to ride. I run a hand along crop tops—perfect for pulling in tips while serving drinks and drugs, but probably not for hanging out with my dad. I want him to think . . . I don't know. There's so much I want to tell him, so much I need to ask.

I need him to be proud of me.

Dio squirms out of my arms and jumps down nose first—a kitty kamikaze. He gives me a heart attack every time he does that. Just like every other time, he lands on all fours.

Cats are incredible little aliens.

He parades through my open bedroom door and into the bathroom like a prince. He's probably just going in there to use his litter box, but still, he's got a point.

I need to just get in the shower and stop procrastinating.

Once I'm clean, I blow dry and straighten my hair. With my luck, it'll frizz up outside anyway, but at least I can say I put in my best effort. I grab my box of makeup and pull out mascara and concealer, then put it back. My teeth sink into my lower lip. I don't know why I'm so indecisive. I should just be me, do my regular thing: a little cat eye and some lip gloss. I reach back in, fingers pushing past eyeshadow palettes and tubes of lipstick before I find my gel liner.

Grabbing a brush, I dip it into the pot, coating the fibers. Gel liner is magic, now that I'm used to it. It glides right on and it doesn't run or smear throughout the day.

Naturally, I completely fuck up my first attempt.

Hand shaking, I draw the flick too thin and too long on my left eye. Scowling, I put the brush down and start hunting for makeup wipes.

"You coming out of there?" Esther raps her knuckles on the door. "I've gotta pee before I get a UTI or pregnant. Or both."

"Jesus," I mutter. I raise my voice so she can hear me. "Don't you have enough kids to worry about? Donny needs to wrap that thing up."

"I like the rush," he says in his velvet baritone.

I fuck up the flick on my other eye.

"At least let me in to pee!" Esther rattles the door knob, but I locked it. I trust Donny, but I always lock the bathroom door when men are around.

Scowling, I reach over and let her in.

"You look nice," she says as she waddles over to the toilet, thighs pressed together. "Oh, damn! What the hell happened to your face?"

I rub the liner off with yet another makeup wipe. "Nerves," I mutter.

"That's right," she shouts over the stream she's unleashing. "Your daddy's back!"

"Please don't call him my daddy." I pick up the brush and take a deep breath. I can do this. I've painted on this pinup look a million times. Tonight should be no different.

"Speaking of daddy issues," she says, flushing the toilet, "did you get anywhere with mine today?"

I close my eyes. Shit. After my chat with Diane, I completely forgot about Esther's case. "I'll pick Glace's brain tomorrow."

Esther's shoulders fall. "Oh. Okay."

"I'm sorry," I tell her. "It was a crazy day."

"I get it." She smiles, her face lighting up. "I really do." Plucking the brush from my hand, she makes a turn motion with her index finger. "Close your eyes."

In just a few strokes, she gives me the perfect wings. She even finishes it off with mascara.

"Don't want you to smear it all over your face, Nervous Nelly," she says.

Guilt sends a bubble up my throat. I let her down, yet she's still a good friend to me. "Thanks. Are you guys stopping by The Wet Mermaid?"

The door opens a smidge. "Everybody decent in here?" Donny asks.

I glance down at the towel wrapped around me. "Sort of."

He pokes his head in. "Essie, I've got Church." His eyes flick to me, then back to her. "Can I take your car? Olivia, you'll give her a ride?"

Her eyes go as round as saucers. "You want me to ride with *her*? The girl who can't even draw eyeliner?"

I swat at her with a hand towel. "I'm an excellent rider."

Help me, Esther mouths to Donny.

He kisses the top of her head. "I gotta go." Without another word, he sprints out of the apartment.

"Where's his bike, anyway?" I ask, putting away my makeup.

"Shop. Some asshole backed into it in a parking lot. Let's get you dressed." She dances into my bedroom, humming to herself. I love that a good lay is all it takes to get Esther singing.

After a few minutes of careful consideration, Esther picks out a gray duster cardigan, maroon tank top, and black jeans for me.

"Keep it simple, stupid," she intones while I dress. She passes me several delicate silver chains of various lengths and I put them on.

I don't even bother looking in the mirror. At this point, I've got to trust that I look all right for this occasion. Otherwise I'll never get there.

I take us over to The Wet Mermaid, riding extra careful because if I put so much as a scratch on Esther, Donny might put *me* six feet under. We head inside, Esther's cloud of curls catching the rainbow lights strobing through the club. A familiar voice croons from the stage. My skin breaks out in a cold sweat.

Oh Vile Eye is playing.

"He's a piece of shit if he doesn't love you," Esther says, putting a hand on my arm.

I put my hand on top of hers and give it a squeeze, more so for my own reassurance than out of appreciation. We walk like that to the bar, my heart slamming painfully into my sternum. I can't work here if *he's* going to keep playing here. All I have to do is say the word to Cliff, and Oh Vile Eye is a band of dead men.

But.

If I always let men solve my problems for me, I'd never keep my power. I am small, and I've been a victim, but I am not weak.

I'll take care of Greg myself.

The strip club is full of the club's hangarounds and regulars —we're still open to the public. Usually, when we throw a party, it's friends of the MC only. I frown.

My frown deepens when I see Cliff standing behind the bar. "Where the hell is Trish?" I say into Esther's ear.

"Who?" she shouts back.

"The little tart who's always fucking up my shelves." I tug her up to the bar with me. There's no telling how much organizational damage Cliff has done. As much as it pains me to say so, Trish is probably a better bartender than the guy who's only just recently had tequila for the first time. "What are you doing back there?" I ask Cliff.

He slides me a shot of tequila. "Sit," he says, mouth drawn.

I glance at Esther. She shrugs.

Cliff slides her a shot, too, then pours one for himself. "You're gonna need this."

I sit on a stool as if my body was made of wood rather than flesh and blood. Oh Vile Eye pulses through me, Greg's voice wrapping itself around my spine and cerebral cord, infiltrating every part of me. I need to focus on the present, not the past. I glance around for Mercy. "Where is he?" I ask Cliff.

"They're all MIA," Esther observes, holding up her shot. "Except you." She nods to Cliff. "¿Que pasó?"

In response, Cliff knocks back his shot, his eyes never leaving mine. "Mercy isn't here."

I don't even blink. "Where is he?" I ask again.

"He had me drop him off at his house."

"The white box?" I salt my hand and grab a lime, then down the shot. "He's there?" I climb down from the stool. He probably wants to look at my baby pictures or something silly like that.

"No, Olivia." Even though he has to yell over the music, his voice is soft.

I turn back toward him. The ache in his eyes sends my stomach plummeting.

He pours me another shot. "He got on his bike . . . and left."

"He left?" I shoot the tequila without even bothering with the salt and lime. "Where did he go?" My voice wobbles, and I nod to the bottle.

Cliff obliges, his eyes sad as he pours. "He went to find Bree."

I blink. "My *mother*?" Eyes watering, I squeeze them shut while I knock back the next shot.

"I'm sorry," he says. He reaches across the bar and entwines his fingers with mine.

I slam the shot glass on the bar. Esther flinches, then gulps down her tequila. "He couldn't even stop in to see me first?" I reach for the bottle, but Cliff puts it back on the shelf.

"He'll be back," he soothes.

I wrench my hand away. Even under the fuzzy blanket of tequila, my anger and betrayal burns. "Is that why the club had Church last minute?"

He nods. "We decided to let him go."

I scoff. "Of course you did." Shaking my head, I take a step toward the end of the bar where there's an opening for whoever's tending. I'm taking that bottle of tequila and holing up in Cliff's room.

Mercy can go fuck himself.

"Hey," Greg croons two inches from my ear.

My entire body freezes. I turn in slow motion, keeping my eyes low so I don't have to look into *his*.

Greg stands so close within my personal space, I could slip a knife between his ribs if I'd thought to bring one. I sidestep him, shoving down memories.

"I'm out of here," I call, then stumble out the door. Before I can think about what I'm doing or where I'll even go, I hop onto the Street Glide, then peel out of the parking lot, far away from The Wet Mermaid and all of the men who have ruined me.

24

CLIFF

I watch her go, chest tightening hard enough to bruise my heart. I fucked this up. I should've broken it to her better. I don't know how, but better. Somehow.

"Watch the bar," I tell Esther, then vault over the thing. I hit the ground hard, the shock reverberating up through my legs, banging around in my knees. I sure as hell ain't eighteen anymore.

Springing up, I race through the crowd. A motorcycle revs—Olivia. I shove past the dick from Oh Vile Eye, just about knocking him over. I don't even bother to apologize.

"Move," I yell as I point a shoulder toward a cluster of dancing bodies. They part and I run through, their bodies stilling as they stare after me. I push through the door, bursting into the cool night air. Olivia peels out of the parking lot, her hair streaming out behind her in frizzy spirals. "Shit!"

I lunge for the Screamin' Eagle, hands and feet working in tandem even when my brain and heart are already chasing Olivia down 63. I barely register when I'm doing. My helmet clatters to the pavement and I leave it. I go after my girl.

When I get onto the street, there's no sign of her. I push the bike hard. I've got to find her. I close the distance between me and a Subaru, my front tire nearly kissing its bumper. The hippie's barely doing 25 on a 45 mph strip. I check for oncoming traffic. Both lanes are clear, so I duck into the left lane and pass the Subaru.

Moving back into the right lane, I push the Eagle to 50, then 60 mph. I pass two Hondas, a Toyota, and a pickup before I get stuck behind an eighteen-wheeler.

I ain't fucking with that.

I follow the truck until I'm nearly in Waterbury. Still no sign of Olivia. I pull into the Mobil at the bottom of the on ramp to CT-8 N. It's a small gas station, so instead of taking up space in front of a pump, I pull off to the side.

Despite the cool air, sweat dampens my hair. Wish I had a bandana or one of Olivia's hair ties. I put it up in a bun once, just to see what she'd do. She laughed so hard, her face turned bright red. I almost didn't want to take it out, because I'd never seen her let go like that.

I put both feet on the ground but leave the Eagle idling. Now I've lost her—I'm not sure in how many ways. I'm not even sure where to look for her, aside from her place or Lucy's. She might've just gone for a ride to clear her head.

Which means she could be anywhere.

I pat down my cut for my cell phone, but come up empty. I don't even have any cigarettes. I left everything at the club. Luckily, I've got my wallet. I put down the kickstand, ready to shut the bike off and go buy a pack, when it hits me.

The house.

She called it the white box. She was only a baby when he went inside, but maybe she and Bree stayed there for a while. I gave the key back to Beer Can, but maybe there's a spare and she let herself in.

I roll out of the gas station and take a left back into Naugatuck.

I've only been to the house once, but I think I can get back there. If not, I'll go back to The Wet Mermaid and get directions from one of the guys.

Before I went in and for the twenty years I served, cell phones were way out of my grasp, but it's crazy how much they come in handy now.

I get lucky again, finding my way back without much trouble at all. It helps that when I pull up, I spot Olivia's Street Glide in the driveway. It's just a little crooked, but I'm grateful she made it in one piece. I should've never let her ride drunk. I slide in behind her bike, then shut off the engine.

If we're breaking and entering, it's probably better to not draw too much more attention.

A single porch light is on. No interior lights. I glance down the side of the yard. Nothing moves.

"Olivia?" I call, checking up and down the street. No one's paying attention.

I stroll into the yard like I live here and call her name again. I don't see her, and she doesn't answer, but I smell menthol cigarettes. I follow the scent until I'm in the backyard.

Another porch light illuminates the yard, shining down on Olivia. She sits at a rusted patio set, its cushions long gone. She holds a cigarette between two long fingers, the light glinting off her maraschino cherry red nail polish. Smoke curls into the air, disappearing up into the night.

I take the seat across from her. Without a cushion, the metal chair digs into my tailbone, already sore from driving back and forth to Pennsylvania. I gesture to her pack of cigarettes and lighter. "Do you mind?"

She nods, eyes luminous. Her lips close around the filter and she shuts her eyes, taking a drag. It reminds me of the first time I saw her, when she lit up the second she slid out of the Uber. The only difference is, then she didn't have a care in the world. Right now, in this dim backyard, she looks ten years wearier.

I light up too. "I'm sorry," I say on the exhale. Those two words are hardly enough. I should've made Mercy stay.

Maybe he thought she didn't need him anymore. Maybe he didn't want to face her after leaving her for the club—after leaving her to the care of strangers. I should've made him see that she needed him to stay, at least for a little while.

I try to find the words to say all of this—words that don't sting. There are none.

I reach across the table, but her arm is wrapped around her torso, her fingers clutching her ribs. Her other elbow rests on the table. She'll have the mesh pattern from the wrought iron imprinted on her skin later.

"If I'd known Mercy was gonna pull that shit, I wouldn't have brought him here," I say. "I would've brought him straight to the club."

She shakes her head. "It's not that," she says, her voice scraping her throat. She laughs. "Well, it *is* that. Too. Two." She brings the cigarette to her lips.

"What else?" I ask softly.

"I mean," she continues, sliding down in her seat a little, "I guess he didn't miss me as much as I missed him." She flicks her finished cigarette into the grass. Then she lights another. "He goes after my *mom*? They haven't even been together since I was born. What the fuck."

I drum my fingers on the table. "Maybe she reached out to him before he got out."

Olivia rolls her eyes. "Lord knows she's always running to the club for help. God, the two of them. Why the fuck did they even *have* me?"

This is a conversation for Lucy. I don't know the right things to say. Not because I think it's a woman's job to deal with another woman's feelings, but because Lucy has fourteen years of Olivia experience on me.

I wasn't there when she lost her parents to the life.

I can't relate to having both my parents walk out on me, but I do know what it's like to have lost them.

"I don't think they know what they're doing at all," I tell her. "I'm glad those two fuckups had you, though."

"You should talk," she scoffs. "Your father makes mine look like Santa fucking Claus."

"You're not wrong." I stretch, reaching for the sky. "I'm pretty sure he killed my mother."

"Get the fuck out." She taps her lighter against the metal. "You never told me that."

"It's more of a hunch. The official cause of death was a suicide, but I've always wondered. Mom didn't have any trouble with depression. She wasn't even on medication or anything." I take a long drag, blinking away the memory of her lying in the tub, fully clothed. "They didn't bother to look into how she got ahold of the fentanyl and Ambien in her system."

"I'm sorry," she says softly.

I need to close that door. I change the subject. "It's kind of romantic that Mercy went after your mom, in a way."

"In a psycho circus kind of way." Olivia sighs.

"He taught you how to shoot. And ride. That's got to count for something," I point out.

"But I must've made that up," she says. "Or remembered it all wrong. How could he have taught me any of those things when he was inside this whole time? I don't even know what he went away for. Maybe it was really bad. Our dads are best friends, after all. No offense."

"Were," I correct. "Mercy told me he was going to kill Bastard if I hadn't."

"The plot thickens." Olivia's gaze drifts into the dark corner of the yard. She bursts into laughter. "What a shit show. You and me, Cliff. I just, wow." Her giggle thickens into a sardonic laugh. "Nothing good comes of our blood."

I want to say that a lot of good could come out of us. I don't.

She scoffs. "We're like oil and water. Fire and gasoline. Napalm and . . ." She taps her lip.

"Napalm," I suggest.

"Napalm and napalm." She finishes her cigarette, tossing it into the dark. "I've got daddy issues."

"Don't we all?"

"That's probably why I can't move in with you. That and Greg."

I straighten in my seat. "Greg?"

"I'm going to kill him," she promises, her voice so cold, I fight off a shudder.

"Who is he?"

"My ex." She reaches for her pack, then frowns. "This is really more of a tequila discussion. Or something stronger than tequila. He's the lead singer in the band Mark hired."

"The one at the bar?" The guy I just about knocked over.

"Yeah, the redhead." She flips open the pack as if she expects cigarettes to materialize. "It's too bad no one actually lives here," she says, glancing at the sliding glass door. "I'd break in and hunt for smokes. Or weed. This is definitely a weed conversation."

"He comes off as a shit head." I flip back through all of my conversations with Lucy about Olivia. She never mentioned a musician ex.

"He's just as bad as Sebastian." Her eyes meet mine.

"You mean Bastard?" I ask, voice hushed.

She nods, just once.

"He hurt you," I say.

"Yes." Her lips tremble, and my heart shatters.

I push back the chair and go to her, falling on my knees in front of her. "I'm here. If you want to tell me, or if you don't. I'm right here." I take both her hands in mine. Her fingers are so cold.

"If I tell you, it'll ruin everything," she whispers.

"Olivia." I hold her hands, hoping the warmth from mine

finds a way into hers. "What he did to you doesn't define you. It reflects on him, not you."

"It might not define me," she says, "but he polluted me. I killed Eli because of him. Because of him, I can't even be in the same room with a man without questioning his motives."

"Eli was coming after you," I remind her. "He was going to hurt you. You didn't have a choice."

"He's got family, Cliff. There's a silver alert out for him. The semester ended and somebody realized he didn't walk that stage." She turns her hands in mine, laces her fingers through mine. "Regardless of what he did, someone loves him and has no idea what happened to him."

"Come here." Pulling her into my lap, I ease us down into the grass, damp with evening dew. "No one is going to find him. You're safe."

"That's not what I'm worried about, Cliff. He's someone's son. Someone's brother. Someone out there has no closure. They're like me, wondering where Bree is. And now Mercy, too. I *did* that to someone."

I wrap my arms around her. I never thought about who I might be hurting by killing Bastard. In my uncle's eyes, I took his brother from him. My aunt and uncle didn't believe Lucy, and I'll never forgive them for that.

There is always collateral damage.

"And it's not the first time," she continues.

"What do you mean?" Cupping her chin, I stroke her skin, my hand almost larger than her face.

"Greg got *married*." Her voice is so low, I have to strain to hear her. "Her name is Cami, and right now, his hands might be around her neck. Or he's having sex with her when she doesn't want to." She tenses in my arms. "I let him do this to another woman."

The blood in my veins turns to ice, then boils. Every muscle in my body contracts, straining, fingers itching to wrap around his neck. My fists feel hot and heavy, battering rams attached to my arms. "He raped you."

"That sums up all of the awful things he did to me, yes."

I'm torn between staying here with her and flying back to the club. I want to yank him off that stage, bludgeon him with his own guitar. Then it hits me.

She told me.

She *trusts* me.

I can't break that by racing off to kill him. Olivia let me in— something I never thought would happen. I'll be damned if I leave her here now.

I pick her up, carrying her to our motorcycles out front. I sit her on mine and straddle it, her arms wrapping around me. She nestles into my back, and I take us back to her place with the heat of her body keeping me grounded. Keeping me with her.

In her bed, I tuck her into my side and hold her until she falls asleep. I don't sleep at all.

All I can think about are the thousand ways I will kill him the next time I see him.

25

OLIVIA

I wake up wedged between the wall and Cliff. At least, what I *think* is Cliff. I roll over and find a body pillow and comforter instead. I sit up, the look in his eyes when I told him about Greg replaying. I shouldn't have fallen asleep.

I've got to get to Greg before Cliff kills him.

That's *my* kill.

I yank on the first clothes I find: a pair of ripped skinny jeans on the floor that should probably be washed, a wrinkled white T-shirt. I can't find a bra, and there's no time. I shove my feet into my boots.

The alarm on my phone blares—my 6 a.m. wakeup call.

"Son of a bitch," I hiss. I can't get to Cliff, kill Greg myself, and get to work on time. Given the choice between keeping my job and keeping Cliff out of prison, I choose him. I can't let him go back in there.

I rock back on my heels. *I choose him.* I turn the words over in my head, trying to decipher them. I don't know what it means. I don't have time to work it out, either. I grab the keys to my Street Glide from the dresser and yank open my bedroom door.

The scent of coffee curls into my nostrils, beckoning me. It's a small ass apartment, so I don't even have to take a step to see Cliff standing at my stove.

Making eggs.

I drop the keys onto the carpet.

He turns, spatula in the air above the pan, mid-flip. "Morning," he rasps.

I go weak in the knees. Like, literally. He stands there barefoot, no shirt, just those dark wash jeans. A tingle zips through my core. I'm hot, panties soaked.

I glance at Esther's door—shut. I think she's home. I don't remember, because the second Cliff tucked me into bed, I went out like a light that desperately needs a new bulb.

"Morning," I say, and bend down to pick up the keys. I turn to just the right angle so that Cliff can watch my ass. The crown of my head points toward the carpet, and my hair falls, a thick curtain of dark curls. I close my fingers around the keys, ass in the air, lips tilted up. I just can't help myself. Not with that sight at my stove.

"Morning," Cliff says again, his voice even grittier than usual. My nipples harden against the cotton of my tee.

On my way back up, I do the hair flip—the one curly girls learn to do, the one that finishes it off after you've scrunched it upside down. It's also the same move strippers use. Different context. I've perfected it over the years, and thank goodness for that.

I'm not sure who to thank for my curls, since both Bree and Mercy have straight hair.

I reach into my room and put the keys back on the dresser. Then I unzip the button of my jeans, kick off my boots. "You should shut those eggs off."

"Why?" Cliff glances down at the spatula and shakes his head as if coming out of a stupor. He flips the eggs in the pan.

I put my hands at my hips, curl my fingers over the waistband of the jeans, and tug them off, dropping them to the floor. I shove them aside. "Because I'm going back to bed." I give him what I hope is a naughty grin, then turn my back to him. I pull the T-shirt over my head and drop it onto the floor, then walk into the bedroom.

A second later, I hear the knob of the stove click to the off position.

I lie on the bed on my side, facing the door. My breasts lean toward the mattress—gravity at work—but my nipples point toward Cliff, my true north. He pads into the room, pausing at the door when he sees me. His eyes trace my form, starting at the points of my toes, drifting up along my calves, thighs.

He smirks. "You forgot to take your panties off."

"Come take them off yourself." I pat the bed next to me.

He closes the door behind him. For a moment, he just stands there, the corners of his mouth lifted. His gaze hovers on the lace of my thong for a heartbeat, then skims up, looping around my bellybutton, settling on my breasts. Without even touching me, he's setting my skin alight, dousing each electrified nerve with water.

His silky black hair falls over his shoulders, brushing just past his nipples. My fingers twitch, needing to wrap it around my hand. He likes when I pull his hair.

"Are you coming?"

That smirk returns. "Not yet. Just appreciating the view for a moment."

"I do have to go to work soon, you know."

"We've got three hours." Still, he unbuckles the leather belt on his jeans. I almost tell him to leave it all on—I'll just ride him through the zipper hole. But I kind of like the languid, tender vibe that's so real, I'm wrapped up in it. He drops the jeans to the floor and steps out of them bared to me.

He slides into bed beside me, on his side facing me. His hand slips through the waistband of my thong and cups my hip, his fingers gripping my cheek. I shiver under the heat of his touch.

His eyes flick down to my hard nipples. "Cold?"

"No." But I snuggle closer, my belly flush with the heat of his length.

His hand wanders down to my thigh, pulling my leg over his, pressing him even tighter against my skin. He threads an arm under my head, his hand holding the back of my neck. His other hand slips between us and takes my breast. Those luscious, full lips of his enfold mine, his tongue running along my bottom lip. I tug him even closer to me with the leg hooked over him. I need all of him connected to me, every inch of his skin bound to mine.

"I'm right here," he whispers against my lips.

I kiss him back, tasting first the coffee with a hint of chocolate, then the sweet spice underneath that's all him. He runs his thumb back and forth against my nipple, drawing a spiral out from the center, slowly moving farther and farther away, rambling down, down. His fingers skim my ribs, exquisite bumps breaking out across my skin. Down, down he continues, the pads of his fingers running along the lace, dipping underneath the fabric.

He traces shapes across my lower abdomen—at least, I think they're shapes until I realize that one of them is the letter L.

I break the kiss. "What are you writing?"

A grin breaks out across his face—the mischievous one that always gives him away. "My name."

Before I can even come up with a response, his hand dips lower, tracing an achingly slow C around the hidden nub. My back arches, leg tightening around him. He twitches against me, the skin of his length and crown impossibly hot. I shift my hips, sliding up on the bed until his crown rests against my center.

I slip back and forth, leaving a trail up and down his shaft. His lips move against mine, tongue prodding into my mouth. Again I taste coffee. I moan into his mouth, a contented sigh.

"Hmn?" he moans back. He clamps a hand around my ass, pressing us tighter together.

I pull my lips from his, leaving just a fraction of space between us. "I was just thinking about how nice it is to wake up to Cliff, coffee, and cock."

"The three Cs." He trails a hand down between my cheeks, his fingers resting just at my entrance. He spreads me apart, sliding himself between his fingers and my lips.

"Four, if you count my clit." I wiggle my eyebrows at him.

"Olivia," he groans.

"It's true, though."

"Not that. I need to be inside you." His words come out even huskier than usual, each syllable exhaled through his strained control.

"Oh." I could spend all morning like this, tangled up with him, our need growing more and more urgent. I do have to get ready for work. After yesterday, I can't afford to be late.

I slide up and down, angling my hips until he slips right into me, his head resting just inside me. He wraps his arms around me and I wrap my legs around him. Inch by inch, he eases into me, each gain sending a sweet pang of relief through me. I hook my ankles together and squeeze, sending him in deeper. Once he's fully buried in me, I sigh.

Our eyes meet.

"Olivia," he says again, his voice full of things I don't want him to say.

So I seal his mouth with mine and push him down until he's flat on his back. I move my knees to either side, digging them into the mattress. Drawing my hips back, I keep our chests together and his mouth shut, my tongue exploring his mouth as if I've never been there before. Then I move against him, sliding back down until he's immersed in me once more.

We find a rhythm, muscle memory taking over, senses gone. Every time I'm with Cliff, I lose myself in him—something I've never done before with anyone else. I don't disappear. I become part of something bigger.

Us.

I tell him what I'm thinking with my body. I lace my fingers through his and put all of my focus into kissing him. It feels different this time, this kiss. He kisses me back with abandon, his mouth saying the things I won't let him speak. No matter how much I don't want to hear it, he finds ways to tell me.

It's the way he stayed with me last night when he could've ridden back to the strip club. It's how his eyes hold all of the light in the world when he looks at me, as if he *sees* me, unclouded by everything I've endured. It's how he strokes my back, holding me both tightly and carefully. It's the coffee and eggs, the graduation party, the motorcycle riding lessons.

He doesn't just think he loves me.

He *loves* me.

The realization steals my breath. I plummet, shattering into billions of stars. Cliff splinters with me. The remaining fragments swirl, suspended in space and time. It's the big bang, the moment everything changes between us. The closing of one door and the beginning of something new, something I don't know what to make of.

Because I think, if I try, I might be able to love him too. In my own twisted way, anyway.

I roll off him and fall onto my back, chest heaving. My lungs feel tight and loose at the same time, like I've just been born and I'm only now learning how to breathe.

"Damn," Cliff rumbles. The sound reverberates through my bones, vibrating through me. I want to lean closer to him, spend some time floating in this.

I *have* to go to work.

So instead of snuggling into his side, I slide off the bed.

"I'm grabbing a shower before Esther gets up," I say. "Lock up behind you."

Before he can argue or offer to give me a ride in, I force myself to walk—not run—into the bathroom. I'll get a ride from Esther back to Mercy's for my bike.

Right now, I need to think.

26

OLIVIA

"Hey there, Rogue One." Glace gives me an exaggerated wink and hands me a case folder.

I stand from the chair in Diane's office, making a mental note to ask Cliff if he's even seen any of the Star Wars movies. I almost roll my eyes at myself. I really just filed away something to say to my boyfriend later. "New client?" I ask Glace, hoping she can't tell that there's something very wrong with me.

"New to you. This one's a bit of a rough case. I want you to familiarize yourself with that folder."

"So, no home visits today?" I study her face. "Have I lost some kind of privileges?"

"No." Glace scoffs. "Before yesterday, my plan was to ease you into this one. I think you're ready now." She motions to Diane's door. "Walk with me."

I trail her through the office, then out into the sunshine. The air smells like spring—that fresh, pastel green scent, clean and open. Glace leads me down the sidewalk lining the parking lot, far past the entrance of the building.

"This one's rough," she reminds me. "I just got it. The foster family made a complaint about the way the case was being handled. Whatever it was, it was bad. Diane yanked the worker who was on the case off. I don't know any of the details."

I'm beginning to think that the sky is the limit in this job. So far, there's no cap to the awful things that can happen to a child. "Where's the social worker?"

She shrugs. "I think they suspended her."

"Shit." Anything concerning the state usually takes ages. So it really must've been bad. "You said 'foster family.' Two parents. Any other children?"

"Grandparents," she says. "Four children, three of them are with us."

I'm afraid to ask. "Where's the fourth?" He or she is probably dead. I can't let myself get worked up if that's what happened. I've got to find a way to detach myself enough so that I don't keep yelling at people.

"Adult child. She emancipated herself at sixteen. She's the one who made the complaint."

I stop walking. "She?" Flipping open the folder, I scan the briefing. The children are Cierra and Abril Figueroa and Ximena Jiminez.

I have to disclose. It's a conflict of interest that I know one of the people involved in the case. If I say nothing, I could lose my job. Hell, that's probably what got the last case worker suspended. If Esther's social worker knew the family somehow— knew Esther's parents, maybe—she would've immediately been taken off the case. I frown.

Maybe the worker started the reunification process on purpose.

"We're supposed to start some kind of permanency plan after eighteen months of foster care, right?" I ask.

"Yeah. It's impressive that you know that." Glace gives me a thumbs up. "Maybe you *are* gonna work out."

"I didn't drink my way through college." I tap my temple.

I don't tell her that I did sleep my way through the men's dorms.

"Everything you need to know about the case is in that folder."

"I'll get started now." I continue walking, heading toward a grassy area on the far end of the building.

"Out here? You can sit at my cubicle, you know."

"Gonna take a smoke break." I wave her off, keeping my gait as casual as possible. I wish I could call Esther right now. I have her entire future in my hands. This has to be the first time the universe hasn't thrown a fuck you in my face. I need to use this power for good.

I'm not telling Glace a damn thing.

I'm going to help Esther keep those kids.

I sit under the tree and take out my phone. I scan the parking lot. There's no one around. I take pictures of every page in the folder. There's a good chance I'll have to give it back to Glace, and I'll definitely need these later. I text copies of the pics to Esther, then drop them into iCloud.

Can't be too careful.

Then I spend the next thirty minutes smoking and reading, soaking up every detail of the girls' and Esther's lives. Their mother, Toci, married Josué when she found out she was pregnant with Esther. When Esther was five, someone anonymously told DCF that Josué was sexually abusing her. DCF placed her with Toci's parents, Salome and León Aguirre.

Toci was "distraught," according to the report. She divorced Josué and went through counseling, and DCF gave Esther back. When Esther was seven, Toci discovered she was pregnant again —with Josué's child.

Cierra.

Another anonymous complaint was made, raising suspicions of neglect and more sexual abuse. The girls were taken again and placed with Esther's grandparents. Within six months, Toci got them back. As soon as her followup home visits with DCF ended, she and Josué took the girls to Arizona, where Josué had family. They stayed for almost a year before moving back to Naugatuck.

The cycle continued: another baby, another state intervention. Toci and Josué were smart. Every time they got those kids back, they moved out of state just long enough to fall off child services' radar.

Then, out of nowhere, Toci took all three of their girls and left Josué. For almost a year, she lived with a friend. She couldn't stay away from Josué long. She went back to him, pregnant with Ximena.

A fourth complaint was made. Naugatuck High's school social worker reported that Josué raped sixteen-year-old Esther again.

Esther took a pregnancy test. It was positive. With the help of the school social worker, she emancipated herself. She was never a ward of the state again. There's no mention of what became of the pregnancy.

The little girls were taken away again, but yet again, Toci got them back.

This case now is the fifth complaint, the fifth time the state has taken those kids.

And they're going to reunify them.

Again.

I don't understand how the state could justify this. Because Toci and Josué aren't struggling with substance abuse problems or mental illness—something a social worker could sympathize with. They're not people trying to get their lives together for their children's sake. They're evil, twisted people who know how to work the system to get away with the things they do.

They're poison, and the system can't touch them. Not with its checklists.

I lower the folder into my lap, the hand holding my cigarette shaking. My other hand curls into a fist, my nails digging into the flesh of my palm.

There's got to be something I can do. If the prior social

worker knew Toci and Josué and tried helping them, maybe Glace and I can overturn the reunification plan and file a motion to grant legal guardianship to Esther. There's plenty of evidence right here in this folder, if anyone had bothered to read it before me.

And Glace.

Glace is on our side.

I'm going to make this right.

27

CLIFF

I sit on Lucy's couch, remote in hand, court TV that I'm not watching on the screen. After Olivia gave me the cold shoulder this morning, I needed a place to crash. There was a chance Greg would be at the club house, so I couldn't go back there.

Not yet.

I *will* take care of him.

Soon.

I rode around for a little while, drifting aimlessly through the streets of Naugatuck and into Waterbury. I ended up riding all the way up 69 to Pine Grove Cemetery in Waterbury. I said my hellos to my friend Devon and my mother Ruth, then headed to Lucy's. Since she's a teacher and everyone else on her street works nine-to-fives, it's always quiet here during the day.

It's the perfect place to crash and think—usually.

This time I can't. Every time I get a little closer, Olivia shoves me away harder, farther. I don't know how to do this, what to be for her. I don't even know what I am to her.

I just know that she let me in on something huge, something so deep and painful, I'm amazed she's even walking around in one piece. She needs time, and I can give her that. I'll just step away a pace, be here when she needs me. If.

In the meantime, I've got to start thinking about my future.

For the past twenty years, I didn't even think I had one. Olivia might not know what I am to her, but I know what she's been for me: possibility, an awakening. For the first time, I understand that there can be more to life than concrete, steel, and iron. I have lost my mother and killed my father, and my aunt and uncle hate everything that I am, but I still have Lucy. She and the little niece or nephew she's incubating are my family.

I think of Ravage, how he told me that someday I'd be President. Even Mercy—Bastard's best friend and VP, who would've been next in line if he hadn't gone to prison—said that the seat at the head of that table is my birthright. I won't even have to take it like I thought.

The River Reapers are my family. They're the ones who gave me a home and a place to punch in and out of every day. They've had my back even when I didn't know I needed someone looking out for me. They covered for me even when I was a Prospect, helped me make Eli disappear. They gave me respect and a rocker.

The MC was once my for-now plan, but now it's my forever plan.

If I want to be President someday, I've got to be as transparent as possible, even now.

I'm taking Greg to the table.

I can't let him work under the same roof as Olivia. I'm not even sure I can let him walk around the same town, breathe the same oxygen on the same planet. I just know I can't kill him without giving the club a heads up.

And I know they'll back me up.

If Mercy stuck around, I know he'd approve. Hell, he'd fight me to be the one to do it. I'm glad he's gone. The monster inside of me has reared its head, and it won't be sated until it's tasted Greg's blood. I'm a killer. Might as well embrace it.

Shutting off the TV, I toss the remote onto the couch and get up. Then I ride to The Wet Mermaid.

"WANT A DRINK?" Trish asks as I pass the bar. She holds up an empty shot glass.

I wave it off. "Thanks."

It's still early in the day, so most of the dancers perfect their moves without the hungry eyes of an audience on their bodies. I nod to Pru and the others, then veer into Mark's office.

Ravage sits at the desk, his boots propped up on it. "Yeah?"

"Where's Mark?" I pull up a chair and sit opposite him.

"Meeting with our accountant. Tax season, I guess." He shrugs. "I'm shit with that stuff."

"Good, because I need to run something by you before I bring it to the table."

He swings his legs off the desk with a sigh. "What now? I thought Olivia was working the DCF angle. I've got Vaughn trying to get into the state's records, see if we can dig up any dirt on Esther's old man."

"That's a felony." I light a cigarette, my eyes on his.

"I know. He's good with that shit. He'll clean up his tracks."

"You ever have him look up our employees? Or associates?"

The corner of his mouth twitches. "What are you getting at?"

"Greg Byrne." His name burns up my throat, leaving an acidic aftertaste. "He have a record?"

"He was in the Navy for a short stint. Only signed up for three years. Came out right after. No issues there. Nothing that shines, either. Why?" His blue eyes laser into me.

"Olivia dated him in high school." I lean forward. "He raped her."

Ravage's eyes darken to a storm gray.

"He tried approaching her last night, right before we took off." I spread my hands on the desk, gripping the wood as if I could reach through it the way I want to break Greg's skull.

He nods once, real slow. "Whatever you want to do, take it to the table. I'll back you up. No one hurts a River Reaper. I don't give a shit whether she's patched or when it happened."

"Call Church," I say, sitting back. I rest my hands on my thighs, vision tunneled to the breadth of my palms, the thickness of my fingers. The solid knuckles, scarred from dozens of fights. Killer's hands.

"That's a felony," Ravage reminds me.

I look up.

A snarl twists his features. "One I'm sure your brothers will be happy to make disappear."

I nod. "Thanks." Pushing back the chair, I stand. The heaviness of my decision pulls me down, a black gravity.

"Thank you for coming to me." Ravage stands, too, and holds out his hand.

I clasp it. He shakes my hand once with a firm, slow pump, those glacial eyes never leaving mine. His black eyebrows bear down on his face, his mouth taught.

"Be in the Chapel in forty-five minutes," he says, releasing his grip.

With a final nod, I turn and walk out of the office.

RAVAGE SITS at the head of the MC's table, the gavel resting by his hand. His whole body is curved slightly, muscles coiled and ready to pounce. "Thank you all for coming."

I glance around at my brothers. Skid, our VP, sits on Ravage's left, his scarred hands clasped. Our Sergeant-at-Arms and best candidate for a dwarf cosplay, Beer Can, to his right.

Next to him is Donny, whose six-plus frame makes him our Enforcer, until you catch the warmth in his eyes. Across from Donny sits treasurer Mark—probably the most normal looking of all of us. The members who don't hold offices fill the rest of the seats: Stixx, Vaughn, Abraham, and me. We'd be ten if Mercy'd stayed.

"We've got to vote on a serious issue," Ravage says, "but first, Vaughn. How far did you get before I dragged you out of your mom's basement?"

The men around the table smirk.

"Actually, I do all my hacking at Starbucks. Public Wi-Fi," he explains, brown eyes crinkling. "I couldn't find any of the DCF cases Donny filled me in on. Except this one. The rest of 'em have all been closed, so there wouldn't be anything else to find. I did find this." He pulls a folded rectangle of paper from the inside pocket of his cut. Unfolding it, he spreads it out on the table.

I lean forward, peering at it. At thirty-eight, my eyes aren't what they used to be.

"Josué Figueroa is a registered sex offender in Arizona," Vaughn announces. "I couldn't scare up any details. It appears to be unrelated to any of the DCF cases."

"The sex offender lists are a state to state thing," Donny growls. "Connecticut might not even know about it."

"I say we call in an anonymous tip." Ravage holds his hand out for the sheet.

"To DCF?" Donny scowls. "Nah. They ain't gonna do shit. I say we find out where he works, someone lets his boss know. Get his ass fired."

The men nod around the table.

"That sounds like a plan," I tell Donny.

He gives me a grateful chin jerk. "Thanks, brother."

Vaughn cracks his knuckles. "Guess my work's cut out for me tonight."

"Talk to your ol' lady," Ravage tells Donny. "See if she can find out where he works. That might be faster than sending Vaughn on a wild goose chase."

"It'll get him out of his mom's basement for a night, too," Beer Can ribs. "Maybe get him laid."

I bang on the table, a steady beat. "Let's get Vaughn laid!"

My brothers join in, keeping time with me with hands and feet. Laughter ripples through the room, some levity to lighten the situation.

Ravage clears his throat, and the Chapel quiets. "I appreciate what we're doing for Donny and Esther. This is outside our area of expertise, but I'm proud of all of you." He glances at me. "Cliff has another public service for us to consider."

I spread my hands on the table, look each of my brothers in the eye before beginning. "I don't know how to tell you all this, so I'm just gonna say it: our live band's gotta go. Namely, their lead singer."

Mark frowns. "What do you mean? Business is up. Our accountant says our revenue's tripled on the nights Oh Vile Eye plays."

"Oh Vile Eye did something vile to our own Prospect," Ravage growls.

"When she was in high school," I clarify, "Olivia dated the lead singer, Greg. He *raped* her. I want him dead."

A collective shock circles the table, my brothers muttering contempt.

"I never would've hired him if I'd known." Mark bows his head.

Skid clasps his shoulder.

"You couldn't have known," I soothe. "None of you could've. We all know how Olivia likes to handle things herself."

Donny snorts. "Yeah, she does."

"I'm not asking any of you to do anything," I say. "I'm just asking for your blessing. I need to take Greg to the river."

Several of my brothers start talking at once.

"Introduce him to the Sludge Spector," Donny says. "Fuck yeah."

"Slit his fucking throat," Beer Can suggests.

"What about the band?" Mark asks.

"The river? Let me earn another X," Stixx grumbles.

"I'll get his address," Vaughn says.

Ravage knocks the gavel against the edge of the table. "We vote. Do we take Greg to the river?" From across the table, his eyes meet mine. "Yea," he votes.

I swing my gaze to Skid.

His chest rises as his lungs fill. "She's a good bartender. A good Prospect. A good ol' lady. And we made a promise to Mercy. Yea."

I nod my thanks, then turn to Mark.

"This is my fault," he says with a sigh. "I'm with you all the way. Yea."

"Fucker should burn in his own house," Stixx says. "The river's too good for him."

"Is that a nay?" I ask, shoulders tensing.

He scowls. "She's a good girl. He should *burn*!"

"Stixx!" Ravage barks. "The how is up to Cliff."

Stixx's pale blue eyes meet mine. "Yea, brother," he whispers, running a hand through his white blond hair. "I'm sorry."

I lift one hand from the table. "My vote's yea," I growl, blood boiling. I need this done soon, before it consumes me, before I implode from the rage coursing through me.

Ravage fixes cold eyes on Abraham. "You with us this time, or is there gonna be a problem again?"

"Yes," Abraham says without hesitation.

I frown, but before I can ask, the vote continues.

"Yea," echoes Donny. "It'll be like old times."

"That girl sure does leave a trail of bodies behind her," Skid says.

"Beer Can?" Ravage asks the stocky Sergeant-at-Arms.

The light illuminates the gray's in Beer Can's beard and at his temples. He shakes his head slowly, fingers absently stroking his beard. "I've known Olivia since she was a baby," he says, voice breaking. "She's like a granddaughter to me. I've always loved Mercy." His brown eyes meet mine, aching and pleading. "Do it. Yea."

Ravage clutches the gavel so tightly, I wait for it to snap. "We'll help Oh Vile Eye find a new singer," he says, then slams the head of the gavel onto the table, the decision made.

My shoulders straighten. My jaw squares.

Now it's only a matter of when.

28

I frown at the house. It's absurd that something so innocuous looking could belong to someone like him. The exterior is teal and friendly, and he is anything but. Looking at him from the outside, I thought he'd be a good time. He smelled spicy and cool, and his pouty lips and long red hair sucked me in.

He was charming, always smiling—until he wasn't.

He could walk out of this house right now and take me out with his Navy SEAL training. If he steps out of that front door, I don't have a single excuse for showing up here.

But I couldn't stop myself.

From the moment I realized he lives right up the street from me, my brain has buzzed in his direction. I'm not much of a walker, but my legs started tingling the second I pulled his house up on Google again.

They're still tingling.

I want to cross the street, march up that front walk, and ring his doorbell. See the look of shock on his face as he registers my presence. Search his eyes for any hint of shame. I'd even take regret. Ask him the question, the one that's burned on my tongue for over a decade. The one that I buried deep in my heart, but still surfaced anyway. Repression only works for so long.

"Why?"

I whisper the word. It slices my lips. It's a futile question, because there's no simple answer. The answers are the kind you get only after years of couples talk therapy. We aren't a couple. I'm not sure we ever really were. Something about him always pulled me in, washing over me until my lungs were full of him. Even now, after all this time, here I am. I couldn't stay away.

Even after everything he did to me.

I know things about him. His wife is a teacher. He's building a mini bridge to the woods in their backyard. They don't have any children. There are also things I don't know, like whether he is sorry, if he thinks about me, whether his wife is safe. I'm good at finding things out but that last one's locked down tight.

I don't know those things but I do know one other thing. Two, actually.

He isn't home right now.

And I'm going to ruin his life like he ruined mine.

The curtains in the front window move. A heart-shaped face peers out at me, her brown eyes watchful. I recognize Cami from the single wedding pic on his Facebook. Instead of turning around and going home, like I should, I take a step toward the house.

The curtains fall back into place.

I freeze in the middle of the street. I should not be here. I'm not ready to face him. I'm not brave enough to face her. The front door opens and she steps out.

"Hi," she calls in a sweet, soft voice. "Are you okay?"

I reach behind me, touch the holster at the small of my back. The metal of the gun presses against my skin, hot from the sun and my own body. It's not a comfortable holster, but my only other options require a jacket—Connecticut is a concealed carry state.

My mind reels for an excuse.

"I'm looking for Mercer," I blurt, the name rolling off my tongue. "Does he live here?"

She shakes her head. "I'm sorry. My husband and I bought this house this winter when we got married."

I glance at the two cars in the driveway. "Is your husband home?" I already know the answer, but I need to know how likely he is to walk out that door.

"He's sleeping," she says with an amused smile. "He works late."

I wonder where else Oh Vile Eye plays, what else he does for a living. "Would he know the previous owner?" I ask, still playing dumb.

"I'm not sure. Sorry," she says again. "Can I get you something to drink? Do you want to come in?"

My tongue sticks to the roof of my mouth. I could use a glass of ice cold water. Or a freezing cold bottle of vodka. "No. Thank you." I clear my throat.

"Do you need a ride?"

I consider it. Two minutes in a car with Cami could get me the answers I need, but then she'd know where I live. He's already too close to me.

"I work at Big Y," I say. "Can you give me a lift?"

"Sure. Let me just grab my keys." She ducks back inside, closing the screen door behind her.

I shift from foot to foot. I should walk away. I should stop coming here.

The door opens again and she flits down the steps, keys in hand. "I'm the Jetta."

"I figured." I glance at the black Thunderbird, remembering all the times I sat in that passenger seat.

I can't believe he still has it.

Then again, that thing was his baby.

I slip into the passenger side of the Jetta, the palms of my hands clammy. I have no reason to fear Cami. Still, as I buckle myself in, I check the front door of the house, the windows.

Nothing moves.

Cami starts the car and pulls out of the driveway, her maneuvering smooth. I find myself staring at her, studying the flawless skin, the way her lips naturally curve upward. Mine curve down, a permanent frown.

She's a teacher, the kind of person who gives rides to strangers. He's a musician, a muscle car junkie. I can't imagine what drew them together.

"How did you two meet?" The words are out of my mouth before I can reel them in. "I love a good meet cute," I say, recovering.

She grins. "Me too. My parents own a deli. Sometimes I help out, especially in the summer. I teach at the high school."

I nod, give her what I hope is an encouraging smile. Big Y isn't far.

"He'd just got out of the Navy. He comes in—in full uniform—and tells me he's starving. So I recommend our Italian combo. He gives me this flirty smirk and says, 'Do you come with it?' *I'm* Italian," she explains with a giggle. "Our deli's Damato's—my maiden name."

That sounds like him, all right. All charm, all the time.

"So you're happy?" I wish I'd flipped down the visor, so I could glance into the mirror, see whether my face looks horrified.

"God, yes. That was in the fall. We've spent every minute together ever since. Except when he's playing. I can't stay awake that late." She laughs, a musical, untarnished sound.

A sharp pain settles into my chest. How is it that he can be so good to her, after scraping me hollow?

Except now I know: he's lied to her at least once. He didn't just get out of the Navy. He got out years ago, when we were dating. He's been in California, pursuing his music.

I swallow bile.

"Are you all right?" she asks as she pulls into the Big Y parking lot.

"My boss's car is here," I manage. "He's *such* an asshole."

She frowns. "Dave? He's always been sweet to me."

"One of the supervisors," I say quickly, reaching for the door handle. "I've gotta go. Thanks for the ride." I push it open and get out, hurrying toward the electronic doors. As I pass through them, I glance over my shoulder.

Cami sits in her Jetta, watching me, her eyebrows pinched together.

I WANDER the store for ten minutes, then check the parking lot. She's gone. I pull out my phone. There's a missed call from Cliff, three from Esther. No messages. I call Esther.

"Can you pick me up? I've got some news about your case." I pace the front of the building, a cigarette in my other hand.

"I've been trying to call you," she says in a hushed voice. "Donny said—"

"Esther, I've got your entire file on my phone."

"What?"

"I texted it to you this morning. There's a lot of information we can use."

"Where are you?"

I skirt a woman pushing a cart brimming with groceries. "I took the bus to Big Y after work."

"Ah, shit, your bike. I was supposed to pick you up and then bring you to get it."

It seems like ages ago that she dropped me off at work this morning. "It's okay. Can you come get me now?"

"Of course, but Olivia? Cliff is looking for you. The whole club is—"

"We'll talk when I see you," I promise. "See you soon." I hang up, scanning the parking lot. Even though I'm pretty sure Cami went back home, part of me expects Greg to pull up in his Thunderbird.

I will Esther to hurry.

I wait twenty minutes before she pulls up.

"You sure took your time," I mutter, getting in.

She blushes. "Donny and I were . . . when you called." She clears her throat.

"Donny and you were what?" I tease.

Her flush deepens. "So what's in my file?"

"Don't you check your texts? Or do you only answer for a Donny booty call?" I can't help it. She's so freakin' cute.

"Don't *you* answer your phone?" she counters, pulling out of the Big Y parking lot. She heads toward The Wet Mermaid.

I hold up my hands. "I was busy."

"Where are your groceries?"

"Oh." My lips tug to the side. "They didn't have what I wanted."

"Cravings, huh? Are you pregnant?" She cackles.

My cheeks burn. "Asshole."

"Hey, you and Cliff bone just as much as Donny and me."

"I can't believe *you* just used the word 'bone.'"

Esther's olive skin reddens to a tomato hue. "Why don't you tell me what's in my file?"

I open the pics on my phone, flipping through them for reference while I fill her in. When I get to the pregnancy part, I hesitate. "It says you emancipated yourself," I hedge. Then I sigh. So much of womanhood involves tiptoeing around delicate subjects. I'm done *not* talking about things. "He raped you again."

She nods.

"He got you pregnant."

She nods again, face pale.

"I haven't talked to Glace yet, because I wanted to run it by you first. If you're willing to testify, we can contest the reunification. What he did to you is plenty of reason for the state to not give those kids back."

"What if they say I'm not stable enough to take care of them?" she asks, voice small, cracking.

"Esther, you're the most stable person I know. You stayed in to study more than I did, and that's saying something." We really were the perfect roommates. I'm going to miss her when she moves out.

"I mean . . ." She takes a deep breath. "What if they say I have PTSD or something? What if they say, because I had an abortion, I can't have my sisters?"

I reach across the console and squeeze her shaking hand. "Even if you do have PTSD, you handle your shit. You're more than capable of taking care of them. And who cares if you had an abortion? Any judge is going to sympathize with you. You were sixteen. Josué is a fucking monster."

She nods, squeezes my hand back. Then she takes a deep breath. "I can do it. I'll testify." She pulls into the strip club's parking lot.

"Shit." I sigh.

"What?"

"I still need to go get my bike." I tip my head back against the seat and close my eyes. I've got way too many plates in the air. I need my bike.

"We are, I promise. Cliff wanted me to bring you straight here."

"Why? I'm not working tonight." I eye the row of motorcycles parked out front. "Esther, am I in trouble?" I wonder if they know about my extracurricular stalking activities.

"No," she assures me. She swallows. "Donny filled me in a bit, but they want to talk to you."

"Filled you in on what?"

Her lips part, then drop open, her eyes locked on something. Or someone. I follow her gaze.

Cliff races out of the club, his mouth a hard line, the tendons in his neck straining. When he reaches my side of the car, he pulls open the door. "You can't be here," he shouts.

"Why the hell not?" I demand.

Esther balks. "You *told* me to bring her here!"

"I'm sorry," he says, and I can't tell who he's apologizing to. "We had a last-minute change of plans." His eyes flick to me. I search them, but all I see are storm clouds.

"What's going on?"

His jaw tightens, his eyes looking past me, through the car and Esther's window. I turn. A Thunderbird roars into the parking lot, music blaring.

A black Thunderbird.

"Oh, fuck," I mutter. Cami might be a good Samaritan, but she *is* a high school teacher. She must've seen right through me.

Pushing past Cliff, I step out of the car. Good thing I wore my gun.

"Where are you going?" Cliff reaches for my arm, but I slip past him. I take several steps toward the middle of the parking lot, directly in Greg's path.

He slams on his brakes.

Through the windshield, I make out his expression. He's surprised to see me.

I turn back to Cliff. "What's going on?"

Mark pokes his head through the door to The Wet Mermaid. "Make sure we do this inside," he calls to Cliff.

"Do what?" I glance from Cliff to Esther. "What are we doing?"

Greg climbs out of the Thunderbird. "Olivia?"

"You almost hit her," Cliff growls. He stalks toward Greg, hands flexing in and out of fists.

"She walked out in front of me!" Greg looks past Cliff, at Mark. "What is this, man?"

Mark lifts his shoulders, spreads his hands.

"*You* called me," Greg says to him. "Said we needed to talk band stuff." His gaze flicks to me.

Cliff stalks toward him. "Don't you fucking look at her." He points a finger at Greg.

Greg stands, feet apart, shoulders wide. Cliff has several inches on him, but there's no telling which way a fight would go. The Navy SEAL versus the ex-con.

I step toward Cliff. "Your parole," I remind him. He so much as throws a fist at Greg, out here with all these potential witnesses, and he goes right back to Lewisburg.

"Olivia," Esther calls.

I ignore her. "Did you bring this shit to the table?" I ask Cliff from between gritted teeth.

"Inside!" Ravage barks.

I gape at Cliff. "You did. You *bastard*."

Finally, he looks at me. His mouth sags open as if I punched him.

Greg smirks. "Oh, Olivia. You always were trouble."

Cliff lunges for him, his hands closing around the collar of Greg's T-shirt. He lifts Greg a few inches off the pavement, then shoves him back, dropping him. Greg stumbles, but stays on his feet. Cliff uses the moment to draw back his fist. It blurs through the air but in frames, as if I've smoked some really good weed and I'm watching a buffering action movie.

I stand there, torn. I should just let him go back to prison. I trusted him with my secret. I've never even told Lucy. I thought he'd understand, or at least give me some space. I should've known he'd go running to the club.

He's just like my father: club first, fuck everyone else.

Gritting my teeth, I yank the gun out of my holster. Pointing it into the air, I click off the safety and discharge a single shot into the sky.

Cliff's fist connects with Greg's jaw.

A stream of blood squirts through the air, splattering onto the pavement. Greg's head rocks back. He stumbles, then rights himself. A second later, he launches himself at Cliff.

The whole MC pours out of the club. Beer Can and Donny grab Greg's arms, holding him back from Cliff.

"What do you want to do?" Ravage asks him.

I lower my gun hand before I shoot all of them. "What does *he* want to do?" I snarl. "What about what *I* want? Any of you think about that?"

They all gape at me.

I wave the gun toward Greg. "Just let him go." I pin Cliff with my eyes. "You'll be lucky if he doesn't press charges."

Greg spits bright red blood onto the black asphalt. "What the fuck is this, Olivia? You fucking the whole MC?"

Cliff lets out an enraged roar. He plants both hands on Greg's chest and pushes, but Donny and Beer Can hold Greg steady. Cliff bounces back. He stands, fists curled, chest heaving.

"I'm going to kill you myself, you don't shut your mouth," Ravage tells Greg. He brings a cigarette to his lips. He crouches between Greg and Cliff, exhaling smoke in Greg's face. "I'm told you raped our Prospect."

Greg spits again. Flecks of blood land on Ravage's cheek.

Ravage grins, the ghastly smile splitting his pale face. "The club voted. We're going to find your band a prettier face to sing for them."

"I'm sorry, Olivia," Greg pleads. "It was a long time ago. I got too rough. I know that now." He wiggles the fingers of his left hand. "I've got a wife. I don't want any trouble."

I think of Cami, sitting in the teal house. Maybe she's cooking dinner for when Greg gets home from his "business meeting," working on lesson plans while she waits.

I want him dead. I *need* him dead. The statute of limitations is long past and, even then, it's my word against his—a Navy fucking SEAL. No one's gonna believe me, especially without any evidence. But I need to know that he'll never hurt anyone again. I need to know that Cami will stay shiny.

But not like this.

It's not Cliff's battle or the MC's.

It's *mine*.

I swallow my betrayal and rage, my contempt. I put the safety back on and tuck the gun into its holster. "I let it go a long time ago," I tell Greg, but I look at Cliff. At Ravage. At Beer Can. "It's water under the bridge. You heard him. He's a better person now. I just . . ." I hesitate for effect. "I just don't want him working under the same roof as me."

"Done," Greg says. "Not a problem. We'll find another venue to play."

Ravage eyes me. "You sure this is what you want?"

"You mean, you're asking me?" I glare at Cliff. "Yes. This is what I want. Get him out of my face."

Donny and Beer Can look at each other, shrug, then release him.

He shakes the blood flow back into his arms. "I'm sorry," he says, but his eyes don't meet mine. Backing toward the idling Thunderbird, he holds his hands up. "I'm sorry," he says again. He ducks into the driver's seat. Slamming the door shut, he throws the Thunderbird into reverse. He backs out of the parking lot, then peels out, leaving a cloud of gray smoke drifting through the air in his wake.

I round on Cliff. "How could you?" Stomping toward him, I shove him with the heels of my hands. He barely moves. I push him again, throwing all my strength into it. Again, he remains standing. Instead of catching my wrists or telling me he's sorry, too, he just takes it. "You *bastard*," I say again.

He flinches.

Stepping back, I hold my chin high. I look him in the eye. "Fuck you, Cliff. We're done." I look from member to member. "Fuck all of you."

Turning on my heels, I stomp back to Esther's car. I get in and slam the door shut behind me, strapping on my seatbelt.

I don't even have to ask her.

She makes a U-turn and takes me away from The Wet Mermaid and Cliff.

29

CLIFF

"You coming down, man?" Donny stands in the doorway to my room at the club house, towering over where I sit on the floor.

I blink through the darkness. I'm supposed to be bouncing the door. I should be downstairs, but I can't make myself move. My whole body weighs twice as much, reminding me of when I was a kid and had the flu.

When I don't answer, Donny sits beside me. "What a shit show, man. That could've been real bad."

My eyes roll toward him.

He tilts his head. "A'ight, it *was* bad. Mark's throwing a conniption. At least you're not back inside."

I'd gladly trade my freedom if it meant I'd still have Olivia.

"She'll come around. You meant well."

I want to be left alone, but Donny's my brother. He's just trying to be my friend.

"I've got an idea." He shifts, then pulls a joint out of his cut. "In a few minutes, you'll be a hundred percent." He lights the joint, takes a hit, then holds it out to me.

I stare at it for a moment. "I've never smoked," I admit.

"Never?" Donny grins. "Aw, this is gonna be fun!" He nudges it closer to me. "For real, man. You'll feel a lot better. It'll be like nothing happened."

I don't want to feel nothing. When I feel Olivia and all that comes with her, I come alive. Without her, I'm sinking to the bottom. For the longest time, I thought maybe I was kidding myself, that I'd just latched onto her while I was drowning, trying to find some kind of footing before I got swept away. Now I know that isn't true.

I love her.

And I've fucked it all up.

Donny sighs and takes another hit. "You know," he says through a cloud of smoke, "for a split second, I thought about just handing you my gun." White teeth flash in the dark. "Sometimes I think I crave the chaos. This club's been pretty tame since Mercy and Bastard. 'Til you two came along." He passes me the joint again, and this time, I take it.

"Am I gonna be able to bounce?"

He scoffs. "I cannot believe you've never done this before. Weren't you eighteen when you went in?"

"My mom," I say, pinching the joint between my thumb and forefinger. I bring it to my lips and take a long pull. The smoke curls into my lungs, spreading through my limbs, settling in my head.

For the first time tonight, it goes quiet.

"Ruth swore she'd shave my head in my sleep if she ever caught me doing any drugs. Even after she died, I couldn't let her down." I hand the joint to Donny.

"You always had long hair?" he asks.

""I might've been a little obsessed with Jim Morrison," I admit. "Except I had black hair, like Ruth's. I wanted to dye it blond, but Bastard never let me."

He snorts, smoke pouring from his nostrils. "Man, I should smoke you up more often. This shit is gold."

"You tell anyone, and I'll beat your face in."

Donny's warm brown eyes go dark. All of the light drains from his face. Those dead eyes meet mine. "You really threatening an officer of your MC?"

I let my own face go flat. At least, I try. When I move the muscles, arranging my features into The Look that helped earn me the nickname Red Dog, I burst into laughter. Donny throws his head back, cackling.

"I can never smoke again," I groan. "This shit'll ruin my rep."

"Don't worry." He claps my shoulder. "I won't tell a soul that Mary Jane is your kryptonite."

"And Olivia." I look down at my hands. The sun sets outside, painting the dim room in streaks of pink and orange.

"Nah, dude. Do *not* go there right now. Let the weed works its magic."

But I can't. She's so far under my skin, nothing will ever cleanse me of her. A thousand, thousand years can go by, and I'll still love her, my heart long reduced to ashes.

Donny's phone rings, the new Backstreet Boys song blaring through the room.

I give him a sidelong look. "You've got to be kidding me."

"Everyone in this club knows I have a penchant for shitty pop music."

"I bet you're holding out for an ESX reunion, too." I shake my head.

"They have Spotify in prison?"

"What's Spotify?"

He throws his head back again. "Goddamn, I love you, Red Dog. I've gotta take this. It's Essie."

I sit up straight. As far as I know, Esther is with Olivia. Or she was, anyway. Through the haze of Skywalker OG, my mind lurches through scenarios—none of them good.

"Hey, baby," Donny greets Esther. "What's up?"

I watch his face, see the muscles tense up, his lip curling, eyes narrowing.

"You see anybody?"

I'm on my feet, pulling on my cut. I've got to get to her. Now.

"Wait," Donny says, holding up a hand. He stands, too. "It's okay, baby. Just stay inside, keep the doors locked. We'll be right there." He flips his phone shut. Two minutes ago, I'd have ribbed him for still having a flip phone. Even *I* have a smartphone.

Everything is different now.

"You okay to ride?" he asks me.

"Fine." Adrenaline surges through my veins, flushing out the effects of the weed. "What happened?"

"Someone slit Essie's brake line."

"Holy shit." I clasp his shoulder. "You seeing red?"

"You fucking bet." He sucks in a deep breath.

"Good thing she noticed before going anywhere. Fuck," I growl. "Do you think this is Greg? Esther took Olivia home. They would've only been back for a little while."

"Nah." Donny grimaces. "There's more, brother." He rubs his hands over his face. "This fucking girl," he mutters.

My spine stiffens. "What is it?"

"Essie dropped Olivia off at Mercy's, for the bike."

That fucking bike. I was supposed to take her back for it, but she kicked me out.

"Olivia was gonna meet Essie back at their place. She hasn't showed yet."

I stomp toward the door.

Donny clamps a hand around my arm, jerking me back. "Chill!" he barks. "Far as we know, Essie's car has *nothing* to do with Olivia. This time." He shakes his head. "She probably just took a ride to clear her head." He leans in, eyes searching mine. "A'ight?"

I nod.

Slowly, he releases me. "Essie thinks this has to do with her folks."

"Shit." I'd completely forgotten about Esther's problems.

"We'll take Beer Can and Abraham with us. You call Vaughn, see if he found out where Josué works."

"Where are you going?"

His eyebrow twitches. "Going to get you a gun, Cherry."

"Cherry?"

"We're popping all kinds of Cliff cherries tonight. Call Vaughn," he tells me again. Then he's gone.

I stare into the deepening darkness of the room. I don't want a gun. It's probably hypocritical as fuck of me, but I don't like them. I don't trust them. My fists, on the other hand—those I can count on. They don't malfunction, and I can reel myself in.

Most of the time.

This isn't the pen. I've got no idea what we're walking into. And if Olivia is missing, my first stop is going to be Greg's.

I pull out my phone and call Vaughn.

"Yeah," he answers.

"We've got a situation. Did you find out where Esther's father works?"

"I was just about to shoot a text to Donny. Josué works at Landon's Landscaping. They're over on Meadow Street, but they've got property on 63. They store all their equipment there."

"Thanks," I say, absorbing the information. "Hey, Vaughn, I need another favor from you."

"Am I ever going to get out of this basement?" he jokes.

"I just need an address for Greg Byrne."

"I dunno, Cliff. After this afternoon, there's too much heat there. Does Ravage know you're asking?"

"Olivia's missing," I lie. At least, I hope it's a lie. "I'm gonna check a few other places first, but if she doesn't turn up, I've got to know she isn't there."

"Sorry, man. I didn't realize. Do you guys need me to come in?"

I pinch my eyes shut. "I just need that address."

"Give me five minutes and I'll text it to you."

"Thanks." I hang up just as Donny bursts into my room.

"You get Vaughn?" He hands me a pistol with a skinny silver barrel.

"Landon's Landscaping." I turn the gun over in my hands.

"It's a Browning Buck Mark. Semiautomatic. They're pretty fucking accurate—good for somebody like you, ain't never shot one."

I scoff. "I'm Bastard's son, Donny. Of course I've shot a gun."

"Then why you holding it like it's gonna bite you?"

I take the shoulder holster he passes me and strap it on. "We going or what?"

"After you, Princess Rimfire."

"I thought it was Cherry?" I toss back as I head downstairs. My voice sounds so calm, but my veins are burning, my hands hot, the joints loose. My phone vibrates in my pocket with a text. I tug it free and scan the address, committing it to memory.

"It's whatever the fuck I want it to be," Donny rumbles.

We reach the landing and Beer Can falls into step with us. Strobe lights pulse through the club, and he's got his cut on, but I know he's carrying, too.

"The Three Musketeers, on the case again," he says, clapping Donny on the back.

If Olivia isn't with Esther, there'll be another body to bury tonight.

30

My thighs hug the Street Glide, fingers wrapped around the handlebars. She hums underneath me, vibrating down into my bones. It's almost deep enough to stifle the scream clawing into my neck, my throat, the hinges of my jaw.

Almost.

If this was a car, I'd bang on the steering wheel. I can't believe him. I thought it went without saying that I didn't want the whole world to know. I trusted him.

He let me down.

I shouldn't be surprised. Not after all the times a man has disappointed me. Especially not less than twenty-four hours after Mercy walked out on me—again. It's the same damn thing, all over again.

Or is it?

I take a turn too fast, the bike going nearly parallel with the road. Everything speeds up and slows to a crawl at the same time. I shift my weight, restoring the balance, and ease up on the throttle. I pull over to the side of the road, heart pounding.

"What are you doing, Olivia?" I ask myself, the rumble of the engine all but drowning out my voice. Closing my eyes, I take a deep breath. I can't let this get to me. There are people depending on me: Esther and the girls, Cami.

Fuck Cliff.

He doesn't get to completely unravel me.

No one does.

I open my eyes, Bad Lane coming into sharp focus. The Street Glide still purrs beneath me. I haven't moved. I'm not dreaming. Yet I'm here.

I turn toward the teal house. Lights are on in all of the downstairs windows. Greg's Thunderbird sits in the garage. I touch the gun at the small of my back.

It could all be over. Right now. If I let myself walk into that house, the story that's been poisoning me ends. He never hurts anyone else. I walk away.

If only it were so simple.

Greg isn't like Eli. There is a whole army of people who love him—literally and figuratively. He probably has dozens of Navy buddies. There there are his siblings and parents, countless friends we went to high school with. People I cut all ties with because I couldn't stand when they said good things about him.

"I saw Greg play in New Haven last night..."

"Greg is such a mama's boy. It's sweet..."

"I run into Greg now and then. He's still so funny..."

My stomach clenches just at the thought of the things they say. So many people walk among a monster and don't even know it.

Still...

If I get rid of him, our story ends, but a whole mess of people will miss him. His sister won't be able to go to the mall without crying, because he won't be there to help her pick out a new record. His bandmates will have to find a new singer, someone who won't even compare but they'll try anyway, until the band collapses. His friends won't have anyone to sit around a fire pit with, drinking beer and laughing until sunrise.

I'll erase my monster, but I'll leave a hole behind for everyone else.

I didn't kill Eli because I wanted to. I had to. I knew, from the moment I actually looked into his eyes, that our story would end with one of us dead. It sure as fuck wasn't going to be me.

Greg is no longer a threat. Not really, despite what my broken brain keeps insisting. He's married, and I'm safe. Maybe he went through therapy, fixed whatever was broken inside him that made him desecrate me. He's sorry—or at least scared enough of the River Reapers to pretend to be. He'll stay away from me.

But I'm not so sure about Cami.

If I knew, if I could be positive that she's safe with him, I might be able to walk away. There's no way of knowing. Not unless I watched them around the clock.

My phone rings, the sound muffled by my saddlebag. I glance at the teal house again. I could go inside. Do it now. Put an end to the memories that keep rising no matter how much I try to shove them down. Exterminate the ceaseless tagged photos that keep popping up in my goddamn Facebook feed. Scrub away any chance of him playing at the next bar I go to.

Trade my peace of mind for everyone else's.

I think of the silver alert, the somebody who's missing Eli. Someone noticed he didn't walk. Somewhere in this town, or state, or even in the country, someone cries for Eli, stares at the ceiling at night wondering what became of him.

I don't know if I can do that to anyone else.

Even after what he did to me.

I open the saddlebag and dig inside for my phone. It keeps ringing, long after a reasonable person would've hung up. It's probably Cliff, trying to apologize. I almost give up, let it go to voicemail. My fingers find it, close around it, pull it out of the darkness. Esther's name lights up the display.

"I know, I'm on my way," I tell her, guilt joining the nausea. "I'm okay, Es."

"Olivia," she sobs. "The girls are gone. Someone cut my brake line, and now the girls are gone."

I hang up, and get the hell out of Bad Lane.

"Shit." Donny hangs up his phone and glances up and down the street we're pulled over on. "Essie's abuela called her. The girls are gone. Her abuelo's brake line got cut, too."

Beer Can leans forward, dangling his arms over the handlebars of his Road King, fingers resting on the fairing. "Anybody call the police? Issue an Amber Alert?"

"We need Olivia," Donny says, turning in his seat to face me.

I spread my hands. "I don't know where she is. Has anyone called the social worker?"

"Essie's grandparents don't want to call their social worker. Olivia's our only shot."

I rub my hands over my face, the stubble scratching my palms. "Do you really think she's going to answer me?" I growl through my fingers.

Donny shoves the kickstand into place and jumps off his bike. He stalks over to me, towering over where I sit on my bike. He leers down at me. "Those girls could be anywhere right now!"

"I'll call Vaughn," I say, grabbing my phone. "He'll get us an address for Josué. We *will* find them."

Donny's hands clench, unclench. "It'd be faster to call Olivia."

"You're wasting time arguing," Beer Can says.

I touch Vaughn's name in my contacts and bring the phone to my ear.

Donny points a finger in my face. "You better be calling Olivia."

Even though I know he's worried about Esther, blood whooshes through my veins. I kick the stand into place and rear above him. "I'm calling Vaughn."

"Jesus Christ," Beer Can mutters.

Donny snatches the phone from my hand and throws it. It disappears into the night. I don't even hear it land. He seizes me by my cut. "I'm your fucking officer!"

"Then take it to the table!" Beer Can snaps. He drags Donny back, sidesteps him, and shoves himself between us. I'm again reminded of how dangerous he can be, even if he's as stocky as a Tolkien dwarf. "Cliff will answer for this," he tells Donny, "at the table." Turning to me, he squares his jaw. "I don't know what your problem is, son, but pull it together. This is not about you. It's not about either of you! This is about three girls we promised to help."

I bow my head.

Donny paces away, scowling.

"Now," Beer Can says, pulling the biggest iPhone I've ever seen out of his cut, "I'm calling Olivia. If you can't handle that, *Romeo*, I suggest you get the fuck out of here." Eyeing me, he presses his mega phone to his ear. He keeps his volume so high, I can hear it ringing as clearly as if he had it on speaker.

I take a deep breath, waiting for her to pick up. Esther needs her, but I kind of hope she doesn't answer. I'm not ready to see her yet. She called me a bastard, flung the word at me, splashing me with its acidic burn. Seeing Greg must've been a shock for her, but she wasn't supposed to be there. I was going to take care of him before he could hurt her again.

Instead, we only hurt each other.

Words have power. That one slur cut deeper, maybe more so than she intended. I might be a monster, but I am not my father. For her to insinuate so is unforgivable.

"I'm going to get Vaughn," I tell Beer Can. Before he can answer or Donny can stop me, I swing a leg over my bike. I bring it to life, the engine growling. Jaw tight, I ride away in the direction of The Wet Mermaid.

I'm halfway there when I realize I'll also have to answer for this. If it means giving myself a little more time before I have to see her, so be it.

I pull into the parking lot and swing off the bike. I tuck the helmet under my arm and surge into the club, moving through the floor with ease. For the first time in days, the club isn't packed to the brim. Oh Vile Eye definitely knew how to fill a house. The club will take a hit on income now, and I'll probably have to answer for that, too.

I duck under the door frame of Mark's office. Lucky for me, Ravage isn't here.

"Thought you were handling something?" Mark asks, looking up from his computer.

"We need Vaughn. I lost my phone." I shove my hands into the pockets of my jeans.

He takes off his thick black rectangular glasses. "The guys lose their phones, too?"

I regard him, saying nothing.

He shakes his head. "You've only been around for a few months, but you know better. Where are they?"

"Almost at Esther's. We had to pull over because she was calling Donny. The girls are gone and her grandparents' car's been fucked with, too. It's gotta be Josué. We need an address."

His shoulders rise, then fall as he takes a deep breath. "Olivia's just like Mercy. You know that."

"Then why did you bring Greg here for me?" I tighten my grip on the helmet.

"Because once you told Ravage, Greg became a security issue that needed to be taken care of. But you know Olivia. There was no way she'd ever be okay with you handling her business for her."

"What was I supposed to do?" I drop the helmet onto the desk and turn away, chest tight. "Nothing? Let him keep coming here, haunting her?" My voice breaks. I clench and unclench my fists, eyes burning.

"I know," he says quietly. "I know." His chair creaks as he stands. A second later, he puts a hand on my shoulder. "We all want him dead, but no one wants it more than Olivia. You've got to let her do this. She's not a princess who needs saving, Cliff. She's the fucking dragon, and she's going to burn us all alive if we get in her way."

Her voice echoes in my head: *Bastard.*

I nod.

"Your head's getting all mixed up with your heart, and you're losing your way. Your brothers understand what you're going through," he says. "Donny especially. He needs to find Josué, because Esther needs him to help slay her demon. She's not Olivia, Cliff. She's the princess, and you've got to back Donny up."

"I fucked up," I agree.

"Yeah." He grips my shoulder and gives it a gentle shake. "Now how are you gonna fix it?"

32

OLIVIA

I speed all the way to Esther's grandparents' house, hoping that this will be the one time Naugatuck cops won't be assholes. That maybe this is the one night they're not hanging around, just waiting to pull someone over. Time is being wrenched away. I can't afford to drive the speed limit.

I also can't afford to get a ticket, or arrested. I slow the Street Glide to only 5 mph above the limit. I should've become a cop instead of a social worker. Then I could fly all over this town.

Approaching a stop sign, I slow down. Naugatuck is all about the three-second stop. When Lucy took me out with my learner's permit, I actually counted out loud, for fear a police cruiser would materialize and arrest me. How things have changed. Now if I see a cop, I'll do the full stop. If there isn't one in sight, I roll right on through.

Everyone here does it.

A squad car pulls up behind me, its front bumper only a few inches from my rear tire. I take the full stop, putting both feet on the pavement. I count to three in my head.

One.

Three seconds is an agonizing amount of time when there's a

cop watching. It's even longer when they're watching and some-one's life is on the line. Tonight, it's three.

Two.

I check my rearview mirrors. He stares at my ass through his windshield. Or maybe he's noting my plate. Technically, I don't have a motorcycle license yet, and the Street Glide is registered under Mark's name.

I swallow.

Three.

I pause, taking a breath. Then, putting both feet back up, I ease forward. Blue and red lights twirl through the street.

"Motherfucker," I grumble, rolling to a stop again. He must've run my plate numbers.

Of all the nights.

He creeps up behind me, again nearly kissing my back tire. The lights wash the whole street in a slow strobe, an effect that makes my temples thud and my eyes ache. He doesn't get out of his cage.

I glance into my mirrors again, without turning my head. I don't want him to see that I'm nervous. Tonight I'm just a girl out for a ride, a girl who obeys stop signs and speed limits.

A girl who doesn't have three kids and a rapist to worry about.

Make that two rapists.

My fingers twitch toward the throttle. On this bike, I can outrun him. I'm not far from the Aguirres's house, so all it'd take is a quick canvas of the neighborhood and he'd find me. Plus I'm wearing my cut, and he's probably already run the plate.

"Fuck," I breathe.

I'm wearing my cut.

And my gun.

I'm fucked.

Completely and utterly done.

If he's run my plates, he knows I'm not the owner. When he asks for my license and registration, he'll know I'm driving this thing illegally. And since he's a Naugatuck cop and a total dick by default, he'll probably pat me down, just to piss all over the MC.

Because even though the police and the club have an uneasy agreement, they're still cops and we're still bikers.

Well, okay. I'm not one of them *yet*.

It doesn't matter, because he's going to find the gun.

Which means I'll be spending the night in jail.

I almost laugh. Cliff and I are about to have a whole lot in common, something we could trade stories on if he hadn't gone all alpha hero and I hadn't broken up with him. There's absolutely nothing funny about this. If I can't get to Esther, they probably won't find the girls. I'm the only one who knows Josué's address.

I sit up straight. I'm not the only one. If I can call Esther, I can remind her to check her texts for the pics of the file I sent her. But if I pull out my phone, he'll probably shoot me. He'll get away with it, too, because technically I do have a gun on me.

Cold sweat dots my hairline, gathers at the small of my back. I wish I could take off this helmet. I've only got one move, so I better use it wisely.

"Hey Siri," I say, voice shaking. I wait for the familiar two-note tinkle. Nothing happens. Fucking Siri. Squeezing my eyes shut, I say it louder.

Nothing.

I open my eyes and check my mirrors again. The motherfucker is still sitting in his car. It's like he's playing with me. I force myself not to glare at him. He turns back to his view of me, and the air vanishes from my lungs.

He looks just like Greg.

I gasp for breath. He *can't* be Greg. What kind of musician works in law enforcement? That kind of kills the whole rock 'n' roll vibe.

Still, the face staring back at me *is* Greg's. Younger, though. I blink, squint at the mirror while remaining upright in my seat.

He *looks* like Greg, but he isn't Greg. His face is thinner, softer. No beard.

I shake my head. It doesn't matter who he is.

"Hey Siri!" I all but yell.

The phone in my cut dings.

"Call Esther."

A second later, I hear the phone ringing. Only, I didn't tell Siri to put it on speaker. I'll never hear her, and she probably won't hear me.

"Fuck," I seethe.

In the rearview mirror, I see the cop's door open.

"Hey Siri!"

The phone chimes, effectively ending my call.

"Call Esther on speaker."

This time, the phone rings—echoing through the quiet street. The cop sticks a leg out of his car. I tap my boot on the ground.

"Please, Esther. Please."

The call goes to voicemail.

"Hey Siri!"

When she responds, I tell her to call Cliff on speaker. I might be furious with him, but I'm not letting that get in the way. Those girls need us, whether we're on or off. But Cliff's phone rings, and rings, and rings. It might as well be in a ditch.

At least he didn't hit the Fuck You button on me.

The officer slides out of his cage. I only have seconds left.

"Hey Siri!"

"Ma'am," the cop calls.

I tap my boot harder, aware of how close he is, how loud he is. How he could so easily fuck up my commands, confuse Siri.

"Text Esther!"

"Please shut off your engine," the cop says.

"What do you want to say to Esther?" Siri asks.

I shut off the engine and close my eyes. "I texted you the file. His address—"

"Ma'am, please stop what you're doing."

"Okay," Siri announces. "Ready to send?"

"Yes!" I yell, putting my hands in the air. I have no idea if the text goes through, and no idea if she'll even see it. All I see is his face, and the name on his uniform.

Byrne.

He isn't Greg, but he is his brother—a face I haven't seen since that night.

33

CLIFF

I push the Screamin' Eagle, weaving through the streets. I'm breaking parole by speeding, but that's nothing new. I should count myself lucky no one called the cops earlier. Since all I have is an address for Esther's grandparents—no GPS, thanks to Donny jacking my phone—I have to rely on my memory of Naugatuck's layout.

Which is next to nothing, considering I hardly drove anywhere before I went inside.

I slow, listening for the growls of my brothers' motorcycles, something to give me a hint. Anything. The night is quiet—especially in this neighborhood. It's the right neighborhood, that I'm sure of.

I cruise down a side street, the blue and red lights of a police car flickering through the trees from the next street over. Good—they're busy with somebody else. Better them than me. I've got to help Donny and Esther, and make things right with Olivia.

Can't do that from inside the pen.

I take a right and catch sight of bikes lined up in front of a brick ranch. Relief washes over me. I'm not too late.

I don't see Olivia's Street Glide.

Sliding in between Beer Can and Donny's bikes, I shut off mine and pull off my helmet. Abraham sits on the front stairs, his long dark blond hair shrouding his features. He shakes his head at me.

"Brace yourself, brother."

I stop, halfway up the walkway. "How pissed are they?"

"They?" He scoffs. "Try all of us. You're in for it." He sweeps his curtain of hair over a shoulder. In another life, Abraham could be a model. He's solid, like me, all carefully maintained muscle. He's also got naturally olive skin and smoky blue eye—all things women trip over themselves for. Unfortunately for them, Abraham is all about his boyfriend Rui.

My chest rises with a tight breath. "I'm gonna make this right."

I head up the rest of the walkway and start climbing the stairs.

"There's one more thing," he says.

I pause beside him, one boot on the top step.

"We can't get ahold of Olivia." He lifts a shoulder. "Guess we're gonna need Vaughn after all."

I rub my face with my hands. "What do you mean, you can't get ahold of her?"

"She'll turn up. It's Esther. She loves Esther." *But not you*, is what he doesn't say.

Or maybe it's all in my head.

"Okay. Thanks for the heads up." I continue onto the porch. Gripping the door knob, I stop again. I don't know whether I'm supposed to knock or just walk in. This *is* club business—half of us are already inside. I don't want to startle Esther's grandparents, though. They've been through enough.

I raise a fist and knock.

"Dude." Abraham chuckles. "Just go in. No one's gonna shoot you."

"Hope not," I mutter. The gun that Donny gave me presses against the inside of my arm, the metal warm from my skin. I don't know if its presence is what makes me think of it, or the fact that my brothers wait inside, each of them armed, too. Inside the pen, the only men with guns were the ones keeping us inside. Every time I had to fight, I only needed my own two fists. Once in a while an inmate would have a shank or a screw, but even those are easier to avoid in close combat than a bullet.

Out here, on the other side of the bars, the rules are different.

I walk inside.

34

OLIVIA

The younger version of Greg blinds me with his flashlight. "Ma'am," he says, sounding not exasperated or even pissed off, but amused. "Do you know why I pulled you over?"

I lift my chin but keep my eyes down away from the light. It hits my face. I bet I'm glowing, I'm so pale from this winter.

Officer Byrne draws a sharp breath. He lowers the flashlight. "You," he whispers.

The lower back holster seemed like such a good idea when I started riding. Now it keeps my gun miles out of reach. I glance at his hip holster, slung low like a cowboy, only inches from where his hand rests at his side.

"I remember you," he says, voice a notch louder but still unsteady.

The sweat from the palms of my hands soaks into my jeans, making my skin clammy. I hold his gaze. If I look away, he might shoot me.

"You were at my mother's house, with Greg," he continues. Even in the dark, his hair blazes, his eyebrows two burning cater-pillars, wriggling toward each other for a kiss. "I heard . . . something, but . . ." The knot in his throat bobs as he swallows. "I knew he liked to get rough sometimes."

"Rough," I scoff.

Sometimes I still feel his hands wrapped around my throat.

Officer Byrne holsters his flashlight. "You're Olivia, right?"

A chill grips my spine, icy fingers walking their way up the vertebrae. It isn't fair that he knows my name but I don't know his.

"Olivia," he says again, shaking his head.

The way he's saying my name nearly freezes my blood. I don't remember much about him, just that he was a punk teenager playing video games—the only other person in the house when it happened. For all I know, he's as fucked up in the head as Greg is.

I wrap my arms around myself in the guise of a hug. My fingers only graze my ribs—still too far from my gun.

"I should've come downstairs," he says softly. "I don't even remember which game I was playing. I didn't want to pause it. Maybe deep down I knew what was happening."

I hold up a hand, remembering too late that I'm dealing with a cop. "I don't want to talk about this." The last thing I need right now is a flashback. If I have any chance of getting out of here alive, I need my head straight.

"What he did is on me." Officer Byrne steps back a couple paces until his calves touch the front bumper of the police car. He sits on the hood, the palms of his hands planted on the shiny metal.

I nudge the Street Glide's kickstand into place, then dismount, every step in slow motion—just in case. I turn, facing him. The longer I look at him, the more his features become his own. His eyes—so light a green, they're almost gray—are so much softer than his brother's. The locks of red hair that fall across his forehead, making him look even younger.

He sighs. "This bike is registered to a Mark Clayton."

"My boss," I explain. "I'm running an errand."

He nods at my cut. "For the MC?"

"For my roommate. Her grandparents live around the corner."

"I'm guessing you don't have a motorcycle license," he says.

I keep my eyes wide. "They're literally right around the corner."

His eyebrows rise then fall. "Uh-huh." He crosses his arms. "Look, Olivia–"

"What's your name?" I interrupt. I don't want to think about that night. I don't want to remember. I just want to forget. Still, I need to know his name. Maybe it'll help me put it all to rest. Maybe it won't. I just need to know.

"Finn."

"Finn," I repeat. "You were in the living room the whole time." The words are out of my mouth before I can catch them, stuff them back down into the dark of my memory.

"Yes," he says softly. "Greg introduced us."

"And then he took me downstairs. To a partially finished basement. There was a load of laundry going, both in the washer and dryer." Each frame of the memory rushes me. It's as if Finn's face is the key to where I've locked it all away. My fingers twitch for a cigarette. They're in my saddlebag, go figure. "Is it okay if I get a cigarette?"

"Please." He gestures toward the bike.

Sucking in a deep breath, I turn toward it, then walk on legs that might as well be weighted by sand bags. I grab what I need and light up, leaning against the bike.

"I saw you afterward," he says while I smoke. "I pretended to be asleep on the couch, but I heard you guys come up. You looked so empty." He rubs his temples. "He came back wrong."

I frown. "What do you mean?"

"I don't mean that night. I mean before that night, when he came home on leave. He was so different. I should've known."

I exhale smoke into the dark. "He didn't seem off to me at first. He was excited to reconnect. I thought he really liked me.

Turns out he just wanted a toy. Maybe he needed to hurt someone to work through all of the things he saw. I don't know."

"Doesn't make it okay," Finn says. "I'm really, really sorry."

I lift my eyes, meeting his. "What about Cami?"

"What about her?"

"Is she okay? Does he ... hurt her?"

He spreads his hands. "I don't know. I don't see them too often."

"That night wasn't the only time," I tell him. "He lied to me over and over. He wanted to try different things. I'd say no, and he'd say no problem, then do it anyway. He always did whatever he wanted with me. It just escalated every time. After that night, I knew I couldn't see him ever again, or he'd kill me." I bite my lip hard, anchoring myself in the present. The salty, metallic taste of blood floods my tongue.

Finn's face hardens. "I can't change the past," he says, "but I can do something now. I owe you, Olivia, and I don't think it'll ever be enough. I'm going to let you go." He slides off the hood. Reaching into his pocket, he pulls out a business card. "This is my cell. Whatever you need, whenever you need it, just call me." He holds it out to me.

I take the white rectangle, rubbing it between my thumb and forefinger. "I'll hold you to that," I tell him.

He nods, then gets into his car. "Take care of yourself, Olivia," he says before closing his door. A moment later, he shuts off the flashing lights. Then he drives away, leaving me alone on the dark, quiet street.

I sink to the pavement, my knees finally giving out. Gasping for air, I crumple the card in my hand. I will never trust a Byrne, especially not a cop.

I throw my pack of cigarettes, lighter, and the crushed business card into my saddlebag. Then I retrieve my phone from where I left it on the seat.

By some miracle, Siri actually sent my text to Esther. It says it was delivered, but there's no read mark—she hasn't seen it yet.

There's no more time to waste.

I flip through my photos, reading through the Figueroa file again, this time scouring for Josué's address. It'd be faster to ride, but I can't read at the same time. While I read, I walk toward Esther's grandparents'. Somehow, some way, I'm ending this tonight. Esther and the girls deserve a new beginning.

35

CLIFF

I stand on a maroon area rug, next to a couch that was made to look like gold but instead came out a mustard yellow. Donny and Esther sit beside an older woman who must be Esther's grandmother. Everyone turns to look at me, the room going silent except for an oxygen machine whirring somewhere in the house.

I don't know what to say to make this right. I can't remember the last time I had to apologize to another human being. For twenty years, I was never sorry about anything—except Lucy.

Donny stands from the couch, unfolding his body and rising, casting a dark shadow over Esther and her grandmother. He regards me with a cool stare.

"Did Vaughn have any luck?" Beer Can asks from the other side of the room. He turns a knickknack over in his hands.

Without meaning to, I reach up and rub the back of my head.

Beer Can sighs.

I drop my hand. "You were right," I tell Donny. "We're better off with Olivia. Where is she?"

Esther and Donny exchange glances. "We still haven't heard from her," she says, standing. "I'll try her again."

I run a hand through my hair. "Shit."

"Guess we might need Vaughn after all," Donny mutters. He lifts his eyes to mine and shrugs. Reaching inside his cut, he pulls out my phone.

I hold my hand out for it, but he doesn't drop it into my palm.

"I still wanna kick your ass, Red Dog. But I know you're going through it, too. We good—for now." He drops the phone into my hand. "Call your girl. Maybe you'll have better luck."

I start to say "She's not my girl." The front door opens, the knob slamming into the wall. Olivia stands in the doorway, her curls wild, eyes lined with dark circles.

"Sorry, Mrs. Aguirre," she tells Esther's grandmother. Her eyes meet mine.

An electric current washes over me, zapping through my limbs and muscles, holding me in place. It's strong enough to snap ligaments and melt bone. The sight of her washes away all of the anger and fear I've been carrying between my heart and ribs. I can never be angry with her for long. My little wolf. I take a step toward her, but she drops her gaze, turning instead to Esther.

"Did you get my text?" she asks.

My knees go weak as the sting of her shrapnel digs into my skin. Mark's words echo through my head: *She's the fucking dragon, and she's going to burn us all alive if we get in her way.*

The problem is, I want her fire.

It's like she's cut my skin open and poured lava inside. I'm wide open, burning, waiting for her rain to cool me down. Waiting forever, probably.

She will never love me.

"No," Esther says, standing. She tugs her phone from the side pocket of her leggings. "Oh." She grimaces. "I left the ringer off."

"Jesus." Olivia sighs. "I sent you the files. You had Josué's address this whole time."

"Where have *you* been?" Donny shouts, rounding on her. "We

needed you 'this whole time,' and you were nowhere to be found, Prospect." He glares down at her, chest heaving.

"Hey!" I step forward, putting my body between them. "She needed a minute. She's here now, right?"

He shakes a finger at us. "The two of you done now? Can we focus?"

I nod. "I've got you, brother."

He sighs. "Olivia?"

"I'm here," she says, looking everywhere but at me. "Toci has an apartment on Andrew Avenue. They've got to be there."

"No," says a wavering voice. For the first time, Mrs. Aguirre speaks. She stands from the couch. "He's paying her rent, but he isn't staying there. He knows he needs to be out of the picture if Toci's going to get the girls back."

I clear my throat. "Why take them, then? I thought they were close to reunification."

"Because I filed a complaint," Esther says. "The DCF headquarters is investigating. The woman I spoke with said it's odd that this social worker is pursuing reunification."

Olivia shakes her head. "Glace isn't pursuing reunification. That was the old social worker."

"Old social worker? The girls have had Glace for a long time. Too long—they should already have a permanency plan," Esther explains.

"So . . ." Olivia runs a hand through her curls. "Why is Glace working toward reunification? And why did she lie to me?"

"Does it really matter?" I interject. "We've gotta go."

Olivia shoots a glare at me, then turns to Esther's grandmother. "Any ideas where they might be?"

Mrs. Aguirre nods. "Try the American Motor Lodge, in Waterbury. It's right off Route 8. That's where they used to meet up." She sighs. "If I could turn back time, I'd have nailed that girl's ass to her bedroom floor."

"Abuela," Esther soothes. "It's going to be okay."

"Essie, you're with me," Donny says. He pulls open the door. I join him, scanning the bikes.

"Where's your Street Glide, Olivia?"

She says nothing.

"Jesus Christ. We don't have time for this!" Donny barks. "Olivia, you're with Cliff. Beer Can, Abraham. Let's go."

"Bring those babies back safely," Mrs. Aguirre begs.

Before I duck through the door, her eyes meet mine. I nod, then turn away. "Let's go," I tell Olivia. I mount the Screamin' Eagle and pass her my helmet.

She pushes it away. "I'm right around the corner. Just drop me off." She hops on behind me, her arms only loosely around my waist.

Chest tightening, I nod. Then I start the engine.

36

OLIVIA

My head is reeling. I need a minute alone to catch up —thirty seconds, even—but I just *had* to walk over rather than take my own bike. New rule: Never put myself in a position where I have to cling to Cliff's back. I try not to press my face into the leather of his cut, try not to inhale his woodsy, clean scent, even over the smells of the road. And I most definitely don't feel all of those muscles, the hard ridges and swells of his back. His hair flies into my face, untamed, the black locks wrapping around my head and engulfing me in the cedar and agave in his shampoo.

I want to shove him off the bike.

He doesn't try to talk to me. He brings me straight to the Street Glide where I left it after Finn took off. I swing off the back of Cliff's bike and walk straight to mine. Halfway there, I freeze, fear locking my limbs.

It's always *after* the action that I freak out.

I glance around, as if Finn's police car is going to materialize any second. It's just Cliff and me, the roar of his Screamin' Eagle loud enough to drown out the turmoil in my head. But it doesn't.

I see Finn's face, then Greg's, and I'm catapulted back to that night, in that basement bedroom, his hands around my throat. The first few times things got weird, I just figured he was into kink, had some odd fetishes.

That almost killed me.

I claw at my throat, fingers touching only my own skin. *I'm safe*, I remind myself. *I'm here.* I look around the street again, turning in a circle. Cliff sits on his bike, brown eyes alarmed.

"Olivia?" he calls out. He starts to say something, but Donny and Esther, Beer Can, and Abraham roar onto the street.

"Let's go!" Donny yells. He urges his Dyna forward, not bothering to wait for us. Casting us a curious glance, Beer Can follows. Abraham doesn't even spare us a look.

"You good?" Cliff asks me.

I don't know! I want to scream. But there's no time to dig into my crazy. I shove the memories down and swing onto my bike. "Come on," I tell him, and start her up.

I fall into formation at the back of the pack—Prospects don't get to ride up front. Cliff hangs back with me, his eyes watchful. I wish he'd stop. He makes it so hard to be angry with him when he so clearly cares—even after I called him a bastard. Not my finest moment. I definitely jabbed his most tender point.

I always do.

We tear down 63 and jump onto Route 8, Esther clinging for dear life on the back of Donny's bike. I'm surprised he brought her with us. I would've left her with her grandma, where she's safe, where she won't have to see what we do to her father. What *I* want to do to him.

Thinking about what he did to her and her sisters sends my blood racing through my veins. Nausea and rage burn up my throat, tightening my grip on the handlebar. I rush Street Glide forward, passing Cliff and putting myself in the middle of the formation.

I haven't been present for Esther. Ever since she told me about her father, my own memories of Greg erupted from where

I must've buried them. In college, I took a psychology class where we did a unit on Post-Traumatic Stress Disorder. At the time, I thought it was fascinating how the brain can suppress memories just to stay sane. Yet the deeper they're buried, the more violent the outbreak, the more vivid the flashbacks.

Some defense mechanism.

It's better to deal with your shit. I know that. From a clinical perspective, I know exactly what I'm supposed to do: ride through the flashbacks, let them happen. I don't want to.

It's like there are two versions of me. There's rabbit Olivia, the girl who froze and stuffed it all down until she couldn't remember anymore. Then there's biker Olivia, the woman who isn't afraid to take back what belongs to her.

A life for a life.

His life for the life I could have had. The person I would be if he hadn't ruined me.

Josué's life for the person Esther might be if he hadn't destroyed her.

The River Reapers veer onto the exit ramp, a short stretch that merges onto South Main Street with a yield sign. Ravage bangs a left, back toward Naugatuck. I'm not familiar enough with Waterbury to know where the hell he's going, but I follow him anyway.

Cliff pulls up even with me, more a faithful old Saint Bernard than a Red Dog. I can't begin to wrap my head around him, his feelings. It's all too big, too much. With Cliff, I feel safe, but that can't be the only reason I'm with him. His love is not enough for this to work.

The American Motor Lodge sign looms above the road. We turn right into the small parking lot, the only real lights from our headlights. I can't explain it, but the whole place just *feels* seedy, like a whole slew of bad things have happened here. I shudder.

Esther climbs down gingerly, her lips pressed together. Donny reaches for her, drawing her in for a hug. Their lips touch for a fraction of a second. I look away, but Cliff is right there, in my line of vision where the pavement or something—anything else—should be.

"Where are you going?" I call out to her, avoiding his eyes.

Her olive skin pales to almost my shade. She swallows. "Going inside to get a room key." She lifts a shoulder. "I look just like my mom."

"I'll go with you." I start the lengthy process of shutting the bike off. I'm still not used to it. Switches and kickstands and keys, oh my. I don't know how Cliff already has it down.

"No," Donny commands. "If they see her, they'll think nothing of it. If they see any of us, we'll lose them."

"That's if they're even here," Abraham mutters.

I shake my head. I can't let her go in there alone. I just can't. Donny's right, though. Right now we've got the element of surprise.

"Wait," Cliff says.

Everyone turns to look at him. I look at his front tire.

"If they see Esther by herself, they'll know she's here for the girls," he says. "If she's with Olivia, they can say they're getting a room because they had too much to drink at HoJo's."

I lift an eyebrow. "HoJo's?"

He chuckles, ducking his head. "Howard Johnson's, back in the day. This motel was a HoJo's, too." He glances over at the bar and restaurant's sign. "Guess it's The Brass House now."

Again I'm reminded of how much older he is. It's another reason why I've got to cut him loose. He deserves someone his age, someone ready to settle down. Have babies. That kind of thing. Things he deserves.

I finish shutting off the Street Glide and swing off. "Okay, then. Let's go." I link arms with Esther, putting on a braver face than how I feel. At least I've still got my gun. That's the only thing that's gotten me through this day: I have a gun, and no one can ever hurt me again.

Esther and I walk under the portico, the sickly yellow glow of a solitary light washing over us. The other light is out. A sticker on the door advertises jacuzzis in certain rooms, by request.

"Nasty," Esther mutters.

"You couldn't pay me," I agree.

The motel doesn't have sliding doors or even a bellhop. I pull the door open, motioning Esther inside, all the while sweeping everything in sight.

Maroon and gold carpeting swallows the lobby, making the space look like a bad acid trip. They should've hired Esther's abuela to decorate, because her place is cozy, coordinated. This place is a drab nightmare, made worse by the green armchairs.

I lead Esther to the front desk, and open my mouth, but she surprises me, speaking first.

"Hi," she says, her voice void of any fear. She sounds embarrassed. "I'm such a moron. I came down to pick up food from next door, but didn't bring my key. Can I have a replacement?"

The clerk—an older white man with liver spots and thin, greasy hair slicked back across his globe of a noggin—stares at her chest. "What's the room number?"

"Oh, God." Esther looks at me. "I don't remember. Do you?"

She's not the best liar, but at least she's smooth. "Hey," I say, playing along. "Don't look at me. It's your room."

"It's actually my husband's." She winks at the clerk. "He's going to be back in a while, and we wanted to surprise him."

The girl learns fast.

"He got a name?" the clerk asks, checking out my rack now.

"Josué Figueroa."

"Spell it?"

With a pleasant smile, she spells it out for him. Her arm tightens around mine.

"Room 1131," he says, activating a key. He holds it out to her. "You gonna take pictures?"

She leans in. "Video," she says with a wink.

He drops the key into her hand. "Any chance you feel like file sharing?"

"Sure," I purr. I tug Esther away, toward the entrance. When we get to the door, I pause.

"We're getting the guys . . . right?" she asks me in a whisper.

I glance at another door, the one that exits to the rooms out back. "Why did Donny bring you?"

She blinks. "To get the girls."

I meet her eyes. "Do you want to be a nanny, or do you want to make that motherfucker pay?"

"I just want to get the girls, Olivia." She puts a palm on the glass of the door. She doesn't push it open.

"It's up to you," I promise. "I'll back you up, whatever you decide. But right now, you and I have this key, and we're already here." I drop my voice. "I have a gun."

"Jesus," she hisses, glancing at the front desk. I look, too. The clerk is gone, probably jacking off in a bathroom somewhere.

Esther pulls her hand back from the door. She taps the key card against her chin. "We *are* already here . . ."

"I don't want to pressure you into doing anything you don't want to do," I tell her, "but I hate those movies where some devastatingly handsome guy kills the baddie who's been torturing the lead actress. It should be *her* doing the slaying."

She sucks her teeth. "I don't know, Olivia. I don't want the girls seeing anything like that. I mean, *I* want to see it, but they're still so young. Maybe it's too late for Cierra, but Abril and Ximena still have a chance."

"It's not too late for Cierra. It isn't too late for you, either." I back toward the other door. "You know my sister, Lucy? Her uncle did to her what your father did to you and your sisters. Sometimes it gets the best of her, but she's doing great, Esther. She's a teacher, and . . ." My voice trails off. She dumped a guy who wanted to marry her. Kind of like how I'm unloading a guy who loves me. I bite my lip.

"You know," she says, taking a step toward the other door. "I'm more angry with my mother. She *let* him do this. She kept going back to him. Over and over. Who the fuck does that? At least your mom kept you away from her toxic boyfriends."

"Well, she mostly stayed away from me in general, but I see your point." I sigh. "If Josué is here, Toci is with him. Let's get your sisters and take out some trash."

"Ay, I need a drink," Esther mutters. She shakes out her arms. "Okay. Let's go."

We sprint toward the stairs, the gun hot against my back.

37

CLIFF

onny, Beer Can, Abraham, and I wait near our lined up bikes, Donny's eyes firmly pinned on the motel entrance. I flick ash from my cigarette onto the pavement, watching the door, too.

"How long does it take to grab a key?" Beer Can crosses his arms.

"Think they called the cops?" Abraham asks.

I scoff. "Cops? This place? Most of their income is from prostitutes renting rooms."

"Then what's taking so long?" Donny inches toward the door. "It's been at least ten minutes."

"More like fifteen." My eyes meet his.

"You don't think . . . ?" He shoots another glance at the door.

"Olivia, maybe," Beer Can concedes. "Esther, though?"

Donny and I stare at each other for a long beat. He sucks in a deep breath. "I'm giving them two more minutes, and then we're checking it out."

I spot movement out of the corner of my eye. Three small figures file from the back of the building. "Over there." I nod toward them.

The smallest lags behind the others, carrying a bundle in both arms.

"Hurry up, Jimmy," the tallest of them whispers.

"Oh, shit," Donny mutters.

The three girls draw closer, their steps slower as they approach.

"It's okay," Donny calls to them. "Come on."

Esther's little sisters crowd around us. In the dim light, I make out a swaddled baby doll in the little one's arms.

Donny kneels in front of them. "Everyone okay?"

The oldest nods. "They bought Jimmy a doll."

"Probably to keep her distracted," the middle one adds.

"Nothing happened, though," the oldest says. "Essie and her friend got us out."

"With Olivia's gun," the little one breathes, her eyes round and awed.

Donny's eyes snap to mine. In a flash, we sprint toward the back of the building.

"Watch them," he yells to the guys, drawing his gun.

"I'm with you," Abraham calls, his footsteps pounding as he catches up.

From behind us, I hear one of the girls ask Beer Can if he's from Harry Potter.

Donny races toward the line of doors. Yanking my own gun out of its holster, I close in on him, pushing my legs to move faster. He lurches through an open door. I skid to a halt behind him, nearly pushing him inside.

From the doorway, I see her. She stands, two hands on her gun, its muzzle pointed at Josué. He sits in an ugly green armchair, his hands resting on its arms. Toci sobs in a heap on the bed, her hair wrapped around Esther's hand. Esther yanks harder.

Donny's eyebrows almost touch his hairline.

I'm not surprised. I know what strength can come from the

fires of human hell, the pain of the evil that people inflict on each other. Those flames flicker in Esther's eyes, tears pooling on her lashes. One blink, one breath, and it'll all break loose.

"Josué," Olivia says, the name oily venom dripping from her lips. "You were supposed to be a father. You were supposed to protect your daughters."

Esther scoffs. "*You* were supposed to protect us," she tells her mother. She twists her wrist, pulling Toci's hair so hard, I can see the red scalp from across the room.

"I wish I had time to make you feel everything you did to them," Olivia continues.

"I didn't touch them!" Josué yells, spit flying from his lips.

"Tonight," Esther says, her voice so cold, chills race up and down my spine.

If I'd had the time twenty years ago, I would've taken my time with Bastard. I would've killed him slowly, draining his life the way he sucked out Lucy's—over many months. In the moment, I didn't think of how to make him suffer. All I saw was my little cousin. All I wanted was to make it stop.

"We can't do it here," Donny says.

Esther jumps, but Olivia doesn't even flinch. "Why not?" she asks.

"Too many witnesses." He holsters his gun, switching it for his phone.

"We should close the door," I suggest, moving into the room.

Olivia glances at me. For a moment, relief flickers through her eyes. A second later, something dark rolls through them, stifling the light.

I know that switch, that moment when the monster fully takes hold. It doesn't matter what your intentions are; the beast is a berserker, taking control of limbs until its revenge is sated.

She pins her gaze back on Josué.

Donny steps inside, too, and I shut the door behind us. The

six of us stand there, none of us moving. Donny presses his phone to his ear.

"Who are you calling?" Olivia snaps.

"Pres," he drawls. "Gonna find out how he wants us to handle this."

"What *he* wants?" Olivia sneers. "What about what Esther wants?"

"The club took this on. It's our call," Donny says.

"Fuck the club!" Olivia squeezes the grip of her gun, knuckles white. "Why is it always all about what *you* want? It's always the men deciding." She shakes her head. "What do *you* want to do, Esther?"

Donny casts me a helpless glance. I shrug. Olivia is right.

But so is he.

"We can't just off them both in a motel room," I say. "We need to be smart about this."

Olivia's shoulders tighten.

"You don't want to go to prison." I take a step toward her. "Let Donny talk to Ravage. Let us figure out a plan."

She shakes her head. "See," she tells Josué, "to me, you're not just Esther's father. You're every man who thinks he has the right to do whatever he wants with a woman's body. I don't need a *plan* because it's pretty simple—to me, anyway."

"I'm with you, Olivia." I take another step. "I went about it wrong, but I'm with you—whatever you want to do. Let's just take a second."

"I don't need a second," Esther says. "I just need this to be over. I want my sisters safe. I don't want to look over my shoulder, wondering if he's coming back for us, praying *she* isn't playing the system." She shoves Toci forward. Pivoting on the balls of her feet, Esther lunges for Donny's gun. Her fingers close around the grip and pull it free from its holster. She presses the barrel against Toci's head.

"Wait!" I shout. In two strides, I close the distance between the bed and me. I grab a throw pillow and hold it out to Esther. "It's not a silencer, but it's better than nothing."

Olivia lifts her head, her eyes meeting mine. She nods, once. I toss a pillow to her, too.

With a sigh, Donny pockets his phone. He peers through the peephole. "We're good." Turning back around, he leans against the door, crossing his arms.

"No one is going to miss *you*," Olivia tells Josué.

Esther prays in Spanish, the words all running together. "Count of three?"

"Your count," Olivia agrees.

"Three." Esther's nostrils flare. "Two."

The digital alarm clock on the nightstand blinks, the time changing from 10:22 to 10:23.

Esther takes a deep breath. "One."

Olivia and Esther squeeze their triggers at the same time. The pillows only marginally muffle the bang of the shots. Josué slumps forward in the armchair. Toci crumples in a heap on the bed.

Olivia holsters her gun. Esther hands Donny his.

I pick up my phone and call Ravage.

"T hank you." Esther wraps her arms around me. Her heart thumps wildly against her chest, reverberating into mine.

I hug her back, feel her whole body loosen. "Any time."

"Yeah . . . let's *not* make this a regular thing, a'ight?" Donny chides.

Esther releases me and steps back, surveying the room, the two bodies. "I should feel sad, shouldn't I?"

Behind me, the men huddle up. They decide Beer Can should stay in the room with the bodies until Ravage and Mark get here, and Donny walks back outside with Cliff. I feel more than see him leave the room, his warmth and energy vanishing with him.

I sigh. "What *do* you feel?" I ask Esther.

"Relieved," she says right away. "Isn't that crazy? I should be freaking out. I just killed my own mother."

"I get it. Now you don't have to look over your shoulder anymore." I glance behind me. Beer Can stands next to the door, his face passive. He might be listening, or he might be running Depeche Mode lyrics through his head.

"I don't even care if I go to jail," she adds. "At least I'll know they're safe. Abuela can take care of them."

"You're not going to jail." I bite my lip, considering how much I should tell her. I glance at Beer Can again.

"Esther," he asks, his eyes meeting mine, "does Donny ever tell you anything about the club?"

"I told him I don't wanna know. That was before." She arches an eyebrow. "I guess it doesn't matter now."

Beer Can steps forward and lays a warm hand on my shoulder, giving it a gentle squeeze. "Your call," he says. "I'm gonna step outside." He pulls a marijuana vape pen from the inside of his cut, then strolls out.

The ugly green armchair suddenly looks inviting. If I sit down in it, I might fall asleep. "You're not going to prison," I repeat.

She shrugs. "I guess time will tell."

"*I'm* telling you. We've done this before. I've done this before."

"What, kill someone's father?"

"We're kind of in the business of killing scumbag fathers," I say. "Scumbags in general, really."

Her eyebrows pinch together.

"Last semester, when someone slashed your tires and keyed your car? That was this guy from my photography class. He's the one who hurt Dio. He came back," I tell her. I'm not in the brightly lit hotel room anymore. I'm in our apartment, hiding in the shadows, the gun in my hand. "I had to shoot him."

She gapes at me. "In our apartment?"

I nod. "I called Cliff. I didn't know what else to do. The gun isn't registered—I got it from Donny."

"Why am I not surprised?" she mutters. Her gaze floats back to her mother's form.

"Cliff, Donny, and Beer Can cleaned up. They got rid of the body—Eli. That was his name. They did a good job. No one's ever going to find him." I think of the Silver Alert, of the anonymous somebody looking for him. "No one's going to find your parents.

I'm gonna have to call this in to Glace, though." I bite my lip again. "I have to talk to the guys, figure out what our story's gonna be."

"Maybe I should've had Abuela call the cops."

"I think I've got that covered," I say. "Come on." I pull open the door and slip out past Beer Can, who gives us both a nod as we pass. Esther and I make our way around the building. The silence is stifling, given how busy South Main Street usually is. There aren't even any drag racers tonight.

I spot the cluster of bikes and men, Cliff standing out. I could pick him out of a crowd. I'm magnetically drawn to him. He holds a sleeping Ximena in his arms, and the sight of it sends my heart reeling. Her head rests on his shoulder, her small thumb tucked into the corner of her mouth.

"Que lindo," Esther croons. "He's a keeper."

I give her a sidelong look. "Don't."

"What?" She spreads her hands. "I'm not saying marry the guy and pop out babies. I'm just saying, he's one of the good ones."

"One of the few," I mutter.

"Truth," she says.

We reach the group. Cierra and Abril rush to Esther, wrapping their arms around her. She holds them close, whispering to them in Spanish.

"We figure out how we wanna handle this?" I ask, glancing from Cliff to Donny.

"We're gonna take them to the river," Donny says.

"What about the girls?" I fix my eyes on Donny's ENFORCER patch, tracing the worn stitching. Anything to keep me from looking at Cliff.

"We'll bring them to Esther's grandparents." Donny frowns at me. "Why?"

"What about the case? Don't you think DCF will find it a little weird that all of a sudden, Esther's parents are MIA?" I put my hands on my hips.

Donny glances skyward, shaking his head. "Why you gotta complicate this, Olivia?"

"Because I work for DCF. They're overloaded, but they're not gonna overlook this. We have to cover our bases."

"Let me guess," he says. "You've got those bases covered?"

I lift my chin, ignoring the burn of Cliff's gaze. "I do, actually." I reach into my saddlebag and run my fingers over Finn's business card. "There's a pig who owes me a favor."

Both of Donny's eyebrows lift. "That so, Prospect?" The corner of his mouth twitches. I think he's smiling, but I'm not sure.

"I'll have him come down, corroborate for us. Esther's parents took the girls, but dumped them here when they saw him in uniform." I nod toward the gas station next door. "Then they took off."

"You got this all figured out, don't you?" He shakes his head. "Cliff, you've got your hands full, brother."

I scoff. "*Cliff* doesn't have anything. I'm a person, Donny, not a piece of ass." Remembering the girls, I wince. "Sorry," I tell Esther.

She sighs. "If that's the worst they experience today . . ."

"All right," Donny says. "Make your call."

A familiar looking SUV pulls into the motel parking lot— Ravage and Mark. Skid trails behind them on his motorcycle.

"Cleanup crew's here. Cliff, pass Jimmy to Olivia. We've got work to do." Donny strides toward the SUV.

Cliff steps toward me, his eyes soft. I hold open my arms awkwardly. He passes the little girl to me. "Got her?" he asks, his hand brushing mine.

The heat from his skin scorches mine, igniting a fuse that threads through every one of my limbs. My pinky twitches toward his, wrapping around his before I have the chance to stop myself. All I want to do is lean into him, let him hold both Jimmy and me, let myself give in to the current. But I know that if I do, I'll sink into him like a stone, falling too deep to ever come back up for air.

Because when I love, I love with my whole heart, with every inch of my marrow. And when I do, I forget who I am, lose sight of what's good and what isn't. Love destroyed me, and I only barely put myself back together. I'm still far too broken.

Cliff deserves better.

His pinky hooks around mine, squeezing for a heartbeat. Then he releases me, relinquishing Jimmy into my arms. With devastation in his eyes, he drops his gaze. Then he walks away, leaving me cold.

39

CLIFF

I can't take this anymore.

This woman has a knife in my chest. Every time I get within sight of her, inhale the same oxygen, she twists the knife a little deeper. There's no doubt in me anymore. She was never temporary. I'm in it for the long haul—or I would be. Something is stopping her, something has a hold on her that's beyond my power. The damage Greg did is too deep, beyond my reach. I would kill for her, but killing him won't save her.

At least not if I do it.

I trudge away, holding my head high but barely holding myself together. I need a drink. As soon as I finish up with the club, no matter how late it is, I'm going to Lucy's. Right now I need to be around someone who doesn't want me to go away.

I need my best friend.

While Abraham and I wrap the bodies in tarps, Olivia calls the cop who owes her a favor.

He looks startlingly like Greg.

My blood boils in my veins. When Esther and Olivia finish up with him and he takes off, Donny brings Esther and the girls home.

Olivia disappears.

Officer Byrne must be Greg's brother. I pace and chainsmoke until Donny comes back with the SUV. I help load the bodies into the back of it, and we take them to the river.

When Ravage held Greg's vote, I assumed "take him to the river" meant weighing the body down and dropping it in. Instead, my President passes out shovels and tells Abraham and me to put them deep. Then Ravage, Skid, Donny, and Beer Can keep watch.

Digging is hard. On TV, they make it look easy, just a bigger version of a sandcastle hole at the beach. Near the river, the soil is wet and heavy. My back aches every time I punch the shovel through the dirt and lift another load. This is Prospect work, but neither Ravage nor Skid made Olivia stay. There aren't any other Prospects. I should try to make conversation with Abraham, get to know my brother a little better. But I'm not in a talking mood, and he never seems to be, anyway.

Not when it comes to me.

By the time we bury Esther's parents, every muscle in my body aches and my eyes might as well be smeared with Vaseline, they're so bleary. Since Ravage and Skid rode Abraham's and my bikes down to the river, I'm free to go.

Until Ravage calls Church.

"Not the way I wanted this to go down," Donny says, his hands splayed on the table, "but I think it played out well."

Ravage's mouth is a hard slash in his face.

"I take it you disagree, Pres?" Beer Can puffs from his pen. If I weren't so tired, I'd tell him to pass it over.

"We need to take a vote," Skid says, but I watch Ravage's face. I'm too tired to defend Olivia if he wants to vote her out. Or whatever it is MCs do to Prospects they no longer want.

Ravage's eyes burn into the back wall. "When we took this on," he says, real slow, "I didn't think they'd take those girls. They almost outplayed us. Who knows what would've happened if we hadn't found them?" He sweeps the room, landing on me.

I swallow.

It's not Olivia I need to defend.

Even though every muscle screams, I stand from my seat and face my brothers. "I fucked up. I should've called Olivia."

Donny shakes his head. "I was pissed," he says, addressing Ravage. "Red Dog's good with me now."

"Sit down." Ravage throws a hand at me. "That's not what we're voting on. We'll get to that."

I ease into the chair, keeping my face blank.

"We need to do better," Ravage continues. "This ended well, but it could've gone very badly. This is twice now that this club had the opportunity to save a girl's life, but almost fucked it up. We need to get organized."

"Organized?" Abraham lifts an eyebrow.

"I want to take this club in a new direction. We seem to keep finding ourselves in this position, so why not roll with it?" Ravage clenches the gavel in his hand. "I'm done tolerating violence against women and children, gentlemen. I vote we do something about it." He turns to Skid. "VP? Anything you wanna add?"

"Guns and drugs are only gonna land us all in the pen," Skid says. "We've got The Wet Mermaid income, which is plenty as long as we're careful. I think those of us who were around in the Bastard era and voted yea all feel the same way about this. Not everyone shares those morals." His eyes flick toward Abraham. "We need to be unanimous."

Mark clears his throat. "Unanimous about what, exactly?"

"Apologies," Ravage says. "It's late and I'm just babbling in the dark. I want to put our resources to good use. I want the River Reapers to be the place people turn when the cops won't do shit. When bad pennies like Greg turn up and rape. When mothers become monsters and let fathers stain children. I'm talking about cleaning up this town, gentlemen. Capisce?"

We all nod.

"Let's vote, then," Ravage says. "Yea."

"Yea," Skid seconds.

"We might have to monetize this service," Mark cautions, "but right now, my vote's yea."

"Stixx?" Ravage asks.

I glance at the tattooed man, who's been so quiet, I didn't even realize he was here. If I'm being honest, the dude unnerves me a little.

"You know where I got my first X?" Stixx asks.

"Do we wanna know?" Beer Can mutters.

The icy glare Stixx slides him makes the hair on the back of my neck stand up straight. "I burnt down a Catholic school," he says with a grin so gaping and empty, he looks lupine. "Walked in on a priest doing things to a kindergartner that no human should ever do to another person. They expelled me. The priest walked. The fire stopped him, though. I was eight." He bares his teeth. "Yea."

The whole table looks at me.

"Cliff?" Ravage asks.

I stare down at my hands. "To be clear," I say, "we're talking about playing judge, jury, and executioner?"

"When the law turns its cheek, yes," Ravage says, gritting his teeth. "You vote nay, brother, and I might kill you with my bare hands, right here, right now."

I scoff. "You really think I'd vote nay? I spent twenty years in federal prison for killing my own father—a veteran. I still want to kill him, whenever I think about what he did to Lucy." I light a cigarette, the back of my neck hot. It's odd, putting my feelings into words. Not something I'm used to. "I've been searching for a purpose. I don't just want to be a biker. I want to . . ." My voice trails off.

"Make a difference?" Abraham sneers. When I turn my glare on him, he holds his hands up. "I'm with you, brother. It just sounds corny. I mean, is this really possible? Do any of you really think we can do this?"

"We've got to try," Ravage says, his voice breaking. "Those three girls . . . They're so young."

I nod. "Lucy, too. And Olivia. I think she was in high school, when Greg . . ." I can't say it.

Beer Can turns away, sniffling. "I'm tired of other men trying to break and control women."

"Me too, brother," I say. I meet my President's eyes. "Yea."

"Yea," Abraham says.

"Yea," Vaughn agrees. "Might as well use these powers for good." He mimes typing on a computer keyboard.

"Do y'all really even need to ask me?" Donny shakes his head. "Of course, yea."

"Yea," Beer Can whispers, still turned away from the table. He dabs at his eyes with the sleeve of his T-shirt.

"Let's kill some rapists," Ravage says, and bangs his gavel on the table. "Get the fuck out of here, boys. Get some sleep."

I crawl up to my room. It's far too late to stop in at Lucy's, and I can't keep my eyes open, anyway. I'm physically and emotionally drained and, outside of my club, nothing feels certain right now. A little sleep will set me right, help me figure out how to fix things with Olivia.

40

I roll from my side onto my stomach, fluffing the pillow under my head. Even though I'm exhausted, my heart is racing. The flutter against my sternum is constant, no matter how many times I do a round of slow breathing on an app on my phone. My entire body is poised—for what, I don't know. I should be passed out cold right now.

Yet the time on my phone reads 3:08 a.m.

Then 3:15 a.m.

4:02.

I download an audiobook and pop in headphones. Despite the narrator's soothing voice, my heart maintains its fast beat. I turn onto my other side, pulling a body pillow close. I listen for what feels like twenty minutes. Just as I slide into velvet slumber, another shot of adrenaline floods my system.

I don't want it, yet it seems I've got a constant supply tonight. Or this morning. Whatever.

If I could bottle this shit and sell it, I'd be rich.

I pause the audiobook and kill the app, then download solitaire. I play game after game, hoping to bore myself into sleep. I *need* to get some rest. Ever since Eli, I've been sleeping like shit, but this is a whole new level for me.

A creak echoes through the apartment, sounding a lot like a footstep. I didn't hear Esther's door open. I stretch out a hand, patting around for Dio. My palm finds his fuzzy head. He makes a short *rrr* sound, a sort of sleepy half purr. Then he tucks his head back into his paws and goes back to sleep.

I tilt my head, ears straining for the shift of weight in the kitchen, or the groan in the floor next to the bathroom. Nothing happens.

Still, I reach for the gun on my nightstand and touch its cool metal. The sensation against my fingertips is reassuring.

Rolling away from my nightstand, I curl myself into a comma. Maybe if I sleep like a cat, I'll sleep just as peacefully. But when I close my eyes, I see Eli stepping through the front door to my apartment. I hear him calling my name, his voice joined by Greg's.

Olivia.

Eli and Greg stand in front of me, their arms crossed, eyes cold. Other figures step in beside them, forming a circle around me—every man and boy who has hurt me. I reach for the gun on my nightstand but I'm standing in a dark room. Their faces spin around me, faster, their eyes and mouths blurring together.

I lurch out of bed, falling to the floor. My hands and knees absorb the shock, my palms slick against the carpet. Dio meows, hopping down from the bed. He bonks his little head against my thigh, as if to say "It's all right. I'm with you."

I pull him into my arms and sit back against the bed. Then I bury my face in his fur and sob, tears soaking his hair. Yet he stays with me until I'm empty and exhausted.

He rolls over in my arms, orange fur alight in the rising sun. I rub his belly, here in this room but also buried in the past. I've heard of trauma survivors unable to remember the event, only to be triggered by something—a new trauma, a situation similar to the event, or something else. It all rushes back, every bad memory.

So much for forgetting.

Grabbing my phone, I Google symptoms of PTSD, then hop from article to article about rape survivors and trauma. Learning the terms for the things I do and the memories rushing back at me helps. I feel less upside down, more in control. I repeat the facts to myself like a mantra.

I forgot what Greg did to me because my brain—in all its misguided gray matter—was trying to protect me.

I remembered again when Esther told me about her history.

I can't stop thinking about every bad thing that he did to me because my brain is processing it all.

Sometimes I lash out at the people around me because I feel so mixed up inside, it spews out, like shaking up a bottle of soda, pointing it at someone I love, and twisting the cap off.

What I'm experiencing is normal for someone who survived the things I survived.

I'm normal.

And I survived.

I still don't know how. Back then, I didn't have a gun. He outweighed me by at least seventy-five pounds. All I had was my voice, and with his hands around my neck, squeezing the air from my body, it wasn't much.

I want him dead so badly, a sweet metallic taste fills my mouth. I almost wish I'd just let Cliff kill him at the club house. I don't know if that would be enough, though.

It has to be me.

Someday, somehow, I will reclaim my life by taking his.

I fall asleep with Dio in my arms, but my alarm goes off a minute later. At least, it seems like it was only sixty seconds. I stumble through the apartment and get ready for another day of work, another day of pretending to be normal. At least I'll be able to get Esther some news about the girls. With her parents out of the picture, she should have legal guardianship of them in no time.

I find her in the kitchen making coffee.

"Want a ride in?" she asks between yawns.

"Why are you awake?" I moan. "You have the privilege of sleeping in, yet here you are, throwing it away." I give her my sternest look.

"I'm not throwing it away," she insists, flipping on the coffee maker. "I couldn't sleep."

"That makes two of us." I take mugs down from the cabinet and set them on the counter.

"Why didn't you come get me?"

"Same reason you didn't," I reply.

"Stubborn," we say in unison.

She laughs. "At first I thought it was because I'm feeling guilty about offing Toci. I'm not, though."

I nod. "I get that." I lean against the counter. "So what kept you awake?"

"I feel so restless," she says. "Like, the girls are gonna be okay, so I don't have to worry about them anymore. But now I have this degree and—no offense—I don't think I wanna work for DCF."

"None taken." The coffee maker gurgles, liquid splashing and sizzling on the burner. I wait for the final drip, then fill our mugs.

"I think I'm gonna get my Master's," Esther says. "Become a licensed clinical social worker. Maybe work in a school. I know I want to work with kids, but I also know I don't want to work with them after they've already been taken away. I want to help them as the shit is hitting the fan, you know? Schools need trauma screening training. I can help with that."

"I think that suits you," I tell her.

"I just hope Donny's cool with it," she says with a sigh. "I'll probably enroll in an online program, but I don't know how it's all going to work."

"You'll have a lot on your plate," I agree, "but I think you can do it."

"I'm gonna find out." She sips her coffee. "Now get in the shower. Clock's ticking. I need you in work on time so you can text me intel on our case."

"For someone so quiet and sweet on the outside, you sure are bossy." But I head toward the bathroom anyway, clutching my mug for moral support. I wish I hadn't gone into a career that requires getting up with the sun.

I pause in the hall, wanting to offer her some kind of reassurance. We both know real life doesn't always have a happy ending, so I don't. Instead I just hope that I can give her good news.

As soon as I walk into the building, Diane waves me into her office. She closes the door behind me, then settles into her chair with a sigh.

"Sit," she says, voice hard.

My spine stiffens, the muscles in my neck tightening. I sink into the chair across from her. I thought I covered our tracks, but there's a good chance I missed something. I'm not a professional, after all.

"God, I'm exhausted, and it's only eight." She pins me with an exasperated look. "You should've told me you had a connection to the Figueroa case."

"I'm sorry. I didn't realize it'd be an issue," I lie. "What happens now?"

Diane scoffs. "*You* are the least of my concerns. Turns out Glace has a personal connection to the case, too. She's friends with the children's mother." She rolls her eyes. "She bypassed protocol and pursued reunification. If your friend hadn't filed a complaint, we probably never would've known."

I try to swallow, but my throat is as dry as a bone. "What does this mean?"

"It means Glace is officially off the case. I've suspended her, but my hands are tied if headquarters decides to fire her."

"And me?"

She scoffs. "You may have left out your relationship with Esther, but you didn't take it any further than that. I have no reason to suspend you. However," she says, giving me a stern look, "you're off the case."

I sit back in my seat, relieved. "Can I ask what's going to happen with the case now?"

"It's being handed to another worker," she says, rubbing her temples. "After last night, the state has no choice but to move forward with a permanency plan."

My shoulders tense up again. "Which is?"

"We'll continue trying to contact birth mom and dad, but it looks like they've skipped town—again." She rolls her eyes. "I'm sure they're aware they've committed a federal offense. We've probably seen the last of them. Your friend should get a date for her guardianship hearing soon."

I exhale, relieved. "In the interest of full disclosure, I'm texting her as soon as I walk out of this room."

"I figured." Diane smiles. "These kids get a happy ending, which doesn't always happen. It's racked up a lot of paperwork, but I'm glad for them. Now," she says, shifting folders on her desk. "I'm pairing you with Harrison. He's a Boomer, so he'll kick your ass if you pull any more stunts. In a case like last night, protocol is to call your superior, not hold your friend's hand. Consider yourself verbally warned."

"Thank you," I say. It could've been so much worse, but I have no intention of playing by the rules. I just have to make sure I don't get caught.

Knuckles rap on Diane's door. A man with blond hair streaked through with silver sticks his head in. His beard and hair slicked back into a short ponytail make him look like a biker. His high cheekbones make him look like an actor.

"You must be Olivia," he says, flicking a glance at me. "Let's go. Got a nasty house to visit." Without another word, he strolls away, leaving the door cracked open behind him.

"You heard the man," Diane says.

At least I have good news for Esther.

I wake up with the blanket twisted around me, my arms empty. The room comes into focus slowly, as if I'd spent the night drinking instead of digging a six-foot deep hole. Every muscle throbs, especially my back.

I take a shower so hot, my skin is red and angry when I step out. But at least my muscles are looser.

I pick my way through the club house, then slog down the stairs. It's still so early, everyone is sleeping, the strip club locked up tight for the day. Bikers are kind of like vampires.

As I near the landing, I hear voices—Pru's smoky velvet, Trish's perky lilt.

"Just talk to him," Trish insists. "He won't bite."

"I know," Pru says with a sigh.

"What are you so afraid of?" Glasses clink as the blonde bartender lifts what sounds like one of the trays for the dishwasher.

I don't want to intrude on their conversation, but I really need a coffee. Preferably Irish. I clear my throat and approach the bar.

Both women look up at me, Pru from under dark waves, her hair still teased up from last night. Trish smiles, her face void of any makeup. Combined with the floral printed dress she's wearing, she looks sweet. I could almost pretend she never said she'd ride my Red Dog.

I smirk at the memory. "Morning, ladies." My voice is smokier than usual from the late night.

"What can I do you for?" Trish asks with a wink.

Nope. No pretending here.

"Feel like making me an Irish coffee?" I stand between where Pru sits and an empty stool, and lean on the bar.

"Sure thing," Trish coos.

Pru eyes me. "Rough night?"

"About as rough as yours." I nod to the bruise on her thigh. "How'd that happen?"

Despite her dark hair and cool complexion, pink tinges her cheeks. "I haven't banged myself up this bad since my very first night on the pole." She nods toward the stage. "New shoes. I slipped."

"Which is why," Trish says, passing me a coffee in a to go cup, "you should *sing* instead of dance."

I take a sip, nodding appreciatively. Trish might suck as a bartender, but she makes a damn good cup of coffee. Or maybe it's the whiskey."You sing?" I ask Pru.

She shoots Trish a glare.

"She's actually really good." Trish slings a towel over her shoulder. "I told her she should ask Mark about Cervical Caves taking Oh Vile Eye's spot."

I lift an eyebrow. "Cervical Caves?"

Pru purses her lips, but holds my curious gaze.

"I'm not knocking it," I tell her, chuckling. I hold up my coffee in a salute and step away from the bar. "See you later."

As I head out the door, I hear them whispering.

"Did he and Olivia break up?"

Wish I knew the answer to that.

It's impossible for a newbie like me to hold a coffee while

riding a bike, so I smoke a couple cigarettes while I finish it. Then I take the Screamin' Eagle over to Lucy's. Halfway there I realize it's a weekday and she's more than likely at work. I pull into her driveway, considering my options. I could go back to The Wet Mermaid and back to bed. I could let myself into Lucy's and crash on her couch.

Or I could find some way to occupy myself.

The problem is, I've got nothing to do, nowhere to be. For twenty years, I got up at the ass crack of dawn. I did my job. I reported to the dining hall for meals. Then I went to bed before lights out so I could get enough sleep. Since coming home, I've had something to do every day. This is the first time that there's nothing.

Without Olivia, Lucy, or the club, I've got nothing.

If Lucy decides to keep her baby, I'll be Uncle Cliff. I can help her out during the day while she works. Save her some money on daycare. But even then, eventually that baby will be old enough for school.

Then what?

I need more. I need something that's just mine, something I can turn to on days like this when I'm kicking my heels.

But I've got no idea what that is.

The realization sends me reeling. I stagger off the bike, stumble my way to Lucy's door. With numb hands, I unlock it and push my way inside. I sit down on the couch, hard.

I don't want to be the guy watching court TV on his days off, ricocheting around until someone needs me. I need Olivia, but I'm not even sure she needs me. I'm not even sure we're a "we" anymore.

I'm just a reaper, haunting the town I grew up in, hovering somewhere between life and death.

I need more than this half life.

I need to build a real life. I don't really know how—I don't have many marketable skills, unless you count killing and burying people. And for twenty years, I worked in a machine tools shop. I don't know if any factories around here will hire an ex-con, but I've got to try.

At the very least, I need a bike that I can call my own, one that isn't a lender from the club. I need a place of my own, too. Living in the club house is convenient, but it isn't mine. I've never had anything of my own. If I can find a second job—maybe a first shift piecing together tools in a factory—maybe I can make a life of my own.

I love the club. I love Lucy. And—god help me—I love Olivia. But I need something that's all mine, something that's constant no matter what.

And there's only one person who can help me find that something.

OLIVIA

"Come on, slowpoke," Harrison calls over his shoulder.

I pause halfway up the driveway and make a face at him. "Why couldn't you park in the parking lot?" I say through gritted teeth. Instead, he had to park down on the street, forcing us to climb this hill.

Well, *me*. Mr. Spry is already almost at the top. It's like he's the one in his twenties and I'm in my . . . whatever age bracket he's in. It's hard to tell. Despite his blondish white hair and beard, Harrison is as tan and muscular as a thirty- or forty-year-old.

"Oh, quit your whining," he chides. "You're young. You ride a motorcycle. I thought you liked thrills?"

The only *thrill* I like is the one that happens when I'm rolling around in a bed with someone, but I probably shouldn't say that. It might be the truth but it could be interpreted as sexual harassment. Not that I'd *ever* jump into bed with this guy. He's a pain in the ass.

"I'm coming," I grumble, and silently vow to start doing cardio at the gym. I've got a cushy state job now, plus I'm still bartending for the MC. I can afford it.

I crest the top and wipe the sweat that's somehow broken out above my lip. Between the heat and this unexpected climb of Mount freakin' Everest, I'm going to be lucky if my deodorant holds out.

Harrison and I stand at the edge of a huge complex of "townhouses" in Waterbury. I've always referred to them as the Gayridge apartments. I'm not sure what they're formally called. Bree used to have a boyfriend who lived here, so I spent a lot of time roaming around outside.

I never climbed this damned hill, though.

I glance down toward the packy, wondering if I can talk Harrison into buying me some tequila after we finish this home visit. He's been taking me on nothing but home visits these past couple weeks. It's like he and Diane don't trust me to do anything else. At this point, I'm a pro. I could repeat the checklist in my sleep.

I'm getting bored, and I'm afraid of what might happen if it keeps going that way. I glance at Harrison again and nearly choke. I'm not *that* bored.

"All right, back down we go," he says, and starts jogging. Jogging!

I gape at his back. "What do you mean, 'back down'?"

"Exercise is good for you. Especially you. You're way too tense." He zips down the hill. I look for something to throw at him.

"So we don't have a home visit here?"

"Nope!"

With a sigh, I traipse after him. At least going down is way easier than up. Still, it takes some concentration. The road winds all over the place, and cars fly up and down the thing like it's the Autobahn. I consider pushing Harrison into traffic, but don't because the club probably wouldn't back me up on this one. I'd back me up.

This old asshole is torturing me.

I find him at the bottom, leaning against his beat up Buick

and smoking a cigarette. At least this is something we can agree on. I light up, too, and hop up onto the trunk. "Thought you were all about the healthy shit?"

"This is my one vice," he says. "I just love a good leisurely smoke."

Maybe he's all right, after all.

"So what *is* on the agenda today?" I ask.

"I make this run every Wednesday," he tells me. "Makes up for the cigarettes."

I roll my eyes. "You realize that makes zero sense, right?"

"Shut it, Millennial. You know nothing. I'm sixty-two and there's not a single cell of cancer in me. I think I'm doing something right. You, on the other hand . . ." He shakes his head at me. "You need more cardio. We're going to do this every Monday and Friday, from now on."

I laugh. "Yeah okay, Gramps."

"Gramps?" He scowls. "I'm young enough to be your father. Gramps." He mutters to himself, something about disrespect.

I smoke in silence, thinking about my father.

It's been over a week since Mercy left, and no one's heard a thing.

He's not the only biker who's MIA, either.

"So what are we doing now?" I flick my finished cigarette into the road.

"Well, as soon as I get the call, we're heading to Naugatuck. Gotta remove a pair of siblings." Bowing his head, he shakes it. "This is the part of the job I hate. Think you can handle it?"

"Why do you hate it? Isn't taking kids from shitty parents a good thing?"

He scoffs. "God, you've got a lot to learn."

I think of my first case, the mother who didn't actually deserve to lose her kids—Renee. "I'm guessing Diane didn't fill you in on my first day."

He waves a hand at me. "I prefer to form my own opinion of

people. It's also part of the job. Lot of the time, the report says one thing, but the truth is entirely different. Besides," he says, opening the driver's door. He gets in smoothly, not a single sign of osteoarthritis or anything. I wonder if he drinks the blood of infants. "Even the shittiest of parents make for a hard case. Until you watch police take a crying child from their home, you ain't seen nothing."

"I didn't cry." I hop down from the car and get in.

"What's that?" Starting the engine, he pulls the Buick through a U-turn and heads back toward Reidville Drive.

"I was a foster kid."

"Ah." He chuckles. "I get it now."

"Get what?" I frown at him.

"Ex-foster kid, came up in the system, wants to make a difference. That about cover it?"

"What's wrong with that?"

"What's wrong with it is it's a cliché. It's also naive. This is the system. There's no making a difference. There's just checking off boxes and moving through the assembly line."

I cross my arms. "I got my first client to cooperate. Glace said she'd been working on her for months." I sound sullen. I don't have a damn thing to prove to this guy.

"Good for you." He swings the Buick onto a side road, the one that connects to the on ramp for I-84 W. The Buick hits a pothole and the whole thing shudders.

I clench the sides of my seat. "Yeah, good for me. Good for the mom and her kid, too."

"Check in with them sometime. Bet you anything the mom's not cooperating anymore. People will say whatever it takes to keep their kids. Even the shitty parents. They don't want the shame associated with the whole thing. What they do is a completely different story."

"You're just disillusioned because you lived through Nixon and Reagan."

"And you've been coddled because you had Obama holding your hand," he shoots back.

"I'm not an idiot," I tell him. The fact that I even have to say it probably means that I *am* naive. My lip curls. I need to stop arguing with this guy.

"All's I'm saying," he continues, merging onto 8 S, "is don't get disappointed when shit doesn't go your way with this gig. The only difference you're gonna make is you'll be a friendlier face when you take these kids away."

I roll my eyes, but say nothing. Right now, while I ride around in this musty Buick, Esther is packing to move in with Donny and her sisters. Even if I only manage to make things better here and there, I've still outplayed the system. Everyone wins when people get happy endings.

If only I could have one, too.

Harrison pulls up in front of another complex, this one in Naugatuck. These actually resemble townhouses, rather than the multi-story Gayridge buildings where apartments are crammed in, the price jacked up. These are single story brick duplexes. They're actually kind of cute. If I was going to move in with Cliff, I'd consider renting one.

Cliff.

Lately, he doesn't show up at The Wet Mermaid until after seven. I don't know where he is the rest of the day, and he leaves as soon as we're closed and cleaned up. We've barely even spoken lately.

It's all my fault, technically.

I'm still mad at him, but I miss him. It's sick, really. How can I want to be with him but at the same time, not want to be with him? I know he meant well when he went after Greg. It's probably for the best that we're done. From the beginning, we were born to die.

My parents will be thrilled.

A police car pulls up behind Harrison and me, its lights off.

"Here's our guy," he says, getting out.

I never understood why DCF needs a police officer to take a child. I didn't cry when they took me from Bree, but that was because I thought I was in trouble. Any time I'd done something wrong, she'd tell me "Don't cry about it, Livvie. Just own up to it."

I didn't know what the hell I was supposed to be owning up to.

I get out and follow Harrison to the police car. Through the windshield, I see the guy's face. My hands go numb.

Finn.

This town is just too damn small.

He climbs out of his car and gives me a nod, but otherwise doesn't acknowledge me. He shakes hands with Harrison.

"I shouldn't even really need you," Harrison tells him. "Just look pretty. Come on, Olivia."

I guess I won't be looking pretty.

Casting another glance at Finn, I follow Harrison to a door adorned with a Christmas wreath. I arch an eyebrow at it.

"Wait 'til you see the inside," he says, and knocks.

Finn stands in the yard with a hand on his hip.

The door opens. A pale, thin face peers out, the eyes surrounded by smudges. The face is all *wrong*, sunken in odd spots, as if some of the bone disintegrated.

Drugs—heavy ones.

I sigh. It's another Bree.

"Yeah?" the woman asks. She glances behind us, her eyes widening. "Oh, shit." She tries to slam the door in Harrison's face, but he sticks a foot inside.

"Now, now, let's not make this difficult," he says.

The woman disappears into the dark apartment.

Finn steps onto the porch, drawing his gun.

"Put that thing away," Harrison says.

"Ma'am," Finn calls, ignoring him. "Do you have any weapons I should know about?"

"No," she snarls.

I push the door open and peer inside. The sparse light from the window illuminates a figure hunched over a coffee table. She finishes crushing a line of pills. I look away, scanning the room for the kids. A light underlines a door in the hall. Maybe the kids' room.

"Put it away," I tell Finn. "She's more worried about getting high." I step inside, Harrison at my heels. "What are their names?" I ask him.

"No idea."

I throw him a sharp look. "This is your case."

"So? Do you have any idea how many cases I've got?"

I look at his empty hands. "Where's their file?"

He scoffs. "You're so cute." He cups his hands around his mouth. "Come on out, kids."

Finn stands beside the woman, shaking his head at her. "Ma'am," he tries. "Can I call anyone for you?"

My chest tightens. I know he isn't Greg, but this whole time, I've still hated him just as much. It's jarring to see him so full of empathy. Maybe he got the dose that was supposed to go to his brother.

"No," she slurs, leaning back against the couch.

The bedroom door opens and two young children creep out. A girl who looks barely six puts an arm around a toddler boy. His diaper sags, brown streaking his legs.

"Jesus," I whisper. "Where are they gonna go?" I ask Harrison.

"Come on," he coaxes them. "Follow me." He shepherds the children outside.

"Wait," I call, but he ignores me. "Do you have a car seat?" I ask the mother.

She slumps back, eyes heavy.

Finn shakes his head at me. "I'll have one of the guys bring me one from the station."

"Better hurry," I mutter. I wouldn't put it past Harrison to buckle the baby into the backseat.

Finn gets on his radio and asks for an ambulance and a car seat. With one last look at the mother, I turn and walk away.

There's one thing I can credit Bree with: she never used in front of me. It was always behind closed doors, with some boyfriend in her bed. Or she'd disappear for days. I knew what she was doing, of course, but only in an abstract way.

I wonder if Mercy caught up with Bree and, if so, what he found. If she's the same woman he fell in love with, or if she's still the woman he left. If he hadn't gone in for the MC, he would've raised me. That I'm sure of.

But he's left me again, which makes him no better than Bree. I will never, ever have kids. I'd rather not live with disappointing them. Considering what I came from, there's no alternative.

That's why it's better that Cliff and I are done. If I'm not with him, I can't repeat history. No one else gets hurt.

I know that, but it doesn't explain the tightness in my chest, the ache in my heart.

I wobble into the parking lot of The Wet Mermaid, barely keeping the Screamin' Eagle upright. I pull into my usual spot at the end of the line of bikes, between Abraham and Olivia.

Olivia.

Her name is a sigh in my mind. Every time I come in, I'm torn between hoping she's working and hoping she isn't. The strip club is a skeleton crew, though—it's always the same people working. We're not a big MC, and Mark likes to keep it family only.

I forgot to stop for a coffee on my way from the factory job my P.O. got me a few weeks ago, so looks like I'm getting one from the bar. From Olivia.

I consider getting back on the bike and stopping at Dunkin' Donuts down the street. It's a shit idea. Balancing a hot coffee while riding is challenging enough. This exhausted, I'd be lucky if I didn't spill it all over myself.

Might as well suck it up.

I head inside. I'm slammed with bass the second I step inside. I don't get this obsession people have with bass these days. The vocalist *sounds* like Maynard James Keenan, but the band is not Tool. Neither is it A Perfect Circle. It's probably another one of his side projects. I've missed twenty years' worth of music. I've got no fucking clue.

I dig it, but the bass is too much. My bones shake. I scan the club and spot Mark, nodding along to it. I skewer him with a glare he doesn't see.

It's probably a good thing Olivia and I aren't talking, because if I gave her my thoughts on the bass, she'd call me an old man.

I drag my feet to the bar and lean on it. Olivia stands at the other end, making a tray of drinks. The guy sitting across from her says something, and she laughs, throwing her head back.

Jealousy snakes through my ribs, winding around them and yanking hard.

I shouldn't feel this way. For one, it's completely normal for Olivia the bartender to flirt with strangers. That's how she makes her tips. For two, she isn't mine anymore.

But her cheeks turn pink as she laughs, and the guy gives her a wink. I grit my teeth.

She turns my way and I pull my face into a blank slate. The smile drops from her lips when she sees me. She makes her way down anyway, her tongue flicking across her lower lip—something she does when she's nervous. Usually it's accompanied by a lot of talking.

I'm a little relieved that I still affect her. I'd rather make her feel other things when she sees me, though.

"Hey." Her hair is sleek and straight, completely unlike its usual curly chaos. "You look tired," she blurts.

Even though I shouldn't read too much into anything, I'm even more relieved that she's babbling. At least she isn't ignoring me.

I could take this one of two ways. I could turn on the charm, try to win her back. Or I could just be straight with her. Since I'm too tired to flirt, and I doubt it'd work on her anyway, I decide to avoid playing games.

"I am." I nod to the industrial coffee maker. "That thing on?"

"It can be." She gives me a curious look, then turns and starts making a pot. "Late night last night?" Her voice is casual, but I hear what she's really asking. She dumps in coffee grounds, barely measuring. I hope it's because she's eyeballing it, not some sort of evil plot.

I guess no one told her. I kind of want to see how she'd react if I was seeing someone, but that'd be cruel. I want to win her back, not drive her away. So I tell her the truth.

"I took a second job."

She flips on the machine and grabs a mug. Setting it down, she turns and faces me again. "Why?"

I give her a look. "Needed something to occupy my time."

Her lips form an O. "Why not just get Tinder?"

"Tinder?" I wrinkle my brow.

She hits the pause button on the coffeemaker and fills the mug. She holds it out to me, carefully offering me the handle. My fingers brush hers, and heat floods me.

It isn't the coffee.

She pulls away, inspecting her hand as if I spilled coffee on it. Blinking, she shakes her head. "It's a dating app. Well, more like a booty call app."

I lift an eyebrow at her.

"Tinder," she reminds me.

I shake my head, taking a sip of the coffee. Olivia makes the best coffee. I don't know if it's because she blindly throws grounds in and hopes for the best, and some kind of coffee god has blessed her, or she's just had a lot of practice at it. But it's her coffee I crave when I'm tired. When I need comfort.

"Not interested in that." I cock my head at her. Is she really that dense? Or maybe she's testing me. Even when I'm well rested, I'm no match for her. Right now, I don't have a chance in hell.

"So, a second job," she presses.

I nod toward the ceiling, indicating the club house upstairs. "I've gotta get my own place."

"Dorm rules getting you down?" Her eyes dance. For a moment, we're *us* again. Neither of us mentions that this subject is what tripped us in the first place.

"It's small. Don't get me wrong," I add quickly. "It's still bigger than my cell. But I need a place of my own." Especially if Lucy needs my help. I can't babysit above a strip club. I don't mention that because it doesn't look like Olivia knows yet. "I also need my own bike," I say, veering the subject a bit.

She laughs. "Me too. Got pulled over a few weeks ago and just about pissed myself."

"Yeah?"

"Yeah." She looks away, eyes dark.

Without thinking, I reach across the bar and wrap my hand around hers. It's such a pointless gesture. Holding her hand isn't going to make everything that hurts her go away.

But she places her other hand on top of mine, smiling sadly. "At least some good came out of it."

"What do you mean?"

"Finn," she says.

"The cop?" Putting the coffee down, I slip my other hand over hers.

"Yeah. I think he'll come in handy. I mean, I think we can make use of him. He feels guilty. It just sucks for me, because . . ." She shrugs.

"He looks just like Greg," I finish.

She nods, sighing. "So many things would be different if I wasn't broken." Her eyes meet mine for a second, then drop.

I frown. She's not broken, she's brilliant—all of her pieces shine. I want to tell her this, show her what I see. But I can't. I can't use words to change her mind about us. I have to let it be.

She pulls her hands away, and the moment's over. "Want me to top you off?" She nods at my half empty mug.

"Olivia," I begin, frantically gathering the things I want to say, the things she needs to hear.

She fills my mug. "Good luck with the new job," she says. Then she turns, leaving my end of the bar.

It's just as well. It's time for me to get to the door. Still, as I walk away, I glance over my shoulder. I catch her watching me, and hope masses in my chest again, a tumor that just won't die.

There it is, the real reason I took a second job at the factory. Hell, I'm considering picking up extra shifts. I don't sleep anyway. Every time I have a spare second, my mind drifts to her. I can't flush her out of me.

I don't think I ever will.

44

OLIVIA

I turn in a slow circle in the empty living room, my face turned up to the ceiling, eyes closed.

"Are you *sure* you don't want me to leave the living room furniture?" Esther asks.

I stop, wobbling a little. Opening my eyes, I take in the neat stack of boxes—the last of my roommate's belongings. Without her things, the apartment is basically my bedroom.

"Olivia?" She crosses the room, stretches a hand out toward me. "You all right?"

"Yeah." I can't smile, so I don't. I stare around the room again. When I replied to her ad for a roommate, I never thought we'd be friends. We're just so different—Esther bouncing from book to book, me bouncing from boy to boy. Now I can't imagine living apart from her.

"You know we're still gonna see each other, right, silly?" she teases, throwing her arms around me in a hug.

Donny strides into the apartment and grabs a box. "Holy shit, woman. What's in this thing? Rocks?"

She smiles sweetly at him, her arms still around me. "That one's just books."

He shakes his head at her, but warmth shimmers in his eyes. Hoisting the box, he carries it out to the U-Haul.

"Well, if you have to go, at least you're going with him," I mutter.

"Oh, Olivia." She kisses my cheek. "How long has it been since you and Cliff boned?"

I exhale, shoulders tightening.

"Too long, then. You guys will make up. You'll see. Then this place won't be so empty." With hearts practically bouncing in her eyes, she releases me.

"I liked you better when you were bossy." I cross my arms.

"Please. You know I'm right. Cliff loves you," she croons.

"That's the problem."

"Problem? Since when is someone loving you a problem? Cliff would do anything for you. He *has*. If I hadn't already snatched up Donny, I'd be throwing myself at that black-haired beauty."

I snort. "Esther, we both know you never throw yourself at anyone."

"It's so much more fun when they're chasing me." She wiggles her eyebrows. "Seriously, though. Maybe you should let it go."

"I can't." I almost flop down onto the couch before I remember there isn't one anymore.

She sighs. "He made a mistake. He meant well. He really did. Dude would kill for you."

"I know." Now that she technically doesn't live here anymore, I wonder if I can get away with smoking inside. My cigarettes are in my bedroom, though, and I don't want it to look like I'm walking away from her. I lean against a wall.

"You *know*, so what's the problem?" she asks.

"Me. I'm the problem. I don't do relationships for a reason."

"*We've* become pretty tight. You're close with your sister. What's the difference?"

I scoff. "I haven't talked to Lucy since graduation." Which is my own fault. I dig my teeth into my lower lip. "I'm not equipped for any relationship."

"Yet we love you anyway." Esther joins me at the wall, leaning against it so we're face to face. "Why not just let us love you as you are?"

I look away, at the scuffed paint on the wall, at the carpet in bad need of a steaming—anywhere but straight into her eyes. "How do you do it, Es?"

She tilts her head. "How do I do what?"

"Let people in. You and I, we've been through something similar. How did you just bounce back? How are you so . . . optimistic?"

Her lips twist to the side. Several moments pass, her eyes distant as she thinks. "I don't really think of myself as optimistic," she says. "I was a sunny kid, but I guess once you're touched by that kind of darkness, there's no going back. But, there are so many things I have in my life that keep me hopeful: the girls, Donny, even you. You gave me a gift that I didn't even know I needed. I'm not saying murder is always the solution, but . . ." She grins mischievously. "It sure helped me."

She pushes off from the wall and pads over to the stack of boxes. Running her fingers along them, she sighs. "I don't think you can ever beat trauma. It's always going to be part of you. It's a daily battle. You just have to do the best you can. You *are*, Olivia. You're doing the best you can. You're doing enough."

I frown. "Am I? Because I let him walk out into the world. I let him get married. How many other women has he hurt?"

"Are you responsible for what he does?" She twists her ponytail around her hand. "Was I responsible for Josué? Is it my fault he got my sisters, too?"

"No," I tell her, my voice stern. "It's not your fault."

"Then it can't be your fault, either, Olivia."

"At some point, someone has to say enough."

She nods. "I get that. Do what you've gotta do. But don't let go of the people who love you. Let Cliff move in here."

"That's not gonna happen."

"Why not? Don't you deserve some happiness?"

I hug myself. "Why does happiness have to equate shacking up with some guy?"

"'Some guy.'" She scoffs. "Cliff is not just 'some guy.' He's *the* guy. Dude popped out of thin air and dropped into your life. Don't let him get away. I've seen that shitty bartender eyeing him."

I wrinkle my nose at the mention of Trish. There's no way Cliff would ever go for her. She's not his type. Pru, on the other hand, is more his type. Not that I really know what his type is.

"You're way overthinking this," Esther chides. "Just invite him over, bang his brains out, and move on. Makeup sex is the best."

"How would you know? When have you and Donny ever broken up?"

"Sometimes we pretend, just for the makeup sex."

I groan. "Why did I ask?"

"You already know what you want," she says. "You're just afraid to take it."

"I'm not afraid," I balk. "I just don't want to be in a relationship."

"Olivia." Esther laughs. "Have you forgotten that I've lived with you for the past four years? If you're not hung up on Cliff, go grab yourself a one-nighter." She crosses her arms and lifts a dainty eyebrow at me.

Rolling my eyes, I walk out of the living room and into my bedroom.

"Ha! I didn't think so," she calls.

I snatch my cigarettes from the dresser and stalk back into the living room. Lighting up, I eye her, exhaling.

"Yeah, that's what I thought." She lifts her chin in triumph. "You can't move on from Cliff any more than he can move on from you."

"What do you mean?" I ask before I can stop myself.

"Quit kidding yourself, and start living the life that's right in front of you." She grins, eyes all big and all but splooping hearts.

"Bossy, mushy, and nosy," I mutter.

"You know I love you." She throws her arms around me again.

The door opens and Donny sticks his head in. "You good?"

"Yeah, we're about done here." Esther winks at him, not bothering to hide it from me. She hefts a box and inches toward the door. "Think about what I said."

"Not so fast." Donny takes the box from her. "These books are almost too heavy for me. Take that last one. It's light." Kissing the top of her head, he leaves us alone again.

She picks up the last box in the pile, labeled DELICATES. "See you later." Leaning over, she kisses me on the cheek. Then she flounces out of what was our apartment.

I guess now it's mine.

I don't want to stay here. Not alone. Probably not with Cliff. I'm not going to ask him to move in with me, like it'll solve all my issues. I'm going to do what I should've done weeks ago.

I'm going to call Lucy, beg her forgiveness for being the worst sister in the history of the world, and ask if I can move into her spare bedroom.

For now.

45

Instead of calling Lucy, I decide to pop in. It's been almost a month since I've seen her face. I'm kind of surprised she hasn't called or stopped by to yell at me for going AWOL.

When I get to her place, I see Cliff's Screamin' Eagle in her driveway. Making a face, I pull in next to him. I can't seem to shake him lately. He's *always* where I am. I know we work together and we have the same circle of friends, but still. He needs to get his own Lucy.

I'm sweating in these damn skinny jeans. I hurry to the front door and let myself in.

I burst into the air conditioning, the cold air rushing over my hot skin. It's too early for this heat in June, but tell that to New England. There's no such thing as moderation or easing into things here.

Lucy sits on the couch, her legs crossed, a mug of tea in one hand. Tea—like it's thirty degrees out instead of ninety. "Hey," she says, grabbing a throw pillow and plopping it into her lap.

Cliff straightens in his seat next to her, then stands. "I'm gonna step outside." He kisses the top of her head. Then, with barely a nod, he eases past me.

I feel the ghost of his hands on my hips—they way he'd touch me before, when we were *us*. Sometimes he'd put a whole hand on the small of my back. Even though he doesn't touch me, my body leans toward him, just a fraction. He slips out the door and part of me goes with him.

I sit in the seat he just occupied, my body reveling in the heat he left behind.

"What's up?" Lucy asks, leaning forward and setting her mug on the coffee table.

"So much." I grab a throw pillow and hug it. "But mostly I needed to see your face. I can't believe it's been weeks! I suck."

She shakes her head. "It goes both ways. I've been . . . quiet." She looks down.

"You all right?" I study her. She still looks like Lucy, but there's something different. Even though she's still pale from winter, there's a sort of sheen on her skin.

Her mouth opens, then closes. She nods, reaching for the tea. "So what do you need?"

I scoff. "Like I only reach out when I need something. Wow, Luce."

She gives me a look, the one that says she's been around and knows me.

"Okay, fine. I don't really *need* it. I just . . ." I sigh, glancing at the door. I hope Cliff has a nice leisurely smoke. "We broke up."

Her eyebrows shoot upward. "What?! Cliff did *not* mention that."

"Oh." I frown. They looked like they were talking about something serious. My shoulders fall. I'd kinda hoped it was about me, that he misses me as much as I miss him. "Anyway," I say, recovering, "Esther moved in with Donny. I've got to either stay there, maybe find a roommate, or maybe move in with my awesome sister who has a spare bedroom." I give her pearly whites.

"You're so subtle, Livvie." She shakes her head at me.

"It'll only be for a little while," I say quickly. "I just don't really love the idea of living alone."

Her eyes flick toward the front windows.

"I'm not moving in with him just because I don't want to live alone."

"That's my girl," she says, patting my knee. Then she tilts her head to the side. "You're bringing Dio with you, right?"

"Of course." I pull a shocked face. "I'd never leave my baby."

"I figured." She pauses for a moment. "How do you think he'd do with a human baby?" Her green eyes search mine, and her throat works as she swallows.

I glance down at the throw pillow in her lap, and it all comes together. How cranky she was during our trip to Lewisburg. How oddly quiet she's been. How she didn't even bat an eye when Cliff and I told her we were together. I count back through all the times we've been together, how many times I've actually *seen* her drink alcohol.

"Damn," I breathe, gauging her face. I can't tell whether she's excited or devastated. "Does What's-His-Name know?"

She tosses the throw pillow aside, revealing her baby bump. "No," she says with a sigh. "Speaking of daddies, Cliff said yours took off." She pins me with her green eyes. "You okay?"

"We are *so* not avoiding the subject. Also, please don't ever refer to my father as my 'daddy' ever again." I try not to think about the fact that Cliff told Lucy about Mercy. I will *not* get started on what that means. I won't. "When are you going to tell him?"

"I'm not sure I'm going to."

"Lucy," I gasp. "You have to tell him!"

She rolls her eyes. "If I tell him, he's going to want to get married. I already said no once." She places both hands on the bump. "I can't break his heart twice."

"Don't you think you're going to crush his heart when he finds out twenty years from now that you had a secret baby?" I scold.

She blinks at me, eyebrows slightly lifted.

"Yeah, that's right. I can be all big sisterly, too. You *have* to tell him."

"Fine," she says, her tone a little too sweet. "I'll tell him as soon as you tell Cliff you love him and want to move in with him."

I scowl. "Never gonna happen."

"Then I guess we know where we stand." She reaches for her tea, wrapping both hands around the mug. "Pretty soon I won't be able to reach anything," she mutters.

"Do you know what you're carrying around in there?" I glance at her stomach and try not to shudder.

A baby.

Lucy is having a baby.

Thank whatever god is out there it isn't me.

"A girl," she replies, her tone awed, but with an edge to it. "It's like karma."

"What do you mean?"

"I mean now I've got this little girl to keep safe in this world." She winces. "It's so awful."

"It is," I agree, "but I'll kill anyone who so much as looks at her wrong."

"Why is it that I believe you when you say that?" She grins.

The door opens and Cliff strolls in, singing the words to a Silversun Pickups son. He stops when he sees us. He closes the door softly, then stands there, looking a little lost. "All good?" he asks Lucy.

He won't even look at me.

I swallow back tears.

"Yes," she says. "Auntie Livvie is gonna move in here."

I groan. "*No*," I tell her.

"You're not moving in?"

"I'm not an auntie. She can call me Olivia or whatever."

Lucy sighs. "Come on. 'Auntie Livvie and Uncle Cliff' sounds so cute—like a unit."

"Well, we aren't a unit." I stand, avoiding looking at Cliff. It doesn't matter, because it's not like he's looking at me. We're definitely over.

"So when are you moving in?" Lucy asks, standing too.

"I can start bringing stuff by whenever." I inch toward the door. Cliff steps away, giving me a wide berth. "My rent is paid for June, so." Lifting a hand, I give the most awkward wave. Then I seize the door knob. "I'm gonna go start packing." Pulling the door open, I see myself out before either of them can say anything else.

Or *not* say anything at all.

Tears slide down my cheeks as I trudge to my Street Glide. I know I broke up with him, but still. I didn't expect to miss him so much. Especially since we're apparently back to barely speaking.

I ride home, pushing the speed limit, my tears drying in the wind almost as quickly as they fall. When I get home, I'm curling up in bed with Dio and Netflix, so I can cry my eyes out.

46

CLIFF

The second the door closes behind Olivia, Lucy turns on me. She swivels in her seat on the couch, angling her body toward me. Her green eyes skewer me. It's the fiercest I've ever seen her.

I take a step back.

"Uh-ah," she says. "Sit."

I drop into a seat as obediently as if she'd cast some sort of spell on me. She might be ten years younger than me, but Lucy is the matriarch of this family.

"Why didn't you tell me you and Olivia broke up?" she demands.

I scrub at my face with my hands. I don't know how to answer without betraying Olivia. I don't want to shut Lucy out, either. "It wasn't my place," I begin. "Besides, you've got a lot going on. There was also that time you told us you didn't want to hear it." I spread my hands.

She slides me a flat look.

"Well, you did. In this very house. I think we were in the kitchen." I give her a lopsided grin, hoping to lighten the mood.

She sighs. "I *did* say that," she admits. "I'm sorry if I made either of you feel like I don't care. I do. I really, really do." She scoots toward me and takes my hands, hers so small. "It was just all happening so fast: I turned down Benjamin's proposal, I found out I was pregnant, *you* called me ..." She shakes her head.

"Aw, Luce." I pull her into my arms, bearing the weight that's crushing her, if only for a moment. "I never thought that, kid. Never. I wish you came to me sooner. You know you can tell me anything, right?"

"I know," she says through tears. "It just didn't seem real. Like, how the hell could this happen to *me*? I was so careful, Cliff. I had a freakin' IUD. Apparently it shifted, and it'll come out when I give birth."

I hold back a shudder as that particular mental image passes. "Uh, thanks, Luce."

"What? It's just biology."

"Yeah, but it's *your* biology, and I don't wanna think about it."

She sniffles, leaning her forehead against my chest. "Yeah, well, you better get used to it. I want you in that room with me."

I laugh. "Good one."

"I'm serious." She tips her head back, green eyes meeting mine. "I can't tell Benjamin. He'll think I kept this a secret from him and then bolted when he proposed. He'll be so hurt. And there's no way I'm having my mother in there with me."

I rub her back like she's eight again. "You haven't told your parents?"

"God no." She leans into me. "And you and I both know that no matter how much Livvie loves me, she is *not* good at this stuff."

"She ... has a lot of her own stuff," I say carefully.

Lucy lifts her head again and pins me with a hard look. "Spill. Now."

"I can't, Luce. I already betrayed her trust. That's why we broke up."

Straightening, she presses her lips together, evaluating me. A finger bare of nail polish taps her chin. Ever since she came to get me in Lewisburg, she's always had her nails done. Usually that natural look that so many women get. A French manicure or some shit.

"You two are so stubborn," she says. "Have you considered, oh, I don't know, begging her forgiveness and telling her how much you love her?"

"I can't. Honestly, Luce, I think that's most of our problem. I've 'caught feelings,' as you kids say, and Olivia . . ." I trail off, staring out the front window. The Screamin' Eagle sits alone in the driveway behind Lucy's car, Olivia's Street Glide long gone.

"Can't handle it," she finishes for me. "Yeah, Olivia's got abandonment issues. I mean, can you blame her? She's been ditched by everyone who's supposed to care about her. Even my parents aren't the warmest."

I nod. No matter how awful Bastard was, at least I had Ruth reading to me at bedtime and telling me how much she loved me —even if only for a short time.

"That's why she blows through men," Lucy continues. "Olivia likes to be the ditcher. That way, she can't get hurt. She's never had anyone chase her, though." She eyes me, lifting an encouraging eyebrow.

"It's not just that, Luce." I sigh. I can't tell Olivia's secret. Not again. It doesn't matter what my intentions were then or what they are now. I know I was wrong. I won't make the same mistake twice. "She's got a lot of demons, and I can't kill them for her."

"No," she says, "but you can help her take out the trash."

I think of the night she called me, how I slid that tarp under Eli's body and took him apart, piece by piece. I never even questioned whether I *should*. I just did it. Then I held her. I don't know if that'll work this time. "Is it really that simple?" I ask out loud.

"Well, this *is* Olivia we're talking about. Nothing is ever simple with her." Lucy puts her hand over mine and squeezes. "Don't you think it's worth a try, though? Tell her you're sorry. I can see how much you regret whatever you did. Let her see that, too. Then just be there for her. Be whatever she needs. Don't try to push her into anything like getting married or moving in together."

I hold up my hands. "Whoa."

"I'm just saying," she says with a laugh. "Olivia and I are cut from the same cloth. We don't like being pushed into corners. I promise you, if you two get through this, you'll eventually *naturally* find your way into an apartment." She says it so sternly, I chuckle.

"I really thought it was the next natural step."

"I know, but Cliff, you've got to remember, even without all the other stuff, Olivia is twenty-one, and you're thirty-eight."

"Way to rub it in."

She snorts. "I see you, getting your septum pierced and switching up your look."

My hand goes to where my goatee's grown back in. "Yeah, well." I shrug.

"I think the septum suits you," she says, "but dude, there are seventeen years between you. That's a love-child-wide gap."

I glance pointedly at her bump.

"Yeah, yeah. Look, you're just going to have to accept that if you want Olivia bad enough, there are certain challenges you're going to have to overcome. You're going to have to stop freaking out about your biological clock."

"I'm not freaking out," I grumble.

She tilts her head at me. "Dude. *Septum.* Need I say more?"

I glower at her.

"If I didn't know you, if I didn't know the *why* behind the story, I'd say you were going through a midlife crisis." She laughs. It's not an unkind laugh, though.

I still keep my glare going.

"Come on. You joined a motorcycle club. Started dating a woman almost twenty years younger than you. Got a piercing most people get in their teens or twenties. Admit it, Cliff. It *looks* like a midlife crisis." Her lips twitch.

"Go ahead, laugh." I lean back in my seat. "You're right, it does look that way. Even I wondered if what I feel for her is just a phase."

"Is it?" she asks, her eyes soft, her hand still on mine.

"No," I say in nearly a whisper. "This is what I want. The club, Olivia. I can't explain it, but it's exactly where I'm supposed to be. I know it."

"I know." She squeezes me hand. "So, you gonna keep telling me, or are you gonna go fight for her?"

"Right now?"

"I mean, there's no time like the present," she says. "You're just wasting time sitting here with me."

"I'm *not* wasting time," I assure her. "I'm here for *you*, not to dissect my problems."

"Honestly, I feel a lot better now. I've got you and Olivia. Secret's out, so that's not eating at me, either."

"Luce," I say gently, "I'm just throwing this out there: you need to tell him. It'd kill me if Olivia and I parted ways, and I found out down the line that she had my baby and never told me."

Lucy sighs. "She said the same thing."

"About my baby?"

"Calm down," she scolds, a playful edge to her tone. "She didn't say anything about you or your fictional baby. God, you really do have a biological clock ticking."

"What can I say? I've always wanted kids," I admit.

"And I never did, yet here we are." She shakes her head. "How about you take this baby off my hands?"

"Yeah, that'll help me woo Olivia," I joke. I sober and pull her in for another hug. "You've got me, though. And her. Even if we aren't together, we both love you."

"I know. Thank you." She wraps her arms around my waist.

Even though everything else is so upside down, in this moment, I'm more content than I've been in twenty years—I've got my best friend. I kiss the top of Lucy's head and my chest loosens. I hate that I've missed two decades of her life, but I'm so glad to be back. Releasing her, I sit back. I'm relieved to see that she's blinking away tears. She smiles up at me.

"So, Olivia's moving in," I say, lightening the mood. "I'm glad she'll be here with you."

"Me too," Lucy says, "though she'll be more moral support than anything else."

"What do you mean?" I ask.

She chuckles. "Can you really see Olivia changing diapers and waking up in the middle of the night for feedings?"

I do my best to picture it, but I can't. "No," I admit. I try not to feel defeated. If by some miracle we get through this, eventually kids will be another sticking point for us. Because I know I want them, and I know she doesn't. We've never actually talked about it, but I *know* all the same. "Don't worry," I say quickly, determined not to let Lucy pick up on my thoughts. "Uncle Cliff is already looking forward to sleepovers, and I don't mind changing diapers."

She grins. "I love the image I immediately get of you, all tough in your MC leather, changing diapers and singing lullabies."

"I changed yours," I say with a shrug.

"You're gonna be the best uncle ever." She beams at me. "Now get out, and go get that girl." She shoos me off the couch. "I need a nap anyway. Why is pregnancy so exhausting?"

"Enjoy your nap," I say as she lies down. I grab a throw blanket and drape it over her.

"Lock me in?" she slurs, her eyes heavy.

"Of course." I kiss her forehead, then ease out of the house. I lock the door behind me as promised. Then I stand on the porch, between Lucy and my bike. I know what I need to do, but despite all of Lucy's reassurances, I'm fucking terrified that it won't matter what I say or how much I mean it.

I'm floating in the most peaceful black when a knock yanks me up from the deep. I sit up in bed, eyes bleary, heart racing. My hand goes to my gun without me even having to think about it.

The knock sounds again, echoing through the mostly empty apartment. A familiar knock. *Cliff's* knock. I leave the gun on the nightstand.

Tossing the blanket aside, I get out of bed but leave the fan in my room running. The second I get rid of him, I'm going right back to sleep.

I stalk to the front door, not even bothering to check my hair and makeup. I couldn't care less. I yank it open. "What are you doing here?" I demand.

He stands on the front porch, hands tucked into the pockets of his jeans, his head bowed. He looks up, that curtain of hair draping over his shoulder, masking part of his face. It doesn't shield his eyes from me—eyes that scorch me, igniting every nerve in my body, sending a jolt straight to my heart.

Then he says three words, words that should be little but together nearly knock me over: "Can we talk?"

It's the hushed, sorrowful tone that gets me, and I know: he's come to apologize. My heart twists. I want to leap into his arms, drag him into my bedroom, and take his apology with my body. I want his words to soothe every scarred inch of my heart, a sort of salve.

Instead I just move aside, letting him in. I don't want to stand out here in my booty shorts and tight tank top, no bra.

He moves past me, leaving me enveloped in warm cedar and vanilla in his wake. I breathe him in, wishing I could bottle it and spray it on my sheets when he's long gone. I follow him inside, closing the door behind me.

He whistles, a long, low sound. "It's so weird being in here without furniture."

"You wanted to talk?" I coax.

"Is that cool?" Something in his voice tells me that, if I told him to get out, he'd drop the whole thing and go.

I might as well get it over with. We've been in a sort of limbo, one filled with longing glances and lingering touches. "I'd offer you a seat, but the couch's gone."

There's no way I'm bringing him into my bedroom.

I sit in the middle of the living room, where I left my cigarettes and an ashtray. I don't light up. I don't want to encourage him to stay.

He sits across from me, folding his long legs. He looks huge in my living room sans furniture. I want to crawl into his lap, let him wrap his arms around me. Put my nose in the crook of his neck and just breathe.

Neither of us moves.

Dio bounds into the living room, charging Cliff. He leaps into Cliff's lap, nuzzling Cliff's hand and purring.

Cliff grins. "Hey, bud." He rubs Dio's little head, the cat's eyes closing in content.

Shit. Am I really about to toss away the man my cat loves? I've got to remember why I'm doing this. I can't be with him when we're whole books apart, never mind on different pages.

"So," I prompt him.

The cat rolls onto his back and Cliff runs his fingers through the soft fur of his belly. He lifts his head, eyes meeting mine. "Olivia," he begins.

The way he says my name makes things inside me melt. The slight burr to his voice, coupled with the way his lips cradle the syllables like they're something precious. The way he says my name carries everything he feels for me.

My chest throbs.

"I fucked up." His hand continues stroking Dio's belly, the cat still purring in his lap. "I own that." He swallows. "I broke your trust. I don't know if you can ever forgive me, but I'm going to do everything in my power to prove to you that I'll never hurt you like that again."

My eyes burn, my throat open. "You meant well," I say, voice husky. "You don't have to prove anything." *Because I know*, is what I leave unsaid.

His shoulders relax, relief flooding his eyes. I see what he's going to say before he even says it. "I miss you."

I hold up a hand. "Don't."

His face falls. "I don't know what you want me to do, Olivia. Am I supposed to fight for you or walk away?"

I shouldn't have sat down. Rising, I grab my cigarettes and go to the open window. I light up, blowing the smoke out the window, careful to keep it away from my fuzzy orange buddy.

"I miss you," he says again. "Tell me you don't miss me. Tell me it's all in my head."

"Cliff," I say, gritting my teeth together. I need him to stop saying things. Especially the right things.

He moves Dio from his lap and sets him down carefully. Then he stands, too. "Say it."

"I forgive you," I tell him again, "but I can't be with you."

His eyes close as he absorbs the blow. "Why?" he asks, voice strained. His eyes crack open, peering at me through a wince.

"Because I don't know if I can do this." I motion to us with the hand holding my cigarette.

"Because I asked you to move in with me." He tips his head back. "You know we don't have to take that step, right?"

"It's not just that," I tell him. "This isn't really even about us."

Sucking in a deep breath, he bows his head. "I know." His shoulders curl. Nodding, he lifts his head, body loosening. His eyes meet mine. "Olivia," he whispers.

Heat tingles down my spine. I lean toward him, my body deciding before I can. I die out the cigarette. "Yeah?" I take a deep breath, trembling in anticipation of his arms wrapping around me.

But the embrace doesn't come. "I hate this," he says, voice breaking, "but you know I'm still here, right? Whatever you need." He joins me at the window, lighting a cigarette.

I nod. "Besides," I say with a wicked grin, "we're still family."

He sputters, nearly choking on his cigarette. Coughing, he shakes his head. "Way to cut the tension."

"Well, we *are*," I insist. "Not in a related sense, but we're both Lucy's family. Then there's the club. That makes us something, no matter what." I swallow. None of this is coming out right. I meant to lighten things up a little, but now I sound ridiculous. It's the equivalent of the ol' "We can still be friends" spiel.

I don't want to be his friend.

We *aren't* friends.

But we aren't lovers, either.

He smiles, and it warms me to my toes. "I know what you mean." He sucks his lower lip. The gentle warmth burns hotter, flaring at my center.

I look away, grabbing my cigarettes from the window sill. I need something to keep my hands busy before I put them on him. I think of what Esther said about breakup sex. I don't know if Cliff and I could survive that. There are too many feelings involved now, and I don't think we can keep it all separate.

The room grows a few degrees hotter, his eyes on me, burning. I glance up, confirming what I already know.

I need to say something, break this heavy silence. I should tell him to go. If I did, he'd respect my wish. He'd walk away, and neither of us would get hurt. Namely him. I *don't* want to hurt him.

I just can't give him what he needs.

He takes a step toward me, and I move forward, too. He swallows hard. "I meant what I said, Olivia." It's like he's saying my name on purpose, like he knows what it does to me. "I'm not going anywhere. Whatever you need, I'm here."

It's an invitation as much as a promise.

"I just don't want you to get hurt," I whisper.

He smiles sadly. "You don't need to worry about me."

That's how I know it's too late. I've taken his heart, and I've broken it—all without meaning to. I don't know how to mend it. I don't even know how to heal my own.

He opens his arms, and I step into them. He holds me tight against his chest. His heart beats under my ear, a steady, quick pulse that sends my blood rushing, too. He holds me as if that alone could put me back together. It's me that should be comforting him.

Tipping my head back, I gaze into his eyes. I reach up and brush his hair out of his face. I cradle him in my hands. Then, standing on my tiptoes, I press my lips to his. I taste salt and something sweet, the equivalent of spring rain. When a drop lands on my nose, I realize I'm tasting his tears.

What I'm holding is too precious to throw away, yet I'm doing it anyway.

Looping my arms around his neck, I tug him down, toward the floor. He follows me, body fluid, each movement synchronized with mine. Except, when I tug at the hem of his shirt, his arms tighten around me. We lay on our sides, facing each other. He hooks a leg over mine, pulling me even closer—his entire body encasing mine in a hug. His lips nuzzle the top of my head, placing a kiss in the mess of my hair.

His fingers run up and down my arm while his other hand strokes my back. Even though I feel him pressed hard against my thigh, he makes no move to remove my clothes. Confusion floods me, filling me with panic. If we're not having sex, then I don't know what it is I'm supposed to be doing.

It's like he's trying to memorize the way our bodies fit together, which is sweet and all, but I'd rather get naked and then fit everything into place. His heart thumps against my ear, slowing to a steady thrum. I slow with him, melting into him, his warmth making me drowsy. Strangely, it reminds me of curling up in front of a campfire, wrapped in a sweatshirt four sizes too big.

He doesn't say anything, just holds me, his hands never ceasing their trek back and forth across my skin. At some point I fall asleep, then wake curled against his body as he carries me through the dark apartment. He lays me in my bed, settling in next to me, again wrapping his body around me. I drift away again, feeling safer than I've ever felt in my life.

Now it's me committing things to memory.

I fall asleep before I can memorize all of it. For the first time in months, I don't dream about Eli. I don't dream about Greg. I dream of a fireplace, its glow filling a living room I don't recognize. I can't see Cliff but sense his arms around me. It's so warm, so peaceful, I never want to leave.

When I wake up, I roll over, lips parting to tell him. But my bed is empty. Cliff is gone.

A fter leaving Olivia's, I kill some time by riding around. I stop at Cara's diner for coffee—cup after cup. I order food, homefries I usually eat by the plateful. But everything tastes bland. I can't stomach food right now.

I pull into the parking lot of The Wet Mermaid, considering ordering a drink. There's a general ache in my bones, and I could use the warming comfort. It's too early in the day. I've got too much to do, anyway.

Not enough to keep me distracted.

There's no such thing.

I step into the cool, dark interior. The place is utterly silent, none of the usual dancers or hungover hangarounds. The only light comes from underneath the Chapel doors. I stop at the empty bar, remembering my first night here. How I stood in Mark's office, then turned around and saw her. It might as well have been a century ago.

I followed her to the bar, admiring the way her hips swayed even as I tried to figure out how to get out of this without Lucy killing us both. Even then, I was trying to protect her.

She never needed it.

I run my fingers along the wood top of the bar, remembering the way she smirked at me. I try to count how many drinks we had together here, how many nights we closed up together and went upstairs.

I don't even know if I can go up there.

There are only ghosts here now.

"In here, brother," Donny calls from the Chapel doors.

I tear myself from the bar and the past, and go to Church.

"You good?" Donny asks in a low voice as I pass.

Shrugging, I drop into a seat at the table, my attention on my President.

"Where we at with the benefit?" Ravage asks his officers, jumping right in.

I pull my face into a blank mask. I completely forgot about our benefit for rape survivors. We've been discussing it here and there since the vote, but my head's been in the wrong place.

"I figured a strip club isn't the best place for this," Mark says, "so I booked us for the thirteenth at the Polish club."

I pull out my phone to set a reminder. "The thirteenth of July?"

Beer Can frowns at me. "When else?"

"Yeah, dude." Vaughn chuckles. "Today's the sixteenth."

"I know what day it is," I growl.

"It's June, in case you didn't know which month it is," Abraham joins in.

Donny clears his throat. "The thirteenth—that's a Saturday, right?"

"Yeah," Mark says, shooting me a curious look. "We'll have the place for the day. Cliff, you're in charge of raffle prizes." He slides a credit card across the table to me.

"Him?" Abraham sputters.

"I've still got a roll of raffle tickets, so you don't gotta worry about those," Mark continues, ignoring him. "Just hang out after and I'll run you through what we usually do."

I close my fingers around the card. It's an immense responsibility—an honor, even, that they trust me this much—but I don't want it. Even though I technically stayed with Olivia last night, I couldn't sleep. I was too afraid that I'd miss something, that later on I'd regret not staying awake.

I just want to crawl into bed and fall into a black sleep where I don't feel this way. The room upstairs isn't home, though. It already felt temporary. Now it's just a reminder that everything is temporary.

"What are we gonna do about music?" Beer Can asks, yanking me back into the conversation.

"I've got that covered. I can plug into their sound system," Vaughn says.

"You gonna put together a playlist?" Abraham ribs.

"We wanna keep this tasteful," Ravage interjects. "Remember, this is to raise money to end sexual violence. We wanna have a good time, but use your heads, gentlemen. You two can figure out the tunes." He motions to Abraham and Vaughn.

Abraham glowers at Vaughn. "This guy has the worst taste in music," he grumbles.

"If you had it your way," Vaughn says, "we'd be playing Shinedown all the time."

"Shinedown is a great band," Abraham insists.

Vaughn snorts. "Every single song of theirs sounds the same."

"I want everyone reporting in to me," Ravage continues, raising his voice over their chatter. "Moving on." He turns to Donny. "How're Esther and the kids?"

"Real good." Donny's smile lights up his face—the whole room, even. "She moved in with me yesterday. Girls are gonna transition over the next few weeks."

"I'm happy for you, brother," I tell him.

"It's gonna be a process. They're already in counseling but their new social worker wants to ramp it up to two days a week. We're all excited, though. This afternoon, they're coming over for a pizza and game night." He shakes his head, still smiling. "Little one kicked my ass at Monopoly last time."

Everyone at the table laughs.

"That's why you're not Treasurer," Mark says.

"Yeah, that's all right. You got the brains, I got the braun." Donny leans back in his seat.

There's an air of content that hovers around the table. I sit outside it, a stranger. It could be the lack of sleep, but I know that's not it.

It's her.

"Let's get out of here and enjoy the day," Ravage says, adjourning Church. "I want everyone outside in five for a ride. It's been a while since we all rode together."

"All?" Abraham looks around pointedly. "Where's our Prospect?"

Every man at the table looks at me.

"It's her day off," Donny says, rising. "See y'all in five."

I get up, too, and follow him out to the floor. I pluck my pack of cigarettes from inside my cut, intending to use my five minutes smoking in the fresh air—away from the curious eyes of my brothers.

"Cliff," Mark calls after me. "Borrow you for a minute?"

Lighting up, I hang back, letting Mark catch up to me. "Yeah?"

"I wanted to run you through the kinds of prizes we normally get. Remember?" His eyebrows furrow. "You all right, brother?"

"Fine." I exhale and try to look attentive. This benefit is important to me, but I'm having trouble caring about much of anything right now. I feel worse than when I first went inside twenty years ago.

"If you say so. You know I'm here, right? We all are. We love you."

"Yeah," I say, running a hand through my hair.

"All right." He claps me on the shoulder. "So, I've got some unisex River Reapers tees we can throw in. I've also got some Mermaid tees. What do you think about that?"

My eyebrows knit together. It's weird that he's asking *me*. The answer's pretty obvious, anyway. "Well," I drawl, "it's a strip club, which a lot of people feel is derogatory toward women . . ." I trail off.

"We *are* known for how well we treat our dancers," he points out. "No illegal activities. We screen. Everyone gets health insurance and other benefits, even our part-time dancers. Our bouncers keep out the riffraff. Anyone causes any trouble, Donny kicks their teeth in." His eyes meet mine, and he says nothing else. Just waits.

My confusion deepens. "We can always throw the shirts in. If no one wants them, no big loss," I suggest.

He nods. "Sounds good. Cool. Now, a lot of the time, we pick up more masculine prizes, like big ass bottles of booze and techie type things. I've got a feeling we ought to mix it up a little."

"Women like booze," I say, thinking of her and her tequila.

"That they do." He chuckles. "We can do the usual hard liquor, throw in a few bottles of good wine for the ladies who like it. Any other ideas?"

I scoff. "Why are you asking me this? I don't have a clue what women want." I don't mean to sound so dejected, but my voice oozes the hurt I feel deep in my bones. I exhale, finishing my cigarette.

"I was thinking we could raffle off a date with you," he says, eyeing me slyly.

"What?"

"I mean, our girls here *love* you," he continues. "I bet we could pull in a lot of cash from that prize alone."

I start to tell him to fuck off, then clamp my mouth shut. It'd just be a date. Completely harmless, and for a good cause. Then I picture Trish the terrible bartender winning and grimace. Olivia would kill us both.

I kind of love the idea of making her crazy, but I can't play games like that. Besides, I'm not in the mood for dating, even if it's for charity.

"Not gonna happen," I tell him, the words firm.

"Even if we vote on it?" He smirks. He knows he's got me.

"This is bullshit," I grumble.

"It's a good deed." Mark grins and strolls away. "Oh yeah, you're gonna want to go up to Vermont for the booze," he calls over his shoulder.

If I didn't need a ride before, I really do now.

Vermont. Jesus Christ. That's forever away, smack in the middle of winter hippie wonderland. I'm not even a Prospect anymore, yet I keep finding myself on these errands.

At least I've got a month before I have to worry about it.

Outside, my brothers mount. The sound of engines starting reverberates through the street. Even in my terrible mood, the purr thrums through me, waking me up a little. I climb onto the Screamin' Eagle and start it, joining the chorus. The bike hums beneath me, trilling through my limbs until we're one. I give myself over to the machine, shedding my heart and mind, no longer a man.

If riding is a sort of meditation, riding with your club is nirvana.

Ravage takes off, Skid close behind him. One by one we fall into formation. I'm last, the latest patched-in member. Normally Olivia would be last, but she isn't here.

I'm simultaneously relieved and sorry.

We become a pack, effortlessly flowing with each other. I lose myself in the peace of it, letting go of the hurt and emptiness, letting my club fill me up again. It's the reminder I needed, that no matter what, I still have my brothers. I've still got Lucy. I even still have Olivia, even if only to a degree. It'll burn every time I see her, even if I live for the next thousand years.

I had to let her go, though.

So I follow my club down 63, through Middlebury and onto Route 8, into the deep green of Litchfield County. The hot summer air fills my lungs, flushing out the emptiness, reminding me of my purpose.

I need to get my head in the game. This benefit is important, not just to me and my brothers personally, but also to our community. To the Olivias and Lucys disguised among us, carrying a pain that tries to rot. If that means going on a stupid date with someone like Trish, I'll deal.

It's the least I can do.

49

OLIVIA

E ven though I need the money, and even though
Harrison is going to kick my ass for it, I call out on
Monday.

"You too?" Diane groans. "There's something going around.
Keep your germs to yourself." She hangs up as if I'm sending her
a stomach bug through the phone lines.

Just like that, I've got the day to myself. Except I'm not sure it's
healthy to lie on the living room floor any longer. Every so often, I
catch a whiff of *him*, his scent still fresh on the carpet. Then I start
crying again.

So maybe it's time to get up.

I really should take a shower, but my skin and clothes still
smell like him, and I'm not quite ready to let that go. It's cool and
gray out, so I dig through my bedroom until I find one of the
many hoodies I've stolen from him. Except I never gave this one
back. It's one of the River Reapers hoodies, with the MC's Sludge
Specter embroidered on it. I tug it on over my tank top and
leggings, the material soft and warm against my skin.

Just like he was last night.

I take a shaky breath. *Olivia*, I tell myself, *get your shit together.*

I've never let myself get all wrung out over a guy. But then again, I've never met a guy like Cliff. Still, the truth remains: I don't do relationships for a reason. Maybe someday I'll be ready, but Cliff and I are miles away from the same page.

It's for the best.

Really.

I swallow hard. No more crying. I'm afraid to look in the mirror, but I do anyway. There's mascara smudged in tracks down my cheeks. The dark circles under my eyes aren't from makeup. If someone from work saw me, they'd definitely believe I'm sick. I *feel* sick—sick to my soul.

My phone chimes with a text. I glance around my bedroom, but it's nowhere in sight. Grumbling, I tear apart my room again. It's such a mess, I might just toss it all and start fresh at Lucy's.

I find the phone under one of my old textbooks. "What the fuck, Olivia," I mutter, waking it up.

Mark: Need you to work tonight, Prospect.

I scowl. Before I became a Prospect, he at least asked. I send him back a "K" and toss the phone onto my bed. Then I grab the Michael Kors convertible backpack that Lucy's parents bought me for my high school graduation. Before today, it lived in the back of my closet—it was always too small for textbooks. Today it's finally coming in handy.

I slide a paperback inside, along with some cash, my driver's license, and house keys. Then I grab the keys to the Street Glide. I push myself toward the front door, then leave the apartment and my phone behind.

I ride over to Big Y, where I wander the aisles for Gatorade and salty snacks. Then I head over to the deli, my arms full. I step into line behind a blonde with a longer bob. I touch my dark curls. Maybe it's time for something different. I straightened it the other day like I was in high school again. It didn't feel like me, though.

The woman turns, and my breath catches in my throat. It's Cami. Shit.

"Hey," she says with a smile.

She's so *bright*, so sunny. It makes me nauseous. Has Greg already begun dulling her shine? I clutch my purchases to my chest, debating whether to drop it all and bolt.

"Day off?" She eyes my wild hair and hoodie, but doesn't comment on it. Her gaze is warm and kind.

How the hell did he land someone like you? I want to ask. Instead, I swallow. "I thought your family owned a deli."

She laughs. "Caught me. I love their Kalamata olives." She points inside the case. "My family keeps it strictly Italian in their place."

"I won't tell if you won't." I look down pointedly at the chips.

She laughs again, an uplifting peal. Again I wonder how the hell she ended up with Greg.

"I never got your name," she says. "I'm Cami." She starts to hold out her hand, then remembers mine are full. A lovely blush splashes across her cheeks.

Bile races up my throat. I cannot let him ruin her. I *can't*.

"Cami," I say, dumping my items on the counter. "I'm Olivia." I watch her, searching for any sign that she recognizes my name.

She only smiles back, pleasant and sweet as ever.

I take a deep breath. "I need to talk to you."

A line appears between her eyes, but otherwise she's unruffled.

"Can we go outside?" I push my items toward the deli clerk.

"Sure." She steps away from the counter.

"We'll be back in five," I tell the guy behind the counter. "I want a turkey and American cheese sandwich when I get back. Don't be a dick about the mayo."

I leave him blinking.

I step into the cool gray afternoon. "Shouldn't you be at work?" I ask her.

"Caught me again." She glances around as if the parking lot of full of spies. "I'm playing hooky."

We have too much in common, Cami and me.

Except she's cute where I'm crude, soft where I'm stoic. Maybe Greg hasn't hurt her because she's everything a straight man with a pulse could possibly want. Cami is family material, the cornerstone of a wife, picket fence, and babies.

"Cami, I need to tell you something, and I need you to take me seriously," I say, fishing in my backpack for cigarettes. Damn. It's the one thing I forgot.

The line between her eyebrows deepens.

"I haven't been honest with you. I came to your house because my ex lives there."

"Oh," she says with a shrug. "Okay."

"*Lives*," I say, enunciating the S. "Greg is my ex. Your husband."

She draws back from me. "What the hell is this?"

"You need to listen. Your husband raped me when we were dating. I don't want him to hurt you, too." I bite my lip. There might've been a more tactful way to tell her. I don't know.

Cami's face moves through a variety of expressions. Her frown turns to shocked disbelief, lips parted, eyes narrowed. Then her upper lip curls, the line reappearing between her eyebrows. She shakes her head and backs away from me, looking for somewhere to sit. There aren't any benches, so she settles for leaning against the brick exterior of the grocery store. "What do you want?" she gasps.

"I don't want anything from you. I just want you to know the truth." I pause for a moment. "I don't work here. I'm a social worker." I fish in the backpack for pen and paper. All I find is a tube of lipstick and the paperback I tucked in earlier. I rip out a blank page and scrawl my cell on it. "I want you to call me if you ever need me. I'm also a Prospect for the River Reapers. They're my family, so they'd help you as a favor to me."

I hold out the paper and she takes it with a shaking hand.

"That's all. I'm sorry to bother you." I leave her outside and go back in. I really want that sandwich and, as long as it doesn't rain, I plan on spending my afternoon reading on the bridge.

I can't control Greg, and I'm not responsible for his actions, but knowing that Cami has my number restores some of my power.

He can try to hurt her.

He'll have to get through me first.

50

CLIFF

I drag myself through my shift at the factory on Monday, then stop in at Lucy's real quick. I'm supposed to be at the strip club, but family first.

Besides, Mark texted me a heads up that he had Olivia come in tonight, and I'm not ready to see her. Not yet.

Lucy sits at her kitchen table. At least, it was a table. The thing is covered in her usual lesson planning paraphernalia, plus about a dozen parenting books and magazines. Smack in the center of it all is a snapshot from her latest ultrasound this morning.

I pluck the sonogram and squint at it. "Totally my niece. She's got my chin."

"How the hell can you tell?" She swats at me with a notebook. "And don't jinx her. No girl needs that chin."

"What do you mean?" I cup my chin, where a goatee's finally grown in. "It's a strong chin."

"Technically you're her cousin. The chances of her getting that chin are pretty slim."

"Damn, Luce." I pull up a seat at the table. "You're brutal when you're pregnant."

"*Second* cousin," she says sweetly. She takes the sonogram from me and studies it. "I really can't tell what the hell she looks like."

"You didn't want one of those 3D ultrasounds?" I ask, sifting through the pile of magazines.

She slides me a wry look. "Those cost money."

I avoid her gaze. "Why not call Benjamin? I'm sure he'd love to have one done."

She swats me with the notebook again, this time harder.

I hold up my hands. "What? You have to tell him."

"I know that," she grumbles. "How about you? Did you talk to Olivia?"

I thumb through a magazine, then peer at an article about DIY baby food like it's the most fascinating thing I've ever read.

"I can't hear you," Lucy chides.

"I did." I put the magazine down and lift my eyes to hers.

"And?"

"And I let her go."

"You what?!" Her voice is so shrill, it nearly pierces my eardrums. "That's *not* the pep talk I gave you."

"Yeah, well." I spread my hands. "It's what had to be done. Just like you calling Benjamin."

She rolls her eyes. "I'm going to."

"No time like the present." I grin, then duck out of the way before she can hit me. Likely with a rolled up magazine.

"Well, since you're here. Moral support and all." She sighs and sifts through all the shit on the table. "Can you call my phone? Oh, never mind. It's over on the counter."

I start to get up to grab it for her, but she pushes her chair back and stands, exposing her very round, very pregnant belly. "Damn, Luce. Where'd that thing come from?"

I wince. No walking that back now. I expect her to beat me over the head with one of her hefty parenting books, but she nods.

"I know, right? All this time, I had this little belly, and then pop! Mom says that's how she was with me. She called it the Seventh Month Pop. Must run in the family," Lucy says, retrieving her phone.

"Just wait 'til I get knocked up," I joke.

Leaning against the counter, she rolls her eyes at me. "Okay," she says, taking a deep breath. "Here goes." She taps on her phone, then brings it to her ear. "It's ringing," she whispers.

"That's what phones do."

She gives me the tiniest crack of a smile before biting her lip. Shaking her head, she pulls the phone from her ear, then hits the speaker button. "Sorry," she mouths.

I don't really know how me hearing Benjamin's side of the conversation is more supportive, but I give her a thumbs up anyway.

The ringing stops as he answers. "Lucy?" His voice is both crisp and warm, the kind of baritone you hear in commercials.

"Ben," she says, as if they're old friends who haven't spoken in years. "Hey."

"Lucy," he says again. "Wow. I . . . did not expect to hear from you."

Flicking a glance at me, she laughs nervously. "I was *not* planning on making this call."

I wince and shake my head at her. "Easy," I mouth.

She throws up her hands and pulls a bewildered face while mouthing "I don't know what I'm doing."

"So," Ben says, drawing out the word. "What's up?"

I get up and join her at the counter, taking her free hand in mine. I give her a nod.

She blows out a slow breath. "Ben, I don't know how to tell you this. I should've called you a long time ago."

Silence on his end.

She surges forward. "I'm pregnant."

The silence deepens.

Her eyes rocket to mine, widening as panic sets in. "Ben?"

He draws a breath. "So, you're seeing someone else?"

"No," she says quickly. "I haven't been seeing anyone. I'm seven months, Ben."

He gasps.

"It's yours," she says, as if that wasn't already clear. Her hand squeezes mine, her knuckles going white.

For just a moment, I wonder if this is the kind of thing Olivia should be handling, instead of me. I'm way out of my element here. Then again, Olivia isn't much better at this than I am. We're both blunt, her more so than me.

Ben's silence stretches. Lucy and I stare at her phone, but the seconds keep ticking. The call hasn't been dropped.

"You still there?" she asks, a hesitant near-whisper.

"Yeah," he replies, with more than a hint of bitterness. "You're telling me this now? When did you find out?"

She clears her throat. "January."

"January." He laughs, but it's derisive. "You've known this whole time?"

"Yes." Her teeth dig into her lower lip. She glances at me again, tears pooling in her green eyes. "I wasn't sure what I wanted to do yet."

"Jesus." The TV commercial cool guy is gone. There's no more warmth to his voice.

My stomach clenches. I take the phone from her, holding it near her as I guide her back into a chair. Her hands shake in her lap.

"Didn't you think I might like a say, too?" he demands.

I grit my teeth to keep my mouth shut. This is Lucy's show, not mine.

"Look, I know this isn't ideal—"

"Ideal?" He laughs, the cruel sharpness cutting through my cousin. Her mouth drops open, then she presses her lips together.

"I asked you to marry me. You didn't want a family! And now you're telling me you're pregnant?"

"I know," she says with a sigh. "It's not the way either of us wanted things."

"Then why didn't you just get an abortion?" he snaps.

Lucy flinches, her face going from white to red. "I didn't," she seethes, "so let's not even go there, okay?"

"So what, you want to get married now?" he fires back.

"No," she begins, but he talks over her again.

"Because that ain't happening. I proposed and you not only shot me down, but also cut me loose. Now *I'm* seeing someone else, someone who wants a future with me. I can't—" His voice drops. "I can't do this with *you*."

"Well, it's happening, buddy," she says, taking the words right out of my mouth.

Despite the situation, I grin. I give her an encouraging nod.

"I thought I'd give you a chance to get to know your daughter," she continues.

"As far as I'm concerned, I don't have a daughter. Is that clear?"

My free hand—the one that isn't holding her phone—clenches into a fist. "Hey asshole," I growl. "This is your responsibility, too."

"Not seeing anyone, huh?" Ben says. I can practically hear the smirk in his voice.

Lucy sighs. "That's Cliff—my cousin."

"The one who went to prison for murder? Jesus Christ, Lucy. What's happened to you?"

She inhales, nostrils flaring. Her face changes, morphing from a viper ready to strike to a teacher whose patience is being tested. "Look, I know this is a lot to swallow, but does it really have to get ugly? Because you know I can just take you to court for child support. Then you'll never have the chance to get to know her."

"Do whatever you want." He hangs up.

I set her phone down with more control than I feel.

"That went well," she says.

I squeeze her shoulder. "Sorry, kid."

"For the record, he knows the truth about you. He's just hurt."

"Darling, you should know by now I don't give a fuck what anyone thinks. What I do care about is *you*. You okay?"

"I want booze." She pouts. "And, inexplicably, a cigarette. How the hell am I supposed to cope with my emotions like this?"

A lump appears in her belly, stretching her stomach before relaxing.

I blink. "Was that . . . ?"

"A foot, yes." She holds out her hand for mine. "Want to feel?"

I hesitate, caught somewhere between curious and a little freaked out. "Dude. There's a *person* in there." Our eyes meet and we laugh.

"Crazy, right?"

"Yeah." I give her my hand, and she places it on the left of her belly. A second later, I feel my second cousin slash niece kick. I laugh in wonder. "Holy shit, Luce."

"I keep thinking eventually this'll get old, but you know what? I'm awed every single time," she says.

"Fuck Ben and his crisp Apple commercial voice," I say. "You're gonna be a great mom. But let me know if you want me to kick his ass."

"Let me think about it. My current hormone level says 'hell yeah,' but I think I prefer you outside of prison."

"Just say the word." I glance at the time on the microwave.

"You have to go." It isn't a question.

"I'm actually a little late," I admit.

"Go!" She shoos me. "Seriously, I'll be fine. I'm gonna eat a pint of Ben & Jerry's and read one of these books."

"Trade you. Olivia's working tonight."

"The two of you." She shakes her head. "Although, this thing would make a great club bouncer," she says, running a hand over her taut belly.

"It's beautiful." I kiss the top of her head. "You're beautiful. Ben's a dick. Text me if you need anything."

"Thanks," she says. She reaches for a book. "Now go. I've got a lot of reading to do."

I leave her to it.

Music pulses through the strip club, shaking my bones. I just want to go home and collapse into bed, but I could really use the money. For a Monday night, the place is pretty packed.

Vaughn raps his hands on the bar, announcing his arrival.

"How's my favorite hacker?" I shout to him over the music and chatter.

"Let's be real, Olivia," he says with a lopsided grin. "I'm the only hacker you know."

I shrug, and my bra strap tugs uncomfortably on my neck. It's not even a bra. Technically, it's a sports bra, and it's at least two sizes too small.

It's laundry day.

"What can I get you?" I ask, dropping any pretense of banter. I'm tired. Cliff is going to walk in here any minute. I want to go home.

"I'll take a Salem Tourist." He folds his hands neatly.

"That's not even a thing." I put a hand on my hip.

He makes a big show of looking around, then he pulls out a stack of ones. "The customer's always right." His grin is crooked, his flop of brown hair hanging in his eyes. "Salem Tourist, please."

"Can we not do the whole torture the Prospect thing tonight?" I plead, resting my elbows on the bar.

His brown eyes soften. "I'm sorry. I heard you and Red Dog split."

"Thanks." Relief washes over me. Before Lucy, I never had any siblings. I always imagined having a brother would be a pain in my ass. But Vaughn is usually the target of good-natured club torture. He's sweet. He's also not bad looking, with a slight dimple in his chin and deep set eyes that make him always look sleepy. Despite the guys' jokes about him living in his mother's basement, he's usually tied down.

Not tonight, by the looks of it.

I perk up a little. Maybe all I need is to toss myself back into the game. I lean toward him. "Empty arm tonight, huh?"

"Yeah," he says, leaning in, his eyes intent on mine. His lips are a little thin—certainly not as luscious as Cliff's—but I can make it work. He cracks another crooked smile. "There isn't a drink in my hand."

I glare at him. "There's *no* such thing as a Salem Tourist!"

"There are plenty of them in October." He wiggles his eyebrows.

"I'm done with you," I tell him. I pour him a rum and Coke—his usual. "Begone," I say, shooing him.

Giving me one last grin, he takes his drink and saunters away.

I lean against the bar, closing my eyes for a moment. The clink of glasses, catcalls, and shitty music are far from peaceful. I open my eyes. Cliff sits on a barstool in front of me, his big hands splayed on the bar.

"Hey," he drawls, and my knees go weak.

I swallow, then deliver my line: "What can I get you?"

"I stopped by Lucy's. I saw our niece."

The way he says "*our* niece" turns my whole body to water. I cling to the bar for dear life. "Oh? How is our little Bunny?" The "our" slips from my lips. His eyes latch onto mine, liquid heat pooling in them. I press my knees together.

"We're calling her Bunny?" The corner of his mouth quirks.

We.

He still says it so naturally.

I know it's for the best that we're not together. I *know* that. But my whole body still aches in his presence. His scent, his voice, his body only a few feet from me—it's all too much.

With trembling hands, I pour myself a shot of tequila. "Well, she's a bun in the oven," I explain, my voice stronger than I feel. I pour him a shot, too, even though he never drinks on the job. I set them both down on the bar.

"I'm good," he says. "Last time we had tequila . . ." He lets the memory hang in the air.

I down both shots. "So how *is* Bunny?" I ask, changing the subject.

His face falls, but he recovers. His expression smoothes over. Must be a perk of two decades in prison. "She's great. I can't tell nose from foot, but I think she's human." His eyes meet mine. "Lucy called Ben."

Shit. I've been so preoccupied with my own stuff, I've barely been there for Lucy. My head's been tuned in to the Trauma Channel 24/7, and even though I know that's normal, that I have to work through it, *Lucy* doesn't know that. She has no idea why I've been MIA.

I take out my phone to send her a text. There's already a text —from a number I don't recognize.

Unknown: Olivia, it's Cami. I need your help.

I freeze, blood pounding in my ears, drowning out the music. I hoped she'd never need my number, that maybe he really had changed. That she'd write off my warning as the rambling of a pissed off ex, because *her* Greg was different.

I hoped, because once upon a time, he *was* different. Before that night, he gave me my first kiss, cupping my chin as we stood in front of our high school, blocking the paths of other students. I barely noticed. Snow fell in light flakes, dusting our shoulders. I barely noticed that, either. My entire existence was wrapped in that moment, suspended in his arms as his lips touched mine.

There was so much gentleness in him, so much good. It's hard to reconcile the boy I fell for with the monster underneath all that. Sometimes I flip back through those memories and they're sweet and warm—as long as I don't think about the rest.

"You okay?" Cliff asks.

I come hurtling back into the present, gasping for breath in the cloying strip club. The air tastes hot, thick with sweat, lust, and stale beer. My hands shake as I tuck my phone into my back pocket. "I've got a work emergency," I say, bending and grabbing my things from under the bar. "I've got to go. Tell Mark I'm sorry."

With barely a look at Cliff, I fly out from behind the bar. My clumsy fingers text Cami back, letting her know I'm on my way. I don't ask for her address because it's burned into my memory.

I burst into the warm night. Sweat dots my hairline, gathers on my upper lip. Yet there's an icy core spreading from under my ribs, pitting in my stomach and making my limbs slow. I try to start the Street Glide but keep fucking up. It's like I've suddenly forgotten how to ride.

Instead of visualizing the steps, I keep seeing the skull-shaped candle he made me, the one that burned down and left a piece of heart-shaped jade. Except I'd forgotten about it, and returned to my room to find my table on fire.

That should've been my first sign.

I carried that heart around with me when he was deployed, pretending it was his and that, as long as I didn't lose it, no harm would come to him. I was so busy worrying about him, I never saw him coming at me.

I won't make that mistake again. This time, I'm making sure he never has the chance to hurt anyone again.

But first, I need my gun.

52

I stop at the apartment first, sidestepping Dio on my way to the bedroom. He lets out the most pitiful meow I've ever heard. I pause for a moment and take him in my arms, holding him tight against my chest while I rub his ribs.

Then I kiss his little head and put him down.

I grab the gun, cursing myself for leaving it behind the one day I need it. I glance around one last time. I tell myself it's because I'm making sure there's nothing else I might need. Truth is, this might be the last time I stand in this living room.

I shake the thought away. I can't think about what might happen or whether I'll be here tomorrow. I need to focus on right now, take it all one move at a time.

As I ride toward Greg's, I try to draft a plan. With Eli, I didn't have time to plan. I just knew I wanted a gun, just in case. Now I have the gun. Now I have to get Cami.

I have no idea what I'm walking into.

I don't know if the text was the last thing she managed to do —if she's alive or dead. For all I know, Greg is long gone and she's alone, palms full of fragments of herself. I have no idea how to put her back together. *I've* barely healed.

One thing at a time.

I turn onto Bad Lane. Dim light oozes from the streetlights, a sickly yellow. In the tainted light, the teal paint on the house turns a dark red—the color of drying blood. A single light shines through a window upstairs, a beacon: *Come to me, Olivia.*

I shiver, the Street Slide purring beneath me. I glance at the Thunderbird in the driveway, then back at the light. My stomach goes oily. He is here, and I can't shake the feeling that he's inside, waiting for me.

No one moves in the window. From what I remember, there were three vehicles listed under his name in the town tax records database. Cami's Jetta is gone. There's a good chance I might've jumped the gun, that she might not even be home.

I pull out my phone and call the number she texted me from. It rings and rings, then goes to a cheery voicemail.

"You've reached Cami. Please leave a message . . ."

I hang up, the sweetness of her voice scraping my stomach. She might not be able to answer. I text her, letting her know I'm here but I don't know where she is. Then I stare up at the house.

My phone vibrates in my hand.

Cami: I'm here. He's gone.

I chew the inside of my cheek. As much as I want to help her, I do want to see my cat again. I hate to put her under the microscope—especially in this situation—but I'd hate even more to be dead.

Olivia: Where's your car?

Cami: ???

I bite into my cheek again, drawing blood. Anyone can text a confused string of question marks. My phone dings again, twice in a row.

Cami: It's really me. He's really gone. IDK where my car is.

Attached is a selfie, except this Cami looks nothing like the woman I ran into at IGA the other day. She's sporting a black eye, her cheek and lips puffy and streaked with blood. Her mascara runs into the blood, turning it black.

But I'm still suspicious.

Olivia: Don't you have three cars?

Cami: JFC. Is this the Spanish inquisition? I need your help. I think he broke ribs and . . . I'm losing a lot of blood. I'm pregnant . . . or I was.

My heart jolts into my throat, shame twisting my stomach. I never wanted to be the kind of woman who doubts another woman.

Olivia: Hold on.

Besides, if he is still here, I've got my gun. I have nothing to fear.

Pocketing the phone, I turn off the Street Glide. For a moment, I consider texting Cliff, letting him know where I am. He'd come roaring in here, and right now Cami doesn't need any more angry men in her space.

It occurs to me that I'm going to have to get her to the hospital. I'm sure as hell not driving that Thunderbird.

"One thing at a time," I whisper to myself.

I climb the steps to the porch, gun drawn. My heartbeat echoes in my ears, the blood pounding through my veins. It's not a helpful adrenaline. Nausea roils my stomach. Seeing Cami's selfie was one thing. I'm not sure I'm ready to see the real thing, to dive into the destruction headfirst. I'm not sure I'm strong enough.

I step inside, leaving the door open behind me. The light from the street barely illuminates the pitch black living room. I'm pretty sure it's a living room, anyway. I stand in the darkness, letting my eyes adjust. When they're as adjusted as they're going to get, I ease forward, carefully feeling my way. My fingers brush the soft microfiber of a couch, the hard edge of what I think is a coffee table.

"Cami?" I call out.

A floorboard creaks over my head, and a groan floats down to me. I swallow. I'm not ready. I cannot do this—even if it means being there for another woman. I bend over, eyes bleary, stomach spasming. I put my numb hands on my knees, suck in a few breaths.

I have to do this. I *have* to.

As if moving through a dream, I float toward a set of stairs. I climb them on legs I barely feel, the soles of my feet pins and needles. Light from an open door floods the hallway and top half of the stairs.

"Cami?" I call again as I crest them.

A thud answers, the sound of someone hitting the floor. I dart into the room, tucking the gun into its holster.

Light flashes, flooding my eyes. I stop short, holding my hands up. Even still, I can't see a thing. "What is that?" I grunt, squeezing my eyes shut. "Cami?"

He laughs, the sound surrounding me.

My knees turn to water. I wrench the gun out, pointing it as I turn in a circle. The strobe light continues flashing, the room only visible in short spurts: a dresser here; a desk there; a half-empty closet, its doors standing open. It's then that I know.

She's long gone.

"The selfie," I sputter.

He laughs again. "You like that? I do all our album covers."

"The voicemail," I say, taking on a pleading tone that I don't intend. I think I'm in shock.

"She left her phone," he says dully. His words come from all directions of the room. Between the stereo sound and the strobe light, I can't tell whether he's even in the room with me.

I've got to focus. I latch onto his words.

"She left you?" I stand still and fixate on a belt on the floor. It disappears then pops back into place, but it's something to anchor myself.

"This morning. I woke up and she was gone. I got served, too." he says.

At least she took me seriously.

I exhale, replay his words, examining them for hints, something I can use. "I'm guessing that's my fault."

"Why did you tell Cami I raped you?" he asks. "I've changed, Olivia. Really. I'm sorry for how I treated you. I really am." His voice breaks.

"You wanna kill the strobe light?" It's too hard to think with it on. More than that, I need to see his face. I need to know what I'm dealing with.

"Put your gun down," he says, "and go into the hall."

I hesitate. He's got almost a hundred pounds on me, and years of combat training and experience. I can't just walk away from my only advantage.

I can't exactly see to shoot him, either.

I don't trust him, but I need him to trust me if I'm going to get out of here alive. Bending forward slightly, I place my gun on the carpeted floor. "Gun's down."

"Come into the hall."

I step out of the strobe light room and emerge into the hall. "Here I am."

I tense, expecting him to grab me. Instead, another door

opens, normal light spilling into the hall. Greg stands framed in the bedroom doorway, red hair disheveled, gray eyes hooded. Before, I'd run my eyes over his perfectly straight nose, the red strands falling into his eyes, and I'd think, *I am the luckiest girl alive.* Now I take in his bare chest, the dark jeans slung low on his hips, and I suppress a shudder. Part of me still thinks he's gorgeous. The rest of me swallows bile.

"I'm sorry," he says.

"I know." My hands dangle at my sides, empty and feather light without the gun. The lie burns my tongue. I want to break his nose and turn and run. I want to go back into the strobe room, grab my gun, and put as many holes in him before he puts his hands on me. Instead I just stand, waiting.

"She left me," he repeats, rubbing his hands over his face.

He blames me. That's the version of Greg I'm dealing with— the one who never takes any personal responsibility. I adjust my plan. I no longer have to save Cami. I've got to save myself.

"I hoped she would." I keep my tone conversational.

"What?" He frowns at me.

I lick my dry lips, but my tongue might as well be made of sandpaper. I inhale, taking in oxygen to steady my voice. "I meant what I said at the strip club. I know you're sorry, and it's all in the past anyway."

His frown deepens.

"When I saw you at the club," I say, taking a step forward, "everything came rushing back: our first kiss, driving around in your Thunderbird." I don't smile. I'm afraid my face is too wooden. "Except now, we're all grown up. You've made something of yourself. You've changed. You said so yourself. You just had to go and get married, though."

"She left," he says again, incredulous. "I got served with divorce papers."

I nod. "I had to get her out of the way."

"Out of the way?"

I take another step forward, stomach clenching. Keeping my eyes on his, I nod again. "She's a nice girl, but come on. A teacher?" I scoff. "You can do better."

"Thought you were with that biker." He crosses his arms.

"Past tense." I wave a hand. "He's long gone, too." I swallow bile. Instead of looking at the monster in front of me, I summon the image of Cliff sitting at the bar, his eyebrow quirking as he turned down my tequila.

Greg makes a contemplative sound in his throat. "I guess we're both single, then."

"Guess so." The two shots I downed earlier churn in my stomach, sour. It's not the alcohol. Cold sweat spikes at the back of my neck. I move my feet forward until I stand in the doorway with him. "Guess we're alone, too."

"Guess so," he says, leaning against the frame. Up close, his bloodshot eyes skim up and down my body. "You look good, Olivia." He pronounces the syllables of my name slowly.

I flick a glance into the bedroom. An Oh Vile Eye poster takes up most of the wall space above the bed. I plant my feet firm against the floor, holding back the shudder crawling up my spine. "So do you," I tell him, leaning in.

He lifts a hand, then freezes midair.

"It's okay," I say, my skin crawling.

His hand remains suspended between us. "You told Cami I raped you."

My entire body goes still. "Yes."

"I didn't rape you," he insists. "I just wanted to spice things up a little. Make it fun. The first time was so bad."

I force myself to chuckle. "It's hard to have good sex in a car."

He laughs, nodding. "Right? I just wanted to be good for you."

My stomach roils. "I get it." The fear pitted in my belly swishes around, boiling into a hard rage.

"I should've been more gentle," he continues. "I'm sorry. But I *didn't* rape you."

Retorts crowd in my mouth, my fingers twitching at my sides. I said no, and he did everything he wanted to do to me anyway. It didn't matter what I wanted. Red tinges my vision. I gather my rage, focusing it. I place my hands on his shoulders. "What if you could do it all over?" I croon, backing him into the room.

His lips furl at the corners, bright blue eyes burning red. "I'd do so many things differently."

"Me too," I tell him. "This time, I promise I'll be a lot more fun." My lips spread, exposing my teeth. I push him toward the bed, then shove him onto his back. I undress, forcing myself to go slow and meet his eyes. I use my fury to fuel me, to keep my fingers from going numb as I strip down. His eyes track my movements, wild and wide, anticipation cresting in them. "Don't just lie there," I command. "Take your clothes off."

He obeys, shedding his jeans. They drop to the floor in a coil. I look through him, into the past, all the times he hurt me playing on a reel.

"Got a condom?" I ask as I approach the bed. I want to touch as little of him as possible.

He reaches for the nightstand, opening a drawer and rummaging through it. I wonder how many times he's brought another woman into his wife's bed. How many women he's sent running out of his life.

It ends here, I promise myself.

At least Cami got out.

The knowledge spurs me on as he unrolls a condom onto himself. My stomach clenches again, and I wish I had more tequila. He rolls onto his back again and spreads his legs in an invitation.

"Let's have some fun," he says.

I kneel on the bed, then crawl into position. Settling my weight onto him, I place my hands on his shoulders, pinning him down. He might have a hundred pounds on me, but now I have what he took from me.

Men are so easy to control, so vulnerable once you get them onto their backs. His eyes flutter as I move, lulling him. They get heavy, heavier, the lids snapping shut. He goes lax, letting me do all the work.

Good.

I shift my weight, moving my hands to his neck, wrapping my fingers around his throat.

I put all of my weight into my hands.

His eyes fly open, alarm pinging through them.

"I'm just having fun," I assure him, clenching. He thrashes underneath me, shock flickering in his eyes. His hands scrabble at mine, but it's too late. "Was it like this?" I ask him. His face goes red, then purple, then marbles. "Was it like this?" I ask again.

The floorboards in the hall squeak under someone's feet, but I don't look away. I'm done making mistakes tonight.

53

CLIFF

A work emergency—I don't buy it. I give Olivia a head start, then follow her. I keep several cars between us, just in case she really is going to work. I don't want her to think I'm some kind of lovesick stalker, like Eli. But when she turns onto her street, I know for sure.

This has nothing to do with work.

I hang back, shutting off my headlight, and watch her go inside. Barely two minutes pass and she's already mounting her bike again. Nothing is different—that I can see, anyway. Still, my gut tells me something is wrong.

So I follow her again.

She takes Spring Street, then turns onto Mallane Lane. I continue by. I don't need to alarm her. She's too focused, body bent forward, shoulders hunched.

Who lives on Mallane?

I circle back down Spring Street, taking a left onto Springdale Avenue. It's the only other way to access Mallane. By the time I turn onto the road, her Street Glide is already cooling down in front of a teal house.

My pulse jumps in my throat.

I consider calling Ravage or even Donny, but there's a slim chance this could be a client's house. Even if it isn't, I don't want to step all over her toes again. That's how we ended up here, this place where we don't talk and I follow her like some kind of creep.

I thumb the throttle, two seconds away from leaving Mallane. This isn't healthy. Olivia's a grown woman. She can take care of herself. Bright white light flashes through a window—a strobe light. I frown. Nothing is adding up.

Something crashes on the second floor, shattering as it hits hard wood. It's then I know. I have to get inside.

I shut off the bike and vault over it, barely registering whether I've moved the kickstand into place. My bike, the street, everything fades away, my focus solely on the house. I lunge up the steps, yank open the screen door. The front door is unlocked. I push it open and race inside, careening through a dark living room. The dim light from the street highlights a framed photo: Greg with his wild red hair, and a happy blonde bride.

This must be Greg's house.

"Was it like this?" Olivia screams from upstairs. Fear and anger sharpen her words.

I fly up the steps, hands tingling, fingers twitching for something to latch onto. I'm going to kill him, if she doesn't first.

I hit the landing and turn toward the sound of her voice. Bright light spills from a bedroom into the hall, a beacon guiding me to her. I take a step toward the door. The blood pounding through my veins pulses even in my eyes. My vision becomes a tunnel of red.

Something thumps—a boot against a footboard, a desperate thrashing.

"Was it like this?" Olivia screams again, pain and fury breaking her voice.

My heart rockets into my throat. He's got her, and he'll kill her if I don't get there now. I close the distance to the door and stop dead in the hall when I see her in the bedroom.

Olivia straddles Greg on the bed, their clothing littering the floor in a trail behind them. Her hands wrap around her neck, all of her weight pressed into his throat. He jerks underneath her, but she's got him in the most vulnerable position a man can ever be in.

I stare as his face turns purple.

"What it like this?" she shrieks again, tears running down her cheeks. She lets out a howl of pain, a growl of vengeance—a battle cry. Even as I gape in shock, my chest aches for her.

I'll never know what it's like to have survived what she survived, but I do know what it's like to reach your limit, when you've had enough. When the phoenix of your broken soul rises, morphing into a beast whose thirst must be slaked. The evil of a man like Greg awakens that beast, and it won't be stopped until its thirst is slaked.

So I watch her take her power back, both shock and awe warring in my heart. I should probably stop her, but I don't.

54

I feel the oxygen draining from his body, his life evaporating with it.

I hold pressure until he goes slack and the life drains from his eyes. Finally, he goes limp inside me. I keep squeezing. No mistakes.

"Olivia," Cliff calls from the doorway.

I flinch, my whole body tensing.

"He's gone," he says.

I start shaking, cold sweat washing over me. He wasn't supposed to see this. As if in a dream, I roll off the bed and start dressing, afraid to look at Cliff. Afraid of what I'll find in his eyes.

I find my phone in the pocket of the hoodie I stole from Cliff. The tremor in my hands makes my fingers loose and clumsy. I drop it.

"Who do you need me to call?" Cliff asks, taking my shoulders. He turns me until our eyes connect.

I see nothing in his.

His brown eyes are dark but void of emotion, as if he's stuffing down his revulsion.

Pressure squeezes my chest and lungs. I try to draw in a

breath, but I can't. I glance at the Oh Vile Eye poster again, my eyes dropping to the form on the bed. I can't look at Cliff.

He wasn't supposed to see this.

Already there are dark red handprints on Greg's pale throat. They're so much smaller than the ones he left on me, yet I already feel the darkness lifting.

He's no longer loose in the world.

Cami is safe.

I am safe.

"Olivia?" Cliff asks, my name emotionless on his lips.

Part of him will always see me in this bed with the man who hurt me, chin lifted, lips spread in a vile smile. Part of him will always be disgusted.

My shoulders are free of the weight I've been carrying, but at what cost?

55

CLIFF

I need a cigarette.

Scratch that—I need a drink.

There is no substance on Earth strong enough to wipe out the last five minutes.

Olivia and I stand a room apart. She's still trying to pick up her phone, still looking everywhere but at me. She is both the earthquake and the house about to cave into the abyss.

I call her name again, but she doesn't hear me. I am out of my element. I thought I saw some fucked up things in the pen, but this . . .

This is something else.

My chest tightens. I've only walked beside her for a short time. I can only imagine what led her to this moment. My only regret is that I don't get to kill him, too.

She stands staring down at her phone, trembling, teeth chattering. Calling her name isn't working, so I do the only other thing I can think of.

I go to her.

"I'm going to put my arms around you, okay?"

She stares and stares, eyes wide and round, shivering. I don't think she's even *here*. She's years ago, before I met her. Her chest rises and falls with rapid breaths.

I hesitate. I don't want to do any more damage.

Tears make their way down her cheeks in crooked paths. Yet she doesn't blink. She doesn't even wipe them away.

She's not having a flashback. She's having a panic attack.

I hope I'm right.

"Olivia," I say gently. "I'm going to hug you."

In the pen, I had nothing but time. I read a lot, mostly old magazines. There were a few medical magazines. I read once that a hug stops the panic response.

I put my arms around her, slowly at first. "I've got you," I tell her. She feels so small, a wisp of a woman. I hold her tight, cradling her into my chest.

It's like hugging a brick, she's so tense.

"I've got you," I say again.

Minute by minute, she relaxes. I cup the back of her head with a hand, holding her as if I can just transfer warmth into her. Her tears collect on my shirt, hot and wet against my skin, a salve to the splitting sensation in my chest.

My woman, my warrior. She is a hero just for surviving, just for walking around with such awful memories.

I hold her, pressing safety into her. I don't know if she can ever believe that, not even now, but I try anyway.

She lifts her head, wet curls sticking to her face. I pull them off.

"You're here," she whispers.

"I'm here." I smooth her hair, my hands suddenly too big, too clumsy.

"You're *still* here." She bows her head. "You weren't supposed to see that."

The ache in my chest deepens. I cup her chin, lift her face until our eyes meet. "Why not?"

She says nothing, just closes her eyes in one long blink.

"Do you think I think less of you now?" I ask.

Those eyes—twin mesmerizing pools of pained determination, as untouchable and beautiful as fog. She blinks again, wet lashes brushing her cheeks. "Do you?" she whispers.

I stroke her cheek. "I could never."

I don't tell her about the shock that kept me rooted in the doorway. I can't. I won't, ever. A shock born not out of revulsion but awe. I witnessed a reclaiming, a rebirth.

Once again, I'm too stunned by her to put my thoughts into words. Because she is stunning, a force that ripped me off my sleeping feet, shook me up, then plunked me down in the eye of her storm.

"You shouldn't be here," she says, heart slamming in her chest against mine. "You have to go." She glances around the room, eyes panicked once more.

"Go? Why would I go?"

She gives me a look. "I can't keep getting you into trouble."

"You *are* trouble," I admit, hugging her tighter. "But you're the kind worth getting into."

She scoffs and puts her hands on my chest. "You *have* to go." She pushes, but I keep my feet firmly planted.

"I'm not going anywhere," I say, and it feels like more, like a promise.

A promise she won't let me keep.

"I thought I didn't need you," she says, more to herself. "Yet here you are, just in time to pull me back."

I close my burning eyes. I can't keep not saying the things I want to say.

Before I met Olivia, I told myself only an irrational woman could fall for me. After I met her, I feared I'd just fallen in love with the idea of her, imprinting on the first woman I saw on the outs. Now I know the truth: I am irrationally in love with her, because love is not rational.

"I'll never stop reaching for you," I tell her, opening my eyes.

"Every time you step too close to the edge, I'll be here, pulling you back into the light."

She nods, once. Then she pulls away, bending down to collect her phone and hoodie.

My hoodie.

I can't help it. I grin. "So *that's* where that went."

She presses her lips together, nodding.

"I'm gonna need that back, you know," I tease.

"Here," she says softly, holding it out to me.

The smile falls from my lips. "I was kidding. You can keep it." I try to press it into her hands, but she shakes her head.

"It's not right for me to keep it." She drops it into my arms and turns away. "I need a shower," she says, her back to me. "Can you call the guys, get the cleanup started?"

"Of course."

I watch her go. When I hear the water running, I pull the hoodie on over my head. As the fabric passes my face, I inhale her scent, the dark jasmine with saffron and pepper. I tug it on all the way, breathing in, ignoring the ache in my chest.

Then I make the call.

OLIVIA

I n the bathroom, I find bars of Dove soap stacked neatly in a closet, still in their boxes. Everything has come down to one question: What do I do next? Find soap. Turn on the shower. Get in. Don't think. Just breathe.

Hot water beads pummel me, beating the soreness from my muscles. If nothing else, the motherfucker had great taste in shower heads. I cup the bar of soap in one hand and trace the Dove logo with the pad of a finger. It's so smooth, so perfect, I almost hate to use it.

But there's no way in hell I'm using one of his.

I jerk my mind back to the soap. It's the sensitive formula, the kind that doesn't suck all the moisture from skin. Not what I normally use, but it's soap. It's clean. It's here.

I didn't think to look for a washcloth, and I don't really want any of his things touching me, anyway. So I wash up with the bar. The point isn't really to get clean, anyway. The point is to . . .

I don't know.

Wash away what I just did?

I didn't even know I was capable of such a thing.

Of killing a man with just my hands.

I touch my neck. The skin itches where he put his hands all those years ago. I sweep the bar of soap up and down, as if I can erase his fingerprints. Prints that are long gone from my skin but still burning deep into my psyche.

Surely this time he would've finished the job.

I should feel lucky to be alive. Instead, my limbs are heavy and numb, the panic attack still pumping through my veins.

"It's over," I whisper to myself. My hands shake. The bar of soap slips from my grasp and hits the tile. It slides down the length of the tub and stops at the top of the drain.

My feet remain planted, reluctant to move.

I need to. But terror keeps me rooted in place. It pumps through my blood, washing out the certainty that carried me through this house. It replaces it with useless frozen adrenaline, a sludge in my veins.

"Olivia?" Cliff calls through the door. He taps on it with his knuckles. "You good?"

I open my mouth—or at least, I *want* to. I hug myself, shuddering.

The bathroom door creaks open. "Olivia?"

Only the rush of water answers him.

It mixes with my tears, disguises the sludge I'm emptying through my eyes. Even though the water is hot enough to turn my skin pink, I shiver. I see Greg beneath me, then above me. I touch my neck again, expecting to find his hands there.

My hands pat my bare neck.

"I'm coming in," Cliff says. "Okay?"

I find my voice. "I'm good."

"You sure?" he calls over the rush of water.

"Positive." I reach for the bar of soap and close my fingers around it.

"I'm right outside—if you need me." The door creaks again, but I don't hear it click shut. Instead I hear his retreating steps, slow and hesitant.

I close my eyes and take a deep breath. Then I straighten. Clutching the soap, I wash again. And again. And again. I scrub my skin until the water runs cold and I can't feel anything with the tips of my pruned fingers.

I'll probably regret washing my hair with bar soap, but at least I don't smell like him anymore.

Stepping out, I take the soap with me. I hold it in my palm. I can't leave it in the shower, and I probably shouldn't put it in the trash. I stand dripping on the bath mat, a new cold fear taking hold.

I've fucked up.

Majorly.

My DNA is all over this shower now. My hair is probably halfway down the drain, just waiting for some CSI cop to find it.

I tug my clothes on, not bothering to towel off. Not that it'd matter.

"Cliff?" I call, darting into the hall.

"Yeah." He strides out of the bedroom, his frame blocking my line of vision inside.

"You *really* should go," I urge. "This is my mess."

I just have no idea how I'm going to clean it up.

He comes to me, hands stroking my shoulders. "Take a deep breath."

"But—"

"Breathe, baby, breathe."

I do as he says, my chest hitching when I realize he called me his baby. Hot tears prick my eyes. "You c-can't go to jail for me."

"No one is going to jail. Okay?"

I swallow. "I shouldn't have taken a shower."

He tips his chin to the side. "Huh?"

"My DNA," I say, hair dripping water down my back. "It's all over the place now."

"We're going to figure this out," he promises.

"Did you call Donny?" I shiver. All I had on under that hoodie was a tank top.

"Yes." He runs his hands up and down my arms. "They'll be here soon." Releasing me, he grips the hem of his hoodie and yanks it off over his head. "Here."

"But it's yours," I insist.

"Right now you need it more than I do." He slips it on over my head. I lift my arms, letting him dress me like a child. Warmth floods my chest. Normally, I'd never let anyone do this for me. But with Cliff, it feels nice. His scent mixed with mine engulfs me, grounding me.

I stand there for a moment, wanting to say something but not knowing exactly what to say. I can't tell him he smells good. I shove my hands into the pocket and my fingers brush against my phone. "I'll call Finn," I blurt.

He lifts a thick brow. "The brother?" He runs a hand through his hair.

I clasp my hands together inside the pocket, resisting the urge to touch his hair, too.

"I don't know, Olivia. That doesn't seem like a good idea."

"He owes me."

"He already helped us with Esther," he says. "Somehow I don't think he's going to go for covering up his brother's . . ." He trails off.

"You can say it." I lick my lips. "Murder."

"That's not what I was going to say."

"That's what I did, isn't it?" I pull my hands from the pocket and cross my arms.

"It was self-defense." His eyes burn into mine. "Self-defense," he repeats.

"It's still murder." I hold my hands out in front of me. They're clean, they smell like Dove, but they're completely different. These hands are an extension of me. "Anyway," I continue, "Finn feels guilty for what his brother did. Somehow I don't think he's going to have a problem with . . . this." I flick my gaze toward the bedroom. I still can't see, not with Cliff standing in front of me.

But I can imagine.

"I don't know." Cliff tips his head back, hands tugging at his hair. "Can we really trust him? That's his brother, regardless of how he feels about what happened."

"He'll help. I know he will. You should leave, just in case."

He cups my shoulders again. "I already told you: I'm not going anywhere. I meant that." He works his fingers into the knots that have formed in my muscles. "We'll figure it out."

A knock echoes through the house—the front door.

My eyes snap to his.

"I think it's the guys," he whispers. Ushering me away from the bedroom, he draws a gun.

As we pass the guest room, I pause. "I'm right behind you," I whisper. I duck into the room and grope around the floor until I find my gun. I grip the handle, the cool metal a comfort on my skin.

When I emerge back into the hall, Cliff is halfway down the stairs. I follow him, my hands shaking with every thump of my heart. I can't imagine who could be knocking at the door. A concerned neighbor would just call the police.

Unless it *is* the police.

I mentally retrace the evening to see if I made too much noise. I don't remember.

Cliff rounds the bottom of the stairs and heads toward the front door, his feet light on the hardwood floor. He stands to the side of the door, angling this way and that to see through the blinds without moving them.

A phone vibrates, making me jump.

"It's mine," he whispers. With one hand pointing the gun at the door, he reaches into the pocket of his cut. "Donny?" he says in a low, hoarse voice.

Donny says something on the other line. Cliff's worried glance toward me tells me all I need to know.

Whoever's on the other side of that door is *not* on our side.

Cliff hangs up and nods toward the kitchen. I stalk through the dark behind him. He crouches down by the fridge. I kneel next to him.

"Donny and Stixx took the van," he whispers, so low and slow, I strain to make out his words. "They drove past. There are cops out front."

I squeeze my eyes shut. "Shit."

"Donny can create a distraction, but you know Naugy. Plenty of cops. There's no guarantee these guys'll take the bait."

I take a deep, shuddering breath. "I have to call Finn."

In the dim light, I see him nod. "Do it. Quick."

I creep back to the stairs, phone already pressed to my ear. As it rings, I sneak back up.

"Officer Byrne," he answers.

"It's Olivia," I whisper, easing up another step.

"Olivia? Is everything all right?"

"More or less." I reach the midpoint. "I need you to call off the checkup at Greg's."

"What checkup?" he asks, wary.

"Please," I beg. "You told me if I ever need anything, to call you. *Please.*"

Knuckles pound at the front door. "Police," a deep voice booms.

"Olivia, are you at my brother's house?" Finn hisses.

"Please," I ask again.

"Is my—sIs he alive?"

"Finn," I snap. "We don't have time for this. If those cops come inside, I'm telling them about your involvement in the Figueroa case."

He blows out a long breath. "Fine."

A second later, the line goes dead.

I sink, my knees rubber. I cling to the railing, but my fingers slip. I sit down hard. That's two felonies I've committed.

All in one night.

The pounding on the front door stops. A moment later, Cliff comes to the foot of the stairs.

"They're gone," he says.

I lean my head against the wall. "I did *not* think this through."

"He didn't give you much of a choice," he says, bitter.

"If I had half a brain, I would've made 'Cami' call or FaceTime me. I should've known." I cross my arms on my knees and put my head down.

"Cami?" he asks.

With my head still buried, I tell him about the emergency text.

"How could you have known?" The stairs creak under Cliff's weight. A second later, I feel the step I'm sitting on shift as he sits beside me. I lift my head. He puts an arm around me, drawing me close.

"Why am I such a psycho magnet?" I mutter.

"I hope that doesn't include me."

My lips part and my mind fumbles for a response. "No" is what I should say, but this night has flipped me upside down. Thankfully, his phone rings again.

"Yeah," he answers. "See you in five." Hanging up, he turns back to me. "Cops are gone. The guys are coming around back." He stands and holds his hands out to me. "Come on."

I let him take my hands, so warm around my cold fingers. He helps me up, bearing my weight as if it were nothing.

Someday, I might be able to shed everything weighing me down.

If we can get through this night.

I open the back door and motion Donny and Stixx inside, tipping my chin at them as they pass.

Donny stands in the center of the kitchen, appraising Olivia. "Is he dead?"

She lifts her chin. "Very."

"Good." Giving her a one-armed hug, he kisses her temple.

Even though I know the gesture is platonic—brotherly, even —my stomach clenches. I want to be the one holding her, kissing away the memories of this night.

But she won't let me.

I'm working on accepting that. I am. I'll keep my promise no matter what, no matter how much the knife in my ribs twists, prodding at my heart with its hot tip. When I look at Olivia, all I see is the future I never thought I could have.

And I won't.

It's a huge disappointment, one that'll take some time getting used to. But I will.

"We're down two rapists this week," Donny says, rubbing his hands together. "If that's our regular quota, we're doing great."

Stixx nods, snickering.

Olivia gives him a long sideway glance.

But I know Stixx's story from the table—something she isn't privy to as a Prospect. Before I knew, Stixx creeped me out a little. Still does. Just in a different way.

"I don't know what you two did to get rid of our friends, but it worked," Donny continues.

"Oh, just a little extortion," Olivia mutters.

"You're coming along nicely, Prospect." Stixx turns to Donny. "Tell them the plan." He leans on the balls of his feet, his grin ghoulish in the dim light.

Donny claps Stixx's shoulder. "Stixx still doesn't think the river's good enough for the dead rockstar." He eyes Olivia's dripping hair. "And my guess is there's enough DNA in here to send both of you straight to the pen. So—"

"We're gonna burn this fucker down," Stixx finishes for him.

Olivia and I exchange glances.

"Don't you think it'll be a little suspicious if the house the cops tried to check up on suddenly goes up in flames?" I ask.

Stixx shrugs. "Dead Red up there was a smoker. Shit happens."

"You two leave the staging to me," Donny says, his face hardening into his businesslike Enforcer mask.

"And leave the burning to me. It's time to add another X."

Someday I'm going to ask him where the other X came from. Then I'm gonna ask Ravage where *Stixx* came from. "What do you want us to do?" I ask instead.

"You two"—Donny forks his fingers, pointing at us—"get on those bikes and get the fuck outta here." He shakes his head. "No doubt those cops will remember there were two motorcycles parked out front. If they didn't already run your plates."

Olivia sinks her teeth into her lower lip. "Fuck."

"Yeah, that's why you leave this shit to the table," Donny says. He doesn't sound annoyed, though.

"I'm gonna have to call Finn again," she mutters. "He'll make that part go away."

"We'll have to vote on it," I say.

She shoots me a sharp look.

I sigh. "That's how shit works, Olivia."

"He's right," Donny agrees. "You wanna be in this club, you gotta play by our rules. We'll take it to the table. For now, *out*." He turns away from both of us, effectively dismissing us.

"Come on," I tell her. I put my hand at the small of her back and escort her to the back door. I open it, gesturing for her to go first.

She steps into the dark, hands shoved into the pocket of my hoodie. Her hoodie. Our hoodie?

The hoodie.

As soon as I fall into step beside her, I light two cigarettes and hand her one—our old ritual. "You all right?" I ask, keeping my voice low.

"I'm better now," she admits. "He's actually dead to me. I don't have to worry about running into him anymore. I don't have to wonder when it'll end. It's over." She takes a long drag, then blows out a stream of smoke into the starry sky.

We walk in silence for a moment, her words hanging in the air. When she says nothing else, I realize she needs me to press. "But?"

She sighs. "Part of me is still under him."

I stop walking. "I'm not even gonna pretend to know how you feel." I steel my nerves. "There's something you need to know."

She takes in a sharp breath and stops, too. "Cliff, don't."

I hold up my hands, palms out. "Not that." I swallow. "You've been carrying this around since before we met. I don't think you realize that you survived. You made it through everything he put you through, everything he did to you. And every day, you keep surviving, even with that hell replaying in your head." I touch her temple. "You survived, Olivia."

She nods. "I know. For the most part. You know, for someone who took all kinds of classes about helping children through this kind of thing, it never occurred to me that I probably need therapy." Ducking her head, she lowers her voice to a whisper. "Bear with me, Cliff." She presses her forehead against my chest.

I drop my cigarette and wrap my arms around her. "Don't worry about me. Just do what you've gotta do." I bow my head. Inhaling the scent of her damp hair, I kiss the top of her head. She wraps her arms around my waist.

We stand in the street like that for another moment. Then I let go. "Let's go home."

OLIVIA

I don't want to be alone, so Cliff follows me to Lucy's. It's late enough that my sister should be sleeping, but when I unlock her front door and we step inside, she appears at the top of the stairs. I glance at Cliff behind me. He gives me an encouraging nod.

So I sit at my sister's table and, with Cliff by my side and a bottle of vodka in front of me, I tell Lucy almost everything. I tell her how Greg filled me with lies, coercing or all out forcing me into doing what he wanted. I tell her about Cami, and how I know that she left him.

While I tell her, she sits with her hands cupping her belly, tears sliding down her cheeks.

After I finish, she gets up and hugs me tight. "I could kill him," she whispers in my ear.

"He's dead to me," I whisper back.

At some point, Cliff slips out. I fall asleep in Lucy's bed while she strokes my hair and promises she'll help me find a good trauma-certified therapist. I don't dream of anything. The upper level of Greg's house burns, reducing him to ashes. The fire department rules it an accident. The town runs a PSA for safely putting out cigarettes.

Cami stays gone.

THE NEXT FEW weeks fly by. I start therapy, three times a week with a woman named Eva. At first, I don't want to talk about Greg. Talking about it isn't painful—it makes me physically ill. Slowly, I become more comfortable with her. I find my voice. I tell my story.

I just don't tell her the ending I wrote for myself.

When I tell her the alternate ending, she sits up straighter. "Do you feel like that robs you of closure?" she asks.

"Nah. I already said everything I needed to say to his face."

Because Eva likes to dig into everything, we talk about everything. Especially Bree and Mercy. Apparently, being taken from your neglectful mother is a trauma in and of itself.

"You've been moving from trauma to trauma," she says, "without ever really processing it."

So I do the work. It's grueling. I practice a lot of avoidance, sometimes threatening to skip appointments until Lucy or Cliff force me to go.

"I feel like this *is* helping," I tell Eva one evening. "The flashbacks are happening less. They're even less intense. But they still come."

"They might always come. They'll knock you down sometimes, too."

I frown. "Gee, that's inspiring."

"You know what to do with them now, Olivia," she says. "You've got all the tools you need so you can keep fighting. Except this time, you're properly equipped."

Over the weeks, I graduate: from three times a week to twice a week, then once a week.

Eventually, we get around to Cliff.

"He's not trauma," I hedge when she asks me about him at the beginning of a session. "I don't need to talk about him."

She tips her head slightly. "Why not?"

"Because some people come into your life for a season. They serve a purpose for you, and then you move on."

"And what was Cliff's purpose in your life?" she asks.

I lick my dry lips. "He reminded me that I'm alive, that I can feel things. For more than one night, even."

"What kind of things?"

I narrow my eyes at her. "I meant alive. Cared for. Whatever. He makes me happy—*made* me happy."

A ghost of a smile touches her lips. "We'll come back to him."

There's nothing to come back to. Cliff finally moved out of the club house, and I moved in with Lucy. I haven't been to his place. I don't trust myself alone with him. I've hurt him enough. If he's ever going to move on, he doesn't need me in his space.

We run into each other at Lucy's and at work, and we're both friendly enough. But I see the hurt in his eyes, feel the pang in my own chest. He's even invited me over a few times for pizza and beer with Esther and Donny, but I always say no.

"Don't you think he wouldn't ask if he didn't want you part of his life?" Eva asks. "Like it or not, you're going to be around each other."

"So why torture him any more than necessary?" I uncross my legs and re-cross them in the opposite direction, tugging the hoodie down into place. After that night, it came home with me again. I tried giving it back—again—but he wouldn't take it.

"Do you mean torture yourself?" Eva smiles gently.

I blink in response.

"It's okay if you have feelings for him."

Licking my lips, I put both feet flat on the floor. "I don't. I mean, I *care* about him. He's one of the best people I've ever met. He's . . ." I shrug. "He's my cousin. Ish."

She purses her lips. A moment later, she resumes her questions, switching topics. "How are things with your adoptive parents?"

"Strained. They know Mercy's out, that I'm upset they never told me where he was. Honestly," I say with a shrug, "they never *felt* like my parents. I love them, because they gave me a safe place and they gave me Lucy. But . . ." I pull my lips to the side, thinking. "I never completely connected with them, and I can't forgive them for ignoring what happened to Lucy."

Eva waits.

"My adoptive father's brother" I say, lip curling, "sexually abused Lucy for years. *Years*, and they did nothing. They had a feeling something fucked up was happening, yet they didn't stop him. Cliff did."

"He did?" She flips through her notes.

"He did twenty years for murder," I say. "He *killed* for Lucy. He'd kill for me." I look down at the patterned carpet, bright swirls of brown, red, and orange that sort of look like leaves. "Yet he knows who I am, and he respects that. He lets me do what I need to do."

She nods. "Sounds like a good friend."

I frown at the word. "He's not my friend . . ."

"Then what is he?"

I blow curls out of my face. "He's, I don't know, *mine*." I cross my legs again, shake my foot.

"You've made excellent progress, Olivia," she says, glancing at her watch. "How do you feel about graduating again? To every other week?"

"Sure." I put my hands inside the pocket of the hoodie. Even though it's July and hot as balls outside, Eva's office is always cold.

"You should be really proud of yourself," she tells me. "Not everyone with PTSD progresses like this. Do you remember what I told you when you first started?"

I think about it. "Something about transforming after PTSD." I twirl my finger in the air, trying to remember the term.

"Post-traumatic growth," she reminds me. "I told you I had a feeling you might experience something like that. And I think you have. You've transcended what was done to you and grown quite a bit. You're a strong person, Olivia. There's no reason why you shouldn't be happy in life."

"Thanks," I say, the only thing I can think of. I take the appointment card she writes for me and tuck it into my phone case. Then I stand and head out of her office. Before I go back outside, I take the hoodie off, tying it around my waist. Then I stride out into the sunlit evening, her words replaying in my head.

I *am* happy—that's what I should've said. I have a great job that lets me help people. I have another job that lets me get bikers drunk. Any day now, I'm going to be an aunt—which is really fucking weird, but also kind of cool. I don't have flashbacks all the time anymore. Actually, most of the time I don't even think about Greg or Mercy or Bree—until I walk into Eva's office.

As I ride through downtown Naugatuck, I tell myself these things as if I were still standing in her office, telling *her*.

I *am* happy.

Yet.

She's right that I'm trying to spare myself just as much as I'm trying to spare Cliff. Because on the nights he stops by Lucy's to check in on her and Bunny, I get the sense that he's also checking on me. His eyes always linger on me just a beat too long. Lately, instead of hurt, I see pride in them. It's like he can see how well I'm doing just by the way I look.

What he doesn't see is how I crank up the AC in my bedroom so I can sleep in his hoodie. Nor does he see how I hesitate to wash it, every single time, even though it no longer smells like him at all. He doesn't see how I try to flirt with guys at The Wet

Mermaid but never let it go further than that because they're not him.

One of my goals with Eva is to start dating again—eventually. Not now. Maybe not even during the scope of my treatment. Someday, though.

Not Cliff, either.

It wouldn't be fair to do that to him. Not when he's doing so well for himself.

I pull into the parking lot of The Wet Mermaid, groaning when I see how packed the place is. Mark begged me to work tonight and, being a Prospect, it's not like I can say no. I did tell him he had to wait 'til I got out of therapy. Not that I told him I'm in therapy. Only Lucy and Cliff know.

I take off my helmet and shake out my curls. Straightening my cut, I walk inside holding my head high.

I head toward the bar, but Trish stops me.

"Ravage said to have you meet him in Chapel."

"Did he say why?" I make an effort not to wrinkle my nose at her. Ever since I broke up with Cliff, she's been circling him. I couldn't blame him if he decided to go out with her. She's gorgeous—even if she doesn't know bottom shelf from top.

"You know they don't tell me anything, hon." She grabs a beer glass and pours a Guinness for one of our regulars.

Taking a deep breath, I stride toward Chapel. When I get to the doors, I throw them open. Might as well go in with a bang if he's going to fire me. I could just tell him the real reason why I cut down on my shifts, but I don't want to. It's bad enough the whole damn MC knows *why* I'm in therapy. I don't want them feeling any more sorry for me than they already do.

Even if it comes from a good place.

Because, damn it, I'm a Prospect and a woman. I have to work twice as hard to earn my way in because MCs rarely patch in women. We can be their queens but we can't go to battle next to them. I don't want to play the PTSD card. I want to prove myself.

So I throw the doors open with all the bravado I can muster, bursting into the room. I open my mouth to shout "Boom, baby!" but clamp my lips shut.

The whole club sits at the table.

I close the doors shut behind me. "You wanted to see me?" I ask Ravage, trying not to look at anyone else.

"A while back," he drawls, "we took a vote. We decided to take the club in a different direction—fighting for people who can't fight for themselves." He rubs the back of his neck, ducking his head.

I daresay he looks a little embarrassed. My eyes widen.

"We made a serious mistake, thinking you were one of those people. I want to apologize for stepping on your toes." His blue eyes meet mine, sincere and bright.

"Um, thanks," I manage, shocked. Ravage is *not* the kind of guy who ever apologizes. "Was that why you called me in?"

I need a cold bottle of water, and I need to text Lucy. She's never met Ravage, but I have to share this moment with *someone*. Since it can't be Cliff, it's gotta be her.

He shakes his head. "We just took another vote. If we're gonna do this—fighting for people who've been hurt, people who no one else wants to help—we're gonna need you."

I swallow the lump in my throat. "Well, you've got me. You make the battle plans, I'll pour the drinks. I know my place, Pres."

"Jesus, kid. Didn't you hear me? We *need* you, as in, all in. Especially if you're gonna keep making executive decisions. You might as well be in on the loop." He sighs, but the men around the table chuckle.

I run a finger along the PROSPECT patch on my cut. "Are you saying what I think you're saying?"

Beer Can slides a RIVER REAPERS front patch and the rocker across the table to me. "Take those goddamn PROSPECT patches off," he says with a grin.

Tears sting my eyes. I blink them away, sinking into a seat. "Shit," I breathe. "I thought I was getting fired for being late."

Mark shakes his head at me. "We love you, Olivia. We'd never cut you loose, kid. C'mon."

"We want to help other survivors," Ravage says, his voice gruffer than usual. "Who better than another survivor to guide us through?"

"Well," I say, fisting the patches. My eyes meet Cliff's across the table for a fraction of a second, then I look away before I burn. "Let's hope we don't have to help anyone else."

"Let's hope," Ravage agrees. "We're still running that benefit. Beer Can. Where're we at with the ride? Everyone pay their fees?"

"Speaking of," Mark says, grinning at me. "I'm gonna need forty bucks from you."

"No problem." I can't help but smile back. My first benefit ride as a patched-in River Reaper will be in support of survivors like me. It's fitting.

Maybe next time I see Eva, I can tell her I'm happy and mean it.

I fight the smile tugging at my lips, and lose. From across the table, I tip my chin at Olivia in congratulations. The vote was unanimous. I don't think she realizes how much everyone at this table loves her.

"Prizes, brother," Mark prods.

Stixx nudges me.

I shoot him a glance, wondering if he's really going to make us all spell his name with three Xs, now that he's burned his third house down. Someday I'm going to ask him where the second X came from.

"Yoo-hoo," he says, ice blue eyes boring into me.

"Right." I pull out the notepad I've been using to keep track.

Vaughn lets out a long, low whistle. "Wow. I knew you were old, but damn, dude. Even Ravage uses the notes app in his phone."

"Watch it," our President barks.

Olivia's lips twitch.

I yank my attention back to the paper. "Booze—check. I got a bottle of SoCo that's almost as big as a two liter bottle of Pepsi." I glance around the table for approval. The men nod—most of them, anyway. Stixx makes a gagging sound. "What?"

He shudders. "I hate Southern Comfort. It's too damn sweet."

"Not if you add cranberry juice and a lime wedge to it," Olivia says.

I bite back a smile. It's so good having her at this table. "I'll throw cranberry juice and limes in, then." She lifts her eyes to mine and my heart stops—actually stops—beating for a moment.

Mark clears his throat. "What else you get?"

I check my list, still not convinced this isn't some sort of test. "A few more big ass bottles." I rattle them off. "Jack, Cuervo, a giant skull of vodka . . . I grabbed a whole bunch of nippers. Stopped at Target and got some toys—the kids should be able to win cool shit, too. And then there's that other thing we talked about," I grumble.

"All set to go?" Mark asks.

"What other thing?" Olivia glances from me to Mark.

"It's nothing." I cross my arms.

"Just a date with our stud," Vaughn crows.

"And Trish'll probably be your highest bidder." Donny cackles.

I glare at them all.

Ravage taps the gavel on the table. "All right, already. So the teal deer of the thing—I'm not that old after all, am I?—is prizes are all set. Let's nail down the final details for the ride, then get the fuck outta here."

We spend the next half hour or so hashing it out, then Ravage dismisses us.

"I want you all here Saturday at 7:45 a.m.," he reminds us as we file out.

Vaughn groans, the sound stretching into a yawn. "I know it's for a good cause and all, but damn. There goes my beauty sleep."

"It wasn't working for you, anyway," Beer Can says as he moves past him.

I yawn, too. "It sure as fuck isn't working for me."

"Work running you ragged?" Olivia asks, her tone casual.

I glance around the Chapel. Everyone but us is gone. "Yeah." I scrape my hair back into a ponytail. "I've been picking up extra shifts."

She nods. "I've got to find out what's happening to my job."

"What do you mean?" I shove my hands into the pockets of my jeans, every muscle in my body aching to hold her.

I'm still working on the whole letting go thing.

"Am I still bartending? Or do they want me somewhere else?"

"I think your bartending job is safe. Trish is still mixing up bottles."

"I swear she does it on purpose, just to fuck with me," she mutters. Lifting her eyes to mine, she presses her lips together.

"What?" I search her face, wondering if the raffle for a date with me is making her jealous.

"Nothing. I've gotta take off," she says.

"You're not gonna ride with us?" I frown. She just got patched in. She *should* ride.

"Nah. I promised Lucy I'd help her put together the crib. Family first, you know?" She tightens the knot holding the hoodie around her waist. My eyes drop down, but only for a second.

We've gotten really good at ignoring it.

Turning, she heads toward the bar. "Be safe," she calls over her shoulder. A second later, she disappears.

Be safe.

She's never said that to me before.

Before I can start overanalyzing it, Donny calls for me. "I'm coming," I shout back. Then I join my brothers, hoping this ride will clear my head.

I've got to get her out of my system.

But somehow, I don't think even a full-fledged transfusion could do that.

I FILL the time between Church and the benefit on Saturday with extra shifts. Practically every minute of my time is spent on someone else's clock. I pause only in five-minute increments. I've even got showers down to five minutes now. It's like I'm in prison again. The difference is, the week flies by, and my paychecks stack up nicely. I put everything that isn't for rent and bills into a savings account for Bunny.

Lucy didn't get a shower, partially because she waited so long to tell us, but also because her parents have been major dicks about the whole thing. I've been scouring Pinterest for ideas, and I think I'll run some of them past Olivia. I like the idea of a "sip and see," a party where people come to visit the new baby, bring gifts, and sip tea. Except, instead of tea, we'll drink whiskey.

Saturday morning, I roar into the parking lot of The Wet Mermaid wearing my cut and the teal River Reapers T-shirt that Ravage's ol' lady Shannon made all of us. Teal, I've learned, is the color for sexual violence awareness.

I line up with the River Reapers. We have a few minutes before the other clubs join us for the ride. Olivia pulls up behind me, her curls tamed under a rolled-up teal bandana. Even with the scent of oil and summer heat, her dark scent reaches me, making my chest hitch. I force myself to stay on my bike, to not cross over and plant a kiss on top of her curls.

This ride's gotta be emotional for her.

She sits atop her Street Glide with her head held high, her face the epitome of a warrior queen: eyes blazing, mouth set.

"Every benefit is important," Ravage says, shouting over the roar of nine motorcycle engines. "This one's personal for us. Let's make sure we conduct ourselves accordingly on the road. I don't want anyone getting pulled over for any bullshit. Let's show our town some pride."

As if on cue, several clubs from Naugy and the surrounding

towns pour into the parking lot, some of them on Harleys, some on other bikes. My brothers nod at them in recognition and greeting. I nod, too, but I've got no idea who any of these people are. All I know is there here to support Olivia, to support us, to support Shannon's non-profit that helps survivors. My throat tightens, my eyes burning.

I don't bother hiding my feelings.

Every River Reaper wears the same expression, and some of the other bikers, too.

Shannon passes out T-shirts to all of the other riders. Some of them tuck them away in their saddlebags, while others put them on under their cuts. The few women riding with us tug them on over tank tops.

Our President revs his engine, snagging everyone's attention. "Thank you all for coming," he shouts. "I appreciate all our friends—and even our rivals—coming together with us."

I follow his gaze toward a cluster of bikers I don't recognize. He gives their President a nod, but none of them are looking at Ravage. They're all glaring at me. I turn toward my President, but his attention is already back on the crowd.

"Let's fucking do this!"

Engines rev throughout the parking lot. Shannon hops on behind Ravage, and I can't help but glance back at Olivia. I kind of wish she was riding with me. Not because I don't think she's strong enough to ride by herself, but because I miss being *with* her.

I suck in a deep breath, exhale.

What's important right now is this ride. Judging by everyone who showed up, we've raised a lot of money. I give my throttle a quick twist, joining the noisemaking.

Then, we take off.

We cruise down 63, a writhing, live teal ribbon. People in cars and on foot slow to stare at us. Some of them sneer. A few—those who get what benefit rides are all about—wave. Whenever it's safe to take a hand off, I wave back.

Every so often I glance into one of my mirrors for a glimpse of Olivia. Her face remains impassive, her knuckles white on the handlebar and throttle. At one point, I catch the long ribbon of teal trailing out behind her—the other clubs wearing today's color proudly. I capture the image, burning it into my mind to remember later, whenever I miss her.

My strong, beautiful queen.

We parade through the town, passing Gunntown Cemetery and Hop Brook Lake. Finally, we arrive at our destination: the Polish-American Club on Bridge Street. Motorcycles pack the pothole pocked parking lot. Some cars, too—including Ravage's ol' lady's. She carpooled early this morning with a bunch of her organization's volunteers and the women who hang around the club. Then Ravage picked her up.

All while guys like Vaughn and me caught up on our "beauty sleep."

A lot of outsiders think bikers hate women, that we beat them, hurt them in other ways. I used to think so, too—especially when I found out my father was one. I'm learning more and more that to a biker, a woman is a goddess to be appreciated and worshipped. If she's his ol' lady, she's his queen. Women like Shannon and Pru put in just as much blood, sweat, and tears into this club as the men do.

I line the Screamin' Eagle up with the rest of the River Reaper bikes, then swing off. Nodding to a few stragglers, enjoying cigarettes before they go in, I head inside.

The second I walk in, Vaughn and Abraham's playlist surrounds me, the melodic sound of A Perfect Circle calming my nerves. I scan the hall for Olivia and spot her near the makeshift bar, talking with Pru.

"Grab a drink, brother," Ravage says, clapping me on the shoulder.

I give him a one-armed hug. "In a second. I actually wanted to run something by you," I say, glancing at Pru again.

"What's up?" He follows my gaze. "You sweet on her?"

"Nah. Did you know she has a band?" I search my memory for the name. "Cervical Caves."

Ravage shakes his head. "They any good?"

"I've got no idea," I say, "but you and Mark should let them audition. Take over for Oh Vile Eye. I think it'd be good for all of us, push back some of that bad juju."

He laughs. "Did you really just say 'juju,' dude?"

"I did. I'm gonna go get that drink now." I rub the back of my head. "Think about what I said."

"Yeah." He lifts his drink in a salute, then ambles off.

I sort of stumble through the party. For the next four hours, I sip at drinks and pick at my food. There's an urgency in my blood, though I can't put my finger on why. I chainsmoke and try not to look at Olivia. She flits around the room, more lively than I've ever seen. It's like the past few months have cocooned her, then released her, a vibrant creature taking flight.

It's made me love her even more.

Trish sidles up to me, laying a delicate hand on my arm. "Hey, Cliff," she says.

"Hey." I take a swig of my can of Dr. Pepper.

"I've been saving my tips." She grins.

"Oh yeah?" I cast around for Olivia, but she's nowhere in sight. If Trish actually wins this auction, will Olivia even care? Or did she stop watching how Trish interacts with me when we stopped dating?

"It's almost time. Where are you gonna take me?" Trish purrs.

I swallow. I know Mark is right. This auction will rake in quite a bit of cash. Women have always liked me. The problem is, I'm not interested, not even for charity. I've had weeks to get used to the idea, but the opposite has happened.

The music cuts out, saving me from answering. Mark climbs on top of a metal folding chair. "Can I have your attention?"

The chatter throughout the hall dies, heads turned toward our Treasurer.

"First of all, on behalf of the River Reapers, I wanna thank you all for coming out today. Whether you rode with us, bought a raffle ticket, or just bought food and drink tickets, we really appreciate your support." He clears his throat. "Speaking of the raffle, we're gonna get started with that shortly. We've got an auction to take care of first."

Someone whistles—probably Vaughn. Trish's hand tightens on my bicep. I bite back a sigh.

"Cliff, you wanna come up here?" Mark invites me.

I trudge over to him, feet heavy but my head held high. I've got to at least pretend I'm interested.

"As promised, we're selling off one of our fine specimens for a date with one lucky lady," Mark says.

A few of the ladies in the crowd *Whoo!* in response. I grin and duck my head.

"We're starting the bid at fifty bucks," he says. "Just raise your hand if you think this stud is worth fifty."

I play along. "Cheap date."

Almost all of the women's hands shoot up—the single ladies, that is. Shannon keeps her hands visible in her lap, a smirk on her lips. Some of the other ol' ladies nudge and tease their partners.

"How about seventy-five?" Mark asks.

A few hands go down.

Beside me, Trish pulls out a wad of cash, her arm straight in the air.

Abraham's hand goes up, too. "What?" he says to no one in particular. "This is probably my only shot."

I hope he wins, because I know he'll let me off the hook. Probably. I can't get a read on him, whether he wants to be friends or rivals.

"How about a hundred?"

More hands disappear. Both Trish's and Abraham's stay up.

"One-fifty?"

Still more hands go down, but nowhere near enough. As much as I want to raise a lot of money, I want to get this over with. I want to go home to my empty apartment and numb myself to sleep with Netflix.

Maybe I should get a cat.

Of course, the thought of a cat makes me think of Olivia and Dio.

"One-seventy-five?"

I scan the room, looking for dropping hands. They all stay up.

"Two hundred," Mark announces. "Any takers for two hundred?" He nudges me.

"Now that's a fair price," I deadpan, feeling like an improv student.

The bid keeps going up. I'm impressed. Shannon has got to be thrilled. I tell myself that by the time I go on this date, I'll be in a much better mood. I'll get enough sleep or whatever I need to do to make sure I show the winner a good time.

"Three hundred," Mark crows.

He could've been a WWE announcer.

Half the hands fall. Both Trish and Abraham still have their hands up.

"How do you still have blood flow?" I tease her.

She preens at the attention. "I know something else that's gonna have blood flow."

I shake my head. Should've known better. "Oh, you," I kid weakly.

"Me," she agrees.

When Mark hits four hundred dollars, only Trish and

Abraham have their hands in the air. "Do I hear five?" he asks them.

They glance at each other. Trish blushes. She shakes her hand, but keeps it up. Abraham shoots me an apologetic look, then puts his arm down.

"My fucking arm is numb," he complains to no one in particular.

"Ladies and gentlemen," Mark bellows, "we have a winner! One night with Cliff goes to our very own Trish."

"Wait," she says, shaking her arm out. "I think . . . I think I've been outbid."

Mark swivels his head from side to side. "By who? You're the last woman standing." The corner of his mouth twitches. "Aren't you?"

She blushes again, shaking her head. Blonde strands of hair escape from her topknot, secured with a teal bandana. "Cliff," she says, putting one hand on my arm. With the other, she points toward the double doors leading to the restrooms and actual bar.

"You better go," Mark urges.

Glancing from Trish to Mark, I frown. "Okay," I say, drawing out the word. I stride toward the bar, hands in my pockets. As far as I know, there isn't even anyone in there right now—maybe a couple veterans enjoying a beer with each other, watching whatever's on TV when football isn't on.

Fall can't come soon enough. I've missed twenty years of games.

I push through the swinging door. For a moment, the change in atmosphere nearly blinds me. I go from a brightly lit room pumping with music and energy to a dim room lit only by sparse light coming in through the windows. Sunlight slants in one direction, spotlighting the woman sitting at the bar. She sits with her fingers splayed on its top, two shots of clear liquid in front of her.

Olivia.

I glance around, but there isn't another soul in the room. Running a hand over my beard, I step forward.

She lifts her head as I approach. She sits with her legs crossed, one foot bouncing in the air. She exhales, blowing curls out of her face.

I stop at the stool next to her. "Had enough of the party?" I nod at the shots.

She shakes her head. "I paid a thousand dollars for these. It isn't even Cuervo."

My eyebrows shoot up. "A *thousand* dollars?"

"Well, okay. Lucy chipped in five." Her teeth sink into her lower lip, eyelashes fluttering.

"Lucy?" I check the bar again. "Why the hell would Lucy drink thousand dollar tequila with you?"

She tilts her head to the side, giving me a look. "They're for *us*," she says. "For the auction."

I sit. "You bid on me?"

"Mmn-hmn." She pushes a shot toward me. "Figured we'd have a drink."

I lift the tiny glass with two fingers. "Don't forget what happened the last time we had tequila," I say, but don't smile. The glass shakes in my grip. I don't dare hope. I'd be a fool to let myself.

She lifts her shoulders and spreads her hands. "Anything can happen." Then she picks up her own shot. Her lips part, but she says nothing, eyes dropping from my face. Her foot continues its spring, back and forth.

She's nervous.

"And here I thought Trish had it in the bag," I say, my attempt at lightening the mood.

She scoffs. "Only because I told her to."

"Yeah?" I clink my shot against hers. I realize there aren't even any limes. Tipping our heads back, we drink, then slam the shot glasses down. The cheap tequila burns all the way to my stomach. I grimace.

"Jesus Christ." Olivia sticks out her tongue. "This is not going as planned."

I catch her hands in mine. "What exactly is the plan, here?"

Her eyes meet mine. She rubs her lips together, the shine of lip balm on them. "To get you drunk," she says in a soft voice, "and then take you home."

"Are you trying to take advantage of me?" I say, matching her hushed tone.

"Only if you want to." Her eyes widen, growing more vulnerable the longer I look into them. Her hands squeeze mine. "I can't move in with you," she says quickly. "And I'm not ready to love you. But I'm ready to let you love me." Her lips tug to the side. "If you still do," she whispers.

I run a thumb across her cheek. "You asked me to bear with you," I say, heart pounding a frantic hopeful rhythm against my ribs. "I'm still here, Olivia. I'm always here."

"I know," she says, her small hand cupping my face. "That's why I can't let you go." Her eyes search mine, swimming with uncertainty. "Do you?" she asks. "Still love me?"

60

My lips tremble as soon as the question is floating between us.

He peers into my eyes, his own hooded and smoldering with devotion. "I do. I don't want to let you go. And I won't ask for more than you can give me," he says, placing his warm hand over mine. His deep voice reverberates in his chest, vibrating through his bones and into mine, soothing me. "Just give me whatever you've got," he whispers, repeating some of my first words to him.

I lean into him, and his forehead meets mine. I lick my lips. "I want to be with you." My voice catches on the words, my lips still trembling. "I never knew I could be so afraid to lose someone. My whole life, I've just let people go. It's always been easy. With you, it's never easy."

"If it makes you feel better, you don't make it easy for me, either." His mouth twitches. "Half the time, I don't even know what to do with how I feel about you, Liv. There aren't any words in any language to capture it."

"You don't have to say it," I tell him, "because I can feel it." I place my other hand over his heart. It thumps beneath my palm. "I feel you, every second of every day."

He lays a hand on my heart. "I feel you, too."

I close my eyes. After a few moments, our hearts sync up, beat for beat. "Do you feel that?" I whisper.

"I do." He clears his throat. "I'm yours, Olivia. I'm not going anywhere."

"I'm yours, too," I reply.

"Can I hold you?" he asks.

In response, I crawl from my stool into his lap. Wrapping my legs around his hips, I curl my arms around his neck. A moment later, his arms wind around me. I rest my head on his shoulder, closing my eyes again, letting myself fade into his embrace, this moment. Our hearts thrum against each other, separated by bone and blood but tied by something bigger. His hands rest against my back, palms radiating warmth into me. We don't speak. For once, we just listen.

His hand strokes my back, his other hand cupping the back of my head. I nuzzle into him, inhaling him.

"I missed you," I breathe against his skin.

"I missed you, too." He buries his nose in the curls at the nape of my neck. His breath sends delicious tingles through the muscles of my head, the curve of my spine.

I lift my head. Lifting a thumb, I run it across his lips. He presses a kiss to the pad. I touch the corner of his mouth, trace the short beard he's grown, taking in all the subtle ways he's changed since I last touched him. Where I'm catching up, he's soaking me in, drawing a finger along the ridge of my ear, rubbing my lobe between two fingers. I arch into the motion, my eyelids fluttering.

"I missed you," he says again, eyes on my lips.

"Do you want to kiss me?" I hold my breath in like a prayer.

"I really, really do."

"Please."

He cradles my face in both hands, his thumbs stroking my earlobes, his exhalations warming my face, intoxicating me the way no tequila ever could. "I don't know how I survived twenty years without you."

"Me either," I joke, cheeks warming.

There are still seventeen years between us. Someday, he might not want to wait anymore, and I might never be ready to move to the levels he wants to reach. In the face of that, reclaiming him isn't entirely fair. I swallow.

"I know what you're thinking," he murmurs. His eyes meet mine. "I don't need all that. I just need you."

He seals his words by fastening his lips to mine.

My eyes flutter closed, my hands going to the back of his head, fingers tangling in his hair. I part my lips for him, letting him in. His mouth crooks against mine in a lopsided, delighted grin. He sweeps his tongue across my lips, hesitant. I flick my tongue out, opening my lips wider for him, letting him probe his way in.

He caresses me with his lips, the kiss fierce and gentle. I sigh against him, my body longing to shed these clothes, to rest my skin against his. To feel his pulse against every point in me.

I dip my head, withdrawing enough to speak. "Is the invitation to check out your new place still open?"

"God, yes." He sweeps me into his arms, cradling me against his chest.

I curl into him, savoring the way I fit into his big frame, how protectively he carries me. "Should we say goodbye?"

"Nah," he rumbles, bringing me to the door and nudging it open with his hip. He hurries into the parking lot, stealing along the building like a thief.

My thief, who stole into my veins and stowed away in my heart.

"I've got to ask," he says as he lowers me onto his bike. He swings on and I wrap my arms around him, resting my head against his back. "Was everyone in on this?"

"Pretty much," I murmur into his colors, the Sludge Specter scratching against my cheek, leather creaking.

He starts the Screamin' Eagle with one kick, and we roll out.

He takes me to Trowbridge Apartments on Highland Avenue. Not once did I ever think to ask *where* he's living. I just knew he got his own place, and left it at that. Anything more was too painful.

He pulls into his unit's spot, killing the engine once the kickstand is in place. Dismounting, he holds out a hand to me. I never need help getting off a bike, but the gesture is sweet. I take his hand and swing down.

"So," he says, gesturing toward the building. He scuffs his boot against the pavement. "I've gotta warn you, it's not much."

"It's great," I tell him, meaning it. I stand on my tiptoes and kiss his cheek. His lips spread into a smile. Taking his hand, I tug him toward the front door.

Inside, we take the stairs. I sense his eyes on my ass the entire time I climb, and I swing my hips just a little wider. At the top, he palms my ass, drawing me into him. Turning, I reach up and kiss him.

"Will you give me a tour?"

"It'll last about twenty seconds." He wraps an arm around me and leads me down the hall. We pass several units before stopping. He nods at a door. "This is me." Taking out a set of keys, he fits them into the top then bottom locks, then pushes the door open, holding it for me.

I step inside and find myself in a narrow hall.

He flips on a light. "This is the hall," he deadpans.

I scoff. "Come on. It's not just a hall. This is the *mudroom*." I kick off my shoes and shove them to the side.

He points to my left. "Bathroom's in there."

"The *powder* room, you mean." I turn right, entering the

kitchen. He turns on more lights. "And this is the chef's galley and dining room. It's an open floor plan," I explain.

"You're ridiculous." He bends down and kisses my temple. "As you can so clearly see, there's no table here."

"It's a work in progress." I wrap my arms around his neck. "Everything is." I tip my head back and look into his eyes, so full of adoration.

He lifts me into his arms then. I laugh, feet flailing in the air. "This," he says, stepping into the next room, "is the living room."

"The *sitting* room," I correct in my snootiest voice.

"Nowhere to sit." He shrugs.

"Your place looks like mine when Esther moved out." I laugh, covering up for how lonely I was. "Good thing Lucy has her shit together—a couch and an actual loveseat."

"It's all right," he says, carrying me to a door standing open. "I spend most of my time in the bedroom."

I try to think of a fancy name for a bedroom, but come up empty.

"The bedchamber," he intones, flipping on the light.

"Good one." I swallow, heart thudding. Biting my lip, I lift my eyes to meet his. There's nothing for me to hide behind anymore: not wild lust, not silly jokes.

"I'm nervous, too," he admits.

Here I'd usually drop some quip to break the tension, maybe something like "Who said we were having sex?" He'd drop me onto the bed and I'd say something about coming over just for a nap.

Instead, I lay a hand against his cheek, lashes lowering as I move in for a kiss. He meets me halfway, lips folding over mine, then pursing, resting against them. He takes in a deep breath through his nose.

"I know," I tell him. "I feel you."

He kisses me again, lowering me to the bed. I lie on my back, the scent of his clean black sheets and comforter engulfing me.

They smell like Gain and the smoky leather scent that is all him. I wriggle back until my head touches a pillow.

Standing at the foot of the bed, he watches me with heavy lids. There's nothing guarded about his gaze. It's as if he's drunk on just the sight of me. His knees touch the bed, the mattress creaking as he kneels. I lick my lips, heart thundering.

If I fall, he will *catch me,* I think, and immediately know it to be true.

He leans onto his hands and slides up the length of my body, pressing every inch of himself against me. I hold him, too, my hands catching his face, my lips capturing his. His hands roam the sides of my ribs, rubbing, squeezing. I knead my thighs together, veins scorching for him.

"Do you feel me?" he asks, between kisses.

"I do." I arch my breasts against him. Rising on his elbows, he palms them, one in each hand. His leather creaks against mine. Even through the layers of leather and cotton, and the lace of my bra, the heat of his hands brings my nipples to life. They tingle, a sacred warmth puckering them, round and ripe. I writhe beneath him, hoping to wake him, too.

Cliff moans into my mouth, his kiss deepening. The air he breathes into me thrums into my core, swirling, pressure building.

A storm is coming, a love born of darkness and tumult, its birth casting brilliant sparks throughout the black sky. I might not be ready, but I'm ready to want it.

I rub up and down his length, coaxing him. He hardens against my thigh. Beneath him, I part my legs, my heat seeking his. The cotton of my panties clings to me. Raising my hips, I strain against him. He leaves my mouth, trailing kisses across my jawline, under my chin, down my neck. He laps my collarbone, drinking me in.

Reaching a hand between us, I palm him. I move my hand up and down, pumping him through his jeans. He thrusts into my touch, one of his hands leaving my breasts, his thumb skimming my belly above my waistband.

"Do you feel me?" he breathes across my neck.

"I do," I reply.

His hand dips below my waistband, beneath my panties. He palms me, his hand slipping against my swollen flesh. "Olivia," he half rumbles, half moans.

In answer, I bring my fingers to the button of his jeans. I pluck at the button, trying to pop it through its slit. But he's so thick and hard beneath his jeans, there isn't enough space for my fingers to get purchase.

"Please help," I almost whine, grinding my hips, pressing tighter into his hand.

His other hand leaves my breast, his thick fingers slipping between us and fiddling with the button. "Fuck," he growls. He pulls his other hand away, leaving me aching for his touch. Both of his hands fumble between us, finally popping the button.

He springs between us, tenting his boxers but rising from the folds of his jeans, his crown proudly nestling against me, homing in. I put both hands on the sides of my skinny jeans and push them down. We each roll to one side and wriggle out, kicking clothing away.

I rise onto my knees, Cliff mirroring me.

My breasts heave against my cut. He puts a hand on my waist and pulls me into him, ours mouths crashing together. I grip the collar of his cut, pushing the sides down his biceps. He shrugs out of it and I fold it in half, setting it aside. He takes my breasts in his hands, palming the leather, rolling them. Then he removes my cut, folding it carefully in half and placing it on top of his.

We face each other wearing only teal T-shirts, chests rising and falling almost in sync. I grip the hem of mine and pull it off over my head. He inhales deeply, an appreciative smile touching his lips.

"You shine, Olivia," he whispers. "All the time. You're all I can see."

I leap into his arms, wrapping my legs around his hips. Our mouths crash together, scorching each other in the sweetest heat. He lies me down again, and tugs off my panties. A moment later, he unhooks my bra and frees my breasts.

I lie bare and open beneath him. Peeking up at him through my lashes, I let him see me—all of me. The rabbit Olivia and the biker, prey and predator, victim and survivor, the mistakes I've made and the ones I've yet to make. All of me.

His eyes soften, his throat working. Without breaking eye contact, he runs a hand along my slit. His fingers pause at my swollen nub, skimming over the aching rise. He circles it, then slides back down. I press into him, back bowing. He works his way back up, circling the sensitive flesh, his rhythm quickening, the pads of his fingers tapping against it.

My nerves crackle, color raining through my core. I twitch, going limp for several blissful seconds.

"I felt that," I breathe.

He smirks at me.

I reach for him, hand diving beneath his boxers and curling around him. With my other hand, I pull his boxers down. My breasts point toward him, aching to feel his chest against mine. "Take your shirt off," I breathe, pumping him. He obeys, twisting out of his boxers and yanking the shirt off over his head in almost one motion.

Parting my legs for him, I pull him to me. His eyes widen, then go heavy and slack with arousal—never losing focus on mine. He descends, his thighs flush against mine. I press his crown against me, rubbing it in a circle around and over my clit. I angle him down the length of my seam, gliding his head along the swollen flesh. Eyes still on his, I fit his head into place.

He fits his lips to mine and, inch by inch, fills me.

When we lock into place, he lifts a hand. Bringing it to my face, he brushes a curl away, cupping my head.

"I'm not gonna say it," he whispers, "but do you feel it?"

"I do," I tell him. "I do." When I blink, my lashes come away wet.

He swipes them away and stirs me with his length. He glides out, again achingly slow, leaving just his crown inside me. I move my hips, taking him back in. He slides each hand under my shoulders, wrapping his arms around me. I hug him back, winding my arms around his neck, my legs around his waist. I meet each of his thrusts, the synced beating of our hearts booming against my chest, reverberating in my ears. The pressure builds, the storm reaching its crescendo. The sky splits, light flashing.

This time, when we shatter, our pieces rearrange, fitting into something new.

Us.

"**S**on of a fucking *bitch*," Lucy shrieks from down the hall.

My gaze rockets to Olivia's. In seconds, we're both racing out of her bedroom and into her bedroom. We crowd her door.

"What's wrong? What's wrong?" I ask her.

"I'm in fucking labor," my cousin says, turning toward us. Sweat beads her hairline. "Holy shit. No one told me it hurt *this* bad! They all grossly understated how much it hurts."

I glance around the room. "I need the keys. Where are the keys?"

"What keys?" Olivia asks, shouldering the bag Lucy packed for the hospital weeks ago.

"The car keys. Where are the car keys?" I turn in a circle as if they'll just appear.

"Those would be downstairs," Lucy says. She and Olivia shake their heads at me.

"It's gonna be okay, Uncle Cliff." Olivia pats my arm.

Clearing my throat, I head toward the stairs. Olivia and I were all cuddled up on her bed, actually watching a movie. I knew

Bunny would be coming any day now, but now that the moment's here, it's a little overwhelming. In just a few hours, I'll have a tiny niece.

I run down the stairs and through the living room, skidding into the kitchen. I snatch the keys up from the same spot they're always in: the table. I shake my head at myself.

"Maybe I should drive," Olivia says from behind me.

I turn, eyes settling on her wry smile. "I'll be all right," I say, smiling back.

She holds a hand out to me, and I take it, the warmth and weight soothing me. We suspend the moment between us, my chest tightening.

Lucy shuffles in behind Olivia. "Do you guys need some time? Because I don't need drugs at all."

Olivia's eyes close in silent laughter. Neither of us have ever seen Lucy like this. I kind of wish I was recording this on my phone right now. Someday Bunny's gonna want to see the moments leading up to her grand entrance in this world.

"Let's go!" Lucy barks, turning and marching out of the kitchen. Out of the house.

"I'd better go get the car." I slip an arm around Olivia and together we follow her.

"That motherfucker," Lucy curses as she settles into the back-seat. "He doesn't even have the balls to watch me go through this."

Olivia slides in beside her, and I jump into the other side of the backseat, sandwiching Lucy.

"Who's driving this thing?" I quip.

My sweet cousin gives me a glare that I'm pretty sure would drop the hardest criminal at Lewisburg.

"Or not." I get out and put my ass in the driver's seat.

I drive to the Waterbury Hospital emergency room, pulling up as far as I can without blocking the ambulances.

"Be right back," Olivia says. She hurries to the entrance, where she snags one of the security guards. A moment later, they head toward us with a wheelchair.

"I can wa—" Lucy's words are swallowed by a guttural groan. She breathes through the contraction. When it passes, she drags her eyes to mine. "I'll take that wheelchair now."

"Thought so," Olivia says. She and the security guard help Lucy into the chair, then whisk her away.

I park. On my way down, I whisper to my mother. She *loved* Lucy. She'd love Olivia. "Please make this all right for Lucy and help Bunny arrive safely."

I don't know if she hears me, but I like to think so.

Eleven hours later, I stand on one side of Lucy, her hand gripping mine, tendrils of scarlet hair plastered to her face. Olivia holds her other hand.

"Just one more push," the obstetrician promises.

Olivia grimaces at me over Lucy's head.

"Liar!" Lucy screams, bearing down. All of a sudden, strong cries fill the room. The obstetrician holds up a squalling Bunny, purple and writhing.

She's pissed.

"Tell 'em," Lucy calls to her baby. "You did so good." Looking up at Olivia and me, she bursts into tears. "She did *so* good."

A nurse wraps Bunny in a receiving blanket. They whisk her away to clean her up a little and take her stats.

"*You* did good," I tell Lucy, kissing her sweaty forehead.

"Remind me to never do this again," she sobs.

"Remind *me* to never do this," Olivia mutters. She pushes damp hair out of Lucy's face.

A nurse places Bunny in Lucy's arms. Olivia and I crowd over her.

Bunny scrunches up her face, lips puckering at the air. She's as red as her mama's hair and her auntie's temper. She's got Lucy's nose and chin, her hair dark—I'm assuming like Ben's.

"Can we say she gets her curls from me?" Olivia asks.

Lucy gazes at her daughter, tired eyes full of wonder. "Sure," she croons, already more herself.

Nurses flurry around Lucy, propping her with a pillow here and there, and outfitting her with an ugly ass pair of mesh underwear.

"Stop looking at my lingerie," Lucy quips while Olivia gapes in horror.

Eventually, the hospital personnel files out of the room, leaving the four of us in a warm haze.

"Think you two will ever have one of these?" Lucy asks, eyes darting between us full of mischief.

"Fuck off," Olivia says brightly.

I reach for Bunny, cradling her in the crook of my arm, her head resting in my palm.

"Jesus, Cliff," Lucy says. "You could hold her in one hand. Oh my god, she's so small."

From across the room, Olivia smiles, her gaze locked on Bunny and me.

"What do you think, Bunny? Want some cousins?" I ask.

"I will kill you," Olivia says.

I know well enough to believe her.

"I'm going to kill him first," Lucy seethes.

"Me? I'm on your side," I balk.

"Stop calling her Bunny." She shoots me a frosty look.

"What else are we supposed to call her?" Olivia says.

"Leigh," Lucy tells us. "Leigh Demmel." She nods to herself. "Both of you have a 'li' in your names."

"She's always gonna be my Bunny," Olivia insists.

With the soft weight of the baby in my arms, I look at these three women—my whole world, all in one room. I would die to protect them. I take a snapshot of the moment for my memory, one to hold in my hands as a reminder of better times.

Moving to Lucy's side, I shift Leigh to one arm and wrap the other around Olivia. It may not be the picture perfect I envisioned, but it's my perfect—*ours*, judging by the way Olivia smiles up at me.

She might break my heart again—she might do it every day, even—but she's worth the risk.

The End

WANNA KNOW IF MERCY FINDS BREE?

The next book in the River Reapers MC series is under way!
In the meantime, find out if Mercy finds Bree. You can only get the novella by joining the official River Reapers MC email list.

Visit *http://bit.ly/RiverReapersMCFanClub*

Got a Cliff/Olivia hangover? You can also join my reader group on Facebook to connect with other fans of the River Reapers MC series!

Visit *http://bit.ly/BaronesBelles*

BODY COUNT

5

ACKNOWLEDGMENTS

First things first: federal parole laws changed in 1987, but for the sake of fiction and both Cliff and Mercy's stories, I'm pretending people convicted of murder and sentenced to life in prison can still get out on parole. Don't @ me.

This book almost didn't make it off my hard drive because it contains a lot of my personal truth. I'm forever grateful to everyone who encouraged me, held my hand, fed me, and read early drafts: Kristen Barone, Sharon Barone, Wendy Bianca, J.C. Hannigan, Michelle Heron, Molli Moran, and Katy Young. Huge thanks especially go to Molli Moran, who somehow knows when to push me to write better and when to pat my hair and tell me nice things.

In 2006, I met my own Cliff, a patient, kind, supportive man who stood by me, supported me, and loved me while I untangled and worked through my own trauma. He never budged, even when I pushed him away. A little of Mike is in every romance hero I write, but a lot of him is in Cliff.

I can't stop gazing at the beautiful, bold cover that Natasha Snow designed. She's a magician who always transforms my vision into something mindblowing that I never could've imagined. This cover is so Olivia, and embodies everything I feel about this book.

Once again, Erica has been a guiding light in my life, supporting me while I navigate PTSD, chronic illness, and life in general. The world needs more Ericas.

After I wrote the second draft, Kayla did a tarot reading for me that shook me up and re-focused my energy. She held me accountable throughout the production process, checking in with me, reading early excerpts, and waving pom-poms.

I'm also thanking myself. This is the hardest book I've ever written, and some weird shit happened both while writing and editing it. Yet still I pressed on. This has been the most agonizing of book births, but so very worth it to shine light on some of my truth. I don't just write, I twirl.

Last but never least, thank you to my readers, old and new. Without you, none of this is possible.

Until next time,

Elizabeth Barone

ABOUT THE AUTHOR

Elizabeth Barone writes books starring badass belles who chose the other path because her life is just as offbeat. Before publishing her debut novel, she was a chef, web designer, apprentice teacher, and retail soldier, but writing is her first love. It took a debilitating autoimmune disease to make her realize it was time to chase her dream.

Elizabeth is the author of over a dozen contemporary romance and suspense novels. She lives in Connecticut with her real-life book boyfriend (husband) Mike and their feisty little cat Squirt.

Connect with Elizabeth
https://elizabethbaronebooks.com
elizabethbaronebooks@gmail.com

facebook.com/elizabethbaronebooks

instagram.com/elizabethbarone

twitter.com/elizabethbarone

amazon.com/author/elizabethbarone

goodreads.com/elizabethbarone